T0147049

PEOPLE PARK

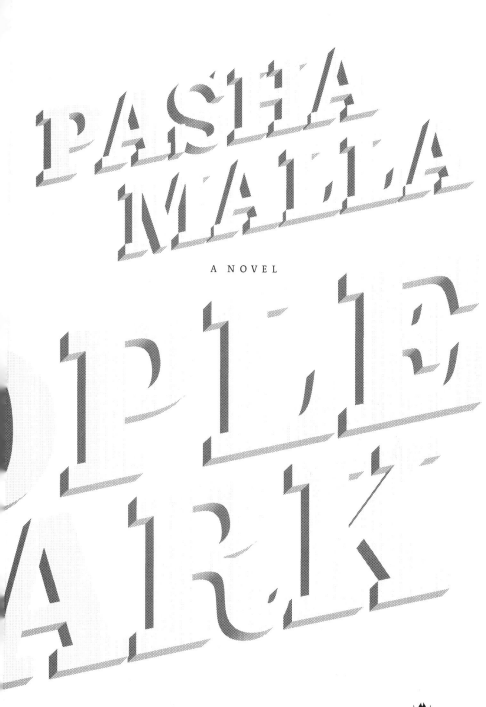

PASHA MALLA

A NOVEL

PEOPLE PARK

SOFT SKULL PRESS | NEW YORK

Cover Design: Chris Tucker
Text design: Brian Morgan
Typesetting: Marijke Friesen

Library of Congress Cataloging-in-
Publication Data is available
ISBN 978-1-59376-539-2

SOFT SKULL PRESS
New York, NY
www.softskull.com

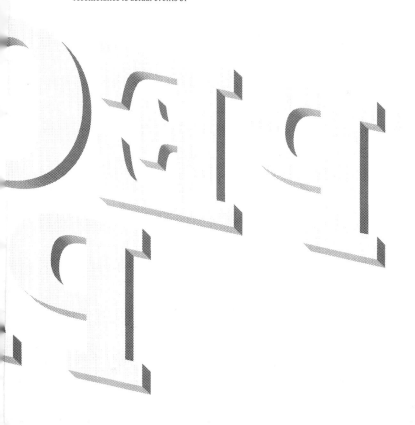

People, people, nothing but people! Yes, I feel it most strongly: I love people. Their foibles and sudden excitements are more dear and valuable to me than the subtlest wonders of nature.

— Robert Walser, *Jakob Von Gunten*

People, people, nothing but people! Yes, I feel it
most strongly: I love people. Their foibles and
sudden excitements are more dear and valuable to
me than the subtlest wonders of nature.
—Robert Walser, Jakob Von Gunten

THE PEOPLE

The Pooles

PEARL: the mother
KELLOGG: the father
GIP: the son, Raven's biggest fan
ELSIE-ANNE: the daughter, who carries a purse, always

The New Fraternal League of Men

GREGORY FAVOURS: the last living Original Gregory
BABBAGE GRIGGS: Head Scientist
"NOODLES" SOBOLIN: Imperial Master
ROSSIE MAGURK: Special Professor
LUCAL WAGSTAFFE: Silver Personality
BEAN: Helper L2, a wily asthmatic
WALTERS: Helper L2, D-Squad
REED: Helper L2, D-Squad
PEA: Helper L2, Snitch
DACK: Helper L2, Ɵnitch
DIAMOND-WOOD: Recruit, on crutches
STARX: Summoner, very big
OLPERT BAILIE: Helper L1 (Probationary), reinstated and reluctant

Island Residents

SAM: aka Mr. Ademus, brother of Adine
ADINE: an artist, sister of Sam, partner of Debbie
DEBBIE: friend to all
THE MAYOR: the mayor
POP STREET: a living protest, a quartered century hence-from!
CALUM: a teenager
CORA: Calum's mum
RUPE: Calum's brother
THE HAND: the girl with the hand-shaped haircut
LEFT AND RIGHT: twins
ISA LANYESS: Face of *In the Know*
EDIE LANYESS: daughter of Isa, Calum's girlfriend
FAYE ROWAN-MORGANSON: Face of *The Fate of Faye Rowan-Morganson*
LOOPY: artist laureate
LOOPY'S ASSISTANT: morose
TWO STUDENTS: a boy and a girl (names unknown)
CONNIE: Sam and Adine's mother (deceased)

And also

RAVEN: the illustrationist

THURSDAY

THURSDAY

How curious that it should begin on a day of
dazzlingly flawless blue.

— Gilbert Sorrentino, *Mulligan Stew*

I

LL WE UNDERSTOOD: at nine o'clock that morning, the illustrationist would be arriving by helicopter.

In the pre-dawn gloom Helpers from the New Fraternal League of Men, mostly middle-aged guys in matching khakis and windbreakers, busied themselves with preparations. The streets surrounding People Park were closed to traffic and down on the common a landing area was marked off with pylons. From these a red carpet cut woundlike across the muddy lawn, up the steps of the gazebo, to a pressboard podium. Affixed to lampposts banners proclaiming the park's Silver Jubilee hung limp as dead sails in the cold still air. At just after six a.m., with everything readied, the NFLM assumed their positions, walkie-talkies crackling, breath puffing in clouds, and waited for the crowds to come.

The towerclock of the old cathedral, now the Grand Saloon Hotel, had barely marked six-thirty when the first people began to appear: families and lovers hand in hand, businessfolk swinging briefcases, Institute undergrads with their knapsacks and hangovers, teens walking bikes, the elderly in pastels, the tall, the short, the fat, the thin, the hirsute and bald, citizens of every shape and creed and trouser, many in Islandwear jackets — Unique! silkscreened into a skyline silhouette.

In a splendid show of diversity and solidarity, with the same look of curiosity and expectation, they came. As night lifted they came, the bruise-coloured sky leaking light while citizens from all corners of the island arrived stamping and squelching onto the wet brown grass, the mud suckled their shoes, their boots, a few thousand strong by the time the lamps and streetlights flicked off at seven-fifteen, everyone wrangled into order by the NFLM.

Atop the bannered poles, on the roofs of the boathouse and the Museum of Prosperity, amid the solar panels of the Podesta Tower, from all around, cameras trained on the crowd, panned over the crowd, zoomed into and out of the crowd, while We-TV commentators readied microphones and ran spit-slicked fingers through their hair. Camcorders pointed at the stage and sky and one another: when two faced it was akin to a pair of young pups nuzzling snout to snout, awaiting the instinct to maul or mate.

Though there were no dogs.

The tower bells sounded eight, and with room scarce on the common, new arrivals were forced up the surrounding hillocks. To the west in the windows of the downtown towers faces appeared framed in steel and glass. Some intrepid souls climbed into the leafless apple trees to the east, or the bare-limbed poplars on the park's south side. In a hilltop clearing to the north a handful of demonstrators wagged placards — ignored and estranged until one young woman was hit with a gritty snowball. Hey! her boyfriend cried. Hundreds of people poured blithely past, the culprit secreted among them.

At twenty to nine by the towerclock the Mayor arrived alone and waving to perfunctory applause, attempted to stride up the gazebo steps — and found herself marshalled sidestage behind a handwritten sign: VIP. Then a signal was given and a faction of Helpers formed a line before the crowd, arms yoked in the manner of paper dolls. They spoke into walkie-talkies, responses sputtered back.

Ra-*ven*, Ra-*ven*, Ra-*ven*, the crowd began chanting and clapping in time.

This was April 16, a bright cold morning warmed by the sun nosing out of the lake. Springtime was coming: stray patches of snow had gone crystalline and grey in their dying days, the asphodels would soon bloom, the trees beckoned leaves with their spindly arms, the crinkle of ice upon Crocker Pond fractured like an eczemic skin. Everything smelled of decay and worms, rich with thawing dirt. High above, a single cloud, a thin little wisp, trailed along — a baby bird lost from the flock. The Ra-*ven* chant faded. Everyone watched the sky because he would come from the sky.

Someone said, It's nearly nine!

Someone said, Shut up howbout, okay?

Someone said, Listen!

There it was: the growl of an engine, faraway. Everyone craned their necks and looked, but in the sky was just the cloud. He couldn't travel inside a cloud. But watching it drift along up there people began to wonder. In locales around the globe the illustrationist had defied many laws of physics and gravity and, more roguishly, the judiciary arms of governments.

There, yelled another someone.

A little piece of cloud seemed to be breaking away. But it was not, the crowd realized, a cloudlet that was now swooping toward the common, graceful and white as a gull against the deepening blue. It was a helicopter. As it approached the air began to thrum, applause splattered through the crowd, there were shouts and yelps and murmurs and with fingers pointed skyward hollerings of: There he is — He's coming — Yeah!

As though lowered on a rope the helicopter descended: one hundred feet from the ground, eighty, sixty, engines snarling. The crowd watched, faces slanted skyward. Those wearing hats were holding their hats. Some people plugged their ears. Puddles rippled and Silver Jubilee banners fluttered and tree branches trembled and all those cameras captured everything, everything. From her pocket the Mayor produced a stack of cue cards she patted into a neat little pile.

Pausing only inches from the ground the helicopter's twin tinted windows were the eyesockets in a polished white skull that tilted this way and that, regarding the crowd curiously. For a moment it seemed it might lift back up and away. Everyone watched, hands clutched hands and squeezed, hearts hoped. And at last as though satisfied the helicopter straightened and nestled between the pylons, and was still.

Two NFLM higherups scuttled out under the chopper's thupping main rotor. The engines settled, the blades slowed from a single whirring disc into four separate propellers, and stopped. The Mayor smoothed her sash and stepped forward, cue cards poised, only to be impeded by a windbreakered arm, a freckled hand. Sorry ma'am, offered the arm's owner, eyes downcast, lashes the colour of lard.

The helicopter sat there on the lawn, gleaming and still — was the crowd watching it, or was it watching the crowd? The feeling was of that cork-wriggling moment before the champagne pops: anticipatory and dreadful. And then the door to the cockpit flapped open and out swung the illustrationist, Raven, a brownskinned man in a white velour tracksuit, baldhead glossy in the sun.

A roar went up. The crowd hollered and thronged and the NFLM held them back. A teenager ululated ironically. Hopping down the illustrationist shook hands with each of the men on the landing pad and whispered into the ear of one, a guy in sport sandals and thick woolly socks, who signalled to his vigorously nodding, goateed colleague, and together they pulled from the helicopter a white, glassy-metallic trunk. With loping strides Raven glided along the red carpet, up the steps of the gazebo, out to the podium. The NFLM hoisted his trunk onstage and retreated.

Raven gazed over the crowd. But as he opened his mouth to speak, from the Grand Saloon clanged the old towerbells. His head sank to his chest, he tapped his fingers on the podium. The hours rang out golden: the first, bong, the second, two more, then three, and in a show of impatience Raven thrust his hand to his forehead, closed it in a fist, and the strikes stopped at eight. Instead of the usual echo and ebb, absolute silence — a tongue cleaved from a singing throat, leaving only breath and flapping lips.

Cameras lowered, everyone looked around at one another, eyebrows arching. But Raven was clutching the edges of the podium now, leaning forward, what would he do next. His fingernails were either all cuticle or painted white. His gaze dragged over the crowd as a net trawling the ocean floor. Beyond People Park there was no indication of the city: its usual hum, its growls and gurgles and honks and whispers — all absent. The island had never been so quiet. Then, with sudden violence, here was the illustrationist: eyes widening, thrusting his arms into wings.

I am *Raven*, he hollered.

The crowd roared in a single voice and the illustrationist bowed to them and bowed to the cameras and bowed in the general direction of the Mayor, waving her cue cards like a winner.

Ra-*ven*, Ra-*ven*, Ra-*ven*, chanted the crowd again, almost pleading. But he looked past them to some place beyond their expectation. He snapped, thrice and crisply. The white trunk heaved open with a groan.

Hush fell. The trunk's insides were as dark as a coffin's. What was hidden within?

The sun continued its slow swing upward. The lone cloud had scattered into droplets — had the illustrationist made it do so, some people wondered. Raven stared out from the podium, the brown of his face and hands, the white of his nails, the white of his tracksuit, china-white teeth bared between parted dark lips, the black of the shadows behind him, the white trunk vesselling night into the daytime. The people waited. The NFLM stood fast — ever-khaki, ever-vigilant. The cameras rolled. The Mayor coughed.

Then the illustrationist sucked in a deep breath and hurled his arms above his head: six doves erupted from the trunk. The crowd applauded, cameras followed the doves upward. Raven pointed a single finger, thumb extended, at the birds as they climbed. A gunshot cracked and the doves plummeted and thudded dully into the sodden field. But they were no longer doves: half a dozen pigeons lay there in the muck.

The crowd whispered, fell silent again.

The illustrationist looked deep into the rolling cameras, and crouching inches from his TV screen Sam watched through a fizz of static and shivered. In the illustrationist's eyes was — what? Nothing.

His eyes are like tunnels, Sam described into the telephone. They're just black eyes.

Contacts probably, said Adine, on the other end of the line. What a doosh.

Summoned by the illustrationist's trembling fingertips the pigeons wobbled to life, tottered about with the wary steps of a litter just born. The crowd gasped and clapped and the cameras zoomed out and the illustrationist bowed. He snapped his fingers — once, twice, three times, the clack of bones.

He's snapping his fingers Adine, explained Sam to his sister.

I've got the volume up, she said, I can hear.

You can hear.

Just tell me what you see, she said. You're my closed captions, okay?

I'm okay Adine. I'm doing the work Adine. I'm doing good communication.

You sure are, buddy. And I appreciate it.

The crowd had gone quiet once more. It was as if a blanket were being ruffled over them, up and releasing their hoots and hollers, down and stifling them silent. A pause. Then the illustrationist flung his arms skyward, the pigeons lifted into the sky, they were white again: doves.

Sam explained to his sister what he saw.

He's done this before, she said.

He's done this before.

It was on TV, at some square in some city, said Adine. One of those places all covered with pigeons. He walked into the square and waved his hand and all the pigeons fell down and everyone thought they were dead and then he did something else stupid and they went flying away, all at once.

They went flying away.

Right. And then he cried a single tear off the main bridge and the rivers started flowing again after like a hundred years or something. God, I just can't understand how anyone buys this guy. *The illustrationist Raven* — it's just so affected and phony.

People like that sort of thing Adine. They like that sort of thing I guess.

People? said Adine, as though the word were a disease. People fuggin suck.

On the TV the doves vanished, the applause faded. The illustrationist peered down upon the crowd and grinned two rows of perfect white teeth from his brown face, arms still extended in the same vast V from which he had released the birds. His eyes were two wet black stones and what Sam didn't tell Adine was that, looking into them, in his gut churned a sick, sour feeling of vinegar and rot.

Slowly, with drama, the illustrationist lowered his arms, returned his hands to the podium, curled his fingers around its edge. He leaned forward. He closed his eyes. He licked his lips.

He's opening his eyes, said Sam.

Look out, buddy, said Adine, here we go.

I am *Raven*, screamed the illustrationist, and everything exploded in thunder.

II

The minivan was trapped in a snarl of traffic along Topside Drive, bumper to bumper back over Guardian Bridge all the way to the mainland, cars and trucks and utility vehicles for sport and vans and other minivans too, though none as spanking fancy as this one, with its sidepanels of woodgrain appliqué. The licence plate was vain, HARRY, and into Harry's roofrack were strapped matching black wheelie suitcases in checked and carry-on sizes, and a hot pink duffel depicting witches and fairies upon a background of castles. Inside Harry were the Pooles: Pearl and Kellogg and their kids, Elsie-Anne, five, and Gip, ten years old and, with each new roar from People Park, more dismayed and defeated to be missing it all.

The Pooles' trip had begun Wednesday morning, post-meds: two pills on a swallow of grape juice, a daily cocktail Gip required for function and focus. Without it, for example, amid teasing on a fieldtrip to a classmate's farm he'd kicked out a schoolbus window and climbed onto the roof, knelt up there screaming and punching himself in the face until the taunts of the other kids had alerted his teacher. Afterward Gip wept. I hate them, he sobbed, chewing the brim of his cap, I'm not a little piglet, I'm a *boy* — I hate them.

Those were what Kellogg and Pearl called Episodes. Meds curtailed Episodes. So did generally just keeping Gip happy. He had problems, sure, but what kid was perfect, no kid was perfect — medicated he was as perfect a kid as anyone's. And while his classmates delighted in the unfortunate coincidence of Gip's physique and his name's written inverse, Kellogg preferred to think of his son as *healthy* — what Kellogg's own father, who had starved in the old country, liked to tweak the boy's small breasts and call him.

At dawn Kellogg piloted Harry along the main street of their sleepy and still-sleeping town. Passing Dr. Castel's office Gip hollered, We're going to see my idol Raven, Dr. Castel — *finally!* and Pearl took Kellogg's hand atop the cassette holder. The Pooles hit the coastal highway and the sky swelled into a great blue expanse mottled with puffy darling clouds. To the west the land rippled dunly, all rolling farms and hillocks and cherry trees just blossoming, while the water glittered indigo to the horizon in the east. Pearl let her other hand loll out the window, the wind buffeted it dreamily. You couldn't worry about a thing, doing a thing like that.

The Pooles arrived too late to check in at Lakeview Campground so they stayed on the mainland at the airport motel, which Kellogg's guidebook commended for its satellite dish and prime rib, though the pool was closed. From there, said the CityGuide, it would be a just a quick zip over Guardian Bridge in the morning — Back to Mummy's hometown, enthused Kellogg, which Gip corrected, Do you mean to see *Raven?* and Kellogg said, You betcha, and Pearl smiled, though her smile seemed pinched and in her eyes flickered something wary.

After ten grey-pink slabs of prime rib between them the Pooles descended a boardwalk to the Scenic Vista, a platform wedged into the cliffside. Across the Narrows the city was a dome of light plunked down into the night. Guardian Bridge twinkled in parallel undulating lines to the chalky bluffs on the island's northern shore.

There it is, said Kellogg, the big city. Where Mummy was a star. How does it feel, Pearly? Is it everything you remembered?

Well I didn't often look at it from this side, Kellogg.

Right. He rubbed a small circle on her lower back, the hand hovered in space, found a home capping Gip's skull, Gip squirmed away and adjusted his hat. But wow, coming back after so long! Guess Mummy was something else for the — what was it?

Lady Y's.

Lady Y's. And there's the arena there! Beside that big round thing! What's that then?

The Thunder Wheel. God, I remember one time I went on it, on a date — what was that silly boy's name? A hairy little guy . . .

Kellogg shrugged, looked away.

Anyway he barfed when we got to the top. Sprayed all the way down on everyone.

Ew, said Kellogg.

He barfed! roared Gip. On a *ride*? Someone barfed *actual barf*?

He did indeed. Poor kid, he was scared of heights, what was his name . . .

More like the *Chunder* Wheel, yucked Kellogg. Anyway I bet my guidebook's got coupons. See it, Gibbles? To the left — other left! Maybe we'll get to take a ride!

The Thunder Wheel was a huge black disc, unlit and unmoving, which rose from the grounds of Island Amusements over the northern fringe of People Park. To its east the orange hump of IFC Stadium glowed like a dinner roll under a heatlamp.

I have to pee, said Elsie-Anne.

Pee in your purse, said Gip, Dorkus. You retard.

I left it inside Harry, Stuppa, retard.

Hey now, said Kellogg, let's not call each other names, huh? But hey, anything you guys want to ask your mum? She was famous when she lived here, a real celebrity. Annie, one sec, okay — but think! That arena's where *thousands* of people came to see Mummy play. Imagine if she hadn't done her knee in? You guys might never have even been born!

Dad? said Gip, looking worried.

Anyway it's been a long time! How does it feel, Pearly? To be back?

Well we're not back yet, are we. We're over here.

Yeah but sure, you know what I mean. And you've got plans to see your old pals too, right? I wonder if any fans will recognize you? It must feel —

It doesn't feel like anything, okay?

The air stiffened. Across the river, the city shimmered and hummed.

Pearl patted her daughter on the cheek. Else, you need the toilet?

Hand in hand mother and daughter headed back to the motel. Pearl's knee must have been acting up: she favoured her left side as she walked, stiff-legged and lurching. But as always there was a publicity and performance to her limp, a showy sort of pain. Down the highway a plane was taking off from the airport. Kellogg watched it rise, roaring and blinking, into the night. Look at that, he said, to one in particular.

Dad? Gip was pulling his father's hand hair. We should go to bed because we have to get there early. Tomorrow, I mean. Dad? Raven's choppering in at nine a.m. in the morning and he's *always* precisely on time, so we *have* to get there at eight o'clock *at the latest* just to make sure, Dad, Gip huffed. To make sure we get a good seat, so we can see everything. Dad?

Got it, said Kellogg. We'll be up first thing. Don't worry, pal.

Later, back in the motel room, while Gip, who wouldn't share a bed with dead-to-the-world Dorkus, snored in his cot, and Pearl ground her teeth with the sound of marbles pestled to dust,

Kellogg flipped through the satellite's endless TV channels. In the high 400s he paused: a large man in a red fez was being robed by a sexy assistant. Kellogg thought for a moment to wake his son, but Gip had no interest in magicians other than Raven. The assistant disappeared offstage — and, to a burst of delight from the audience, the performer collapsed, pitched backward, and went still. The screen cut to black. Kellogg shivered. Somehow it was one-thirty.

AT THE FIRST SHUDDER of light through the curtains Gip was up, shaking his parents awake and whipping the covers off his sister. Come on, come on, we have to get across to the island, Raven arrives today! As his family showered he danced around the room — Hurry Dorkus, hurry Dad, hurry Mummy, *hurry*!

Kellogg waited for Pearl to dress, then while she administered Gip's meds coordinated his outfit with hers: pale bluejeans, grey crewneck, ballcap. Emerging from the bathroom he announced, Matchy matchy! and Pearl covered her face in her hands. Come on, Kellogg laughed, we're on vacation, it's fun.

At breakfast Kellogg was loudly good with his kids, everyone's plates heavy with sausages tonged in pairs from the buffet — except Pearl's, she had yoghurt and fruit. All the other diners would surely look over at their table and think, What a nice normal family on a nice normal family vacation, holy.

How healthy his marriage had become again, Kellogg thought, like an amputee striding about on fresh prosthetics. He and Pearl talked things out, they were communicative and open, infidelity was inconceivable, Dr. Castel would be proud. And here they were, taking a holiday. They'd see some magic and camp and visit all Pearl's old haunts. On the south shore of the island was a beautiful beach, said the CityGuide, Elsie-Anne loved swimming so much, the little fish. And Kellogg would just be happy to make it happen, to make his family happy.

After breakfast, packed up and ready to go, in the parking lot Kellogg took Pearl's hands and said, Hey, we okay? Just kidding around, I can put on a different shirt if you want. Pearl said, Kellogg, hey, no, I know. Just feeling a little stressed, a little weird is all. Coming back is weird. With Harry's door ajar and dinging, Kellogg corralled his wife into his arms. I love you, he whispered into her neck. I know, said Pearl. I know.

Come on, screamed Gip from inside the minivan, it's past seven o'clock!

Elsie-Anne had wandered off down the boardwalk. Kellogg found her leaning over the railing at the Scenic Vista. A drainpipe jutted from the cliffs twenty feet down, she claimed an eel lived in its depths, she'd named him Familiar. Gently Kellogg pried her away, and as he folded her into Harry's backseat she whimpered, But I loved Familiar and he loved *me*.

Kellogg followed the ISLAND signs down to the water, where they hit a jumble of cars queued at the Guardian Bridge onramp. Pearl's allergies were acting up, she blew her nose, discarded the tissue on the dashboard, punched an antihistamine tablet from a blisterpack, swallowed it dry.

Just a little traffic, folks, no big deal, said Kellogg, grinning into the backseat.

Dorkus is talking to her purse, said Gip. It's weird.

Gip, why not try a trick from your book? suggested Pearl. Else, hey, wouldn't you like to see your brother do some magic?

While Pearl readied their documents Gip leafed through Raven's *Illustrations: A Grammar*. Tapping a page, he announced, Situation Thirteen, in which Dorkus picks a card, any card. Cunningly he fanned a deck on the backseat. Kellogg smiled at Pearl: how sweetly their kids played together, what lucky parents they were, and he reached over and squeezed his wife's arm as though testing a fruit. She regarded him with confusion — a look that suggested she didn't, for a moment, know who he was.

Hi, it's me, Kellogg — is that who I am, according to those things? You're fine. It's the kids: Gib Bode, and his lovely sister L.C.N. Goode.

But you have proof you're from here, which gets us in — right?

Let's hope, said Pearl.

After a rambling, theatrical process that required Gip to consult Raven's *Grammar* four times, Elsie-Anne refused to admit, with a shake of her braids, that she'd chosen the nine of clubs. What? Gip said, brandishing it at her. This is your card, Dorkus. No it isn't, Stuppa, said Elsie-Anne, mine was jack. Impossible! her brother screamed, and swept the rest of the deck onto the floormats.

Gip, barked Pearl — but Gip only gazed out the window, while the minivan crawled onto the lip of the bridge.

Why are we going so slow, he said. We've barely moved at all.

Just a little backup, said Kellogg. Got lots of people heading over probably just as excited as you, pal. We'll get there, don't you fret.

Gip leaned into the frontseat. But gosh, it's nearly seven-forty a.m. in the morning, Raven's arriving at nine o'clock sharp, and what if we don't make it for eight, which is when I said we needed to get there, if you remember. Don't you even listen to me?

Oh hush up, said Pearl. We've got plenty of time.

We'll get there, said Kellogg. Everyone's going the same place, traffic's got to go somewhere. Just likely making sure everyone's got their tickets and permits in order, and Mummy's from here so we'll just whip on through. Okay?

No response.

One spot ahead of Harry was a maroon pickup truck with a bashed-in taillight. Its driver, a wild-looking man in a dirty blond ponytail and prospector's beard, leaned out the window to spit. The spit, even from this distance, was goopy and brown.

Disgusting, said Pearl, and sneezed.

Ten minutes passed, traffic barely budged, the pickup driver spat four more times. Gip ignored his dad's suggestion to try the trick again. Instead he began humming, a sound somewhere between the whine of a cicada and the bleating of a distant car alarm. Kellogg and Pearl exchanged a look. The driver of the pickup hawked out the window again, pulled forward eight inches. Harry followed, stopped, and Gip kept humming.

You guys excited about, Kellogg began, couldn't think what to say, turned on the radio: static. No signal out here I guess, he said. Weird.

Pearl turned the radio off.

Gip is humming, Elsie-Anne said. Mummy, Stuppa's humming.

Stop it, said Pearl.

The humming continued. Pearl cracked her window.

Little cold out for that yet, said Kellogg. And what about your allergies?

Pearl looked at him. He winked. She rolled up the window.

And Gip hummed.

Elsie-Anne covered her ears with both hands. The traffic jam stretched ahead, a steel-scaled python slumped over the bridge. The guy in the pickup truck stuck his head out the window, made eye contact with Kellogg, spat, and retreated back inside the cab. Nothing moved. Pearl pointed at the vacant opposite lane. Just go there.

I can't — sheesh, Pearly, here's a lane just for the Pooles I guess? He checked Gip in the rearview, who hummed back. When Kellogg spoke again his voice was oddly boisterous, infused with the forced mirth of a waiter singing Happy Birthday to a table of businessmen. Hear that, buddy? Get us arrested why don't you! We'll get there, guys. Look, see, cars are starting to come the other way. And hey-ho! We're off now too.

But something was wrong: traffic was being routed back to the mainland.

A car swished past, the faces of the driver and passengers resigned. Gip's humming stopped. The clock on the dash ticked over to 8:00. Gip unleashed a scream like a bottle hurled against a wall. No no no no no no no no no, he sobbed, kicking the back of his mother's chair.

Kellogg cried, Wait! — but Pearl was already diving into the backseat to tackle her son. Kellogg's technique would have been soothing, soft words and a gentle hand on his knee. Discipline was useless, he thought, watching Gip jolt and squirm in Pearl's arms. Episodes weren't his fault, you had to be patient — you subdued him with kindness, not force. Why didn't the boy's own mother understand that?

The pickup wheeled into a three-point turn and the shaggy guy absconded, spitting. In the rearview Kellogg watched Pearl cuff her son's wrists in one hand and clamp his mouth with the other while Gip thrashed and moaned. Hesitantly Kellogg put the minivan in gear, pulled forward, said, Look, champ, here we go.

Gip went still. Blinked. Inhaled a trail of snot.

That's it, coaxed Kellogg, we're at the checkpoint, we'll see Raven soon, don't worry.

In the middle lane sat a man in khaki at a child's schooldesk. Kellogg was summoned from the minivan with curling fingers.

Take Elsie-Anne, Pearl told him, still restraining Gip. Show him our permits.

Kellogg wanted to see something beyond resignation on his wife's face — love! Instead in her eyes was the beleaguered look of someone suffering a chore. Go, she said.

Annie, come with Dad, said Kellogg, and together they approached the guy at the desk — Bean, said his nametag.

Bean nodded at Harry's plates. You have a resident in the car?

Former resident, my wife. She used to star for the Y's?

Leafing through the papers, Bean eyed Elsie-Annie. Who's this?

That's Elsie-Anne — L.C.N., see? Someone must have —

Bean held up a hand. And Gib?

With my wife. He's ... sick.

Sir, you realize no one in your quote-unquote *family* has the same last name?

That's maybe not our fault though?

You're suggesting it's ours.

No! Just a miscommunication maybe? It happens . . .

Bean swivelled, spoke into a walkie-talkie. Took a puff from an inhaler. Eyed Kellogg with the ambivalence of a bored shopper sizing up a lettuce.

Kellogg gazed down the bridge. Along the island's shore was more gridlock, a call-and-response of horns, long blasts echoed by long blasts, all of it useless, nothing moving.

Mr. Poole, we're going to need you to get processed once you're islandside. Your wife is fine — Bean stamped her permit forcefully, handed the others over — but the rest of you need special permission before you can join the Jubilee celebrations.

But! No, we can't do that — my son, he's . . . We'll miss Raven's arrival!

Bean checked his watch. Not much chance of you making that anyway. NFLM on Topside Drive are expecting you, they'll direct you to Residents' Control — that's the Galleria foodcourt, five minutes from the bridge. Good lookin out!

Thanks, said Kellogg, and headed back to the minivan wondering what he'd thanked him for.

Elsie-Anne raced ahead to the bridge's railing, hopped up, leaned over. And went rigid. Dad, she called, pointing below. Look.

A naked woman was walking — precariously, slowly — out onto one of the iron trestles that extended from the structure's underside. Two hundred feet below lay the river, a ruffle of black silk spangled silver, and as the woman stepped, one foot then the next, the wind tousled her hair like the hand of some benignly drunk uncle. Pigeons burbled somewhere, but Kellogg couldn't see any pigeons.

The woman seemed oblivious to everything: to the traffic, to Bean and his flares, to Kellogg and Elsie-Anne, to the world and all that was in it. Her back was hunched, her buttocks alabaster. At the end of the trestle she stopped, arms extended for balance. If she were to jump it seemed she would be leaping not down, but outward, into open space.

Oh my god, said Kellogg. Elsie-Anne, get in the car.

Dad?

Kellogg snatched her by the chin. You listen, if that person jumps and we're the only witnesses, it will *ruin* our vacation. You won't get to swim, Gip won't get to see his magician — we'll be at the morgue, answering questions. They might even blame us! So forget you saw anything. Get in the car. Say *nothing* to your mother. Hear me? Nothing.

Elsie-Anne nodded.

Good girl, said Kellogg, knuckled her cheek, slid open Harry's door, ushered her inside, slammed it closed — and looked over the railing. The woman hadn't moved: a porcelain, otherworldly figure who seemed to float in the brisk morning air.

Kellogg opened his mouth to call to her, to tell her — what? But it was too late: a great tumble of hair, and the trestle was empty.

Trembling, Kellogg rushed to catch the body's splash or see it swept away in the current. But Bean was calling him: Sir, sir, in your car, please, sir. So Kellogg stopped, apologized, returned to the minivan. In the backseat Pearl, sniffling, stroked Gip's hair. Elsie-Anne stared vacantly into her purse. Okay, said Kellogg, moving his foot from brake to gas. The engine vroomed, he pressed harder, Harry went nowhere.

You're in Park, said Pearl.

Oh, said Kellogg, shifted to Drive, and lurched another ten feet closer to the island.

III

13

BY TEN-THIRTY it was all over.
Raven stepped into his trunk, waved a brochure from the Grand
Saloon, said, I believe this is where I'm staying, and closed the lid
on himself. A moment later the helicopter seemed to come alive of
its own accord, lifted up from the common, looped over Crocker
Pond, and landed atop the hotel. The doors to the penthouse suite
opened and Raven stepped onto the balcony, blew six kisses at
the crowd, bowed, and ducked away.

The trunk sat innocuously in the middle of the stage.

There was nothing else to look at.

And so with a collective sigh people began to shuffle back to
their lives.

From the top of the northern hillock the protestors withdrew,
trashed their placards out back of Street's Milk & Things. Today
Debbie, Pop and the two Island Institute students whose names
Debbie kept failing to learn were joined by the most militant
members of the Lakeview Homes Restribution Movement: a
man called Tragedy — walleyed, squat, and gnomish, smelling
of salsa — and his lean, lisping, wispily bearded friend, Havoc.
They'd shown up to their first meeting only two weeks prior and
pulsed with something weird and feral that might euphemistic-
ally be described as energy.

Debbie watched the crowd thin and scatter, far below. You wonder if anyone even knows we're here, she said.

The one who hit me with a snowball did.

Here were the students, clasping hands.

That sucked, said Debbie. People just don't think sometimes. You okay?

The girl nodded shyly, the boy shook his head. A patchwork of cause-oriented pins covered her knapsack. Over his woolly jumper hung a pendant in the shape of a fist.

Down the path to the common Tragedy was trying to tear a Silver Jubilee banner from a lamppost. He was too short though, and couldn't get decent purchase: he jumped, clutched, flailed, swore, sulked. Havoc lisped, Let it go, man, it'θ only a θymbol. Be real.

Meanwhile Pop was heaving himself up the steps of his houseboat, which presided on the lip of the clearing over People Park. He was in his sixties, and large, flabby even, somehow yellowing, every breath was a gasp.

The houseboat was a boxcar on blocks, scabbed with rust and flaking paint. Maybe she'd help fix it up sometime, often thought Debbie, and felt guilty now having only ever thought this thought. Pop unfolded a lawnchair and plopped into it. One minute, he said, wheezing. Yet in his eyes, as always, was that manic glimmer. When three years prior Debbie had come to interview him for *In the Know* he'd stormed out of Street's Milk & Things ranting about *restribution*, every few sentences screaming, Get this word for words, reporter! After a four-minute diatribe he'd announced, I have to work, and disappeared into the store. Debbie, assigned to write about Mr. Ademus's mysterious and hugely popular sculptures — the Things he sold, the Things of Milk & Things — had written nothing.

Lark, called Pop from his lawnchair, arms raised, poncho spread (RESTRIBUTION! markered across the chest). Gather!

Debbie pushed close with her notebook and beamed at him with what she hoped passed for reverence.

In the baritone of a preacher Pop began: Thank you all for attendenating here with me today. The city's going to hear us! — Tragedy responded, Fug yeah! — We may be small, but we're big. This Mayor, this NFLM, this *Jubilee*, they envision our spirits as flattened as they flattened Lakeview Homes? That a quartered century hencefrom we've forgotten this so-and-so-called park was once impersonated by *people*? Say it with me: No!

No fuggin way, said Tragedy.

Feverishly, Debbie took notes.

No! Not this time. Not any time. Not *this* time!

Shame, warbled one of the students — the girl. Shame, echoed her boyfriend.

Shame! Pop pointed at them, eyes narrowed. You've said the magical word. It *is* a shame. What transposed here, a quartered century hencefrom — a bloodied shame.

Bloody fuggin cogθuggerθ! screamed Havoc.

And they think they can just erect a memorial to make it okay-dokay? A *statue*?! Well I've got a statue of limitations for that sort of thing!

Pop's eyes gleamed.

The memorial unveiling's tomorrow, added Debbie. Hope everyone can come?

Pop saluted, hoisted himself to his feet, howled, Restribution! and waddled off, puffing, to open Street's Milk & Things for the day.

A pigeon wheeled overhead, perched on the roof of the houseboat, eyed the gathering, scratched itself under a wing with its beak. Tragedy threw a rock, which went sailing into the bushes. The bird shat a greenish dribble onto the roof and glared defiantly back.

Guess that's it for us then, said Tragedy, lighting a wilted Redapple.

Some halfhearted goodbyes were offered (Θolidarity, proposed Havoc unconvincingly, and passed around a fist-bump) and he and Tragedy, swapping the cigarette between drags, took the path down into the common, past an elderly man caning his way up the Crocker Pond Slipway to Parkside West Station.

The students hung around. Debbie wished she'd been more like them in her twenties: all secondhand alpaca and shy, dreamy ideals. Instead she'd been an athlete.

Thanks for coming, guys, she said.

We saw the posters on campus, said the girl, at the Institute.

We didn't know anything, said her boyfriend, about this. Before.

But we're glad we could come.

The boy shuffled, his girlfriend nudged him. He spoke: We wanted to tell you, though, we're leaving town. Tomorrow. We won't be around for the rest of the weekend.

It's just, we're going camping. Back home.

Can you tell Mr. Street we're sorry?

Oh, that's okay, said Debbie, feeling flattered. Just nice you came out today, right? And have a nice time camping, that'll be fun for you guys.

Yeah, we feel bad is all. There aren't a lot of people out.

Most kids we're in school with are happy to just party at the Dredge till they're sick.

And watch themselves after on TV.

We'll totally be up for whatever when we're back. With the um, Movement.

We're just a little worried.

What about? said Debbie.

The boy and girl exchanged looks. We've heard Mr. Street tends to —

Kick people out. Of the Movement. For disappointing him?
Like almost everyone?

Yeah, sighed Debbie, that happens. We're currently in a rebuilding phase.

A second pigeon joined the first: an elderly couple, grey and waiting.

Hey, said the girl. We heard you're writing a book about him?

Debbie laughed — a sharp, awkward bark. Well it started as a script but my boss didn't want it. I mean, you can't really capture Pop Street in a four-minute segment.

That was for Isa Lanyess? You write for In the Know, right?

Not that we watch it, clarified the boy.

Yeah, said Debbie, though I only do occasional stuff now, got to pay the bills, right? Mostly I run a program in Blackacres, for neighbourhood kids. Out of the Room?

The students stared back. Were they judging her? What was their judgment?

She plunged ahead: But yeah, I have all these notes about Pop and the Homes and everything, and someone should write about this stuff, it's just so hard making it all come together, right? We should get a cider. I could tell you more about it, about the book.

We've got class.

We would though, totally. Otherwise.

Oh I didn't mean now, ha. A bit early for drinks! Just sometime, anytime — whenever! You guys should give me your number. So we can stay in touch. About Movement stuff.

The girl said, Not sure I've got a pen, and dug around in her knapsack: no pen.

From the houseboat, the birds cooed in chorus, ruffled their wings. Their poop was an eggy froth baking in the sunlight.

Debbie said, Okay, off with you then, get to school. She tried to sound light, but it came out hurried, dismissive. And when they left, Debbie felt abandoned — and embarrassed, she still hadn't gotten their names. The students were heading the same direction as her, toward Parkside West Station, but she hung back, didn't want to sidle up alongside them after saying goodbye. It'd seem too desperate, even pathetic, and too much like pursuit.

YELLOWLINING WESTBOUND on a packed train Debbie got out her notebook. On the first page were a few attempts at a prologue: *For twenty-five years Pop Street has been camped out behind his old store in a* ~~stoic~~ *steadfast protest against People Park, living out of the houseboat he used to keep at the Bay Junction piers, the ceiling so low the man has developed a permanent hunch* . . . Or: *For most islanders, People Park is a place we only associate with joy: it's where our kids go to daycamp, where we go on dates for picnics, enjoy the Summer Concert Series at the gazebo — but for one widely misunderstood former resident of Lakeview Homes, it's a monument to forgetting, and a place that embodies everything that is wrong about this city* . . . Or: *What is justice?*

Though like many of her teammates she'd majored in Communications at the Institute, Debbie had never considered a career in journalism, the accountability made her nervous. But when Isa Lanyess, a star from the pre-Y's era of the Island Maroons, saw her We-TV fixture, *In the Know*, become the island's preeminent news source, she hired a few ballers who weren't turning pro to write her scripts. I'm the Face of this thing, Lanyess told them, so think of yourselves as my makeup artists. And what's a makeup artist's job? To make the face look good. And also? To make their own work invisible. All anyone should see is my face.

It was a job. For a year Debbie churned out reports on local goings-on with the mechanical proficiency of a windup clock, yet failed to find satisfaction hearing her words spoken on TV by someone else. But the meeting with Pop left her feeling forced to the edge of her own life: she stood there peering down into it, blank and bottomless. When she'd returned to Isa Lanyess's downtown office, Debbie suggested a piece about the Homes might be more interesting than one on Pop's Things.

Lanyess gave Debbie a withering look. People don't care about that guy, she said. Unless *he's* Mr. Ademus. Is he? No, right? Mr. Ademus and the Things are *hot*. So how the fug did Pop Street, who's never been lukewarm by anyone's measure, become the guy's dealer? *That's* what people want to know. So *that's*, are you listening, what you, who I hired, write about. Not some fat loser living in a trailer who can't forget the past.

I just thought there was a bigger story here, said Debbie. Right?

Wrong, said Lanyess. I brought you on here because you struck me as a hard worker, someone who knew how to be part of a team. Was I mistaken?

Debbie had stood there, fists clenched, heart pounding. Lanyess had a way of speaking to her that made her feel not only indebted, but small and young. Like a scolded child, in hateful silence you could only wait until it was over, she told Adine that night, drinking ciders on their couch.

Fug Lanyess, said Adine. Fug that show. I mean, props to Pop Street for making bank selling it, but trash nailed together into funny shapes? That's art now? I guess, according to the superdooshes of this dumb town who buy it up like it's gold.

Debbie tipped back her cider. He can't be making much, she said. The guy's the closest thing this town's got to an ascetic.

Is he? Whatever he is, he's just like, off. Even when me and Sam were kids our mum didn't let us go to his store alone. The Human Polyp, we called him. That's what he's holding on to? He needs to let go of Lakeview Homes, everyone else has.

But, started Debbie — and stopped herself.

What does he even *want*?

Restribution, Debbie said automatically, and Adine rolled her eyes, wrangled Jeremiah into her lap, and buried her nose in his fur.

Now, on the train, Debbie leafed through her notebook, and felt she was closer to a real reason — and the person himself, the two were linked. In her notebook were dozens of Pop's attempts at aphorisms: *If you've an advantage, do it*, e.g., and *People come in a multitudany of kinds, but we've all got the same heart.*

In a way Pop had thrown Debbie's life into relief. To live as he did, a living protest, one had to forgo everything else — social mores, relationships, basic hygiene. His dedication made Debbie feel flaky and capricious. So she'd begun attending his rallies, not as a journalist but as a participant, committed to the Movement, even fancied herself his second-in-command. Though there always lurked the danger of being banished, often for random, arbitrary, and baffling reasons. Most recently Pop had expelled three of Debbie's friends for *Insufficient restritubutive doctrination*. Requests for clarification had been ignored.

So around him Debbie took notes, listened, deferred, and always, always agreed. But what really kept her on his good side was the prospect of being written about: Impart this in your book, he would say, and then enunciate, syllable by syllable, so Debbie didn't miss a word. Being around someone so firm in his vision of the world, and of his purpose upon it, was comforting. And by writing about him Debbie was getting closer to clarity about her own life as well. Because her own life, thought Debbie, as the train slowed into Mustela Station, felt so vague and shifting, a precarious trudge through churning sand: no matter how firmly she stepped, it always felt to be swirling off course, or backward. She wasn't even lost: how could you be lost when you didn't know where you were heading? And so she reeled people in, she surrounded herself with people, she felt all she could do was try to be good, to try in her floundering way to be useful, to help.

A SATELLITE INITIATIVE of the Isa Lanyess Centre for Westend
Betterment, the Room occupied an old crabshack at F Street and
Tangent 15, right on the water, a building on stilts scummed with
algae and around which rippled the lake. But because Upper Olde
Towne Station was under renovation and had been for months,
Debbie preempted her ride at Knock Street and took the escalator
to streetlevel while the train slipped north into the Zone.

On foot she passed Lower Olde Towne's B&B's and Islandwear
outlets and expensive artisanal concerns, horse-drawn buggies
clopped by depositing great steaming dung knolls upon the
cobblestones. At the top end of Knock was the Dredge Niteclub,
a block-long, three-storey partyhouse that had once been a func-
tioning dredge meant to scour Lowell Canal. Past it was the canal,
a gutter of sludge the colour of dead TV screens. Crossing the foot-
bridge Debbie held her breath, the canal's off-gases shimmered
like noxious aurorae, its lustreless surface reflected nothing.

Released into Upper Olde Towne, Debbie gulped cleanish air
and headed up F Street. The east–west Tangents ascended, the
neighbourhood bustled: greengrocers hawked produce, two girls
in throwback Y's jerseys lobbed a ball back and forth in a concrete
parkette, a young couple on a bench smoked Redapples and took
turns ashing into a cup. In shadows under the Yellowline's tracks,
the westside of the street was edged with razorwire that fenced in
disused lots and docks. Debbie stayed on the sunlit eastside, where
rejuvenated properties alternated with boarded-up vacants, the
latter supervising the neighbourhood with the staid melancholy
of blind widowers.

At the corner of F and 10 was the Golden Barrel Taverne. Already
drunks milled about on the sidewalk, taciturn and twitchy, jingling pockets of coins. Debbie smiled, was ignored, kept going

north. This had once comprised her jogging route, abandoned when concerned locals kept flagging her down to ask if she was being chased. The Zone wasn't pretty or quaint but it boasted a certain authenticity, Debbie thought, and though way out on the island's western fringe it struck her as the city's heart, vibrant and essential — or maybe its guts.

At Tangent 15 Debbie waved to Crupper, sweeping the front step of the newsstand opposite the Room. He gestured across the street. Seems they got you last night, he said.

Debbie looked: the Room's front windows had been painted black.

Are you serious? she said.

Crupper shook his head sadly. Animals, he said.

Debbie went up to the window, scratched. The paint came off in a jammy curl under her fingernail, tarlike and still wet.

As always the Room smelled of the faint salmony tang of children and their half-eaten lunches. Debbie hung her coat in the office, checked the messages — none — filled a bucket with soap and water in the bathroom. But before she washed off the blackup she had to attend to the business of her daily We-tv address, which she loathed.

Debbie turned on the camera, readied her spiel: two minutes of tape to satisfy the Island Arts Division trustees and the school-board people, who claimed these updates were meaningful to the parents, but what parents would watch it? There were better things on tv than their kids building papier mâché piñatas and Debbie breaking up fights over pastels.

Adine had tuned in to her bit exactly once and that night she'd mimicked, in a perfectly fake-bright voice: Hi, Debbie here! This is the Room's um, channel! Today's Tuesday and we're making time capsules! Debbie had shut herself in the bathroom and moaned, Why'd you watch it, you know I hate doing it, why have you forsaken me? while Adine cackled on the other side of the door.

Eyes shifting around the room, never quite settling on the lens, Debbie covered the date, the day's crafts (gluesticks, shoeboxes, glitter), and explained the Room would be closed for the long weekend — though, with a three-day tape-to-broadcast delay, she was unsure why this information mattered. When all this was done Debbie shut the camera off and, as its recording light dimmed, felt oddly lonely, unnerved less by the prospect of being watched than by the thought that people, given the choice, might opt not to.

IV

Within the orchard on People Park's eastern fringe, teenagers, some with cameras, watched the last few stragglers filtering back into the city. While Edie videoed, Calum clutched her from behind at the hips, nuzzled her ear, the whisk and swish of her hair against his cheek, his cock throbbed dully in his jeans. But when he winnowed a thumb into the waistband of her skirt Edie squirmed, lowered the camera, and said, We should go to school, and Calum grinded into her and said, Sure? and Edie said, What's wrong with you, and pulled away, and Calum was left with what might be wrong with him, a bit.

IN THE FINAL DAYS of winter he'd gone to a party at Edie's, her parents were away somewhere tropical on their yacht. From his family's apartment in Laing Towers Calum walked south, over the Canal, down Knock Street, and up the cobblestone hill to the Mews, the gated harbourside community that lofted over Lower Olde Towne, where, after a call to Edie, the security guard buzzed him through.

Calum passed mansions festooned with pillars and arches and ornately trellised decks, to the Lanyesses' landscaped yard. On the front porch, smoking, was a girl with her hair shorn into a hand shape, the nape and sides shaved right to the skin. The

Hand. Calum ducked behind a bush. Why was she here, how did she get past security? With her were two kids, hoods up, a pair of goblins. Calum shifted, snow tumbled from the top of the bush in a little avalanche. Laughter, cruel and shrill — they'd seen him.

Hey, the Hand called, why you hiding, party's in here.

So Calum, caught out, made the long dreadful walk up the driveway.

The threesome barely shifted to let him past, he had to squeeze between them, for a moment he was face to face with the Hand, she blasted smoke in his face. Don't lock the door, she said. We'll be right in.

In the living room Edie and a half-dozen of their friends sat in a stiff quiet circle, six ciders on the coffee table, six labels peeled to shreds, a boardgame unpacked and so far unplayed, everyone's pieces loitered on START. Did you see who showed up, Edie whispered. Calum nodded, didn't go over to kiss her.

And the door opened and in gusted the winter and here they were with their shoes on.

Great party, said the Hand, laughed, as sharp as a slap, the laugh hung fizzing in the air. Nobody moved, nobody said anything. Then there was a cry of, You're on TV, and one of the goblins plucked a camera off a tripod in the corner and did a slow pan over everyone's dazed faces, then said, Don't worry, I'm not taping, and gave the camera to Edie, who held it to her chest like an infant.

Towing her sidekicks the Hand withdrew to the foyer. Footsteps headed downstairs.

Go see what she's doing down there, whispered Edie.

Calum stared.

You know her better than any of us. Go!

The goblins sat at the top of the basement stairs, their whispers followed him down. The recroom's open screendoor admitted an icy draft, the deck was dark, but the pool lights were on. Kneeling on the diving board was the Hand.

If you're supposed to be checking up on me, she said, you'd better come out here.

He thought of Edie, of this house, of her parents. When he was over they talked to Edie as Calum's interpreter or warden: And how does your friend do at school, etc., while a mute housekeeper served soup in bowls of bevelled glass. This was what he was now supposed to defend.

The Hand reclined on the diving board. Calum stood in the doorway: what might she do? Snow dusted the flagstones. The pool steamed. Deeper into the backyard was the tennis court, and beyond that, down the hill, Kidd's Harbour, a fleet of pleasurecraft nudged about by waves.

Here's a game, said the Hand. Find a star. Find one.

The sky was the broad back of something huge, turned away.

You can't, can you? Because of all the lights. There's too many lights here so there's no stars. What's the point of being up here if you can't even see the night?

The Hand sat up and spat into the pool: a little raft of phlegm floated atop the water. This is your girlfriend's house, right? The poor little rich girl? She sucks.

Careful, said Calum.

She snorted, moved to the edge of the board. Careful, she said. Careful's nothing.

In a single, swift gesture she pulled her shirt over her head. Her shoes came off next, kicked onto the deck. And finally she stepped out of her jeans. The pool's ghostly light shimmered over her body: parts were dark and then lit, parts were always light, parts were always dark. Calum looked over his shoulder, into the house. And back at the Hand.

Her mouth twitched at the corners. See? she said simply, and flopped into the pool with a splash. She surfaced, just a head, the water mangled the rest of her body into jagged indistinguishable shapes. This was tantalizing, if the waves settled it would all turn clear. Calum imagined diving in, swimming up, touching the smooth wet skin. He tensed, leaned forward on the balls of his feet, toward her —

Well, said the Hand, see you round.

Her legs kicked up and she dove. Calum waited, waited, the ripples stilled — and she didn't come up. He moved poolside: the pool was empty. Giggling came from the house. The goblins rushed out cackling, scooped the Hand's clothes off the deck, and tumbled in wild somersaults into the water. When the bubbles cleared they were gone too.

Later, when Edie and Calum went to bed they realized the brass doorknobs to the master bedroom were missing. I can't believe you let that happen, she said, and rolled away. Overhead glowed the star-stickered ceiling of Edie's room. He thought about the Hand's body in the water, the slick shimmering gibberish of it, and tried to assemble the pieces into a naked whole.

Edie, he said, edging across the mattress, pressing against her. The replica galaxy shone down, dull and green. Hey, Calum murmured — nudging, grinding, stroking. Edie, hey. Edie? But she was either asleep or pretending.

LOOK, SAID CALUM, his voice coaxing, squeezing Edie's hips. Look at these two appleheads, he said, and Edie sighed and looked: a couple, thirtyish, pushing a fancy stroller up the hill toward Orchard Parkway. Calum waited for Edie to ask what was so wrong with them. When she didn't he said, I bet they don't even do it. Edie let his words hang. He crossed his arms around her waist and pressed himself into her backside and said, Hey?

She wriggled away and left Calum holding air. Voices called from within the trees, their friends emerged, watches were tapped, they should go to school. School? said Calum. Come on, Edie. We could go back to my place, my ma's at work all day. But

Edie shook her head firmly. No way, Calum. You might not care about your future but I do. I want to graduate, thanks.

Their friends were moving up the path, behind the stroller couple, in pairs. Calum gazed across the common, at the stage where the famous magician had wowed everyone that morning, and he wondered how it felt to have so many people, together and all at once, say your name.

THE MONDAY after Edie's party Calum awoke to his mother, Cora, leaning her head into his bedroom, eyes ringed with dark, voice a reedy crackle: Okay Cal, up you get, go to school. But he just lay there thinking. After a time his little brother Rupe appeared in the doorway. Ma said you have to take me to school. Take your fuggin self, said Calum, and went back to sleep.

That afternoon he walked up F Street, slushy and unplowed, through the Zone, past Blackacres Station, past the Room, into Whitehall, the factory district, and the ICTS Barns, where the trains went to sleep every night, unlaced sneakers flopping and soaked through to his socks. Past the Barns he entered the industrial district: abandoned warehouses, factories, plants, various Concerns no longer concerned with much, their gerundial purposes (Shipping, Receiving, etc.) painted onto pale splintering wood. At last he came to the massive concrete panpipes of the Favours Brothers silos, long decommissioned, where Calum ducked through a peeled-back section of chainlink. The loading dock was open. Inside was dark as a throat.

He peered into this blackness. There was no sign of the Hand or any of her people. But this was their way: invisible unless and until they wanted to be seen. Yet the gloom seemed to dance with firefly sparkles — dozens of eyes, catlike and glittering, watching him . . .

Calum ran. Back through the fence, out of the docklands to the Piers. Here he hopped out along the blunt-headed stumps of a drowned jetty to the breakwater, the most western point in the city, and sat, heart hammering and dangling shoes refracted in the lake. The air smelled of wet wool and sewage. To the north was the mainland: tan-coloured fields, chalky cliffs, a gravel beach prodded and coaxed with waves — close enough to swim to, but Calum had never been.

HE REACHED FOR EDIE, to hold her, to hold on to anything. But her back was to him. He tapped her shoulder. A half-swivel of her neck: an acknowledgment of what he'd done, but not him.

What?

Nothing, said Calum.

Well are you coming? There was exasperation in Edie's voice. You can't skip, you've already been suspended. Calum?

The only people left in the park were the NFLM, hollering, taking down barricades, rolling up the welcome rug, collecting garbage on spiked sticks, their voices resonated as the woofs and hoots of animals.

One of the men splintered off from the group. He was coming over, crossing the common in a delicate mincing way. Calum said, Look at this guy, but Edie was moving up the hill to join the rest of their friends, waiting to go to school.

LOOK AT THOSE KIDS, said the one named Starx. Hey, partner — look.

Olpert Bailie stopped struggling with the guardrail. Teenagers loitered in the hillside orchard on the eastern edge of the common.

Go tell them to get the fug out of here.

Olpert blinked. Me?

Yeah you. You're the security guard, right? Effortlessly Starx, a man-shaped monster, lifted a barricade into the back of the cube van, hopped up, hauled it alongside the others, and stuck his head out again into the daylight. Get going, he told Olpert. And quit being such a foreskin.

So Olpert went trembling across the swampy common, mud spattered his slacks. It was impossible to tell how many teenagers were gathered among the trees, they shifted in and out of the shadows, they made Olpert's stomach jump and twist. The trains were always full of kids this age, they jostled him, they said things about him, it took such effort not to listen to what they were saying, if you met their eyes they had you.

Surely Starx would have been better at this sort of thing, the man was a giant, a menace, a coil of rage. Also he had on boots. Olpert wore loafers and anger was a language he'd never learned. In fight-or-flight moments he preferred to just stand, to stand and wait. To Olpert life was a negotiation of terror — at the world, but also at himself, as a part of it.

He'd only met Starx the week before, his first visit to the NFLM Temple in two decades. Prior to that he'd sat through the unveiling of his grandfather's portrait alongside the other departed Original Gregories, afterward been granted conciliatory Full Status: Helper Level 1 (Probationary), funnelled the ceremonial pint of schnapps, sat while his legs were shaved by a hunting knife, sprinkled the clippings into the Hair Jar, thanked everyone profusely for the opportunity, and never returned.

Twenty annual newsletters arrived over twenty Decembers, each one junked. In that time Olpert took a job as overnight security at the city's Department of Municipal Works, ten p.m. to six a.m. shifts paging magazines in the building's marble-pillared foyer. At dawn he was relieved by a woman named Betty and took the ferry from Bay Junction to the Islet, then walked home to a roominghouse where the four other lodgers existed only as crusty dishes piled in the shared kitchen sink and occasional thumps or groans from behind their bedroom walls. Also one of them was stealing Olpert's apples.

So went Olpert's life through his thirties, into his forties, punctuated with the sporadic glory of the Lady Y's, his season tickets renewed devotedly each campaign. His body aged: the rusty mop atop his skull thinned and withdrew, his torso softened, the mightiness of his pee stream dwindled. As a kid he'd been an old soul, sombre and serious, taking nightly walks around the Islet with his hands clasped behind his back, and had always assumed in adulthood he'd at last find a home within his own body. Yet at forty-two he still felt apart from himself. Betty suggested a girlfriend might help, instead Olpert took to keeping moles: half his small room was taken up with a terrarium in which they burrowed and lived their delicate, private lives.

In March one of his housemates had taken a message: *Olprt Balie call Griggs*, and there was a number: 978-0887. A bland, almost robotic voice answered — NFLM Temple, Head Scientist speaking — and explained that *all* Helpers, even inactive ones, were required at a mandatory meeting that weekend. You work security, Bailie? asked Griggs, and Olpert told him sort of, yes. Well we can use you then, Griggs said, make your grandpappy proud. And at this Olpert felt something shrivel in his chest.

The following Thursday night he ferried to Bay Junction and switched to a Yellowline westbound to Lower Olde Towne. The Temple was two blocks up Knock Street, housed in what had at one point, before the Mayor's sweeping reforms, been a police station. The building's history was hinted at over the doorway: in rusted steel lettering, OLDE TOWNE POLICE SIA ION — one-and-a-half T's had fallen, the half having maimed a postwoman, the lawsuit was ongoing.

Olpert paused on the doorstep, flooded with memories of that year spent trailing his grandfather into the bi-weekly meetings, less at the old man's side than in his blindspot. As a Recruit, he'd have his mouth ducktaped and spent meetings wedged into a Little Boy Desk. Later everyone but the Recruits pounded schnapps and staggered into the neighbouring Citywagon Depot to unleash orange splashes of meaty man-vomit.

The door swung open and standing there was a six-foot-tall moustache. Bailie! Remember me? growled the moustache. He tapped his nametag — Reed — and hauled Olpert into a handshake that felt like losing an arm to a trash compactor.

I was L1 when you were a Recruit, said Reed. L2 now though.

Olpert recognized him: a manic character keen on workshopping masturbation techniques, his own involving slit fruit.

Reed rattled his bones with a clap on the back, screamed, Diamond-Wood, ready for your ducktape? and leapt away to wrestle a kid on crutches into a headlock.

At a sign-in desk inside the doors, between hauls on an inhaler a Helper named Bean handed Olpert a nametag — in a child's scribble: Belly — and told him. You're the only call-up, you know that? You start your own club or something?

Olpert faltered.

Just fuggin with you. Great to have you back. Now head on in, guys're just getting their shine on.

Little about the Temple had changed. The walls were still panelled in a plastic approximation of wood, the floors the chipped tile of an elementary school gymnasium, track lighting flickered by the bathroom doors — one denoted with an M, the other with an upside-down W. Queues to both toilets choked the corridor, and whenever a man came out the next one went in fanning the air in reverent disgust.

Everywhere men performed manhood: punching, wrestling, grunting, roaring — there was so much roaring. All the Helpers wore nametags, official NFLM golfshirts, khakis, and the generic black sneakers of elementary school custodians. Olpert's own uniform, resurrected from his leaner, lither Recruit days, spandexed his body, and his shoes — loafers, always loafers — seemed conspicuously unsporty and brown.

From the recroom came the burnt sour smell of too-strong coffee, pingpong ticktocked within a rumble of voices. Helpers sprawled on recliners, the bigscreen chopped between classic episodes of the incredibly popular *Salami Talk* and the NFLM's own We-TV fixture (mostly pingpong). In the library things were more docile: a half-dozen men swirling snifters of schnapps debated the topic of Helping. Beyond this Olpert hovered as a child might outside his feuding parents' bedroom.

Well people here just don't seem to appreciate how we hold the city together, a man was proselytizing, to murmurs of agreement. Most people, he continued, most people wouldn't know what to do if we stopped helping. It'd be chaos!

A different man jumped in, lisping: Juθt baθic θurvival, people have no idea how to θurvive if they have to. They've got it too fuggin eaθy.

Dack, come here, growled the first man, let's see how you'd get out of a chokehold.

Some shuffling, a pause. The first man was flipped on his back.

See? he called from the rug. *That's* how we do.

That'θ how we do, confirmed Dack.

Another man spoke up: My neighbour, you know what he's got in his garage? Nothing. Honestly, it's amazing, shelf after empty shelf — not even a *hose.*

Amid jeers and snide laughter, Olpert thought of his own garage: the roominghouse didn't have a garage.

He drifted back through the foyer into the dimly lit, high-ceilinged, pew-lined Great Hall. The walls were the same fake wood as the rest of the Temple, but stained darker, suggesting the kitschy austerity of a stripmall funeral parlour. Ringing the room were portraits of late Original Gregories — and here, by the door, was Olpert's own grandfather, face youthful and taut, gazing down along a pelican's beak of a nose.

From the front of the Great Hall came a smashing sound — a gong, the Summons, the night's assembly would soon begin. One by one the High Gregories emerged from a semi-secret portal that led to the Chambers and took their seats upon the dais. In the shadows, wielding a felt-tipped mallet, stood a massive, bullet-shaped man with no discernable neck — the Summoner — beside whom the gong hissed into stillness. Had he always been there, Olpert wondered, lurking in the dark?

With a great crash the Summoner struck the gong again. Last up from the tunnel appeared Favours, pushed out in a wheelchair by a ducktaped Recruit. Favours, the final remaining OG, appeared to have been unearthed from the grave: a face made of dust, eyes that ambivalently surveyed the living world as though already glimpsing the other side. The Recruit positioned him upon the dais and retreated.

Affixed to the wall above Favours' head was a six-foot version of the NFLM crest: atop an outline of the city, a naked woman and winged man entwined in coitus. Above this image was written *New Fraternal League of Men: The Mighty Ones of Eternity,* and below it the four pillars: *Silentium. Logica. Securitatem. Prudentia.*

The gong exploded again, again, again, and Olpert slid into the end of a pew as Helpers shuffled in, some twirling pingpong paddles. The High Gregories took their seats on the dais, flanking Favours. At the far end of the table was Wagstaffe, the NFLM's current Silver Personality and host of We-TV's *Salami Talk,* which featured interviews leavened with a barely euphemistic sausage-making theme. In person he was even more orange-skinned and drastically chinned than he seemed on TV.

Beside Wagstaffe was Magurk, the Special Professor, a ratlike and savagely hairy man. As an L1 he'd wrestled Olpert into a half nelson and demanded to be told which pressure points it was possible to kill a man by striking. Out of nowhere Olpert's grandfather had come barrelling down the hall, dropkicked Magurk in the lower back, and, as he crumpled, suggested, That one?

To Favours' right, in the Imperial Master's chair, sat a tense, taciturn man Olpert remembered as Noodles — older than the rest, in his sixties, golfshirt tailored into a turtleneck. Framing a stoic, pink face were a white brushcut and matching goatee. Noodles rarely spoke, just icily observed, yet was always nodding, as if his head were physically affirming its own secret thoughts. He worried Olpert even more than Magurk.

Griggs, the Head Scientist, took the podium. His hair was puttied into twin crisp halves, beneath which his face remained expressionless and waxen, almost animatronic in its movements, the way the forehead crinkled and flattened, the nose dipped obediently when he opened his mouth to speak. Quiet now, he said, in a voice like wind over water.

Pivoting on his hindquarters the bullish Summoner wound up and bashed the gong a final time. The murmuring around the room faded. Everyone stood for the Opening Oath, led by Griggs in a droning monotone from the pages of *How We Do*, the ongoing codex of NFLM ideology and activities. Olpert joined where he could remember: Let us all swear an oath . . . A new year is dawning . . . Stay awake to the ways of the world . . . sworn and bound . . . in eternal execration . . . the last days and times . . . from generation to generation and forever . . . the mighty ones of eternity . . . all men.

The gong sounded again, the NFLM lowered into the pews, and the Summoner, perspiration ringing his armpits, squeezed into the empty seat beside Olpert. He nodded, a downward bob of his neckless head, his shoulders were foothills that sloped into the mountainside of his face. With a glance at Olpert's nametag (his own read: *Starx*), the man took Olpert's hand and whispered, Good lookin out, Belly.

Starx's hand was weirdly tiny for such a huge man. The handshake felt to Olpert like having his fingertips gummed by a small, toothless lizard.

Hi, said Olpert. Good looking out.

The meeting got underway: Griggs conceded the mic to Magurk, who took it in his furry fist and began strolling the aisles. Terrified he'd be recognized, singled out, perhaps even attacked, Olpert slouched and averted his eyes. From the back of the Hall four Recruits crammed into Little Boy Desks, ducktape over their mouths, videotaped the proceedings — that was new, the cameras. One was the cripple, Diamond-Wood.

The rest of the men were the same as ever, broad and tense, with a primordial intensity in their eyes that goaded: Try and test me, just try. All of them, save Griggs in his socks and sandals, wore those same black sneakers. Olpert covered his left loafer with the right, then the right with the left. For some reason he found himself trying to estimate how many individual testicles were in the building — and had to shake his head to rattle the dangly jungle this conjured from his brain.

Magurk's speech, whatever it had been, was over. My people, he said, you ready to show this city the best weekend of their lives? Are you with me? Are you fuggin *with me*?

Yeah! roared the men.

Starx punched the air, grinned at Olpert, whispered, Gotta love this stuff.

Magurk passed the microphone to Wagstaffe, reassumed his seat at the edge of the dais, rabies frothed at the corners of his lips. Positioning himself in the Great Hall's most photogenic light, Wagstaffe spoke rousingly of courage, the four pillars, the NFLM's responsibilities, history, order, the cameras rolled. The speech seemed a little too performed, infused with a mannered nonchalance meant to deny the presence of a viewership beyond the Temple. But people would be watching. They always were.

Was it less of a lonely life to be watched like that? To know you were seen? Olpert thought of his own life, the furtive hush of it. As a child he had more than anything wished to be invisible, to just drift through the world without being heard or judged. Two pews back was Reed, stroking his moustache. Did Reed have a wife? A family? Or was the NFLM his only family, and was that enough? The New Fraternal League of Men, thought Olpert: like a religion, except all they had to believe in was one another.

Wagstaffe handed the mic to Noodles, who pressed it to his lips, nodded, nodded, the room was silent, expectant — and with a final nod tendered it to Griggs.

Applause.

Helpers, Griggs began, though Olpert lost focus — Starx had shifted, his arm pressed against Olpert's. It was a hot, heavy arm. He was very close, he smelled of boiled cabbage and wet towels clumped on the floor for a week, his nostrils flared and whistled. There was something almost soporific about his breathing, the steady in-out rhythm of it, it lulled Olpert, he listened and lost himself a little —

And now Starx was elbowing him, standing. Everyone was standing.

Olpert flushed and jumped to his feet.

Starx moved gongside. What had Olpert missed? He checked his watch, an hour had passed, how? Everyone rose for the Final Oath, which Olpert lip-synched as best he could. Starx banged the gong a final time and came at Olpert, seized him by the upper arms. Olpert tensed to create muscles there (biceps, triceps, whatever).

What do you know, Belly, said Starx, me and you: partners. B-Squad.

Me and you?

Yeah. Pretty big honour. Us as the magician's official escorts or whatever.

Starx still held him, Olpert was growing exhausted from clenching his fists. Around the room like a prisonyard dance men had partnered off muttering in low tones. Starx's eyes scanned Olpert's face — and at last he was released.

Me and you, Belly, said Starx, smacking a small fist into his palm. Big time. You work security? Good. Here's our lanyard. You take it, it won't fit me — Starx gestured sadly at his colossal head. Nice to get a Citypass though. Ever drive one of those wagons?

No. I don't drive much really. I get a little nervous on the roads —

Great. Seriously though, Belly, this kinda makes me think they're grooming me for a bump, if you know what I mean. Maybe even to HG. I mean, because you're still, what? Technically only Probe or something, right? Because you quit or whatever.

It's Bailie.

So you'd think they paired you with me because I'm like, senior or whatever. Bigups have gotta be due soon. I know Noodles has his eye on the top spot — I mean, Favours isn't going to be around forever.

Across the room the old man, deserted on the dais, had spun himself around. He bumped against the wall, a disoriented animal trying to tunnel its escape.

Poor guy, said Starx.

My name, I mean, Olpert tried again. They spelled it —

Belly! Heads up, here comes the We-tv crew.

A Recruit sidled up with a camera. Starx hauled Olpert under his arm, displayed him with paternal pride, and beamed into the lens. Me and my man Belly here, Raven, if you end up watching this, we're gonna make this the best weekend you ever had. Welcome to our fair city! He squeezed Olpert roughly. Anything to add, Belly?

Olpert Bailie looked at his hands. His fingernails dug ridges into his palms. Bailie, he whispered. My name's Olpert Bailie.

Best weekend you ever had, Raven, repeated Starx, through a teeth-gritted smile.

The Recruit moved off to shoot a pair of Helpers by the Citypass cache playing tug-of-war with a lanyard. Starx fixed Olpert with a stare. Hey, dingledink, I know you've been away awhile but we use patronyms in this here outfit. Everyone's first name Gregory, last name whatever — in your case, Belly. Got it?

Olpert tried to meet Starx's eyes. But they were hard eyes to meet, twitching over everything but settling nowhere. What did they see?

CALUM WATCHED the gingery man highstepping his way through the mud to the bottom of the hill, where he did a salute sort of thing over his eyes, squinted, and, in a voice like a feebly blown flugelhorn, told them they needed to leave the park. School time! he said.

From the top of the hill one of Calum's friends said, We've got the morning off.

Well the morning's over, right? said the man. He wore a name-tag: *Belly.*

Grumblings, mild protest, but there had already been talk of going to school. Calum felt apart from them, from everything, standing there alone at the edge of the orchard.

He looked past Belly, into the sun, high above the treetops now. When he'd been little, Cora had told him never to look at it directly, it could blind you. So now he stared not just at but into the sun. He wouldn't go blind. Nothing would happen to him. But after a few seconds Calum looked away, blinking and queasy.

THE NIGHT AFTER being suspended for skipping class Calum lay awake in bed until his mother's gentle snores came wisping down the hallway. He tiptoed out the door, slid his shoes on in the stairwell, and, ducking in and out of shadows to evade Helper patrols, ran all the way to Whitehall, where he waited by the loading dock. Past one a.m., past two, to that nothing hour when the moon sagged and dimmed and the night became infinite. It was only then they appeared from underground, a faceless hoodied mob toting cans of paint and rollers.

From behind someone grabbed his shoulders and Calum tensed — but the Hand was leaning in, the soft warmth of her cheek upon his cheek. So you're with us? she whispered in his ear, and Calum told her, Yes.

He'd been delirious with it, the silent stealthy rigour of the herd slipping through the streets, so many of them, he stayed at the Hand's side. It was random yet purposeful: someone picked a window and someone else unfolded a stepladder and up Calum went, taping the top of the frame and around its upper corners while someone else did the bottom. Then the painters stepped forward with their rollers and the quiet filled with the zipping sound of acrylic pasted over glass, and when they were done Calum tore off the tape and there it was: a blackup. And on to the next window, wherever it might be.

Time disappeared. Calum lost count of the blackups. He felt giddy. At some point the night began fading, he'd just finished taping the vitrines that fronted a pretentious hardware store. When he came down the Hand told him, This'll be the last one, and pressed close and her breast was against his arm and she said, Fun, right? and he said, Yes, and she laughed and went off to gather the troops.

Calum admired their final piece, the big bright window negated into a dead black thing. He patted the wet paint and transferred a handprint to the wall. Stepping back he saw himself in the five-fingered outline on the bricks and thought how being a person was at once such a big incomprehensible thing and so, so small.

But the Hand had returned to curse him: What are you doing, that's not how we do it. She spat. You think you're special? You don't get it, we're all part of this, no one's above anyone else.

She turned her back on him. Everything withered. The group tramped away and so did the Hand and Calum stood there deserted in the middle of D Street while the sky lightened into morning, his handprint growing more stark and black and stupid as the bricks around it blanched, and knew he was a fool.

YOU TOO, OKAY? said the man, Belly, to Calum. Time to go to school.

At the top of the hill Edie and everyone else were waiting for him. Above them, rising out of Orchard Parkway towered the Redline Station. But why go? Being suspended had been liberating, all that time alone with his thoughts.

Hey? said Belly.

He was about Calum's mother's age. He was struggling to be brave, something he wasn't. He couldn't meet Calum's eyes. You could tell he was no one.

Calum moved out of the shade. Belly wavered. From up the hill Edie called, Cal, hey, we're going, let's go.

Belly still wouldn't look at him, he cast a sidelong glance over the common, muttered, Okay now, thanks a lot.

Calum took another step downhill, turned his head, hawked from deep in his throat, then spat a jiggling gob that landed at the man's feet.

Hey, said Belly. But his voice was weak.

One of his classmates said, Did Calum just spit at that guy? and Edie called: Calum, hey! Calum, what are you doing?

Belly watched the spit foaming on the grass, the little bubbles popped one by one. For some reason, he closed his eyes. He swayed.

Calum hawked again and spat. Belly flinched as it struck him in the cheek, but his eyes stayed shut. Edie screamed. Yet she didn't

come running down the slope. In fact there was a sudden emptiness to the air that suggested she and the rest of their friends had
fled. How did Calum feel? He couldn't feel anything.

His spit wiggled down Belly's face.

And then from somewhere came a sudden rush of something
swift and huge. A second figure in the same beige shirt was steaming up the slope, and Calum barely had time to cringe before a fist
caught him in the face. A sparkle of lights, his legs gave way, the
earth swam up to catch him, cool and damp. An enormous pair of
legs stood over him — black sneakers and khaki trousers — and
from high above a deep godlike voice boomed: You fug with my
man Belly? You're nothing, you hear me? You're nothing, nothing,
nothing, you're fuggin nothing.

V

ITH JEREMIAH nuzzling her feet, Adine channel-upped past people showing off their musical skills, giving hotplate cooking lessons and walking tours of their neighbourhoods, hawking used electronics, performing standup routines, etc., all those endless lonely voices, each one calling into We-TV's echoless ether, all the way to 73, where the woman, Faye Rowan-Morganson, drained and draining and tragically fascinating, the lure of a stranger's tragedy, was just beginning her daily introduction.

Well it's Monday, she sighed, welcome to *The Fate of Faye Rowan-Morganson*. Though if anyone's even watching, for you it's Thursday by now. I hope you're having a better Thursday than my Monday anyway. I'm having a hard day.

A pause, which Adine, seeing nothing, had to fill with her imagination. Maybe Faye Rowan-Morganson was just staring into the camera, at herself reflected in the lens. Maybe she had stepped out of frame for a moment, maybe she was getting a drink. Adine raised the volume a couple clicks and listened for the knock of a mug or glass placed back on the kitchen table.

Of course, since Adine saw nothing, this table was just one detail in a world she imagined for this stranger every noonhour, the rest of the kitchen sparse and dimly lit, more scullery than culinary suite, just a sink, bare countertops, with this pale and drawn woman hunched at a plastic table with her arms outstretched, thin arms, reaching toward the camera and toward anyone who might be watching. Or not watching: listening.

THAT NIGHT, back in February, when Debbie came home to Adine painting the goggles black she joked, Is this so you don't have to clean out the mousetraps? Later, in a more delicate tone, she asked, Is this about your accident when you were a kid? Adine pulled the goggles over her eyes and stared into the emptiness concocting some acid response.

Finally she said, No. It's about trying to be alone.

The air went taut.

Adine sensed Debbie hovering, wounded. Then the bedroom door closed and from behind it came whimpering. Adine turned on the television: two Helpers were elucidating the merits of a backhand serve. After a few minutes she called Sam. Tell me what's happening, she said. And happily he did.

Watching TV without seeing: this became her work. Not *investigating blindness as phenomenology*, not *a (sub)liminal exploration of nonvisual space*, not an *inquiry* or *critique* of any sort. Not lost in words. She just wore the goggles day and night, flipping channels, seeing nothing beyond the pictures her imagination painted inside her mind. Maybe one day her hands would paint them. Maybe not.

At 1:00 and 5:00 and 9:00 Sam would call and narrate the action in two-hour chunks. Her brother felt so faraway out there on the Islet, it was good to connect again. Before We-TV's closed-circuit democratized the airwaves, they'd grown up together with television: cartoons and gameshows and the overwrought daytime dramas in which soft focus signified both memories and dreams.

Meanwhile Debbie was out saving the world with her endless friends and colleagues and contacts and networks and indomitable faith in the city and its citizens. Adine found it all exhausting: pleasing so many people fractured Debbie into many different people herself. From the moment they'd met she'd struck Adine this way, trying to please her even as Adine ranted and raved and shoved her against a wall.

This had been at an IAD gala, a semi-formal banquet celebrating the new arts-dedicated floors at the Museum of Prosperity. The exhibits included a retrospective of Loopy's work, four sculptures by the mysterious Mr. Ademus, and, thanks to Isa Lanyess's on-air lament, Adine's Sand City, which technicians had unearthed from Budai Beach and shellacked and preserved under glass. Though she'd been invited, Adine played event-crasher, ninety-five pounds of rage storming past security, her hair a brushfire, right up to the host of *In the Know*.

I'm just the show's Face, explained Isa Lanyess. She pointed across the room at Debbie skulking by the punchbowl. *She's* the one whose idea it was, *she's* the one who wrote the script, *she's* who's responsible for your sculpture getting saved. Talk to her.

You? Adine railed, driving a finger into Debbie's chest. You're responsible for this? You want to *save* Sand City? Do you understand *anything*? Who even *are* you?

I just thought it was a waste to have such beautiful work washed away, Debbie whispered, steering Adine into the coatroom. She begged her to go for a coffee or a cider or a meal or something, please, she'd only loved the exhibit and —

Exhibit? You and your fuggin *exhibit*. Adine produced a notebook from her pocket and in a voice of mockery recited: . . . *that infinitesimally detailed replica of the city, heartbreakingly rendered, building by building, in sand-sculpted miniature. What a travesty to have such a magical creation just erode into the lake.* You doosh, she sighed, destroying it was the fuggin point! But her rage seemed to be waning.

They should talk more, this wasn't the best time or place, Debbie told her, she just wanted to support what was good. Please, she said, I'm sorry.

Fine, ciders. But you have to come to my neighbourhood.

Ciders became dinner (wings) and more ciders, a soft and nervous goodbye, another round of ciders the following week, a midnight walk down to Budai Beach, a kiss on the sand, and a few nights later, back at Adine's apartment, the two of them collapsing sweat-slicked on either side of the mattress. Debbie whispered, Let me hold you, and Adine cracked up, a snort that exploded into goosy hoots while Debbie disappeared under the duvet. I was just trying to be nice, came her voice, muffled by the covers. Adine cackled: *Let me hold you* — what a precious swan you are, it's adorable.

JUST AS FAYE ROWAN-MORGANSON was signing off — Well if there's anyone even watching thanks for listening, hope it wasn't too depressing — the phone rang.

It was Debbie: You sound out of breath, she said.

No, said Adine, just working.

Oh? Oh good. Me too. Except guess what? I got blackedup. Can you believe that?

Sam's going to be calling soon.

It's just you'd think they'd respect, I don't know, that this is a place for kids. No?

At one. What time is it?

Nearly Lunchtime Arts. But listen, that old friend of mine? Pearl? She's in town tonight. And I'd told her I was planning this big reunion —

Pearl . . . Your former colleague.

Teammate.

Teammate, whatever.

Ha, well she was a million times the player I ever was. I mean, she went pro, for one thing. But I haven't heard back from *anyone* from the old team. Do you think you could join us? So it's not just me and her?

Ew, Jeremiah's doing that bum-licking thing. I can hear it. Ew, ew. He's really going for it. Get in there, buddy!

Adine, hey, it'd be nice if you came. I mean, you don't have to decide now or anything. If it's last minute, that's fine. Just, you know, keep it mind. She'd love to see you.

She would? Or you feel bad you couldn't raise a crowd?

Please?

Are you coming home first?

Didn't I tell you about this thing out in Whitehall? With one of the older kids? Calum?

He's — ew. Should we put one of those cones on him? Listen, I'll hold the phone up.

Adine?

Did you hear that? It's like, *slurping*. Do you think he has worms?

Anyway I might write it up for *In the Know*, this thing, it's some sort of concert or something. And before you say anything, I know, slaving myself to Lanyess again, but we need the money. Or I do anyway. And then meeting Pearl, so. See you after? If not before?

What about dinner? Picture me, alone at the kitchen table eating corn from the can.

Meet us! We're just going to the Barrel for wing night, it's two minutes from the apartment. And if not to eat you could at least come by to say hi?

Silence on Adine's end of the line.

The door jangled and slammed: the first kids arriving for Lunchtime Arts, three of them smacking one another with their knapsacks. Debbie held a finger to her lips, the kids hushed. Adine, she said, you there? I have to go.

Love me.

I do. I do!

Of course you do. You love everyone.

AT THE STROKE OF ONE, Sam called his sister.

It's one o'clock Adine, he said. Time to do the work. Time's a machine right Adine?

It sure is, Sammy. Thanks for calling. What's on?

Salami Talk Adine, said Sam, and switched the phone to his other ear, clamped it against his shoulder. On 12 a tearful Knock Street florist was raving to Lucal Wagstaffe about being blackedup. When she finished, he leaned in with half-lidded eyes and murmured, How terrible, madam — but what are your feelings on spicy meat?

I can't do this, said Adine. Anything else, please.

Flipping the dial Sam said, Are you ready for Monday Adine?

What's Monday, buddy?

We're thirty-six on Monday Adine. The end of the third hand.

Ha. Right.

And then it's the end of the work right Adine? The end of time's third hand when the machine stops and goes backward. All the way back to the beginning right?

Buddy, I get a little lost when you —

Then time's machine will take us to thirty-six years ago okay, when we were zero and together okay Adine. Right Adine?

You want to get together for our birthday? You want to come out here? Sure . . .

Sam smeared his thumb into the worn arrow on his remote, the TV chunked from one channel to the next, through the hissing blizzard of channel 0, at 99 pictures appeared again. He paused on an infotainment program where neon graphics splashed across the screen to the zipping sounds of lasers. Sam watched.

What are you watching? What channel are you on?

He's doing his trick tomorrow night at nine Adine, said Sam.

What? What channel?

Raven. This is what Isa Lanyess, *In the Know*, is saying now okay. Channel 83. She's not saying what he's doing yet — Raven.

Raven, ugh. Just the *name*.

It's going to be in the park Adine. But it'll be on TV too. Not even tape-delayed. *Live.*

Hey, buddy, the talking stuff — I'm good, okay? You don't have to tell me that stuff. I can hear fine. It's just seeing. So if there's something to see, jump in there.

Sam said, Yes.

He watched and listened while Adine listened. Isa Lanyess, *In the Know*, was talking about the downtown movie theatre, Cinecity, where people could come if they wanted to watch what was happening everywhere else, all at once, on the bigscreen.

With all the We-TV Faces' feeds, *plus* all the public cameras, there'll be coverage of every neighbourhood in the city, Isa Lanyess said. So anything that Raven does will be projected live to anyone who wants to see it!

That's kinda crazy, said Adine.

Who knows what he'll do? said Isa Lanyess. We're all really excited.

The woman doesn't so much talk as *bray*. Don't you think, Sammy?

It's kinda crazy, said Sam. Why's it kinda crazy Adine?

Buddy, that they can even *do* that sort of thing. Turn the city into a movie set, I mean.

And then don't forget, said Isa Lanyess, starting on Saturday, Cinecity's going to be broadcasting the Jubilee *Spectacular*, all weekend. And don't forget *All in Together Now*, the movie for the people, by the people, that *you* all helped write and create!

Oh, wait, said Adine. *This* is the worst ever.

Ever Adine?

Ever.

The report ended. An ad for *Salami Talk* came on, a feline slink of bass guitars and saxophone beneath the sultry voice of its host: Tomorrow on *Salami Talk* we'll —

Adine hit MUTE. This fuggin show, she growled. This fuggin guy.

They're having Raven on tomorrow. As a guest.

Right.

Lucal Wagstaffe's chin, said Sam, is a very big orange chin.

Hey, Sammy? How's that thing on your face? Are you taking care of that?

Can we watch this interview Adine?

Don't pick at it. Remember what the doctor said. And you got that ointment, make sure you're putting that on. And food? Today's grocery day, right? Make sure you go.

Yes. Adine? Raven's on at one o'clock. That's perfect, that's when we do the work.

It is.

Adine?

Sammy?

I'm sorry.

You're sorry.

Yes.

For?

Because you can't see okay.

Oh. Ha. Right. Well thanks.

But we're doing the work right Adine? We're doing good communication. And it's only Monday when it's our birthday and we're thirty-six and time's machine —

Indeed, buddy. I appreciate it.

Adine hung up and Sam sat for a moment with the phone pressed to his ear, waiting for the dialtone to be replaced by the machinations grinding away beneath the city's surface. When it emerged, the sound was faint. Did that mean the machine was slowing? Sam wasn't sure. He checked his three watches. The first two had stopped, their six hands aligned at midnight, the final watch's three still wheeled. He put the receiver back in its cradle, looked around his room at the various parts and elements, trying to decide if a last-minute cog or gear required adding before the end.

Sam touched the scabby crust along his jawline, felt a loose flake, and pulled. The pain as it peeled from his cheek was lemony and sour, his eyes watered. The air was cold on the raw spot. He brushed his finger over the sore, paused, then stabbed inside. The hurt was sudden and sharp. Sam closed his eyes and said, This is time's machine and not a dream, and gouged, and finally, gasping, pain blazing in his face, examined his fingertip: capped in a thimble of blood.

ON THE FERRY to Bay Junction Sam stood on the deck with his hands on the railing, the boat's engines growled, the water frothed and sloshed, the day dimmed. An Islet-bound ferry passed transporting workers home from their downtown jobs, their own work. Citybound it was only Sam and an elderly man with his cane on his lap, whom Sam avoided. It was important workers were unseen, and good communication with Adine was important too, though Sam's own work had many elements: good communication, proper attire, dream checks, systems maintenance — all of it, all the way to time's reversal, and then they'd be at the beginning again, before everything went wrong and changed.

When the ferry arrived at the mainland Sam did not head down into Bay Junction Station as the old man did. He could walk to Street's Milk & Things, though it was much farther than it had once been. When he and Adine were kids they'd lived so close that if his mother Connie needed milk for her coffee he could run over and get it before the water even boiled, though they had to go together, the Polyp's products were often expired: you had to know the calendar, you had to check the dates.

Normally Sam walked, head down, up the path from Lakeview Campground into the woods, past the Friendly Farm Automatic Zoo and out beside the People Park Throughline, then down into the common and up through more woods, finally entering the clearing and past the houseboat to the glowing white sign of Street's Milk & Things. But today Sam stopped at the edge of the poplars on the southern ridge of the common and stood for a moment, looking.

The common was empty, the muddy ground golden in the late-afternoon light. On television that morning the whole park had been teeming with bodies, all those bodies that existed within time's machine, each body held a brain that made it a person, and each person had a mother and maybe a sister, or a brother, and friends, or at least other people they knew, and those people had brains and families, and more people attached to them, and it was endless, a great sprawling lattice of people and their brains upon people with more brains that grew and looped back upon itself and grew again, forever, yet everyone was so separate. Though soon time's machine would bring them all together.

Deep underground (and monitored on Sam's wrist) turned the three final hands, most people were oblivious, they just lived their lives. Which was fine. Only a select few could be responsible for the work, though Sam had to remind himself that anyone among the city's bodies could be a worker — you didn't know, you were only permitted to connect with two other workers. And his connects were Adine and the Polyp.

Atop the Grand Saloon Hotel the towerclock's hands were locked at nine. Sam recalled Raven putting his fist to his forehead and his eyes opening and the nothing within them, they were just holes, and the clock had stopped. It had only two hands, was not official, its rotations were marked by minutes. So Sam stared at the clock and counted to sixty. The hands did not move. He counted again: nothing. Yet upon his own wrist his third watch still chipped away, seconds to minutes to hours . . .

Sam listened: birds chirruped and the leafless branches of the poplars creaked in a tired wind and on Parkside West cars went by with an airy, breathy sound — but there was no grinding of gears, no clank of levers, no steady drone of engines or tick of meters or hiss of valves from underground. The earth didn't vibrate and hum. The towerclock was still. Sam touched his scab and felt pain. This was real. He looked out over the common and said, Hello? But to whom. The park was empty. There was nobody there.

STREET'S MILK & THINGS hadn't changed since Sam was a kid: the sad clinking of the bells over the door as you entered, its owner the Polyp affixed to his stool behind the counter, everything furred with dust, you came out feeling grimy and damp. Near the door was a rack that held one yellowing dirty magazine and a poorly folded map, the scantily stocked shelves were organized by container type: boxes of cereal and detergent and nails, canned goods huddled together below — corn-in-a-can, catfood, motor oil, a labelless can, in black marker it asked: BEANS?

In the back of the store was a sign that heralded: MR. ADEMUS'S THINGS. Upon these shelves Sam filed the parts to be collected by another worker who passed them along to another worker to maintain time's machine. Now though the shelves were empty. Everything was in place. The work was done. There was nothing to do now but wait for Monday, the end. But what about the towerclock, locked, and the silence —

Mr. Street the Polyp came waddling out from behind the counter. Hello, Mr. Ademus, once again. Old friend! As you can envisage for yourself, you're a sellout. Success!

A hand came at him: a bulge of meat that slumped into a wrist, an arm, up to a humped shoulder, a neck lost under a sludge of chins. Grinning lips, yellow teeth, from the mouth a bad smell. But first the hand.

Grudgingly Sam took it: now Street had him, he squeezed. The fat man started ranting, nothing Sam wanted to hear — restribution this and historiographically that — all the while pumping Sam's hand with his fat, hot hand. At last he pulled away grinning. Mr. Ademus!

Hi, said Sam, Mr. Street, but what about time's machine? It's stopped or I can't hear it okay. And it's supposed to be Monday that the machine reverses and time turns back, the third hands I mean. And do you think it's Raven Mr. Street? Who might stop the work?

Pop shook his head sadly. Almost without refutation, he sighed. This charlating they've plotted upon our fair island, how could he not be balsamic of all your whoas?

And so? Should we do something Mr. Street?

Mr. Ademus, prehaps more work? More *things*, prehaps?

But should we try to stop him Mr. Street?

Unrefutably! He must — Pop looped an arm over Sam's shoulders, placed his mouth to Sam's ear, dropped his voice to a whisper — *be stopped*.

Okay.

Now, said Pop, clapping, Mr. Ademus, about you endowning me with new works.

Sam told him no.

Ah. So today you endown me only with shopping?

Sam told him yes.

Then beplease yourself and shop till you've dropped!

From the freezer Sam took a stack of nuclear meals, put them on the counter, and waited for Pop to ring them in.

Once again, Mr. Ademus, please consider these on my house. As grace for your things.

Sam took his groceries, turned to leave.

Until tomorrow, Mr. Ademus?

If there even is a tomorrow okay, said Sam, and headed out the jingling door, home.

VI

THE GRAND SALOON'S penthouse was in the cathedral's former belfry. On either side of the suite's door stood the watchmen of B-Squad: the Summoner — Starx — and Olpert Bailie.

Inside the room napped Raven, he needed his sleep, though who knew what he got up to in private, thought Olpert. There was something strange in his eyes — or, more, it seemed they weren't there at all. The illustrationist had requested the A/C cranked, so the air was icy and brittle. While Starx fiddled with the walkie-talkie clipped to his belt, Olpert shivered, blew into his hands, hugged himself.

Starx looked him over from head to toe and said, You haven't thanked me yet, Belly.

Bailie, said Olpert. My name is Olpert Bailie.

Sure, sure.

You want me to thank you.

I knocked that kid the fug *out*!

A kid. You punched a kid.

He spat on you. And you were just standing there. What's wrong with you?

Olpert had no idea what to do with this question.

You got a lady, Bailie?

A girlfriend.

Starx nodded.

Not currently.

You go out a lot?

Out?

To meet ladies.

Olpert thought about the last date he'd been on, nearly a year ago. His colleague Betty had set him up with her sister, Barbara, of the recent divorce and red leather pants. Things had been going fine, considering, until the nosebleed.

He shrugged. Sometimes, I guess.

Starx's walkie-talkie crackled — Griggs, with instructions: at six p.m. they were to escort the illustrationist to the hotel's banquet hall. The NFLM had taken the liberty of booking Olpert off work until Tuesday. So he's all ours, said Griggs, all weekend. Then he recited the four pillars, traded Good lookin outs with Starx, and the radio went dead.

Listen, let me buy you a cider, said Starx, turning to Olpert, when we're done tonight.

A cider.

Or two. Or nine. You ever been to the Golden Barrel?

In Upper Olde Towne ?

You sound nervous.

Nervous?

You'll be fine with me. That's my hood, been out there since — a while. Tell you what, we'll do our business, bust outta here say eightish, and be over there to make wing night. The Barrel's got a *killer* wing special till nine.

Wings.

Holy shet, yes.

Somewhere, the A/C came on with a whoosh. Olpert closed his eyes, shivered. Opened them.

And standing there was the illustrationist.

Olpert's bowels slackened, but didn't release.

Gentlemen, said Raven.

Starx took an elongated stride backward and stooped — more of a lunge than a bow.

Raven said, You are my escorts to this dinner, I understand. This celebratory *homage*.

We are, said Starx.

Good. Your names?

Starx.

Olpert. I mean, Bailie.

You attended my arrival this morning.

We sure did, said Starx. Really amazing stuff, sir —

Fine, yes. But may I ask how the morning's events made you feel.

Sorry, said Starx. Made us *feel*?

Yes. What emotions did you experience. When I touched down, or made the illustration involving the birds, or when I trunked away. How you — Raven's hand twirled in an evocative gesture — felt. Please explain.

His accent could be described only as foreign, something bad actors might adopt to suggest *somewhere else*, all rolling r's and hacking k's, but even then nothing was consistent — a sentence later the vowels might drawl and twang.

Olpert said, I felt a bit nervous.

I don't think that's what he was after, said Starx. He's always a bit nervous, this guy.

No, no, said the illustrationist. Nervous is good. What else.

Um, scared.

Scared, good.

I was sort of hungry, said Starx.

Raven's eyes flicked briefly to Starx, back to Olpert. His gaze was vertiginous — like an undertow, that helpless sensation of being tugged under.

Mr. Bailie, how else did you feel.

Anxious. And frightened. And worried, uneasy.

Starx elbowed him. Those are the same as nervous and scared.

Perhaps they are, said Raven. But continue. Why, what made you feel this way.

Something felt . . . wrong.

God, Bailie, don't tell him that.

No, this is good, said Raven. This I can use. You see, as the one making these illustrations, the emotions they might evoke are alien, almost unimaginable, to me. Precisely because I am at their centre, I remain at an experiential remove — the eye of the storm, so to speak. So your neuroses interest me. Come, let's sit down.

Olpert and Starx followed him inside the suite. The illustrationist seemed to glide across the marble floor.

Sweet digs, said Starx, collapsing onto a plush white settee. Olpert joined him.

Raven moved to the window that overlooked People Park. Yet when he spoke his voice seemed somehow inside Olpert's head: Now, Mr. Bailie, what else fills you with fear?

What? Else?

I ask because I wonder what it was about this morning that struck fear into you. Perhaps it is at the heart of something. As I've said, as the generator of the experience, all this is beyond me. I want simply to understand. To achieve some . . . clarity.

Raven's voice seemed come from somewhere out the window.

Perhaps we are on the wrong track, said Raven. At the risk of sounding forward, could you tell me your dreams, Mr. Bailie. Your most secret dreams. Are there motifs.

Sorry?

Motifs, Bailie, said Starx. Patterns, themes. Stuff on repeat.

In the scary ones? There are snakes sometimes.

Snakes, said Raven.

Though that might be because of Jessica.

Starx perked up: Who's Jessica?

What else appears in your dreams, said the illustrationist — he sounded now high above, hovering against the ceiling.

Other than snakes?

Yes. Tell me.

Something heavy and hot clamped upon his shoulders — Raven's hands. Olpert tensed, but from the illustrationist's fingers a soothing, sedative warmth spread into his body. When Olpert spoke the words came slow and didn't seem his own: Motifs in my dreams are less things in my dreams than things not in my dreams. Absence as a motif. And by that I mean total absence. I'm all alone and there's nothing else there.

Raven let go. What else, Mr. Bailie?

Well I have this one dream … Olpert had no idea what he might say. But the words just kept coming, tumbling more quickly now one to the next: I'm on this big ship, as big as a building, one of those ships that's so big it feels like a mall or something.

An aircraft carrier? said Starx.

Mr. Starx, please, said Raven. Then, to Olpert: Go on.

Okay, the ship's so full of people I can't move. You can't imagine how many people. Millions. And everyone's lined up for something, but I'm for some reason smaller than everyone else so I can't see what it is. I can't see over their heads. I'm a kid. Or feel like a kid, clarified Olpert, though none of this was true, he'd never had this dream, it spilled out of him from nowhere. Anyway, he continued, everyone's looking at this … *thing*, whatever it is, at the front of the ship — starboard? aft?

The bow, said Starx.

The bow, indeed. Thank you, seaman Starx, said Raven. Continue, Mr. Bailie.

So I want to see it, Olpert said, or at least find out what it is, but when I go to talk no words come out. I can't ask anyone, and getting to the front is impossible too because the crowd is packed so tightly in. And it's then I get this feeling, this *wash* of a feeling, that I'm alone. All these people are united by this thing and I don't even know what it is. And that's when the crowd starts spreading out from me. Like we're on an iceberg breaking apart. Nobody's actually moving but the space around me just gets bigger and bigger, and it's not even that I don't want to move, I don't know where to go. There's no one in the crowd I know, no one to go to, but the feeling of being alone like that — I can't even describe it to you. I can't. And the deck of this ship is expanding all around me, and the crowd is fading farther and farther away. I stand there and stand there and let it happen, until the crowd is eventually gone — they've disappeared. They've vanished.

Vanished, whispered Starx.

Oh, Mr. Bailie, said Raven, without even pressing you, we learn so much about your heart! Now, continue, please.

Well then I'm just alone, on this big open grey deck of something that used to be a ship, but now it's just . . . everything. It's the whole world, as far as I can see, and I'm there, and it's the same everywhere I look, just the greyness, and the sky is sort of colourless too, and I'm totally, completely alone. I'd walk somewhere but I don't know which way to walk. And who would I walk to?

And this makes you afraid.

It's the most terrifying feeling I've ever experienced in my life, said Olpert Bailie.

Starx's eyes were wide, astonished. The room felt spellbound.

And then what, Mr. Bailie.

And then?

Olpert straightened. Starx blinked. The trance was broken.

And then? And then I guess I wake up.

AFTER RETRIEVING her papers from the Galleria's security office Pearl wandered back to the foodcourt, where Kellogg and Gip and Elsie-Anne queued for nonresident processing. Go on, Pearly, said Kellogg, be a while here yet, we'll meet you at the campground, and flashed a big thumbs-up. But Pearl couldn't take her eyes off her son, who gazed at his mother with an uncomprehending, anaesthetized look.

She'd never seen Gip like this, almost catatonic, and though Dr. Castel claimed that a double dose of meds wouldn't be harmful as a one-off emergency, she wondered. He'll be fine, he's a tough little guy, Kellogg had assured her, crushing four pills into a can of apple juice. Usually her husband's brightness bolstered her, now it wearied her into surrender — hadn't Gip himself looked frightened, swallowing the potion down?

One of the Helpers took her by the elbow, steered her away. The line shifted, her family disappeared. From within the crowd came Kellogg's desperate, warbling cheer: See you soon, Pearly!

She was taken out of the foodcourt, past the shops, to the Galleria's southern exit, where the Helper said, Welcome home, gave her a little shove onto Paper Street, and locked the doors behind her.

And there it was: the city.

All that concrete and glass and steel seemed ushered up from underground. Pearl imagined the buildings folding in at their rooftops and blocking out the sun, she had to lean against the Galleria's wall to steady the ensuing vertigo. Though down below was no less disorienting — people, so many people, barrelling around and past and between each other, a choreography of chaos, a percussion of footsteps pattering this way and that. How did each one remember who they were, or where to go —

Pearl laughed. She was being ridiculous. Though she'd been away a few years, the city had been home for most of her life. She stepped away from the wall and levelled her thoughts and tried to look at things rationally, anthropologically. What had changed? She knew the buildings along Paper by name: Municipal Works, the caustic Podesta Tower, We-TV's HQ on the corner at Entertainment Drive. The few new businesses bore merely cosmetic changes in signage, the architecture original and unchanged.

Even so, everything had the slightly skewed look of some dreamworld rendering, nothing matched her memories, not precisely. Though she'd never felt comfortable downtown, its joyless parade of suits and high heels, so she took Paper east to Parkside West, crossed over and stood at the hilltop looking down. And with the park spreading out before her, she tried to summon how it felt to be home.

Nothing surfaced.

A breeze got the bare trees creaking.

A few blocks south, a Citywagon pulled into the City Centre lot.

A train came gliding into Parkside West Station, high above, traded passengers, then went north. Pearl followed on foot beneath the tracks, caught up at Bridge Station, the Yellowline reversed and headed back toward Bay Junction. Traffic still choked Guardian Bridge all the way to the mainland, where, wedged into the cliffside, was the Scenic Vista upon which the Pooles had collected the night prior.

Pearl headed east. Passing Street's Milk (& Things — newly amended) she was first surprised, then relieved, to see an OPEN sign in the window. The place hadn't changed, though had it ever been new? Pop's store had always seemed in need of upkeep, the paint faded and flaking and the windows forever smudged with an orange, oily type of dirt.

A half-mile along the park's northend she came upon the grounds of Island Amusements, rollercoasters twisting like scoliotic spines, the ice-blue slides of Rocket Falls, the Thunder Wheel's all-seeing eye glowering down upon everything. (OPEN

JUBILEE SATURDAY! boasted a sign pasted to the fence.) But it was the Stadium that Pearl wanted to see, so she pushed farther east. Ten minutes later she stood at the players' entrance. The new sponsorship and ubiquitous Island Flat Company signage provoked a slight proprietary jilt, but just seeing the place felt good: a bulbous island amid a sea of stark concrete, banners in Y's maroon hung from the roof at each of the six gates.

The players' entrance was locked, so Pearl had to go around to general admissions. On gamedays, when Pearl arrived for warm-ups she was always greeted by fans clambering and begging for autographs. Though the lack now of fans, of other players — of anyone — felt ceremonial and right.

A notice in the box office window seemed apologetic: *Thanks for another great season, get next year's season passes now, call* YS-TICKT *(978-4258).* From here Pearl walked the perimeter of the stadium, stopping at each gate, cupping her hands to the glass, scanning the mezzanine for custodial workers or administrative staff or maybe even a keen rookie, out here alone to train.

But there was no one, and no way in. By the time she made her way back to the box office Pearl was huffing and felt a slight twinge in her knee. Leaning forward, catching her breath with her hands on her thighs, she allowed herself a cruel little laugh: returning to the place she'd once been a star, she'd worn herself out trying to get in.

IN THE GRAND SALOON's banquet hall waiters hustled about to a tinkle of silverware and the burble of fifty conversations, the pepper-and-steel odour of roast meat wafted smokily from the kitchen, schnapps-based aperitifs had given way to cider, the bubbles lifted emberlike in each crystal flute. Distributed among the two dozen tables in blacktie and ballgowns were local dignitaries: various reps of cultural associations, several pink-drunk pillars of the business community, stars of the Lady Y's tautly muscled and stuffed into too-tight eveningwear, nervous academics from the Institute and their embarrassing spouses, the beautiful and rich, the vapid and canny. A cameraman crept between the tables, dropping to one knee every so often to shoot scenes he'd edit later for *In the Know*'s weekly Party Town featurette.

Upon the stage worked the island's artist laureate, Loopy, a squat woman in a paisley caftan and matching beret. Loopy's assistant, mousy and morose behind a curtain of bangs, handed over chisels and picks with which Loopy hacked a potentially avian shape from a block of ice.

Two tables were stationed at the front of the room: one for the NFLM's High Gregories, where a ducktaped Recruit struggled to napkin wheelchair-bound Favours, Griggs flipped idly through channels on his walkie-talkie, Noodles sipped a glass of water, and Magurk quizzed Wagstaffe: How'd you come at me with a blade? With a shy giggle, Wagstaffe wagged his butterknife. Wrong, said Magurk. Like *this* — see? Punch and cut, punch and cut. Good lookin out, said Wagstaffe.

At the other head table, with the central positioning of newly-weds at their nuptial feast, sat the Mayor and Raven. She'd doffed her mayoral sash in favour of a powersuit, though a nick in her stockings had run from ankle to knee. He'd clipped a bowtie to his tracksuit, his head seemed especially polished, all discoball sparkle and gleam.

Here were the appetizers: atop an IFC flat, fish bladders in a buttery broth, an antenna of sparrowgrass sprouted from their midst. Laughter stabbed into the air, glasses clinked, waitstaff in IFC uniforms cranked limb-sized peppermills and in the kitchen refilled empty cider carafes from a rubber tub by the compost bin.

The Mayor watched Raven stir his fish bladders. The whole

menu tonight comprises gourmet selections from the Island Flat Company, one of our local businesses, she said. Everything's local, the cider's from the orchard on the eastside of People Park…

Raven wasn't listening: he plucked a bladder from the bowl, examined it with a dubious squint, and tentatively slid it into his mouth. Face contorting into instant horror, he gulped cider, replicated the horror face, signalled a waiter, made sure the milk wasn't local (it wasn't), commanded the largest glass possible. Then, to the Mayor: You were saying?

There was more to her little treatise, once upon a time she could dovetail any subject with civic pride. But she'd lost the thread. Gazing around the room she tried to feel something for her constituents beyond mild loathing. In the last half-decade of her incumbency she'd begun to feel first distant from these people, then estranged. Life on the island had become too easy, everyone took her reforms for granted, no one considered how things used to be. Look at them, she thought: these people owe their comfort to me and they don't even realize it.

Well I should probably say something, said the Mayor, pushed back from the table, closed her eyes for a quick personal affirmation — touch green! — before addressing the guests. But when she opened her eyes Raven was standing on his chair, arms extended in victory. Yes, he cooed. Yes, yes!

Around the room people struck glassware with forks. Every head in the room swivelled toward the illustrationist, faces alight, what would he do.

Yes, yes! he cried, conducting his audience like a maestro. Put down your forks, please. Friends — welcome. Yet here I am welcoming you when it is I who should thank you for being welcomed. For you have welcomed me here — graciously. And so it is with grace I thank you for this welcome.

He bowed. Everyone tinged their glasses again, they couldn't resist, the banquet hall was a cauldron of delight. Ignoring this, the Mayor carved into her fish bladder. Out hissed a little gasp, a nautical aroma.

Please, no more tinging, said Raven, please. I've been all around the world, and this city — I've rarely had so keen a welcome. Don't applaud. Seriously, stop it. *Listen.*

He climbed down from his chair and began to walk around the room. The Mayor slipped the fish bladder into her mouth, the moist withered cyst of it.

Passing the NFLM table Raven nodded, the High Gregories nodded back.

Tomorrow night, he continued, though I have yet to discern the specifics, I will be illustrating something truly, I think, spectacular. As always it will be a magic that of course already exists, but remains unseen. My job as ever is just to reveal this magic to you, to illustrate what in your hearts you already know, what you already believe. My work is only to remove the fog that obscures the truth.

The air had gone tense and glassy. The Mayor chewed, mouth flooding with a sour, silty mucous.

Raven paused beside Loopy and her sculpture. A raven? he asked. She curtsied. He patted her beret in approval, then was on the move again: Friends, tomorrow night all I can offer is an uncovering. Each of my illustrations is only that, merely scratching at a frosted window to reveal the hidden wonders on the other side. But with a shift in light, every window can become what? A mirror. He smiled, snatched a napkin off a nearby table — its owner, the Institute's oft-cuckolded provost, yelped — and held it up. Madam — sorry, *sir*, if you'll allow me. Please, all of you, follow along with your own serviettes.

Everyone in the ballroom folded their napkins as they were shown: once in half, once diagonally, doubled over, pinched in, and tucked. Choking down the fish bladder, the Mayor swept up her napkin and endeavoured to catch up. Nearby, Griggs, Wagstaffe, Magurk, Noodles, and Favours' Recruit were doing a bangup job, while with each step the Mayor's creation looked less like Raven's, like theirs, like anyone's or anything.

The illustrationist said, Now we have envelopes. And what do you think might be inside this envelope? Perhaps we should open it to see.

Around the dining hall, the packages were unfolded — the Mayor's collapsed — and murmurs rippled around the room. At the neighbouring table, Wagstaffe displayed his creation: seared into the fabric was the Silver Personality's self portrait. And so it was with everyone, hundreds of effigies of the attendees' own faces, rendered in striking realism. The Mayor's own napkin bore only a brown smear — hideous, possibly fecal.

See? the illustrationist laughed. Now you see. Just a simple illustration.

The Mayor launched to her feet, clapping. Wonderful, wonderful. On behalf of us all, thanks a bundle for the trick. But now let's eat, you're our guest, not our entertainer. And we're here to celebrate the park, after all, twenty-five years of People Park, let's not forget. It's the *Silver Jubilee* — she sensed hysteria mounting in her voice, paused, breathed. Please, sir, relax, enjoy the IFC's fine cuisine. A round of applause for our guest!

Hands tapped.

The main course arrived: squab with toasted almonds atop the requisite IFC flat, steamed sparrowgrass on the side. Raven slouched in his chair, draped his napkin over his face, appeared to nap. Though the Mayor's meal tasted weirdly bilious, she ate every bite, sawing the sour grey meat into little cubes that she chewed to oblivion and swallowed, until all that remained were bones, a rubbery dimpled flap of skin.

The dessert carts began to circle the room. Raven peeked out, snatched the napkin from his face, leapt to his feet, snapped three times, and screamed, Who wants to see, before we retire, one final illustration?

Hooting. Feet stamped, laps were drummed. An apple flat was held aloft in salute.

Raven slid behind the Mayor, took her napkin, and placed his hands, as heavy and hot as fire-baked stones, on her shoulders. She squirmed, he squeezed. From his fingers heat entered and spread through her body, along her arms into her fingertips, through her torso down to her feet. Her face tingled, relaxed. Raven released her, turned to a passing dessert cart, said, May I? to the young woman wheeling it, swept all the flats into the white cloth, shook the bundle, and opened it: empty.

Wild applause.

Please, Mrs. Mayor. Please, if you could just lie upon this cart.

The crowd cheered: Mayor, Mayor, Mayor!

Summoned with a curling brown finger, as a patient called to a surgeon's table the Mayor lay down on the dessert cart, her legs hung off at the knee. She felt nothing beyond distant, dreamy worry, almost a memory of the emotion even as it occurred. The illustrationist draped the sheet over her midsection. In his hand materialized a whip with a grip of two knotted snakes.

Cutting a woman in half, intoned the illustrationist, is delicate business. It is most important to ensure that she remains — Raven fingered the whip — alive at both ends.

He tossed her napkin up and snapped the whip: the fabric fluttered in two halves to the floor. The brown stain had vanished. Wagstaffe yelled, Huzzah!

All this seemed vague, the room shimmered, the Mayor felt herself not quite falling asleep — but *fading*. She was only hazily aware of the illustrationist looming over her, grinning, eyes like two black slots.

I hope you can forgive me, he whispered, for what I am about to do.

The crowd waited.

The illustrationist stroked her midsection with the whip, lazy and serpentine. He closed his eyes. Once, twice, three times he stroked the Mayor's body with the whip. Then, with drama, he cocked it behind his head. It has been said by one of my predecessors, said Raven, that one receives just desserts in accordance with one's beliefs. His eyes opened — in them the Mayor saw herself, reflected — and he screamed, So be it! and the whip swooshed through the air.

There was a moment of silence and stillness, as if everyone in the dining hall had inhaled at once. This was broken by a clumsy, clumping noise, like a piece of furniture knocked over. A gasp resounded around the room.

And then silence.

The Mayor felt a surge of satisfaction: the trick had failed!

But they were applauding now, a few scant claps that swelled quickly into a standing ovation. People roared and shrieked. Someone smashed a glass. Favours cackled. Noodles nodded. Magurk whispered, Holy fug, look at that. Wagstaffe fell to his knees, tears in his eyes. Even Griggs' waxen face seemed to have come alive with delight.

You see? laughed Raven, nudging the cart forward.

The Mayor looked down.

By its wheels, her legs lay in a heap on the floor.

VII

ROM WITHIN THE HOOD of his sweatshirt Calum watched his mother's back, or the bones of it beneath her dress, the coathanger of her shoulderblades over which the dress draped, through its thin fabric her ribs and spine. Eyes on the little TV propped on the kitchen counter, Cora stirred the pot of corn-in-a-can with a mix of tenderness and fatigue, slowly, round and round.

Calum turned his attention to the empty plate before him, pressed down on the tines of his fork and angled the handle upward. Across the table, in a matching sweatshirt, his little brother Rupe began to do the same thing.

Calum snatched Rupe's fork, a flare of pain shot down his cheek. He touched the tender, puffy skin around his left eye, wondered if something was broken, if you could break your face.

Rupe watched him carefully.

Be nice to each other, said their mother. It's so rare we're together, be nice, please.

Yeah, Calum, said Rupe.

In a careful voice Cora said, How's Edie?

Calum folded the fork around his wrist, admired his new jewellery.

Cal? I said: How's Edie?

No idea.

His mother stirred the sauce. On the TV, Isa Lanyess, so classically, equinely handsome, with her cheekbony grin and thick batting lashes, counted down the week's most popular Faces. At number three, she said, what do you know? It's me, Isa Lanyess, *In the Know*. And then she threw to a clip of herself that morning, hair whipping around her face as Raven's helicopter descended into the common.

She's up two spots from last week, said Cora.

Calum imagined a punch landed between his mother's kidneys, the wet paper crumple of that pitiful body around his fist.

So, Cal, are you going to the Room after dinner?

Her voice was the faint whimper of mice in the wall.

Cal?

Yeah, he said. But talking hurt, his eyes watered, he blinked away the tears.

It's so nice you do that, Cal, with those kids. You're so talented — and generous too! Cora gave him a proud look. The sauce sputtered. Calum hid inside his hood.

Isa Lanyess was back: At number two, holding strong from last week, *Lady Y's Lingerie Pillowfight Extravaganza*. It's the quarterfinals —

Well we don't need to see *that*, said Cora with a nervous laugh, snapped the set off, and announced, Dinnertime!

Onto the table she slid Calum's and Rupe's dinners, a splat of corn over an XL flat apportioned half to each of her sons. None remained for herself. She put in some toast.

You boys eat, she said. You're young, you've got appetites. I'm just an old biddy thing, what do I need all that food for. Then she rocketed to her feet moaning, Cheese, and rushed to the fridge. She returned with a plastic tub. There you are, sorry.

He shook some on, ate a forkful. Chewing was agony. Good, he said.

Is it, oh I'm glad! You've always liked my flats, Cal, since you were a little boy.

Rupe said, It's really good, Ma, thanks.

The rest of the meal passed in silence save the chime and scrape of cutlery. Calum longed even for the TV's inane chatter. Despite the pain, he shovelled food mechanically, rapidly, into his mouth. Meanwhile Cora sheared corners from her toast and chewed each one pensively, watching her boys eat until they were done.

Thanks, said Calum, and rose with his plate.

Don't clear up, his mum shrieked, standing. I'll do it, you go, you've got places to be, and then seeing his face she startled. Cal, honey, what happened to your eye?

He shook off her hand, slid his plate into the sink, pushed past. As he put on his shoes at the door Rupe appeared. Cora wants to know when you're coming home.

Late. Tell her, late.

Then he was bounding down the stairwell past blocks of black painted on the walls, the tang of urine, to the street. He leapt over the final, broken stair, landing upon the flagstones of Laing Towers' courtyard, the impact split his lip, he tasted pennies, a sour ache radiated through his face. Calum tightened his hood and headed up F Street, where the streetlights were just coming on, one then the next, in gradual consensus admitting the night.

KELLOGG JIGGLED THE POLES, buckled down the final clasp. The tent flapped a bit in the wind up from the lake but seemed secure.

What say you, fair wife of mine? A shipshape castle for the lady in her manor?

Pearl took two ciders from the cooler, knocked the tops off on the picnic table, handed one to Kellogg. Ahoy, she said, and drank, and giggled, and said, Ahoy-hoy.

You think Gip needs another round of meds? said Kellogg.

Across the campground their son sat reading *Illustrations: A Grammar* in Harry's backseat. At sixish Kellogg had pulled into the site to find Pearl sitting on the picnic table with a warming sixpack, two empties at her side. She'd sprung up and climbed into the van before anyone had a chance to get out.

I missed you guys, she said, lavishing boozy kisses upon each of the Pooles in turn.

Gosh, Pearly, said Kellogg. We missed you too. But we're all together now, right?

Gip had ignored his parents' requests for help setting up camp and refused to get out of the van. The day's already ruined, what's the point, he'd sulked, arms folded over his chest. Now, with dusk settling, he still hadn't moved, nose buried in his book.

Let me see how's he doing, said Pearl.

Kellogg was left at the picnic table with Elsie-Anne, whispering into her purse. An errant braid hung in front of her face, Kellogg tucked it behind her ear. She permitted this stiffly, as she might an inoculation.

Annie, hey, who you chatting to?

Familiar. He's telling me about Viperville.

What's that then?

She cocked an ear, leaned down, nodded, smiled.

Oh, is that your friend from this morning? The snake?

Eel, she said. In Viperville Familiar says babies don't come from mums and dads. They come from themselves.

Do they now.

Shhh, she said, and bent to listen.

Kellogg tipped back his cider.

The van door opened. Pearl swung her legs out, sat there rubbing her face.

Everything okay in there? said Kellogg.

Gip's hungry, she said. I am too. All this cider on an empty stomach —

I'm *starving*, Dad! screamed Gip.

Well sheesh, champ, then why don't we get a move on and find something to eat?

WELL, SAID DEBBIE, that's it for today, I'm Debbie, thanks for checking in, we're off for the Jubilee Weekend but we'll be back Monday, hope to see you then.

She turned the camera off. Calum, sprawled on a workbench, was shaking his hooded head.

What?

Nothing.

I don't like doing it! Come on, Cal. You know this isn't my thing.

Right.

Just let me finish up here and we can go, okay?

Sure.

Debbie tacked a drawing on the gallery wall — a spring theme, a lot of green and great lurid bushels of flowers, with clear skies topping the pages in blue stripes or rain dashing down from grey washes of cloud. The newest addition was a picture of the Zone: the twin rectangles of Laing Towers anchoring one end, the ramparts of F Street rowhouses, above everything the traintracks ran like a headline. No people. A cat sniffed a fire hydrant and over a fat pale spider of a sun flapped two m-shaped birds. Most striking was an alley in the picture's centre, markered so black the page puckered. In the bottom right corner, the artist had signed his work: -P.

Pierre's latest masterpiece, said Debbie. See how he's using what you taught him about perspective? And that alley! Look how dark he's done it. Very mysterious.

Yeah.

Hey. Debbie sat down beside him. Everything all right?

He pulled his hood away.

Your face!

One eye was swollen shut, the skin puffed and glossy, black crust scabbed his lips.

What happened?

Calum moved to the back of the Room. By the bay window stood an easel draped in a sheet. Past it the lake was purple in the dusk. Twenty yards out waves met the breakwater, a ridge of cement that resembled the petrified spine of some beached aquatic beast.

Debbie said, You going to work on your painting?

Calum shook his head.

If you want to talk about it, I'm here. Right? Calum?

Yeah.

Was it an initiation or something?

The Room's timbers groaned, waves glipped and swished against its stilts. Calum watched the lake.

Well should we get going? said Debbie. When does this thing start?

Dark. When it's dark.

And what is it exactly? I know you explained sort of but . . .

I saw you got blackedup. There's still paint on the front windows.

Yeah. I mean, a little frustrating because we have kids here and, I don't know . . .

You don't think you deserve it.

I don't know. Do you think I deserve it?

Calum pulled his hood up again. It's getting dark, he said.

Sure, let's go then, said Debbie. Put the benches up for me?

In the bathroom she washed sparkles and marker from her hands, locked her office. When she came back Calum was still standing at the window, staring at the lake.

You're not going to write about this for TV, right?

Calum, no. I told you. You don't trust me?

This is just to see. You want to know what's going on out there, what we're doing, well you can come see. But it's not for anyone else, right?

Sure. Wait, what do you mean?

You can come but it's not . . . He trailed off. It's just, it's for us.

Oh.

He flipped his hood up and moved past Debbie, toward the door. Grab a flashlight, we should go, he said.

And Debbie went after him, trying to feel trusted, trying to feel good.

AT FIRST WHEN THE pickup and trailer pulled into Street's Milk & Things, Pop assumed he'd only have to disappoint hopeful patrons of Mr. Ademus. In the doorway he held up his arms in a gesture meant to convey: *Sold out, apologizations!* But out stepped two men in the khaki uniforms of the NFLM, one carrying a briefcase, the other with a Citypass lanyard around his neck, both with terrific moustaches. At last the birds fly home to roast, said Pop.

He locked eyes with each of the men in turn, closed the door, turned the sign around so NOT OPEN faced out. The men looked at the NOT OPEN sign, at the proprietor posed defiantly behind it, one of them knocked, the other gestured at the pickup. Pop didn't move. From the briefcase papers were produced and pressed to the glass. At last Pop addressed them as per their nametags: Bygone with yous, Misters Walters and Reed!

The Helpers exchanged words. Walters tore off a crinkly carbon copy, rolled it into a tube, and wedged it in the doorhandle. Then they got back in the pickup and pulled around behind the store. Pop's breathing shallowed, a vein throbbed in his throat. Finally he threw the door open and in socked feet went waddling after the two men.

With Walters waving him along, Reed was reversing into the clearing. The trailer slid underneath the houseboat with a clang. That's my home!, screamed Pop. What is your strategization? It's condemned, said Walters. We're just picking it up. You've got a problem, go through the proper channels. We gave you the paperwork.

Just doing our job, called Reed from the cab.

Pop wailed, Injust, degencrational, vandalistic, totalitary! Unsuppositionant, predominary, predilicted, no, reprehensitory, no, unfoundational, no, declensionive, no, anti-popularly, no, not fair, not fair, not fuggin fug fuggin fair.

Meanwhile Walters secured his houseboat on the trailer, strapped it down, locked everything into place. Listen, he said, smoothing his moustache with thumb and forefinger, just check the paperwork. There are processes for this sort of thing.

Processes? roared Pop. I'll tell you a processional thing or two. If it didn't mean defiliating the hollowed ground of my establishment I'd process my foot through your cranial lobe right now, both of yous, evil ones!

Walters nodded at Pop's stockinged feet. Would you now?

This is my home, Pop said. He fell to his knees. My *home*. A quartered century hencefrom. Whereupon am I supposed to sleep?

Reed honked the horn.

Read the paperwork, said Walters, and hopped into the cab.

Pop knelt in the gravel, watched the pickup pull onto Topside Drive, houseboat swinging behind atop the trailer, slid into traffic — and just like that his house was gone.

AS REED PILOTED them west toward the dump, Walters opened his briefcase and took out a packet of Redapples. He offered one to his partner. No, sir, said Reed, quit those things years ago.

Smart, said Walters, unrolled his window, lit the cigarette, took a long, deep drag, and blew smoke into the oncoming traffic. On the shoulder, someone had painted over the Guardian Bridge turnoff sign with a solid black rectangle.

Look at that, said Walters. Those fuggers are getting bold, coming this far east.

Try blacking out the Temple though, said Reed, and they'll see what's coming.

Or, you know, they won't.

Won't?

See what's coming, sighed Walters. Hence the surprise, Reed, of whatever *what* is.

In the sideview mirror Reed checked the trailer. It rolled along steadily behind the pickup, a boxy shadow back there in the purple evening. From the cupholder he took a walkie-talkie, confirmed the seizure and signed off: D-Squad, Good lookin out.

Poor guy, said Walters between drags. You got to feel sorry for him.

Reed merged onto Lowell Overpass. How do you mean?

Oh, he's a total applehead. I mean, what's he doing, living in a parking lot? It's amazing it took this long to get him out of there. Still though, he said. Still . . .

Enh, said Reed. You heard the HG's: this weekend's supposed to go smooth, no hiccups. Who knows what trouble that guy might have had planned. What did Magurk call him? *A genital wart on the dong of the city.*

Walters ashed out the window, inhaled, blew smoke into traffic.

You think too much, Walters.

So what? We're just doing our job?

Exactly. We're just doing our job.

DURING THE DAY THE ZONE was a storybook of wonders: why did that person have a parrot on her shoulder? What was happening down that alleyway with three men arguing around a dolly heaped with copper? This litter of thousands of orange paper dots — who, how, when, what? But in the cold, still night with the only life her own jammering heart and the cloudpuffs of her breath, Debbie's curiosity shrivelled. You bundled against the cold. You were wary. Any shadow could morph into a thief slinking at you with a blade.

After sunset the Zone always felt a little chillier, the air a little thinner, than the rest of the city. It didn't help that the breakwater subdued the tides, or the lack of lights in the old stockyards cast the western side of F Street in gloom, or that UOT and Blackacres emptied at dusk: the soup kitchen and shelters and Golden Barrel began to admit their nocturnal clienteles, the shops lowered their shutters, families withdrew into their houses for the night. The only people out would be patrols of Helpers, whistling cheerfully as they strolled the streets, clubs hidden in their pantlegs. At night anything could happen here, and often it did: instead of a place of stories, it became a place where stories happened to you.

Following Calum up F toward Whitehall, Debbie talked unceasingly, if only to distract from their footfalls, calling out to be chased.

So you're really in with these folks now, huh?

Sure.

They're okay?

They're okay.

You're not worried about —

Calum clicked his tongue. There's nothing to worry about. You have this idea that these people are like, not people. Maybe they just figured out something different than you. Maybe they look at what you think's a normal life and are just like, that's not for me. Maybe it's too safe and boring and there's nothing, there's no *edge* to it. So they make something else. And maybe their something else isn't for you.

Well why take me there then?

So you can see.

Does this mean you've been before? You've hung out with them lots? Calum?

He quickened his pace.

At F Street and Tangent 20 the Yellowline sloped downward and continued at streetlevel into the Whitehall Barns, and it was here that Calum veered inland. He led Debbie down a laneway between empty warehouses, through the hole in the chainlink, to the silos. In there? she said, and he told her, Yep — though he seemed to waver, and it was Debbie who went first.

Inside, the moon sliced through the shattered windows and played jagged patterns over the concrete floor. Flashlight, said Calum. Debbie turned it on: a dab of yellow quivered at their feet, down a flight of slatted metal stairs to the basement, where bunches of candles burned on either side of a door propped open with a chair.

Then they were in the service tunnels angling down beneath Whitehall, the temperature warmed, Debbie shed her coat and sweater, carried them heaped in her arms. An industrial noise came grinding up the tunnel. As they descended it intensified, a grating drone that set Debbie's teeth on edge. On and on they went, deeper and deeper underground. Finally the tunnel released them into a sort of grotto, where the sound exploded: a terrible music that was huge and cruel and everywhere.

Debbie killed the flashlight. Motes of colour swam before her eyes, she plugged her ears and blinked at the sparkling dark. Gradually she was able to pick out industrial lamps strung along extension cords ringing the room. Beyond their alcoves of weak light the room was a fathomless smudge. Slowly the shadows took shape, they seemed to swell and pulse and writhe — people.

Were they dancing to this tuneless music that rattled Debbie's bones inside her skin? There were people around the periphery too. In one of the nearby light nooks a hooded figure held out a forearm to someone else dragging a piece of glass across the skin: the blood swelled in black bubbles, wiped away with a rag. They noticed Debbie watching, turned toward her, faces just shadows inside their hoods.

Where was Calum, he was gone. Debbie squinted. How many people were there? Thirty, forty, hundreds, she couldn't tell. And even with her ears plugged the music throbbed inside her head. Though this was hardly music, no instruments, no one was singing. It was noise, yet somehow immediate and intimate, even alive. It seemed, thought Debbie, to billow mistlike from the room itself and swirling to consume everyone within.

Tentatively she took her fingers out of her ears, let the sound come screaming in, tried to make sense of it. The whining through the middle range was reminiscent of the staticky screech of a distorted guitar, the pulse beneath it seemed percussive, but there was no sign of either guitars or drums. Just people, ringed by a dozen or so megalithic towers of speakers and amps, wires webbed overtop in a ropy ceiling. Inside these towers the crowd milled and shifted — slow, almost purposeful.

Calum stood at the edge of the cipher, backlit, talking to a girl wearing what appeared to be a glove for a hat.

Debbie caught his eye and waved. He ignored her, kept talking to the girl. But then he eyed Debbie again and finally came over and slouched in front of her like a child humouring a parent he wants to escape.

What is this music? she yelled. What do you call it?

Calum pulled away, looked around, leaned in again, didn't speak.

Is there a band? Where are they?

Calum's lips moved but Debbie heard nothing.

The band, Debbie screamed, and placed her ear to Calum's lips.

There's no band, he said. We're the band. He gestured above, at the network of wires overtop the dancefloor. Those are sensors.

The sound comes from us, moving around. However we move is whatever we hear. You hate it, don't you?

He seemed almost gleeful. Cal, said Debbie, why did you bring me here?

Why? So you could see.

But there's nothing to see!

A sour look Debbie couldn't quite read passed over his face, frustration or regret. He muttered something and drifted away, back toward the girl in the odd hat — not a hat but hair, Debbie realized, palming her skull.

This girl spat, said something to Calum, who looked at Debbie, quickly, then away. The urge to calm whatever she had unsettled fluttered up, but the girl took Calum by the hand, moved out of the light and into the crowd.

And Debbie was left alone with the music. It was horrible — like a hand over her mouth, like hands on her throat, like hands tightening on her shoulders and stomach and thighs. It stabbed into her ears, filled her face, centipedelike went scuttling down her spine, spread pulsing back up into her chest, expanded, tingled all the way to her fingertips and out again, into the world, as shreds of exhausted light. She tried to find something in it, to trace some melody or beauty. But she couldn't. She didn't understand.

Calum and the girl had vanished. The two who'd been cutting each other were gone too, all that remained in the lamplight was a shard of bloodied glass. Everyone was inside the circle now. Except Debbie, who groped toward the tunnel, found its opening, entered, the walls rough as gravel. She remembered the flashlight: it strobed wildly ahead of her as she went splashing through puddles that hadn't been there on the way in, the cavernous hall chased her with its screams.

After a time the music faded to a distant drone, farther along the only sounds in the tunnel were Debbie's footsteps and the rasp of her breath. She leaned against one of the walls: moist, almost spongy, she recoiled from it shivering. Behind her and ahead, the flashlight shone into blackness. Hello? she called. Her voice didn't even echo, just seemed swallowed by the dark.

She couldn't go back, not to what was there. And so she continued on — the corridor sloped down, leading her even deeper beneath the city. She turned back and there was the music, faint but screeching. So down again she went. What was this lightless place, where would it take her, the smell was earthy, the floor became dirt and the flashlight wobbled over it, was it fading? A knot bobbed in Debbie's throat, she blundered on.

And up ahead was a shaft of light.

Debbie raced to it: a grate, high above, and a ladder leading up. She pocketed the flashlight and climbed. The grate swung open — the street, and air, sweet and cool, and the night sky, the vast burnt skin of it bruised by citylights.

And people: a crowd of students lined up along the street, an ordered line behind a velvet rope of girls in too-tiny skirts and boys in too-tight tops, and beneath everything thumped a dull and steady bassbeat.

The Dredge Niteclub. She'd come out in its gutters.

VIII

T EIGHT-THIRTY a Yellow-
line train dumped the Pooles into Mount Mustela, a neighbourhood known for okay restaurants and furshops and Bookland,
the city's oldest bookshop, said Kellogg's CityGuide. From the
platform the escalator lowered him and Pearl and Gip and Elsie-
Anne, conversing with her purse, while Kellogg enthused, How
about that *train*, eh, guys? Can you believe there's *no one* driving
those things, pretty amazing. You want to talk magic? And those
moving sidewalks — just whoop, all aboard! And off you go.

They were spit out where Mustela Boulevard deadended at
Tangent 1, a turnaround from which the 72 Steps switchbacked
down the bluffs to Budai Beach. From here the alleged mountain
(more modestly, a hill) lifted to the Mount Mustela Necropolis
at its top end. On either side were residential neighbourhoods,
fractals of courts and crescents, each house and duplex and walkup
glowing golden with the lives lived inside. Surf rumbled, the
night held the island in its fist, the air smelled of deepfry and
the fishy lake, and Kellogg took it all in, beaming.

We're *here*, he said. The Pooles have *arrived*.

I'm hungry, said Gip.

Well how about some island flats? The local specialty, isn't
that right, Pearly?

You bet, she said. Inkerman's at Mustela and Tangent 4. Best flats in town.

Best in town? Is that what my guidebook says? I thought —

It's what *I* say, said Pearl.

Gotcha. Kellogg pointed to a streetlight: a buttery flame danced inside a wrought iron cage. Check it out, guys — fire!

Gas lamps, said Pearl. That's new.

Why does no one care about me? said Gip. I'm *hungry*, I said, a million times.

The Pooles swept north, Kellogg in the lead brandishing his CityGuide, Gip next in his knapsack, then Pearl holding hands with Elsie-Anne, who whispered into her purse. At Inkerman's they were greeted with a HOLIDAY HOURS SORRY notice over padlocked metal shutters.

Great, said Gip thinly, just great. What now? Are we going to starve to death?

Did you take your meds? said Kellogg, then to Pearl: You gave him his meds, right?

The gas lamps seemed to slow and gutter. At the fur concern next door a man wheeled display racks off the sidewalk, shaggy pelts jostling as if still alive, and closed up for the night. A few doors up a woman was folding up a sandwich board — BOOK-LAND: NEW AND USED BOOKS. Kellogg sprinted toward her yelling, Hey, hey you there!

The proprietor slipped into her shop, studied him through a little window in the door.

Hi? said Kellogg. Sorry, we just want directions.

I'm closed, she said, voice muffled. Open by appointment only.

We're just looking for island flats, he said. Or anything really. Food.

Pearl came up, holding Gip's and Elsie-Anne's hands. Raven! screamed Gip, and pointed at the storefront display, a tower of *Illustrations: A Grammar*.

My family, said Kellogg, gesturing grandly.

The woman spoke to Pearl: It's food you're after? Flats?

Or anything. Anywhere to eat.

Only stuff that's open now this far north is in UOT. But you don't want to go there. Not this late. You'd do better down on Knock Street. Lots of restaurants there.

For tourists, said Pearl.

The woman stared.

My wife's from here, Kellogg explained.

Oh, said the woman.

We're here for the Jubilee!

Well good luck, said the woman, and trotted off into her store.

Pearl snorted, shook her head. What a charmer. See why I left?

Oh come on now, said Kellogg. Probably gave her a shock is all! But how bad is OUT?

UOT, Upper Olde Towne. I guess there are patrols and stuff now, they've cleaned it up a bunch. My friend Debbie lives out there. It's where we're meeting later.

So then, really, said Kellogg, how bad can it be?

THE BANQUET HALL was in darkness. From Loopy's bird sculpture, packed away in the hotel's meatlocker between two gory sides of beef, one of the catering staff chiselled a few feathers into his end-of-shift schnapps, chugged it, then locked everything up and went home for the night. All but one head table had been cleared and folded up and stacked in a backroom. At this table, swirling a goblet of milk, sat the illustrationist. Beside him was the Mayor, or the two halves of the Mayor: her torso erect on the top shelf of the dessert cart, and below, heaped on the lower tier, her legs. She had the defeated look of a child promised a pony and whose parents instead have divorced.

The illustrationist spoke: This is not what I intended. I had thought to fill these folk with trembling and awe. With desire.

He sighed, swirled his milk, took a sip, swallowed.

The Mayor stared into the shadows of the banquet hall, saying nothing.

Something, anything. I wanted to make them *feel*. But they long only to be entertained. If that! One wonders if they know what they truly want . . . I'm a showman to them, nothing else. One would assume a show then is a means to attract their attention, to ignite some flicker in their spirits that gives way to —

Please fix me, said the Mayor.

Raven shook his head, continued: That gives way not to empty sentiment, Mrs. Mayor, but true, desirous *feeling*.

I feel something, if that counts. I feel annoyed. I feel you should fix me.

Oh, my sweet queen. That's not at all what I mean.

PEARL LED THE WAY OUT of Mount Mustela, around a bend, down an alley painted black from road to roof, and out onto a different sort of street: one side all crumbling rowhouses, the other pawnshops and cheque-cashers, windows barred. Trash clotted the gutters, many streetlights were burnt out, the air was sickly and foul with sewage and rot. At the first corner huddled men who went silent as the Pooles approached. Pearl held Gip's hand, Kellogg hoisted Elsie-Anne onto his shoulders, her purse atop his head, her legs yoked his neck. They hurried past the quiet men with a rigidity Kellogg hoped conveyed purpose, rather than fear.

No problems here, he whispered, in his pocket lacing keys between his fingers.

The Pooles went west along Tangent 7, the rowhouses of A Street gave way to the squat shapes of warehouses and storage facilities between C and D, many of the windows punched out in spiky dark shapes. At F Street they headed north. Beyond the empty stockyards to the west shone the oily glint of the lake.

The only sounds were footsteps: Kellogg's, with Pearl's and Gip's echoing half a block behind. The air was still and cold.

Pearl called, The Golden Barrel's just ahead.

A motion sensor light flicked on as Kellogg passed what he mistook for another painted square, but a breeze wafted from it — an alley. He gripped his keys, ready should a drunk stumble out of the dark, to shred the man's face with a razory punch.

Around the corner on Tangent 10 the Taverne's blinking sign lit the sidewalk in orange flashes. Upon its roof was a movie-screen–sized billboard: the obelisk of the Island Flat Company's logo and Food at the edge of forever scrawled beneath.

Suddenly Kellogg's footsteps were without echo. He stopped, looked back: no Pearl, no Gip. The corner sat in darkness, they'd somehow not tripped the motion sensor.

Pearl? Kellogg called. Gip?

Nothing.

He lowered Elsie-Anne into his arms. Guys?

No reply.

Clutching his daughter he jogged back down F. The motion sensor triggered. Kellogg stopped. The light went off. He called his wife's and son's names again, with Elsie-Anne held close his heart thudded through both their bodies. He faced the alley: a murk too dark to be shadows, a void that existed beyond light.

Kellogg moved to the alley's edge. He squinted. Nothing became clearer, nothing took form or shape. Pearl, Gip, he said, his voice weak. The blackness seemed wet. His pulse filled his ears, surged through his hands.

He hitched Elsie-Anne onto his hip and stepped forward. The shadows closed in. Another step, the ground sloped down. He pushed in a little farther and thought he saw movement. Then, faint and faraway, came a rushing, airy sound, and the breath of something huge whisked hot and cobwebby over his face.

Kellogg wheeled, stumbled, whispered, We're okay, we're okay, into his daughter's hair, ran and nearly fell inside the Golden Barrel.

The bar's half-dozen patrons swivelled to inspect him, and in disinterest or disappointment returned to their drinks.

Kell!

Pearl and Gip were in a booth by the bathrooms. Kellogg took the seat opposite, moved Elsie-Anne off his lap, gaped across the table at his wife and son.

What's going on? said Pearl. You look like you've seen a ghost.

Yeah, Dad, said Gip. Your hands are shivering. Dorkus, what'd you do to Dad?

Elsie-Anne spoke into her purse.

I don't, began Kellogg. You were . . . behind us. What happened?

Kell, sorry, I'm confused. What are you so shaken up about?

Sensing the whole bar watching, Kellogg hid behind the menu. So, he said, what's good?

Mummy already ordered, said Gip. Wings.

Hope that's okay, they don't have flats. Pearl touched his arm. Kellogg?

Wings! he shouted — too bright, too loud, with a maniac's grin. Hear that, Annie? Mummy's ordered wings, who needs flats . . . He trailed off. On the floor was Gip's knapsack. Be right back, he said, scooped it up, and tumbled out of the booth.

In the bathroom he dug past Raven's *Illustrations: A Grammar*, his CityGuide, the extra sweaters he'd packed (just in case), their permits, apple juice, a first-aid kit, until his fingers closed around the cold smooth container of Gip's meds. He tapped two of the white tablets onto his palm, looked from them to his reflection in the mirror — wide-eyed and weak — shook out two more, opened the tap, filled his mouth with water, and choked all four pills down.

PUT MY LEGS BACK.

Back? Mrs. Mayor, who is to say they were ever otherwise?

Who? Me! I do!

Bah, said Raven, waving his hand as if to waft away an unpleasant odour. It's all perception and perspective. You say tomato, I say thaumato.

Listen here, I've been very patient. I'm all about keeping my constituents happy. And they seemed to very much enjoy this … trick. But, now, come on. It's been hours.

The illustrationist drained his milk.

Please.

No.

You have to.

With a forlorn expression he contemplated the creamy residue inside the glass. You try, is the thing. You try and try and try. And people will just make of whatever you do whatever they want. Or, more — whatever they think they want.

He stood. The Mayor wriggled toward him, lost her balance, toppled onto her chest. The view was of her own legs on the lower tier: the skirt hitched to reveal a glimpse of silky slip. She grasped for it — hopeless — and let her arm hang, hand dangling.

Well, said the illustrationist, if people want a show, a show is what they will get.

He placed the empty goblet upon the dessert cart and drifted off into the shadows. The Mayor started to tell him to wait, but was preempted by a ruffle, a flapping, a whoosh. And then silence. The air felt sucked from the room.

Hello? she called.

The word echoed. Hello, replied the shadows.

Hello, hello, hello.

CALUM FLOATED WITHIN the screaming darkness. Everywhere were people: hands ran down his chest, someone's lips fastened onto his neck, who was anyone, he patted the tops of heads for the distinctive frizz of the Hand's buzzcut. But instead his palm met fabric — hats, hoods, stockings, masks — or greasy nests of hair, flat and damp, and he recoiled as though he'd fondled a corpse.

None of these people was her, where was she, he saw nothing. Someone caressed him from behind, looped their arms around his waist, pulled him close. Calum broke free, was hauled instantly into the arms of another stranger. Who? Nothing was discernible in the dark. Sound scorched his ears, jangled his nerves. He slipped into the arms of someone else and felt their head: a woolly cap.

The Hand was here somewhere, she had to be. Or had she left — had she abandoned him? Calum floundered into the naked flesh of someone else, he was held, though cruelly, aggressively, and the rusty music grated and shrieked, and now this person was lifting Calum's shirt to press their hot wet skin against his — and were they now fumbling at his belt? He squirmed but was held fast, the arms were strong — and even in the dark there was something faceless about this person, something phantasmal or maybe masked ... Calum wriggled, pushed, was released with a giggle.

From the periphery glowed those feeble pockets of light: in this one figures writhed on the floor, faintly illumined in the next a shadow pinned another shadow to the wall, in the next a tangle of limbs unravelled and four, five, six people stumbled back into the central darkness. The screaming shifted, sharpened. Where was the Hand? Calum pictured that shirtless character finding her, cornering her, her body trapped and rubbed and licked. And her licking back ...

Fingers laced through his and squeezed. The touch felt familiar, safe. A cheek pressed to his, nuzzled, at the temples the smooth skin gave way to stubble, the head was crowned with a bristly patch. Come on, the Hand said in his ear, and he was taken out of the circle, beyond the music, past the ring of lights, to a tunnel, and down through the darkness, and down where it was quiet, and down and farther down.

THERE YOU GO, said Starx. Her husband's leaving.

Olpert swivelled on his barstool. In a corner booth, a man and two children were abandoning a woman with a half-drunk pitcher and a basket of bones.

Starx punched him in the thigh. Shet, Bailie. Don't *look*.

Sorry. I just might know that woman. If she's who I think she is, she used to play for the Y's, blew her knee in her second season and —

Pints appeared. Drink, commanded Starx. You want hot or mild wings?

Mild, said Olpert, drinking, and Starx said, Wrong.

The Taverne smelled of stale popcorn and cigarettes and pee. It had the mood lighting of a supermarket, there was no music, the sounds were the clop and chime of glassware, subdued conversations like rain upon soil, all of it supervised by the bartender, Pete, an abundantly sideburned older guy in big square glasses and a tuxedo.

Okay, said Starx. You like that ballplayer?

Olpert rubbed his thigh. That'll bruise, he said, I hope you know.

Starx motioned to the mirror behind the bar. You want to check her out use that.

Olpert was bad at mirrors: what was reflected there never made much sense to him. He couldn't use a rearview to park a car, and, shaving, he often floundered with the razor on the wrong side of his face.

I don't *like* her, Starx. She was just on the team for a bit, I recognize her. Gosh, I probably have her card!

Card?

Y's cards, they come with season tickets. I've got every set way back to when I first started going to games with my grandpa.

One of the OG's was a Y's fan?

Well back then they were the Maroons, Starx... This received only a blank stare, Olpert drank. Had he said something wrong? From behind his glass he looked along the bar at the three men down the other end, each one steeping in the boozy puddle of his world, and then up to the mirror: there was the booth, and the women — it was her, the former star, Pearl, and she was staring back at him, hard.

HER EARS STILL RINGING, Debbie entered the Golden Barrel gently, almost apologetically. The usual pallid faces ringed the bar, a foursome of recent Institute grads nibbled wings. The only other patron sat by the bathrooms, some sad grey woman alone with a jug of cider. How tired and defeated this person looked — and then she was standing and waving and Debbie realized it was Pearl.

You haven't changed a bit, Pearl told her, they hugged long and hard, and pulling away Debbie wished she'd worn a shirt that showed off her tattoo.

Kell and the kids just left.

Whoa, you brought them here?

One sec, said Pearl, and slid out of the booth wagging the empty jug at the bartender.

Order me wings, said Debbie, please, studying Pearl as she limped away. Did she know what life had done to her? This scared Debbie, the thought that life might happen beyond one's understanding, with its truths manifest in a hunched and heavy walk or the lines on one's face, those cicatrices of every trial and sadness.

Pearl returned, set down the refill. Those two at the bar are checking you out, she said. The big guy and his little friend in matching shirts.

Not you too? So I get both?

Nobody checks me out anymore.

Aw, Debbie said — how condescending this sounded. But what else to say?

Pearl poured two pints. Behind the bar, the phone started ringing. Pete stared it down until it stopped, then went back to twisting a towel inside a spotty glass.

Cheers, said Pearl. They clinked drinks. And then came the question Debbie was dreading: So who all's coming?

BAILIE, here's the thing about you: there's no life in your life.

There's life!

Example?

I have moles.

Freckles.

No, no. As pets, Starx. I keep moles. In a terrarium. But they'd call it a larder.

Starx shook his head, drank. The phone started ringing again. The bartender scowled at it, held up his hands to deny responsibility, disappeared into the kitchen. Ha, said Starx. You gotta love Pete.

Starx, hello? Moles don't count? Those aren't lives?

Fug, Bailie, that's not what I meant. There's no life in your life *outside your life*. Look, I've only known you for, what?

Cumulative? Less than twenty-four hours. But we met two weeks ago.

Whatever. Listen to me. You've built this little life and you live inside it, and anything outside it is — there's nothing outside it. You don't let anything in.

Wait, I'm sorry, moles don't have lives? Whatever! Do you even know anything about moles? Keeping a mole is really hard. The thing with moles is that they have to feel at home in their world. They have to be able to burrow, they like to feel safe, they feel safe by burrowing. They need to be surrounded in their homes. And they're delicate. I only keep one at a time. If you put two together they'll mate, and you don't want all those babies. That's if you're lucky. Usually they'll just kill each other.

Are you going to talk to that woman over there or what?

The little gal I've got now is called Jessica. I just got her. Poor Kathy passed on the eighth, just over a week ago now. Before her was Alfredo, I just realized it would have been his sixth birthday last week! Moles are sensitive, is the thing. You have to keep them dry, and the temperature has to be regulated. They don't like loud noises either — loud noises can kill them. Just from shock. That's how Henry died, I think. One of my housemates —

Gal. You call your mole a *gal*.

What? Do you even know how much moles *eat*? Often half their weight in bugs a day! I get a lot of slugs from under stones around the Islet, and since I live with slobs we've got roaches, and I have a worm bin too, under my bed. They like variety in their diets, moles.

Starx tipped back the end of his cider.

What I'm saying is that you want to talk about *alive*? Well moles are very much alive, Starx. Are you listening? Are you even *listening*? They're very, very alive.

BUT THINK, said Debbie, if you moved back home you'd get to see everyone, whenever!

Home? You mean *here*? No thanks.

Never?

What's there for me here? For my family?

I don't know, this is a great city. I mean, there's problems, but there's a lot of good people here. You should have seen this thing I went to earlier tonight, it was amazing —

Yeah, obviously I'd have a real community to come back to.

Well people get busy, right? And to be fair it was kind of short notice —

Pearl waved it away. She drank.

So, said Debbie, you playing any ball at all ever?

With my knee?

Yeah, me either. It's less of a shame for me than you though. I mean, you were a for-real star! But anyway, I've just got so many other commitments.

Adine.

That commitment, yeah.

How's she?

Good! Really good. She says hi. She'd love to meet you but she's — you know how artists are. She's working hard on a new project, it's really cool, it's about all sorts of really smart stuff. She's so smart. But we're good, yeah.

So everything's good.

So good! What about Kellogg? Things okay? I mean, last time I talked to you —

Things are fine.

And your kids! They must be like little people now. What's the younger one?

Elsie-Anne. Else.

And Gip was like two or something when I visited — that was fun, remember that? Who'd have guessed you'd end up living on a *farm*?

Deb, wow, you're such a big-city girl. It's not a farm! People grow things on farms.

Ha, yeah. I guess even the idea of grass is like, so rural-seeming to me.

What about the park?

Debbie waved her hand. Don't get me started on the park.

No?

No. Debbie looked at Pearl carefully, felt the gulf of this conversation opening up before them — it was better sidestepped. Debbie conjured light to her eyes and grabbed her old friend's hands across the table. It's just so good to see you!

THE OTHER WOMAN's laugh was like fireworks, it came tinkling down in silver lights: head thrown back, neck exposed, such a clean perfect neck to put your lips to — once, again, again, forever for the rest of your life, every night. But then in the mirror Olpert's eyes met Pearl's, suspicious and mean.

He stared into his cider.

Quite a mating call on the other bird, said Starx. Eh?

I know.

Whoa, wait a minute! Look at you, all fawny and — you're smitten, aren't you, Bailie.

Starx.

You *are*. Well go get her.

Ha, yeah right. Her friend already thinks I'm probably a rapist.

Starx stiffened. Don't say that, he said.

Oh. Okay. Sorry.

Their wings arrived. Olpert ate one, a sweat moustache came, he wiped it away, another appeared in its place — why was his body so relentlessly humiliating?

Starx licked sauce from his fingers. Good lord but that's the stuff, he said.

This is embarrassing, said Olpert.

What?

What, what? Everything.

Stop talking to me. Go over there.

Just go over there, just like that. *Hey sugar, hey babe,* or something, *nice hotwings, great legs, do you want to give me your phone number?* Right. That'll happen.

Are you scared?

What, right now?

When else?

I don't know.

What are you scared of?

Olpert drained his glass. The bartender dove upon it, filled him up.

Good man, Petey, said Starx. My man here's nearly living.

I'm getting drunk, said Olpert. I don't do this. It's not normal.

Well it's normal in bars, said Starx. That's what guys who are living do: get drunk in bars. Speaking of fuggin which, let's gun some schnapps. Pete! Shots!

Shots appeared. Starx cheersed the guys at the end of the bar, who ignored him, and then faced Olpert. Look me in the eye, he ordered. Olpert did, and noticed his partner's face had softened. Starx said, To you, getting laid, and slammed his schnapps. Olpert followed suit and came away gasping. Starx thumped the bar.

Mutherfugger, he howled, that'll put hair on your shaft!

JESUS, listen to those guys.

Aw, they're just having fun.

Pearl spat cider back into her glass. Deb? Wow, that's not like you.

Like me? What do you mean?

You used to chew up guys like that. No smartass comments? Look at them — wait, don't look at them, they'll think you're interested.

I just figure everyone's got a right to a good time. They're not hurting anyone. I mean, not in this instant. Outside of here, of course, they're the *enemy.*

Huh. You used to be so funny.

I'm still funny.

Are you?

I don't know. Adine's funny, in her way. Maybe she's funny for both of us.

Pete arrived with Debbie's wings, held up their empty jug with a questioning look.

One more, said Pearl.

You don't have to be back? For your kids? What time is it?

But Pearl was watching the bartender return to his post. Is he going to get that phone?

Pete dispenses drinks and wisdom, said Debbie. Don't expect much else.

Pete. How long have you been living here?

Let's see, I'm thirty-one, I came to the Institute when I was eighteen, so —

No, in UOT.

Years, now. Since I moved in with Adine.

Right.

Debbie smacked the table. I forgot to tell you! Though, wait, now I forget . . .

What?

Someone from the team's coaching now. Coaching the Y's, not at the Institute . . .

Who?

I can't remember! Isn't that terrible? It's just, I haven't really been up with ball-related stuff. I'm trying to think, though, who it might have been . . .

Pearl waited.

Anyway. Neat, right?

Whoever it was.

Debbie took a wing, eyed Pearl. I feel bad, she said, nibbling, that no one else came.

It's fine.

No, it's not. Wouldn't it have been great to get everyone out? Could have been a perfect excuse for a little reunion. And short notice, I know I said that, but it's no excuse, right? Blame me. As I said, I've been a little AWOL from that whole scene.

Doing what?

I've been doing more like, activism-type work, with a different crowd. Stuff around the park. So I've met some new friends through that. And Adine, of course — I see her. Though lately she doesn't see me, ha. Anyway you barely ever come home. I feel bad.

Stop saying that, *home*. My home is very, very far from here. This isn't a *homecoming*, Deb. It's a vacation. And we only came *here* because of my son.

I just mean —

I'm not *home*. Do you understand?

But your parents —

No plans to see those two appleheads this weekend either.

WE MAKE A GOOD squad, Bailie — even if you're a fuggin asphodel. Maybe *because* you're such a fuggin asphodel. And I'm weedkiller! So we're balanced or whatever.

Um. Thank you.

Though you still need to lighten up.

I'm lightened! I'm wasted. I feel like I could float home.

Starx ordered more schnapps. Olpert was still chasing the first one's burn with cider, it fizzed in his nose, he pulled away snorting.

Easy there Bailie.

Olpert wiped his face with a napkin, looked at Starx. I've been meaning to say: you shouldn't have socked that boy. Even if he spat on me. That wasn't right.

Socked. Bailie, the words you use. I hardly socked him. Just a little love-tap.

Love-tap? You could have killed him.

Killed? With a little knock like that? You don't ever dust it up, as a security guard?

At Municipal Works? Who would I dust it up with?

What do they got you carrying? A nightstick? Spray?

Sometimes staff come in to work latenights and I have to check their ID badges. I've got a scanner for that. Starx was searching his face for something. What?

Bailie, listen. You have no idea about anything — you don't understand people, what people can do. You probably think those blackups are the reason we started Zone patrols.

Does this reason also explain why you go around socking children?

Someday, Bailie — someday I'll tell you a story.

Not now?

No.

Pete brought two more shots and another round of ciders. As he turned away the phone started ringing again. He swept it from its cradle and banged it down, hard.

Starx?

Go talk to that woman.

Starx sipped his drink in silence. Olpert shredded his coaster onto the bartop. The phone was ringing. Scowling, Pete disappeared into the kitchen. Starx burped. The phone silenced. And started ringing again.

I HAVE TO ADMIT I was a little wary about meeting out here. Never mind bringing the kids, though Kellogg had some sort of freak-out.

Oh yeah?

Well you know. UOT. This used to be one of the neighbourhoods you just didn't *go*. After Lakeview Homes closed.

Right.

Though I guess people are really starting to move out here?

Her glass halfway to her mouth, Debbie paused. I'm sorry — *people?*

Pearl blinked.

What people?

You know. People.

Debbie put her drink down.

People like us, whatever.

And what are we like, Pearl?

Forget it.

No, come on, I'm not being confrontational, honestly. You said people are moving here — *people like us.* I just want to know what people you're talking about.

Forget it, okay? I'm very proud of you for living here. You're very brave —

No, no. That's not what I mean. I'm just interested is all.

Pearl opened her mouth, closed it, pushed back from the table, looked at her watch. The air over the table had turned jagged and static.

What? Are we done?

It's past eleven.

Right, well at this hour the trains only run every fifteen minutes. The next eastbound Yellowline is —

Now you're telling me how to get back? I *grew up* here, Deb. You're not even from here. I love people like you, who move —

People like me? I'm sorry, are those different from people like you? Because a minute ago we were the same. We were *people like us,* remember.

This conversation is stupid. This is not a conversation. I don't know what this is. Pearl stood. I have to go to the bathroom, she said, and moved with care, one step after the next, toward the toilets.

Debbie gazed mournfully at the empty seat across from her, tried to pinpoint the moment things had swung so drastically in the wrong direction. If only she could rewind the night somehow, and reset it on a different, more affable path. She looked around, avoiding eye contact with the guys at the bar. The Institute kids had cleared out. The place was quiet. She realized the ringing in her ears was gone. Two hours earlier she'd fled that awful sound — and come here, to this: drunk and alone, with a basket of bones.

LOOK, she's solo, said Starx. Make your move.

From Olpert came a panicked bleat, like a vexed sheep.

What was that? Is that your alert siren?

I'm too drunk.

You're not. You're the perfect amount of drunk.

Olpert lay his head on the bar. Her name was Debbie, the other woman had said it. She was a full person now: Debbie.

Don't do that, with your face. It's disgusting. Who knows where that bar has been.

Olpert didn't move. Time passed, the phone began ringing again, the room pitched and reeled. He concocted scenarios with this Debbie: a phone number, a date, a kiss, a whole life together, and every night ended with their heads on the same pillow and Olpert whispering, *Goodnight, Debbie, I love you.* And her saying it back.

From the real world came a clatter. The phone had stopped ringing — Pete had it to his ear screaming, What the fug? What!

Olpert blinked. Okay, he said.

Who's that on the phone then, Pete, said Starx.

Okay, I said, said Olpert. I'll do it.

His cheek was stuck to the bar, he had to peel himself off. Eyes bleary and bloodshot, Olpert wavered on his stool, buffeted by a secret wind.

That's it, Bailie. Starx lifted his cider in salute. Live, it's time for you to live.

Olpert searched his partner's big face for mockery. But Starx, though flushed a ripe-cherry purple, looked stoic, even sincere.

Easy, Bailie. You look like you're about to kiss me. It's only our first date.

Sorry, sorry...

No, that's the spirit. Just, you know, direct it over there.

Olpert swung off the stool, stepped down. The room carouselled around him. Starx gave him a push that sent him staggering toward the corner booth. He reached for something, a chair maybe, to steady himself, it toppled. He came closer, his mouth began to form the words he was meant to say — simple words spoken all the time: *Can I have your phone number.* Because that was all you needed, a number, to begin.

Debbie was a person-shaped blur, Olpert's stomach churned, then heaved with a more troubling sort of violence. Oh no, he said, and felt Debbie watching him as he stumbled past to the men's, her eyes full of revulsion — or, worse, pity. Hands pressed to either wall he shimmied down the hallway as a miner down a mineshaft, face tightening as vomit threatened at the back of his throat.

He swung through the door: the toilet was occupied. Olpert rattled the handle and a woman said, Take it easy. He staggered and fell against the sink, slid to a sitting position on the tiles. The stall door opened and he had a view of jeans and sneakers and from somewhere above them a female voice was demanding angry questions Olpert didn't understand and couldn't answer because here it came, surging and gurgly and sour, a hot spray down his uniform, all over the women's bathroom floor.

IX

1TS FINAL S FLICKERING, the
STREET'S MILK & THINGS sign lit the parking lot in a milky pallor.
The store's lights were off. Debbie tried the door, found it locked,
cupped her hands to the glass, and looked inside. Pop sat behind
the counter, the great mound of him motionless in the dark. His
hands were not madly gesticulating, no invectives poured from
his mouth, no perspiration darkened his poncho. He seemed sad
and hunched, a shadow of himself. She'd never seen him like this.

Debbie knocked. He looked up. Fear flashed in his eyes. She
waved. The look faded, he nodded and came around to let her in.

Mr. Street, hi, sorry, said Debbie, trying to steel the boozy slur
from her voice. I rushed here as quick as I could.

I dilated your phone number, I spoke to someone —

Adine.

— whom told me of your presence at this drinking bar. After
localizing the number I called recurrently, and called. Ultimately
upon the midnight hour a man responds, and thence you are.
Should I have slept in my store, what of the Movement then?

Mr. Street, sorry. I would've come quicker if I'd known —

They took my house. After a quartered century hencefrom,
they took my house.

I know. I know.

The men who took it — I lend you insurance, was I younger...
With his hand Pop made the chopping motion of a cheese slicer.

We should try to catch the last train. Do you have stuff?

He held up a plastic bag. It seemed to be filled with candy.

Pop locked up and led Debbie around back. Where the house-boat had been a handpainted LAKEVIEW HOMES RESTRIBUTION MOVEMENT placard lay in the gravel, which Pop collected and stroked as a sad dad might a photo of his lost child. My domicidal return can be petitioned on Monday, he said. After this Jubilee has transposed.

This is so unacceptable. I've got a friend who's a lawyer —

They are desirous for my eradification. Sincerely! For I am the lone recalcitrant of history, of what *presupposed* what *is*. I'm the sole one who cares anymore.

Debbie, following Pop down the path into People Park, said, Well.

Lark! I'm the sole one.

Are we supposed to be in the park after midnight? I thought there were Helpers —

They can't tell me whence to be or not be, said Pop.

Okay, said Debbie, swaying down the path behind him, still drunk.

They bulldoze my home and then sagefully proclaim this park better? Bah. To whom did they consult among us, the populace, the impersonatory people? This Mayor cares about people as the eagle of malignancy cares about the earth from which it plucks the worm of hope — the earth this worm has *toiled*, stay mindful.

I will, said Debbie.

The night sky had clouded over, the moon glowed dully behind a smoky scrim. Debbie followed Pop into the lightless common — a vast pool of spilled ink.

This here, he said, was the beginning of the alley behind F-Block, I impersonated unit F-802. All the way aghast this hill were backyards. Of course it was planified then also, there was no hill. Perhaps difficult to visualize from here.

I think Adine's family was in Block H, said Debbie. That was near your shop, right?

But Pop was on the move again, heading around Crocker Pond to the Slipway, which they'd climb to Parkside West Station. At the boathouse he stopped to catch his breath. The clouds parted: a perfect full moon splashed little crags of silver upon the pond.

You okay?

He nodded, produced a blowholish grunt. Atop the hill the train station glowed like a spaceship. See, you see? He gestured vaguely with his bag of candy, gasping. Thence was my place. You see?

Do you mean when you had your boat in Crocker Pond or —

They made me move from the pond! Claiming that upon my own property would be an endurable arraignment! And now the squab has come home to roast.

I know, but was your house near here too? Sorry, I'm just confused.

The hawk, he whispered, and grinned. I'd forgotten about him, what was his name, what did we call him? The walls were so thin that if you heard mice you couldn't be sure if they were from next door or your own unit. And if you had mice there was a hawk, someone had tamed a hawk. This man brought his hawk to your house and you would go out and come back and the mice would be gone, all of them. But what was his name?

The man's?

No, said Pop. The hawk's.

He had grown so lucid. He even breathed more easily — but he snorted and wheeled. Lark, why am I pontificating this story? About a hawk! Not exactly utilitary.

It's a great story. Our cat Jeremiah's useless with mice. He —

Cats, bah.

Clouds slid over the moon.

Climbing the slipway, between gasps Pop muttered, Stories are just stories.

I thought it was nice. Crazy maybe, a hawk let loose indoors — Nice and crazy maybe is *not* utilitary.

Well it's just nice to hear a story that's not about how dangerous it was here. In the Homes, I mean. You hear about the violence —

Pop grunted. You entreat me of violence? Of course there was violence. Whence is there not? But is it not just as violent to force citizens from their homes? To uproot us like so many roots from the soil, with the spade of unjustice?

I wasn't —

Violence. Bah.

Debbie and Pop cut through a final thicket of shrubs onto the sidewalk. Ahead loomed the monorail station, up on stilts and halogenically lit, tracks extending north and south, and into which an escalator rose, whirring.

With his hands on his knees Pop rested, candy bag hanging. Sweat dripped from the end of his nose and splattered the sidewalk. Across the street, the Cinecity marquee read: JUBILEE LIVE FRIDAY/ALL IN TOGETHER NOW STARTS SATURDAY! Beyond it, the Podesta Tower lofted high above everything, twirling twin searchlights into the night sky.

Debbie never came downtown at this hour, the abandoned streets reminded her of afterhours at the Bebrog bar where she'd worked before signing on to *In the Know*. At the end of each night, with everything hosed down and the stools stacked and the place vaultlike and the morning lurking outside, it never seemed that the night's revelry, or anything resembling life, could ever happen there again. And now, with the streets empty and the office towers vacant and the escalator winding up and down, untrafficked, the absence of people in this world they'd built filled her with that same melancholy.

Something moved under the Cinecity marquee. A strange shape jerked through the shadows with a scraping, rattling sound. At first Debbie thought it might be a person in a wheelchair, but the figure seemed too tall — a homeless person piloting a shopping cart maybe. But there were no homeless people downtown, not anymore.

Pop toed the escalator, retreated. How does one make an ascension?

What do you mean? said Debbie.

You think, with all I do, that I have time to gallivate around the city? Pollycock!

Wait — you've never taken the *train*?

Across the street the figure had heard them: it melted inside the entryway to the theatre. There's someone there, Debbie whispered, but Pop was edging onto the escalator.

No problem, he said, swept upward, here I go.

With a glance over her shoulder — the person across the street cowered, motionless — Debbie followed Pop, the escalator lifted them to the turnstiles. Up the tracks a train eased south from Guardian Bridge Station. Good timing, said Debbie, and Pop nodded, eyes fixed upon it in terror, as if what approached were a shuttle to his own grave.

THE MAYOR WAITED until the train pulled out before moving. With a dust shovel scavenged from the banquet hall fireplace she land-paddled out from under the marquee and wheeled right onto Paper Street. From atop the dessert cart she punted along, legs heaped on the lower tier. One foot had lost its pump and dragged on the pavement, the tights split, big toe flaking skin like sparks.

At Municipal Works' executive entrance the Mayor keyed in her code. The doors opened, she paddled down a long, empty hallway, out into a marble-pillared rotunda, surveillance cameras blinked red lights, past the security guard, Betty, to the elevator at the base of the Podesta Tower. And then she was lifted into the sky: the island swelled glittering to its edges, where it ceded abruptly to the lake.

Released one hundred storeys up, the Mayor flicked on the lights and rolled out onto the viewing deck, a bubble enclosed by glass on all sides that turned, languidly, clockwise. And though the viewing deck boasted the best and most comprehensive panoramas of the city, at this hour, with the lights on inside, the Mayor saw none of it: not the sleeping city, not the night sky, not the polished coin of the moon, not, as the viewing deck rotated south, the vast emptiness of the water, a second sky hollowed out beneath the sky. Everything was lost in the room's reflection.

And at the heart of this reflection the Mayor saw herself, spectral and translucent, floating out there in space, a thousand feet above downtown. The dark shapes of her eyes hovered in a gaunt face, every wrinkle a gulley, her hair a tussled silver nest. She stared into the eyes out there, on the other side of the glass, her eyes, but couldn't see her own eyes: they were just absence, two holes punched into the night.

Had she left the lights off, as the deck swivelled north, then east, she would have been treated to a straight shot over People Park, and across it, the tower of the Grand Saloon Hotel, the clockface a sort of second moon, the hands at right angles where the illustrationist had frozen them that morning. On the roof's edge sat his helicopter, nosing out over the brightly lit penthouse suite. The balcony doors had been cast open, the curtains billowed in the A/C's steady draft. And with each ruffle they revealed the illustrationist atop the sheets in his tracksuit, fast asleep.

He needed cold air to sleep and light, lots of light. The penthouse was all marble and polished dark wood and brass, everything gleamed in the brilliance sprinkled down from a row of crystal chandeliers. Atop the nightstand was the CityGuide that lived in every guest's bedside drawer, bookmarked with a feather four pages from the end.

Raven's position atop the bed's black silk sheets was perfect symmetry: on his back, arms at his sides, legs a fist apart, face to the ceiling. His baldhead gleamed. His tracksuit was velvety. His eyes were open, yet he was sleeping, this was how he slept, and his eyes seemed to have no irises but just pupils swollen into pits, and his body produced no movement or sound, his chest did not rise and fall, there was not even a hiss of breath, and anyone happening upon this person would have assumed him dead.

The illustrationist seemed to stare upward, but his brain registered nothing of the outside world, only his dreams — if he had dreams. But Raven did not dream.

FRIDAY

FRIDAY

And when he had called them together, he spake as follows —
— Plato, *Critias*

I

THEY WOULD ALWAYS remember the day their mama stopped believing in God, a hot August Sunday when Sam and Adine were seven. With the tower bells ringing the entire congregation was set free into the Cathedral parking lot, Sam and Adine held their mama's hands, her grip went tight when they reached their parking spot: no car, just a sprinkling of what appeared to be beach glass. In her nice blue dress their mama sank down onto the curb, face in her hands. All around the bells chimed joy and past them flowed people in their Sunday best, smiling and saved. No one stopped to say anything or help.

Once everyone disappeared and the bells went quiet their mama stood and without a word started walking west, into the ruins of Lakeview Homes. Sam and Adine trailed behind her exchanging looks: What was happening, where was their car? They followed their mama in silence through the wreckage of buildings half-destroyed by diggers abandoned for the weekend, sitting there like the shells of larval bugs, and the spindly stalks of apple-tree saplings lined up along the fence that penned in the wrecking site.

The sun burned above and the asphalt of South Throughline burned below and the churned-up earth burned from somewhere deeper. The heat was brackish, stifling, they could taste the tarry smoke of it in their mouths. Their mama stopped at the fence: beyond it was the dug-out pit where A-Block 100 had once stood. All the A-Block residents had already been packed up and bussed across town, trucks had taken their things. As the demolition swept north into B- and C-Blocks, more and more people would be shifted to what people were calling the Zone, the westend neighbourhoods north of Lower Olde Towne. And when the bulldozers reached H-Block Sam and Adine and their mama would have to move too.

A Park Project diagram mounted on the fence showed how what had been A-Block would become a forest of poplar trees that stretched all the way to a campground at the lakeshore, where there would be a beach. Centre Throughline would be moved underground, tunnelled beneath the park all the way from the southside to the island's northern shore, overtop of which would be a field and a pond. It was impossible to imagine what was pictured ever becoming real: Lakeview Homes looked as though a meteor had struck and incinerated its entire southern half, how could anything grow here, it was just a dead empty hole or a giant mouth gaping wider and wider until it swallowed the whole complex down.

Their mama took off her pumps and with one in each hand wiped her forehead with her sleeve and threw her shoes over the fence, one then the next plunging birdlike down into the shadows. The back of her blue dress was dark with sweat. Okay, she said, and barefoot continued home along what had once been sidewalks and now was just dirt. Sam and Adine followed her up Centre Throughline, north through B-Block and C- and D-, west along North Throughline into the 50s, then north again to their unit, H-54, wedged amid a row of identical units, where the screendoor smacked closed behind her.

If you had your car stolen you were supposed to call the police, yet their mama did not. She sat in the living room smoking cigarettes with the front curtains drawn until the matching ashtrays Sam and Adine had made her at school overflowed. After church their mama always fixed lunch but today there was no lunch. She got up only to take down the cross that lived above the kitchen sink and dump it in the trash.

From that day on their mama became a pinched-in version of herself: smaller, and taut, and when she talked her mouth barely opened. It seemed something was hiding inside her that she couldn't let escape. Though sometimes whatever it was would claw to the surface and come stabbing out in screams and slaps. When she found Sam inside the living room armoire dismantling her hairdryer he cried not because it hurt to be hit, but because of the surprise.

By the time school started in September the demolition had swept into C-Block and everything changed. Their mama switched to nightshifts at the factory, so there was no longer time in the evenings, she said, to cook or say Grace. Instead she heated TV dinners from the freezer, slid the trays onto the kitchen table at her kids. Eat, she said, putting on her coat as they peeled off the tinfoil covers and folded the warm edges into the still-frozen centres. While Connie was at work Sam and Adine would watch TV until they couldn't keep their eyes open, and in the mornings she'd often come home to them still sprawled head-to-toe on the couch. Go to school, she said then, and she would go to bed, and they would go to school.

In October Sam and Adine came home one afternoon and a bicycle was leaning against their front steps. Inside a hardhat sat on the kitchen counter and mud had been tracked down the hall to their mama's bedroom, the door was closed. At dinnertime she came out with a man she told Sam and Adine to call Uncle Bruno, but he was no uncle of theirs, they called him nothing. Bruno never said much to anyone, and around him their mama spoke in a whisper like she was embarrassed or sorry for something. He drove the crane, they learned, that swung a big ball on the end of a chain into their neighbours' units and turned the walls to dust.

As the weeks went on and the Park Project crept north Bruno moved in, frying bacon every morning that he never shared with anyone, at night he took over the TV with his workboots up on the couch. With their mama at work and nothing else to do Sam and Adine hid inside the armoire and told each other the stories of TV shows they'd watched, including the one with the terrorist who made a bomb from batteries he was going to use to blow up an airplane — before, of course, he was stopped. They were always stopped.

The day of the first snowfall of the year, Sam and Adine came home from school to their mama crying in the dark in the living room, two bits of bloody paper towel stuffed up her nostrils. The matching ashtrays were smashed on the living room floor and there were cigarette butts everywhere. Bruno was gone. Adine swept up and then she and Sam sat with their mama, one on either side of her on the couch, each holding a hand. That night in the armoire they made up a new story, and it was about bad strange people coming from the outside and ruining everything, and it ended with revenge.

The next morning, a Saturday, Sam and Adine woke up and their mama was still sleeping. As quietly as they could, they rounded up all the batteries in the house, emptying flashlights and smoke detectors and other various small electronics — and put them all in the tin can of bacon grease that Bruno had left on the ledge above the stove, and last of all dug a pack of matches out of one of the drawers. We need more batteries, said Sam, so they stole one small bill from their mama's purse and went to Street's Milk and from the Polyp behind the counter bought the biggest battery they could afford.

This was November, the Park Project was demolishing C-Block. Then work would break until the spring, when Sam and

Adine and their mama were supposed to move to some new big building across the city. The workers took weekends off too, though their equipment — backhoes and diggers and tractors and bulldozers — remained onsite. So this is where Sam and Adine headed: through the fence, their makeshift bomb ready, toward the big tall crane and its wrecking ball, inside the shadows way down in the pit.

IN THE TRAUMA ward of City Centre Hospital, Sam stood beside his mama as the doctor explained what had happened to Adine's eyes and when his mama said, So she might be blind, it seemed she was almost wishing it. There was a cold, white sharpness to her voice. The doctor said something about surgery, and recovery, and that it was good she was young — but Sam's mama just said again, She's blind, and rocked a little on her feet like she might fall. Sam put his hand on her lower back to steady her and at his touch she stiffened and wriggled away. Thank you, she said to the doctor, and sat down on the other side of the waiting room. The doctor looked at Sam and smiling in a soft kind way asked if he wanted to see his sister. Sam did not but he had nowhere else to go.

They went through two sets of doors and down a hallway and stopped outside a room. In a bed underneath a window slept a person that was almost Adine. Beside the bed was a chair. The doctor gestured at the chair and left. Sam didn't move. Bandages hid his sister's eyes. Across her cheeks were dark ridges and speckles of dried blood where gravel and battery acid had sprayed up from the ground. A big cut on her chin had been stitched with crude blue knots. Tubes ran from her arms to machines that beeped and hissed. Another tube ran to a box on the floor. Under the blankets Adine's chest rose and fell, rose and fell. Sam leaned over the bed, watching his sister breathe.

What the fug are you doing, said his mama's voice from the doorway, and Sam stepped away from the bed.

He didn't know where to look or what to say. His insides felt hollow, scooped out.

You aren't even going to cry, his mama said. You haven't even cried.

She leaned against the wall in a small hunched way.

You did this to her and you can't even fuggin cry?

Sam looked out the window: a pretty sunset over the city, big fat bands of gold and pink that darkened into mauve, indigo, all the way to black.

The last thing he'd seen before the explosion was Adine squatting over the coffee can, igniting the fuse, the fast sizzle of it, the thunder of the bomb blowing, a cruel ripping sound as the can sheared in half, and so much light.

It left a tone in his ears like when the TV went to coloured bars at midnight. He sat up, discovered Adine sprawled with her limbs at weird angles, the coffee can split and blackened between her feet. Sam went over. Through the thrashered mess of her face she seemed to be looking up at him for an answer. The gore was black in places, wet and raw in others. You couldn't see her eyes.

On the taxi ride to the hospital his mama screamed Fug fug fug in the backseat with Adine's head in her lap, his sister's face not so much bleeding as just opened up, as if the top layer of skin had been wiped away. Sam noticed that he'd torn the knees of his jeans — and for a moment thought that *this* would be why he'd get in trouble.

A nurse appeared and whispered something to Sam's mama. Outside the sky had gone purple. Okay, said his mama, Sam, we're going home. There's nothing for us to do here now. There's nothing we can do.

At home Sam sat inside the armoire thinking about blindness, that his sister could be blind. He closed his eyes to see what a blind person saw: black. But still he could perceive a thread of light between the armoire's doors, facing it the darkness behind his eyelids brightened.

He heard his mother shuffling down the hallway and called to her.

What do you want, said her voice. Why are you in that thing.

Mama, said Sam.

There was a pause and three short barks that was his mama coughing. And Sam looked and there she was, through the crack between the doors, her cigarette sparking orange in the dark and the light from the hall flooding in behind her. Don't call me that, she said. Mama, don't say that to me.

Sam scrunched his eyes so tightly they ached. Is being blind like this.

His mama's voice was tight: You call me Connie, hear me. No more Mama.

Like this, said Sam, when it's all dark. When I close my eyes it's dark and —

Your sister can't see nothing, his mama, Connie, said.

Nothing?

Nothing. You did it to her, and now she can't see nothing at fuggin all, said Connie, and then she went down the hallway and shut herself in her room.

Sam sat there thinking about nothing. Nothing was a cold black space, an empty coffin. But then a coffin had walls so it was something. And a clump of smoke scudding over a field was something. And the deepest darkest depths of the ocean were something. And the farthest outlying nowhere of the universe was something. Even the air was something if it kept you alive, and even if not. The idea of nothing was impossible, it couldn't exist because for it to exist it had to be something, which it wasn't.

And Sam thought about what Adine's world would be with eyes that saw nothing and it seemed too big to think of or too small. There were no words for what it was because every word was a thing and nothing meant no things. What was nothing if even the dark was something — if even black and empty had to be seen?

Sam tried to make his brain go blank so it was nothing but even the blank was something because he was thinking about the blank and it was a wide white disc. He scrunched his eyes as tight as he could and when he opened them they ached and the air sparkled the way the TV did when everything dissolved into static.

Maybe death was the only way there was nothing. Heaven was a place to go when you were dead but if you did not believe in heaven, if you'd stopped going to church, there was nothing. Then your life slipped from you like ash caught in a draft: it went swirling away and your body was left a hollow husk. Then instead of burying you your family pushed that body into a fire where it burned to ash and ash was something that could get caught in a draft and go swirling away and be gone.

THE NEXT DAY Sam began his mission to become nothing. He sat by himself on the frontseat of the bus and spoke to no one and kept his eyes closed and tried not to let his brain register the darkness he saw there or the jostling of the bus or the whoosh of cars passing by or the wind or the other kids shrieking. Sometimes the kids would come to him in pairs or in threes and call him Welfare or demand what he had for lunch, because instead of flats and apples he usually had crackers and a candy bar, and the kids would want his candy bar. Sometime he fought for it and sometimes he was too tired so he just gave it away. But today he was nothing so if they came they would come to no one. But they didn't come. Somehow they knew.

At school all the kids spilled out of the bus and Sam slipped silently after them into the school and down the hallway to his classroom where he slid behind his desk. The desk made a noise when he opened it so he stopped and went slower, in increments, and stopped every time the hinges squawked and bit by bit opened it. He took his things out and laid them as softly as possible on his desk, his binder and pencils and workbook, and lowered the lid.

Sam did not put his hand up when the teacher called for answers even if he knew the answers. He did not laugh when a kid said something funny and the whole class laughed. He did his work in silence.

When the bell rang for recess Sam filed into the back of the line and glided out after everyone and then walked across the playground alone while the rest of the kids shrieked and hollered and chased one another around. From the ballfields came a mad scramble of voices cheering on other voices or disputing calls or championing themselves. Usually Sam hung around the ballfields, just in case someone asked him to play, but today he did not. He stationed himself by the parking lot and waited for the bell to ring, trying to clear his brain of everything.

Lining up to go back inside, sometimes the other kids would talk to him or about him but today he was nothing so they didn't. Sam stared ahead and said nothing. Then everyone filed inside and back into the classroom and it was math and then lunch and at lunch Sam sat alone and ate slowly and on the playground once again retreated to his quiet corner and stood with his eyes closed and waited for the bell and back in school waited for the final bell and then he walked home, alone, through the crunch of autumn leaves he tried not to feel or hear and the vinegary smell of apples rotting on lawns he tried not to smell. And even though he'd been nothing all day he couldn't believe that no one had asked him about Adine, not even one of the teachers, though by their quiet careful way he knew they knew. Everyone knew, yet no one said anything.

At home there was a bicycle against the steps. In the living room Sam found his mama, Connie, on the couch with her shirt hoisted to her neck and Bruno on his knees slurping at her breasts. Connie's eyes were closed, her head tilted back. Bruno looked at

Sam standing there in the doorway, then went back to sucking and licking and kneading. Connie moaned. Sam ran down the hall to the armoire and shutting himself inside closed his eyes and vowed to Adine, fiercely, that he would never open them again.

SAM OPENED his eyes. Out the basement windows the sunrise blushed the lawn. But he didn't get up. He lay in bed and thought about the illustrationist — about those eyes, the emptiness in them. Sam tried to understand them but could not. He put on his watches, lined up on the bedside table, the final one still ticked. And yet, from time's machine, silence. Though upstairs too there were clocks.

After listening to ensure that none of his housemates were awake and about, Sam headed up to the kitchen. The microwave said 7:09. He waited. It ticked ahead one minute. Good. He placed a nuclear breakfast in the microwave, and while it nuked his food Sam watched the bulbs gleam and the digits tick down, and lost himself in the light.

Time disappeared then. Where did his mind go? In a panic Sam caught the microwave only four seconds before 0:00 — very close. He opened the door, took out the meal, ate thinking about the towerclock and Raven and the work, took an apple from the fridge for later, went to the bathroom, and in there was a miracle.

It was the uniform worn by the men in charge. The full uniform — pants, shirt, jacket, everything a brownish yellowish non-colour, the colour of the sleep crust he knuckled from his eyes. Sam touched it: in places the material had gone crispy, and an orange stain yawned down the front of the shirt. But still: this was a gift, and a sign, it had been left for him. His face tingled with nervous joy, was he dreaming, he fingered the scab on his jaw and felt the real-world sting.

Back in his basement room Sam laid the uniform on his bed, the pants where his legs would go, the shirt and jacket overtop. For now though he dressed for the work: the black suit with the black shirt underneath, the perfect clothes for being unseen. And then, with all the other residents still asleep, he slipped out of the roominghouse, walked to the ferrydocks. Boarding the first island-bound boat of the day Sam thought he heard thunder, off in the distance, despite the clear skies and across Perint's Cove the island trembling like a mirage in the bright morning sun of Good Friday.

II

FROM THE TOP of the Podesta Tower the Mayor surveyed the city — around and around the viewing deck had spun her, all night. She'd eventually killed the lights and spent the past six hours sleepless atop the dessert cart, perched there plantlike, the kindling of her legs piled on the cart's lower deck, watching the island reveal itself beneath a steadily paling sky. When at last the sun rose it lit everything purple, then pink, then gold. In the blooming daylight a spattering of traffic grew into steady cords up and down the city's main thoroughfares, the trains crawled out of the Whitehall Barns and began to whip around the city, and as the deck rotated east and the park came into view, coppery in the morning light, the Mayor, touch green, allowed her spirits to warm a bit.

The view swung south, to the Islet off the island's southeastern corner, the first ferry chugging across Perint's Cove to Bay Junction, then the Mayor was looking west along Budai Beach to Kidd's Harbour and the mansions of the Mews lording over LOT, north to Mount Mustela and Upper Olde Towne, to Blackacres, to Whitehall again in the northwest, an industrial ghost town, its unused Piers, where no ships had docked in a decade.

Even from this distance she could sense the neglect, all those weeds sprouting through cracked cement, a riot of green wavering shoots. In a city, the Mayor believed, nature needed to be tamed, or it choked you. And this corner that escaped human control was irksome, the view seemed to linger, she waited impatiently to see something else. The tower obeyed, rotating for sightlines over the Narrows. With the city at capacity, the NFLM had closed the bridge to traffic. Until Monday, no one was allowed in or out.

And here again was the relief of People Park, its ordered borders of forest, the southside grid of poplars matching the orchard to the east, the ellipse of Crocker Pond (rowers lit out from the boathouse and skimmed across its surface) a watery yolk amid the greater ellipse of the common, the discipline of the gardens — or, best, the rigour of hedgerows: the nonsense of bushes carved into walls, made geometrical and sane. And on the park's southern edge was Friendly Farm Automatic Zoo, a perfect square, and Lakeview Campground, the beach, the surf upon the beach, the lake.

But something dark and resentful slithered alongside her pride. Twenty-five Easters before, a collective exuberance had consumed the city, they'd come out by the thousands to be part of a new beginning. The Silver Jubilee was already less a celebration of People Park — or even the citizens, the people — than a forum for the whims of the dastard illustrationist. It felt symptomatic of a larger problem: her citizens were complacent, too comfortable, bored, and like dumb moths charmed by every flickering light.

SINCE STARTING ON nightshifts Olpert Bailie's sleep schedule required a seven a.m. bedtime and rising in the early afternoon. Friday morning, at the hour he'd normally be tucking himself in, his walkie-talkie buzzed. The voice integrated into his dreams: here was Starx, chasing him through the clouds, Olpert breast-stroking along with the city miles below . . .

Bailie! Get the fug up! B-Squad's gotta put in work!

Olpert rolled over, hit TALK: Hi, yes, I'm awake, okay.

I'm just leaving the Temple. Meet me in forty-five at Bay Junction.

Okay.

In the bathroom Olpert supported himself on the sink, head sludgy from the night before, throat raw, inspecting his face in the mirror: red-rimmed eyes, hair a brambled disaster. But looking past his reflection he felt his stomach drop. He was sure before bed he'd scrubbed and hung his NFLM uniform in the shower to dry — yet it was gone.

The bathroom hamper held only mildewed towels. Back in his room there was no sign of it either. What punitive humiliation might How We Do decree for misplaced khakis? Dropping four wriggling worms into Jessica's terrarium, Olpert only hoped it would be quiet and private, something behind closed doors, nothing televised or broadcast or even, with any luck, seen.

His radio buzzed: Bailie, you on the move?

Starx, hi, I've got a little problem.

Didn't have time to wash your duds? No problem. Your partner's got you covered.

Olpert let the misunderstanding ride, thanked him.

That's how we do, said Starx. Now hurry the fug up, you sack of nuts.

Sometimes Jessica would nose up from the soil to see what was going on. Today though there wasn't time to coax her out, and Olpert left the house forgetting a thing people did called breakfast, and on the ferry ride across Perint's Cove the dregs of the previous night's wings and cider rose up acidly in his throat. When the boat docked he came reeling ashore — greeted by Starx, spotlit in a sunbeam, a bottle of some fluorescent orange liquid in one hand, a spare NFLM uniform draped over his arm.

Drink this, he told Olpert. Then put this on.

The drink was disgusting, carbonated in a tart, fermented sort of way, with a tinny, bloody aftertaste. Ugh, what is that?

Secret recipe. My wife's hangover cure.

Wife?

Ex-wife. Long story. He reconsidered: Well, short story. A story for another time.

Olpert sipped, winced. And this will make me feel better?

Should, said Starx. There's nothing orange in it. Just goes that colour, for some reason.

Olpert drank, handed the empty back to Starx.

Bailie, nice work last night! No way those dames'll forget you anytime soon.

Kill me, said Olpert.

Kill you? No way! That, my friend? That's what some of us call *living*.

Oh.

Though I'm feeling pretty rotten myself, thanks for asking.

Oh. Sorry.

Not much of a people person, are you?

I beg your pardon?

I mean, we've hung out two days now and I know everything about you, from your job to your living situation to your fuggin moles. What do you know about me?

Um. You were married?

People, Bailie — see, normally the way this goes is that I'd ask you something, you ask me something, and in such a fashion of reciprocated dialogue, we'd get to know each other, ta-da. Like fuggin magic.

Oh.

Starx's expression was hard to read: not quite hurt — disappointed maybe.

Olpert said, What sort of work do you do?

Work? Thanks for asking. I'm in construction, Bailie.

Construction.

Right. Buildings. Or not exactly buildings. More roads. I have the same boss as you, Bailie — the city. We're civil servants, servants of civics. Civilized.

What do you do?

You know how the road sort of sparkles? Well you think that happens on its own? When they're tarring roads I'm the guy walking around with a little pouch of powdered glass who sprinkles it over the road. They call me the sparkle fairy.

You're making fun of me.

Swear! I used to do more hands-on work but I got hurt on the job, they tried to put me in an office, no way. This way I still get to be outside. Sparkle fairy.

Olpert struggled to picture that giant body lumbering around with a pouch of pixie dust.

Starx smacked him on the back, handed him the clean uniform and their Citypass lanyard. Hop along little buddy, you can put your duds on in the car. First stop after we pick up Raven is We-TV Studios. Hey, maybe Wags'll let us on *Salami Talk*?

Maybe, said Olpert carefully, and followed Starx, the asphalt glittering beneath their feet, to the first available Citywagon in the lot.

THE ELEVATOR DROPPED to the ground floor, fetched whoever was coming up the Tower, arrived with a thud at the viewing deck. Pushing away from the window, the Mayor smoothed her blazer and snapped the lapels straight, ready to face whoever it was.

Out stepped three Helpers in khaki: two luxuriantly moustachioed characters flanked a skittish-looking kid on crutches. Strapped over the boy's shoulder was a callbox, its cord drooped in ringlets at his hip. A fat strip of ducktape covered the lower half of his face. His eyes were afraid.

To what do I owe, etcetera, said the Mayor.

We represent the NFLM, said the man to the cripple's left, fingering his lanyard.

He's Reed, said the other, and I'm Walters.

The cripple said nothing.

Mrs. Mayor, we realize you've been put in a compromising position, said Reed, so we've brought this Recruit here, Diamond-Wood, to be of assistance to you until . . .

Until the Jubilee is over, finished Walters.

The HG's really appreciate what a sport you're being about this.

Sport? said the Mayor.

There's talk, said Walters, of erecting a statue of you. We're already talking to Loopy about it. How do you feel about *solid gold*?

Though you do have to admit, said Reed, it *was* spectacular — that illustration, I mean.

Three sets of eyes crawled over her body to the lower tier of the dessert cart.

Anyway, said Reed, Diamond-Wood here's at your service. Anything you need.

A personal aide, if you will.

Not that you'd normally require such a thing. Just —

— in your —

— current —

— *situation* —

— we're happy to provide logistical assistance.

And he comes with a portable phone, with a direct line to the Temple should you require anything else.

From the HG's. They want you to know that you can —

— call anytime.

It's a fax machine too.

Well touch green and colour me golden, said the Mayor.

Yeah! No problem!

We'll leave you then, said Walters.

Lots to prepare for tonight! Sure you've got work of your own…

And of course, Mrs. Mayor, as always, you'll be the guest of honour.

VIP!

Obsequious goodbyes followed (two-faced fuggers, thought the Mayor), instructions were whispered to the cripple, and the elevator took the Helpers back down to ground level. Out the window, the view was of the park.

This is their idea of a joke, isn't it? said the Mayor, and, turning away, missed the boy's attempt, heaped over his crutches, at a vigorous and earnest shake of his head.

Make yourself useful. By the door is a keypad, see it? Enter this passcode: forty-five, ten, twenty-two, forty-four hundred, but before you go thinking you can come up here and mess around anytime you like, it changes every day.

From behind her: the tap of crutches, a pause, a digital, affirmative-sounding chirp.

Now hit STOP, she said. Solar-powered, you know that? Another of my initiatives.

Another chirp. The viewing deck shuddered to a halt.

Look at it, she said. People Park, *a park for people*, is how I pitched it to council. And here we are, twenty-five years later. I bet the park's older than you are.

The cripple made a noise: Mmm.

And you know, don't you, I hope you know — though who knows what they're teaching you kids in school these days — that the park was all my doing? Of course engineers designed the amusements, and the actual *building* was taken care of by contractors. But the concept, the layout, the landscaping — all mine. I know people just think of me as a figurehead and nothing else. Most of you have no idea what I've done for this place.

Mmm.

I wanted a park for everybody. Young, old, handicapped, fat, whatever. Oh, some people criticized my greying measures — but how does a greenspace stand out without a little contrast? Look at it now, how it practically glows! Or will, touch green, in the spring.

Mmm, said Diamond-Wood, nodding.

Do you know what this city was before People Park? It was nothing. It was a nothing place. It was disconnected, all these neighbourhoods flung off in all the corners of the island, and in the middle was a cancer. That's what it was, a cancer. But think of a city as a person   what should a person have in its centre?

She swivelled atop the cart: A soul. Before it had a cancer, and then it had a soul. I put the soul in. And People Park is the soul, the Mayor said slowly, of *everyone*. That was its purpose and what it remains. But here we are meant to be celebrating it — *twenty-five years* of this soul, keep in mind — and instead your organization has brought in an outsider, a fraudulent, ridiculous conjurer intent on humiliating us and stealing our souls. Because that's what he's here to do, make no mistake. I mean, look at me.

Diamond-Wood's eyes were on the floor.

I said *look at me.*

He glanced up, quickly, then back down.

You can't! This is your fault. It's all your stupid organization's fault.

The Mayor gazed out the window. I don't think people know what they're celebrating this weekend. They just want to be awed. They've forgotten. This magician — what does he have planned? Do you know? Speak, for fug's sake!

He pointed at the ducktape.

So take it off! Oh. I bet those appleheads have some sort of regulation — well come here then, said the Mayor, and tore the gag from his mouth.

Ow, he said.

So?

Sorry, no idea.

Ah. Good thing I ungagged you then. She rubbed a hand over her face. So you have no idea what's going to happen tonight.

Tonight?

Tonight. With the — what's his face. Crowboy the Illuminator.

Raven? Honestly, I'm just a Recruit, hence the ducktape, and I certainly wouldn't —

No idea.

None. The HG's haven't even been told anything. I don't even think *he* knows. I guess he has to explore the city to figure out what he's going to illustrate? Honestly, we've been told how to arrange the stage, and we're working with Cinecity to make sure the live feeds are running, keeping the bridge blocked. That's it. And *I'm* here with you!

The Mayor turned away. In the park preparations for the evening's show were beginning: a cube van had arrived, cartons and crates of various sizes and shapes were being unloaded into the common.

Mrs. Mayor?

What.

It's going to be amazing, I think. Tonight. It's going to be —

Oh would you please just shut up.

The first spectators were arriving, staking claims with towels unfurled on the muddy grass. The Mayor sighed — and looked at Diamond-Wood.

Hey, she said. Come closer.

Sorry?

You enjoy magic? She beckoned with a finger. Let me show you a trick.

Diamond-Wood leaned in, wobbling on his crutches.

Closer, the Mayor whispered, closer, and once his face was near enough to kiss, she plucked the ducktape off the dessert cart, slapped it onto his mouth, smeared it flat, and announced: Ta-da.

GENTLEMEN, said Raven from the backseat, if I could request a detour.

It's gone eight already, said Starx, wheeling out of the Grand Saloon's driveway and south on Orchard Parkway. We're supposed to be at the studios at half-past —

A *brief* detour. If you could take me to the bridge. Just to see it.

We're heading south, said Starx. Bridge is north. Road's closed anyway.

Ah, but my understanding is that it's your people who have blocked off, what is it? Raven flipped through the CityGuide in his lap. The Topside Drive? And it seems that one can turn around at the bottom of this street, and really it's not far from here at all.

Starx's eyes moved between the road, steady with traffic, and the rearview. Olpert, Starx's XXL shirt billowing around his body, checked the mirror: the illustrationist reclined in a pose both sanguine and erotic, one knee up, hands behind his head, grinning.

Might no one, he said, have more authority to traverse these blockades than us?

At the bottom of Orchard Parkway Starx merged onto the roundabout at Cathedral Circus, but didn't exit onto Lakeside Drive, just went looping back around. Another Citywagon slid in ahead of them, peeled off toward Bay Junction.

Mr. Starx? said Raven.

Fine, but let's keep it brief, said Starx, and from the drinkholder scooped the walkie-talkie, told Griggs what was happening.

Olpert's hangover had found its way into his temples, where it thudded and stabbed. With each surge came flashes of the previous evening, shameful razory nicks — nevermind the great gaping wound of how he'd ended his night. As Starx turned onto

Topside Olpert cracked the window, pointed his face into the breeze like a pet.

At the Guardian Bridge exit the Helpers ushered them through the barricades. Starx nodded officiously, pulled onto the shoulder, and killed the engine. The bridge arced toward the mainland. Beneath it the Narrows swept briskly to the east, twinkling in the sunshine.

Well here we are, said Starx, turning to the backseat. What can we tell him, Bailie?

IFC Stadium, where the Lady Y's play — it's just back that way.

He's a fan, said Starx.

Olpert shrugged shyly.

Fine, fine, said Raven. Now, gentlemen? If you'll give me a minute.

He swung out of the car, glided up onto the bridge.

Starx watched. What do you think he's after? Wait, why's he lying down?

Shhh, said Olpert.

You think he can hear us?

Starx, come on.

Look at him, what's he doing? Is he *smelling* the road? Bailie? Can you tell?

I don't know what he's doing.

Oh shet.

From his knees, Raven was summoning them from the car. Gentlemen, he hollered. Please, I need your assistance and expertise.

Reluctantly they joined him.

Mr. Bailie! Mr. Starx! Tell me about this structure.

This . . . bridge? said Starx. Sure. Well it's called Guardian Bridge —

Delightful! Why?

Um. Bailie?

I don't know, said Olpert. That's just its name.

That's just its name, enthused Raven. Fabulous, Mr. Bailie! What else?

Well, said Starx, it's the only way on or off the island. Except by boat, or I guess plane.

Or helicopter, added Olpert.

They've been talking about building a second one from White-hall for ages, but ... it's not really happening. Whitehall's sort of a disaster anyway.

Raven shaded his eyes with both hands, looked west. A disaster?

Yeah. It's fugged up out there. People living underground, running amok. We do what we can to keep them in line. Isn't that right, Bailie?

But Olpert was watching the illustrationist. He lay on his belly, stroked the pavement, licked his fingertips, nodded.

Yes, said Raven. Yes, yes, *yes*.

III

ADINE WOKE TO the sound she'd fallen asleep to, or in spite of, or had kept her up all night, she wasn't sure: Pop's snoring. Despite Debbie having closed and Adine then locking the bedroom door, his snores drifted into their bedroom from the den in a phlegmy, spectral mist. It wasn't yet seven a.m., her pillow was hot on both sides. Had she slept? Maybe she'd just dreamed of sleep, in some inchoate, semi-conscious state of dreaming. Though if she *had* slept, Pop's snoring had found its way into her dreams too.

Overnight, Adine had learned this snoring like a song: the in-breath a gravelly scrape, a pause, a gleek and rattle, and the exhale contained a groan, a sputter, a cough, or a jammy smacking of lips, sometimes even the pasty slop of his tongue — and had at some point he cried out, Please, yes, oh? Adine hoped with all her heart she'd been dreaming.

She lay there in her shorts and T-shirt and blackout goggles, covers long flung off in a prickly fit. Beside her Debbie slept, she could sleep through anything, her breath swished in, out, in, steady as waves. Upon Adine's feet she could feel Jeremiah, his little body rising and falling. It felt conspiratorial, the two of them slumbering so peacefully, while Adine had lain awake half the night, or all the night.

She dug an elbow into Debbie's back until it elicited moans.

Ow, what are you doing, what time is it.

He's out there, said Adine.

So?

I can't see, remember. What if I trip on him or something. When's he leaving?

Debbie pulled the covers over her face, said something muffled. Adine yanked them away. Do something with him, Deb. I had to listen to him snoring all night and —

Hi, said Debbie. Good morning. Are you going to ask me how my night was?

Oh. Do you want me to ask?

Yes.

Oh. How was it?

Thanks for asking. It was fine. We drank too much. I feel sort of ugh.

And ... your old colleague?

Teammate. Pearl.

Pearl.

Pearl is, I don't know. The same but different. Or maybe it's me who's different. I mean, I know I'm different, but ...

What?

Pearl seemed tired.

Tired.

Like tired from her life. Not *of* her life — *from* it.

Her marriage. Her kids.

Maybe.

I don't tire you, said Adine, do I?

Debbie smiled. No, you wake me up. Sometimes with violence.

Are you going to kick that guy out of here so I can go pee?

No, wait. That's a good point. That's the difference, right? Don't you always want someone who wakes you up? Like even when things are lousy you'd rather be up, awake, than too tired to even ...

Adine's eyebrows did a provocative bounce — up, out of the goggles, then back down.

No, not just that. A stimulant life, not a sedative life — isn't that what you want?

I guess. I mean, once you guys head out I'm probably going to take a nap . . .

Debbie shook her head, laughed, flicked the lenses of Adine's goggles. I miss your eyes, she said. When's this project going to be done?

Adine shrieked, Never! and with both feet pushed Debbie out of bed.

What are you doing today, said Debbie, pulling on her house-coat. You want to come down to the memorial protest, or?

Work.

Right, said Debbie.

Pop's snoring intensified as the door opened — and faded as it closed. Adine scooped Jeremiah off her feet and hoisted him onto Debbie's pillow, tried to find his face with her nose, felt a whisk of tail, and realized she was nuzzling the wrong end.

AT HOME MORNINGS to Pearl were the enemy. She treated those first few daylit hours as an adversary to tackle and vanquish and with the fierce resolve of a mad sergeant drove Gip and Elsie-Anne with bum smacks and handclaps from bed to breakfast and out the door. She seemed to be in three rooms at once, threatening, In the van in ten minutes or you're walking to school! and when the garage lifted and Harry tore out of the driveway Kellogg invariably was left to drink the mug of untouched coffee she'd forgotten cooling on the counter.

So on Friday morning it was odd for Kellogg to be up with the kids, crouched over the camping stove with instant oatmeal dustily awaiting hydration in plastic bowls, while Pearl slept in the tent. Come on, Dad, let's get a move on, said Gip, kicking his father's feet, we have to get there early to get a frontrow spot. Remember yesterday? I don't —

Hush now, said Kellogg, Mummy's still sleeping, and he smoothed a bedheaded tuft of his son's hair, it sprung up again in defiance.

Elsie-Anne sat at the picnic table in her pyjamas, her purse in her lap, a spoon in one hand and a blank expression on her face. From all over Lakeview Campground the sounds of other rousing families sifted through the trees: car engines growled, radios jangled, the patter of morning routines — dads, mums, kids, everyone starting their days, the big day, thought Kellogg, and the Pooles were part of it! Birds warbled and chirped, a gentle breeze came hissing up through the poplars from the lake, and if you listened close, beyond it, the shush of waves splashed the beach.

Kellogg only faintly remembered Pearl zipping herself into the sleeping bag beside him at some point after midnight — had he imagined the sickly smell of booze filling the tent? What if it had, she'd been with old friends, why not have a few? And so what if she slept in, it didn't mean anything was wrong. They were on vacation. Maybe it meant things were going right.

Dad, whispered Gip, eyes urgent. We need to *go.*

Champ, hey, we're a five-minute walk from the park. It's barely gone eight. We'll have some breakfast and when Mummy gets up —

Mummy? We can't wait for *Mummy.*

No?

Do you want yesterday to happen again?

Kellogg stirred the water. Bubbles were just starting to percolate to its surface. Beneath it, the butane roared and blue flames battered the pot. No, he said. I don't.

After breakfast and Kellogg had given Gip his meds and the dishes were washed up and everyone brushed their teeth at the communal tap (*Not potable*) and the kids put on clean clothes (No showers, Dad? asked Gip and Kellogg pulled a cap over his son's jaunty hair and said, We're on vacation!), it was almost nine and Pearl still hadn't risen. Kellogg cocked an ear at the tent as a hiker might outside the cave of a hibernating bear. Gentle snores. He winked at his kids. Looks like Mummy tied one on last night.

Tied one what on, Dad? said Elsie-Anne.

Never you mind, Annie.

Should we untie her?

No.

Elsie-Anne, looking worried, pulled her purse over her head.

Along with Raven's *Illustrations: A Grammar* Kellogg packed Gip's knapsack with a blanket, snacks, juice, meds, sunscreen, mosquito repellent, a first-aid kit, a book of crossword puzzles, and waterproofs (the sky was cloudless), the guidebook got tucked in his backpocket. Then he wrote Pearl a note, wedged it under a pot lid on the picnic table, and told his kids, Okay, guys, Mummy'll just have to meet us when she's up. Annie, take that bag off your head, we've got to walk now.

His daughter emerged blinking. Familiar's concerned about Mummy.

Dorkus, will you please *shut up*, Gip said. Mummy just got tied up. It's not a big deal.

Shut up, Stuppa.

Mummy's fine, said Kellogg. Though let's not call each other names, huh?

Gip shouldered his knapsack, so stuffed the zipper puckered.

Kellogg looked at the tent. We're doing the right thing, right, guys?

We're doing the right thing, Dad, said Gip.

Oh, you think so, champ? Good. I think so too. I mean, ideally we'd all be together, but — she'll meet up with us soon. Mummy, I mean. Right?

Right.

Okay! To People Park! Annie, come here, take my hand. And stop looking in your bag, you'll fall down, you've got to watch where you're going.

Here we come, Raven, said Gip, then deepened his voice: For tonight's illustration will surely be a spectacle for the ages, one which nary a soul will soon if ever forget.

POP WAS TOO big for the couch, he'd opted for the floor, and there he was, right in the middle of the living room, a blanket clung to him like giftwrap, from his face came that sinusitic scraping. His clothes were everywhere, jeans draped over the recliner, a sock on the kitchen counter, another inside a stray teacup, the pale dead moth of his underwear splayed on the endtable — this Debbie's eyes raced away from, a brownish tinge to the white cotton — and, by the door where he'd flung it the night before, his poncho, while in the closet dangled empty hangers. A high whiny fart arpeggiated a minor-C triad, Pop rolled onto his side, from within the sleeping bag came the gritty scritch of fingernails raking pubic hair, and then he was snoring again.

Even more than his sounds and things, it was above all Pop's smell that had invaded: a musty, tangy odour reminiscent of stale cardboard boxes and humid cheese. Debbie pushed open a window. From outside came the growl of traffic, a train rumbled through Blackacres Station. Across the street, at the corner of E Street and Tangent 3, the owner of the laundrette was scrubbing her windows with a soapy mop: she'd been blackedup in the night.

Pop spluttered, turned, flopped an arm over his head, buried himself in his own body, and kept sleeping: snore, whistle, snore. Debbie edged by him to the bathroom, locked the door, dropped her robe, stepped straight into the shower.

When she emerged ten minutes later in a towel, Pop was at the stove, the element glowed orange beneath a pot of water. This is an alienated stove, he said, not turning to face her. I am habituated of one which flames.

Hang on, I have to get dressed, Debbie said, and slipped past into the bedroom, where Adine was sitting up in bed in her goggles.

Is he still out there.

He's boiling eggs.

Amazing. We've taken in a refugee.

Refugee. You say it like it's a joke, but that's what he is. He's homeless! What are we supposed to do, let him sleep on the street?

I mean, that's his name, right? If he'd been born, say, Pop Apartment maybe —

Stop that. I need to lend him your housekeys. I mean, if you're not going out today . . .

What.

Come on, said Debbie. Just for the night. Maybe Sunday too. But on Monday we're going to figure out what's going on and get him home.

Great, said Adine, flatly.

You okay? said Debbie. She sat on the bed, put her hand on Adine's leg.

But behind those goggles, it was impossible to tell what was happening.

CALUM JOLTED UPRIGHT, the garbage bags taped over the mattress crinkled. His sleep had been deep and leaden, coming out of it now felt akin to being chiselled from a concrete slab. At some point in the night the Hand must have released him, he hadn't even stirred — anything could have happened and on he would have slumbered. On her empty side of the bed was only an apostrophe-shaped impression, where her body had curled against Calum's. The supply closet's only supply was a headless mop leaning in the corner. The dusty shelves were empty, the air stale, the stripe of light under the door suggested a world Calum wasn't sure he had a place in.

From somewhere out there came voices, a silent pause, an explosion (of glass?) followed by laughter, cheers, hoots.

Calum unballed the hoodie he'd used as a pillow, pulled it on, then jeans, then sneakers. From beyond the closet came another crash and delighted whoops. He opened the door, light came searing in, he squinted, the swollen eyesocket ached. Everything was quiet. He felt himself being observed.

His eyes adjusted. Sitting on stools in the middle of the silo were two small figures in sunglasses. Near them, on the floor, was a pile of fluorescent tubes, frosted glass pipettes the length and width of saplings. Through the loading dock's open doors poured water-coloured light, a choir of hoodies lined the threshold. On a couch against the far wall lounged a shirtless guy in a welding mask, the visor reflected the room. Someone lying with their head in his lap sat up — the Hand. Calum waited for a greeting. She yawned and lay back down.

The welding mask leaned in, seemed to whisper in the Hand's ear.

The Hand laughed, sat up again. With her eyes locked on Calum's she snuggled close to this shirtless, faceless person. Her fingers splayed around his bellybutton. The thumb snuck into the waistband of his pants.

Calum watched.

From within the mask a voice said, You want to play?

This prompted from the hoodies a squawk of sharp, mean laughter.

The Hand looped her arms around the masked guy's neck, swung her legs onto his lap. In front of the couch was a table littered with papers and bottles and cans and packs of Redapples, a tin of corn-in-a-can overflowed with butts, burn marks pocked the tabletop. From a paper bag the masked character produced a flat, which he fed to the Hand: her lips caressed his knuckles, her tongue flicked and curled, all wetly pink. She giggled.

Calum looked away.

The kids on the stools seemed about Rupe's age, faces expressionless behind those sunglasses. They perched with perfect, crisp posture, hands on their knees — *ducktaped* to their knees. At their feet was broken glass, a few glossy red dots that had to be blood.

The masked guy spread his arms, indicating a space into which Calum was now welcome — or implicated. Ready to take on my sister?

A bout of laughter, brief and dreary, lifted from the figures at the door and dispersed among the rafters like smoke.

The Hand came over, scooped up a fluorescent tube, smacked it into her palm, something inside rattled and tinked. She held another out to Calum, who took it but couldn't meet her eyes.

The figures by the door crowded in. Their shadows stretched into the room, the light went patchy and sinister. From the couch the guy said, You think you can beat my sister? You know what she did? Last year? You know what this kid did?

Whooping from the hoodies.

This kid right here? She gets up on the struts under the tracks at UOT Station and waits for the night's last train, it comes through slow, right, because of the construction, and when it comes she, get this, *grabs one of the bars underneath the train!* And rides it like that all the way to the Barns, just hanging there, we're all running along underneath, and when it lowers she jumps off and is just like, What. My sister, man.

The Hand twirled the fluorescent, laughed a shrugging sort of laugh.

Calum had heard this story, everyone had. It existed in his imagination as a movie. Walking underneath the Yellowline he'd often look up and imagine the weightless thrill of being zipped along, how it might feel to pass through airspace that no other human body had ever troubled, parted, touched.

Now the story had a hero, and here she was: Let's go, said the Hand. You versus me.

Terse, ironic applause.

You want to go first?

First?

The rules are this, said the Hand. You call a twin and hit it, you get to sit down. You call one and hit the other, you got to take their spot. You miss three lights in a row, you take the spot of the kid you called last. You hit the kid and the light doesn't break, you got to break the light over your own head. Got it?

The shirtless guy called, Good luck! in a cheery, chilling way.

Everyone laughed again, a rhythmic swell and ebb that felt rehearsed, artificial. It left behind a vaporous sort of silence that swelled and pulsed in the still air of the silo.

I'll go first, said the Hand. Watch me, I'm the best. She had barely prophesied, Left, before her tube was flying from her hand in spinning flashes of light — and exploded on the kid on the left's forehead. He crumpled from the chair, sunglasses skittering across the floor. Everyone went crazy.

The kid rose to his knees with a spidery wound opening on his temples. He shook his head, droplets of blood scattered in a little arc, and in a gargly voice choked, Hit.

More cheers.

The boy took his spot back on the stool, swaying slightly. One of the figures behind Calum came forward with the stray sunglasses, slid them back onto his face, and retreated. The kid hawked a thick, gory splat of blood onto the floor.

Your turn, said the Hand.

The tube felt heavier now.

The Hand said, Which one.

Beneath all that blood the left one's face was pale. The other kid waited in silence.

Right thinks she's tough, said the Hand. Hit her. Now!

Calum lobbed the tube weakly — it landed a foot short of the stools, skidded, stopped unbroken. Amid boos the girl kicked it back at Calum.

I'm done, I won, said the Hand. Two more for you though or it's you on the stool.

Come on, son, called the shirtless guy from the couch. The Hand went to him, he folded her into his arms. The visor was blank but Calum sensed a sneer beneath it, he felt mocked. And the way he was holding her, it was familiar . . .

And he was back down below the night before, the darkness full of screaming, grabbed by those big strong hands, that humid skin against his own, the suffocation, Calum had felt so feeble — and the sense that whoever it was had no face: here he was now, in his mask, holding the Hand, who dreamily stroked his chest. He placed one hand atop her head, onto the pattern of hair, and confirmed what Calum feared: a perfect fit.

Calum's next throw went pinwheeling wide and high. The intended target watched it sail overhead: the light landed, popped, loosed a dusty puff up from the warehouse floor.

Jeers, screeches, catcalls, whistles. Someone cawed. Someone mooed.

Calum took his final tube from the pile. His reflection warped in the cloudy glass. He could hear the Hand taunting him and the guy — her brother? — taunting him too. But he wouldn't look at them. His thoughts blurred, their words became noise.

Behind the girl's sunglasses were the faint shadows of eyes. But they were dead eyes. There was nothing in them. They were nothing Calum could understand.

Calum cocked his arm. From the depths of Whitehall came the rumble of a train pulling out of the Barns, clacking up onto the tracks, heading south into the city. As its sound faded the boy on the other stool collapsed, hitting the floor with a dull thud. Blood trickled from his headwound, drastic and crimson on the cement. Calum lowered the tube, waited. But nobody moved. If anything, the air went rigid with impatience.

Come on, said the Hand. Throw!

Calum tried not to register the kid passed out and bleeding on the ground.

Throw! roared a dozen voices.

So he threw.

IV

 HE 10:30 MEMORIAL unveil-
ing would not be covered by *In the Know*, or any We-TV corres-
pondents. A small crowd gathered in a clearing in the southeast
corner of People Park known as Circle Square. Surrounded by
poplars, in its centre was an inactive fountain clotted with dead
leaves and bounded by the Community Gardens, the Hedge Maze,
and Friendly Farm Automatic Zoo, where, when activated, mechanical beasts (animaltronics) lurched into educational couplings.

The attendees comprised a few patrons of the arts in extrava-
gant hats, a pair of cardigan'd archivists from the Museum of Prosperity, a shifty photographer, a curious family in Y's paraphernalia
on their way to the common. In the shade at the square's southern
edge a special area had been designated for protestors — Pop
and Debbie — and though the sun arcing above the park was
bright and warm, a chilly breeze whistled up from the lake.
Debbie shivered. Lark, intoned Pop, peeling a hardboiled egg, a
nip bequeaths the air.

Loopy, of course, was the belle of the ball. With her black-clad
assistant at her side she waited impatiently for the Mayor to in-
augurate the unveiling. Other than its materials (debris salvaged
during the Homes' revitalization), Loopy had kept quiet about
the Lakeview Memorial. A white cloth draped over the sculpture

suggested a ghost, six feet tall and hovering there starkly. Somewhere under that sheet was a plaque, Debbie knew. Pop had been consulted on the text, though he and the archivists had clashed over the word *restribution*, and in the end it comprised only the names of every resident of Lakeview Homes, 51,201 in all (It is I, claimed Pop, the extemporaneous one!). A tombstone of sorts, thought Debbie, though that seemed morbid. Better: a document and testament. It was, at least, something.

A few pigeons scrabbled and pecked at the cobblestones. With nothing else to shoot, the photographer pointed his camera at a passing cloud, which to Debbie resembled a vulture. She shivered again, and thought, with a bitter twinge, that she'd attended Loopy's last opening too — she was becoming a regular Loopy groupie. As with most of Loopy's exhibits, aside from the retrospective that consumed the second floor of the Museum of Prosperity, her previous show, *Us:*, had gone up that past September at Loopy's Orchard Parkway gallery, Loopy's, at which Loopy commandeered an underpaid, high-turnover staff of students from the Island Institute, her current assistant was one of these. *Us:* featured portraits of the most popular Faces of We-TV.

Even before it opened the project was celebrated on *In the Know*: What a diverse proclamation of municipal pride, Isa Lanyess had gushed. This truly is the best city on earth, and who better than Loopy to show the people of our beloved island to us, in all their and its glory. Loopy also guested on *Salami Talk*, flirting along to Wagstaffe's inane questions. How do you like your sausage, soft or hard, he yucked. Oh, I like it hard — *very* hard, Loopy said, batting purple eyelashes, and they both took big bites out of rods of cured meat, and winked. At home, Adine threw the remote at her TV.

For divergent reasons (politics, indignation), Debbie and Adine decided to crash the opening. From the sidewalk outside Loopy's they watched the city's sophisticates congratulate each other for being there. Photorealist paintings wallpapered the room from floor to ceiling, art appreciation burbled out onto the street alongside a tinkle of inoffensive jazz.

Debbie hid behind Adine. What if we get kicked out? For sure Lanyess's in there. We weren't invited. I don't want to —

Can you relax? said Adine, and by the elbow steered her inside. Fifteen minutes later Debbie was following an irate Adine up to the rooftop patio of a pub above Cathedral Circus. A jug of cider arrived, they drank in silence, Debbie eyed Adine warily across the table while traffic wheeled through the roundabout below. Down in the park the poplars swished in the breeze, with the late-summer twilight just starting to settle over the city.

Debbie said gently, It's nice here.

Except for all the people, said Adine. See, here's the thing: people suck.

Aw, come on. They don't.

And by people, I mean people in this city especially. They think the world ends at Guardian Bridge, and all a superdoosh like Loopy needs to do is hold a mirror up to their stupid insular world and they'll love her for it.

Debbie listened. As far as she knew, Adine had never been off the island.

Was that *art*? No, art challenges people, but people don't want that. They just want to be reassured, to see themselves, to see each other, to feel comfortable in the world. What kind of art only makes you comfortable? Paintings of We-tv? What the fug is that?

Well, said Debbie.

But Adine was on a roll: As if that whole culture isn't inward-looking enough. You'd think if you were going to paint people from tv you'd, I don't know, have something to say. But no, she just replicates what's already there. And people love it!

Wait, inward-looking? Don't you think that if people were a little *more* inward-looking then maybe —

You're not hearing me: people suck.

But, Debbie said, wait . . . Isn't there merit in showing people that there are other people like them? Being a person's lonely, what's wrong with art that makes us feel less alone? To create a space where people can connect, with a common language —

No way. Adine tipped back her glass, swallowed. *Whose* common language?

Don't get me wrong, I didn't love the show either, but don't you think it was at least an attempt to show some diversity —

Diversity! That word's a fuggin joke. If it was diverse then you'd have a diverse crowd. But everyone there, all those rich dooshmasters — what they were doing? Shopping. *Patrons of the arts?* Yeah right. They're fuggin *customers*.

Debbie resisted defining the word *patrons*, instead reached across the table for Adine's hands. She scowled, but offered one, which Debbie stroked. Maybe it's your job then to make stuff that shows people something they haven't seen or thought, that's apart from their lives? That challenges what they think they know?

Right, I should be working. That's what you think. You think I'm lazy.

No! I didn't say that.

Fug that, said Adine. Fug that, fug you, fug everything and everyone.

Something hitched in Debbie's throat.

Adine filled Debbie's glass. You know what I mean. Come on, let's get drunk.

Two hours later, with Adine asleep on her shoulder Yellowlining home, what had begun as a slight yelp of hurt burrowed down into Debbie's guts and gnawed away down there, persistent and parasitic. She was sad — not at being attacked, that had passed, but at the chasm she felt opening between them.

Until that night, whenever Adine told her of any conflict — with neighbours, motorists, gallerists — Debbie had sided with her wholly: the world was wrong, Adine was right, and the unwavering allegiance helped stitch them together. But Debbie had enjoyed *Us:*, it'd been nice, inclusive, heartwarming. Of course she kept this to herself, and so at home in bed, feeling disloyal and duplicitous, Debbie did the only thing she could: took Adine in her arms and held her, as close and long and hard as she could.

THERE HE GOES, said Starx, turning on the car stereo — too far, too hard, the grind of distorted guitar filled the Citywagon.

Olpert watched Raven disappear into the We-TV building with Wagstaffe and a pair of pages while Starx banged away on air drums. This music wasn't music, it was noise, Olpert looked at the radio, thought about turning it down.

We've got an hour to kill, screamed Starx. What do you want to do?

Do?

We can't just sit here, can we? Let's just drive around. Find some trouble.

But.

Your turn to drive though.

Drive? I don't really —

But Starx, weirdly quick, had already circled the car, opened Olpert's door, and now waited there massively on the sidewalk while a sax solo wailed from the speakers.

Though there wasn't much traffic due to the holiday, navigating downtown's one-ways, plus his hangover, plus his natural anxiety behind the wheel, plus Starx's music, plus Starx with his seat slid into the backseat, thumping the dashboard, howling, Drag you down, drag you down, drag you mutherfuggin down, caused Olpert's grip on the steering wheel to tighten into white-knuckled panic. As he turned onto Paper Street, the song climaxed in a commotion of cymbal crashes and throaty howling.

Olpert cracked his window.

What are you doing.

It's, Olpert yelled, it's just a little loud. The music, I mean.

It's freezing out.

I don't drive very often. I'm, Starx — I'm finding it hard to concentrate.

Not a Cysterz fan, I guess. Starx snapped the radio off. Better, princess?

Olpert pulled to a stop at Lakeside Drive. He turned, hand over hand, toward Bay Junction and the southern edge of People Park, while Starx played with the powerlocks: chunk, chunk. Chunk, chunk.

A barricade blocked the roundabout's exit to Parkside West, two Helpers sat in lawnchairs arm wrestling atop a cooler. Olpert leaned out, displayed his khaki, was waved through onto the empty street.

Where are you going? said Starx.

You said just drive around!

By the park? What if the HG's see us, figure we're shirking duties? Think, Bailie!

Down the slope Crocker Pond shimmered in the sunlight. Spectators, already numbering in the hundreds, filled the common.

Hey, said Starx, I need to express myself. Pull over.

What?

Urinate.

Here?

Yeah here, I'll go in the trees. Nothing quite like urinating in the open air.

Can't you wait?

Bailie, what the fug, mine's not your average flow. Starx clawed across the frontseat, grabbed the wheel, and yanked the Citywagon over two lanes toward the curb.

A thump — something smacked the windshield, something white and sudden from above. Instead of braking Olpert stomped the gas, the car shot under the Yellowline tracks, veered into the Citywagon lot, and with a succession of explosive highfives, tore the sideview mirrors from a row of vehicles parked along the median.

Bailie, whoa, what are you doing?

We hit a bird, moaned Olpert, we killed a bird.

Brake! Fuggin Bailie, brake!

I'm braking, I'm braking.

The car slowed, Olpert signalled, checked his blindspot, pulled over, stopped.

We hit a bird, said Olpert.

Yeah, I saw that. Quite a performance, Bailie.

The bird, he said, do you think it's dead?

Starx got out of the car. Olpert trembled, tried to steady his breathing. The walkie-talkie crackled and Griggs, in a typically listless monotone, droned, Silentium. Logica. Securitatem — and before Prudentia Olpert clicked the thing off. In the rearview he watched Starx survey the debris, shake his head, move south.

Oh man, Bailie, he called. You gotta come see this.

Olpert joined him: at the end of a trail of shattered glass and plastic, lying in a heap of feathers against the curb, was a dove.

Oh no. It isn't.

Fuggin right it is.

No.

Have you ever seen any other doves in this city? In the *wild*?

It's not a pigeon?

What, an albino? Come on, Bailie. You know exactly what and whose that thing is.

I didn't — I didn't even *see* it, it came out of nowhere.

At the end of the street, the two Helpers had their hands raised in identical exaggerated shrugs — like, What the fug?

Starx waved. Nothing to see here! Back to work!

Hey, don't! What if they come look? What are we going to do?

Whoa. Hold on. *We?* This was all you, pencildick.

Me?

Yeah you. I wasn't the one driving.

That's — that's not *fair.* You grabbed the wheel!

Which reminds me, said Starx, and he headed off into the bushes, unzipping.

Olpert crouched beside the dead bird. One wing was folded, the other splayed, the head tucked into its chest, the tiny gnarled treeroots of its claws. No blood. Though Olpert imagined the damage was internal, its organs pulverized to stew. Dead, dead, dead — and he had killed it.

Starx returned. He nudged the dove with his shoe. Then, in a single, swift movement, he scooped the little corpse under his toe, lifted it up, and launched it into the bushes.

There.

That's where you peed!

Bailie. It's dead.

Olpert stood. Still, some respect . . .

Respect? Starx grabbed Olpert by the shoulders. Listen, you were driving, the bird should've been smart enough not to fly into traffic. Maybe that magician dopes his birds. Maybe he abuses them and they get suicidal. Whatever, it's not your fault. The guy lets these things loose in the city? You figure he figures he'll lose a couple. Partner, am I right?

Yes, but —

Hey hey hey. No buts. This is not a big deal. Dead bird? Who cares. A million of those things die every day crashing into skyscrapers.

Really?

Probably. Listen, why don't I drive the rest of the day?

Will you?

Starx put his arm around Olpert and walked him back to their car, sweeping the broken sideview mirrors under the parked Citywagons as they went.

Sliding the driver's seat back Starx said, Those Helpers won't sell us out. Don't worry.

Are they friends of yours?

Not really . . . but *silentium*, right? It's the first fuggin pillar.

Olpert looked over his shoulder: past the line of Citywagons, silver and symmetrical and identical, the two Helpers were taking turns putting each other in grappling holds.

And hey, Bailie, said Starx, what about that chick last night.

Debbie?

Yeah, that's the one. Before your . . . upset, I thought she seemed into you.

You think?

Sure. Just, next time? See if you can chat her up without puke-painting your khaki.

You really think she was into me?

You bet. Now let's get out of here before that bird's pals show up for vengeance.

POP LEANED IN and on a gust of eggy breath said, Lark! Birds.

A half-dozen pigeons had made their way to the foot of the sculpture. Get those stupid things out of here, Loopy told her assistant. The girl looked at Loopy, then the birds, and with a sigh tiptoed over flapping her arms. They scuttled around behind the sculpture, more aggravated than scared. The assistant followed at a crouch, clapping, and the pigeons hopped along, circled the sculpture's base, and the assistant gently shooed them around again, around and around. Debbie watched with interest.

At the next pass Loopy went hurtling at the pigeons with the wings of her caftan spread wide, cawing and shrieking, and the flock ruffled up and came to rest on the lip of the fountain, cooing and cool. Returning to her spot by the covered sculpture, Loopy didn't take her eyes off the pigeons, ready to pounce at the slightest provocation.

At last the Mayor arrived, wheeled by Diamond-Wood, who clattered behind on his crutches. Stop, she called, with a wary scan of the cobblestones. We'll be fine here.

Those who had heard tell of Raven's bisection gawked. Debbie wasn't sure what she was seeing: a white sheet draped over the dessert cart gave the impression of an enormously wide-waisted skirt supported by a trestle the size of a writing desk.

Hello, good to see you all, said the Mayor. Now let's get this shet-show on the road.

His ducktape gag peeled aside, Diamond-Wood offered a few hastily rehearsed words about the arts, the importance of community, and how firmly the New Fraternal League of Men were dedicated to these things, though the High Gregories extended regrets at not being able to attend personally. To Loopy Diamond-Wood said, Thanks, most of all, to our artist laureate for this wonderful sculptural work to commemorate our park's twenty-fifth anniversary —

At which Pop growled, That's not the point of it, evil one!

Diamond-Wood retreated to scattered, tepid applause, slid behind the Mayor, and retaped his mouth. All eyes fell upon their civic leader. Of the two white sheets hiding secrets, it was clear which one they wanted removed. The Mayor gestured irritably at the sculpture. Do it now, for the love of green.

Loopy bowed. I give you ... the Lakeview ... Memorial!

But before her assistant could perform the big reveal the pigeons came flapping at her in a ragged formation. Overwhelmed, the assistant tripped, grasped at the white sheet, which whisked away — and there was nothing beneath it. No pedestal, no sculpture, no plaque. Only emptiness. It was as if the cover had been floating there all along, inflated by some internal wind.

What the fug kind of art is that? said the Mayor.

That's not it, shrieked Loopy. My work's been stolen! Someone's stolen my work!

Disgrateful, said Pop, shaking his head. A complete and utterful disgrate.

Debbie giggled. Which met with scowls from all around.

Hardly the time for humours, Pop chided.

Her smile faded. If only Adine were here, she thought. Adine would find this funny, would supplement the scene with the perfect wiseacre crack to tip Debbie's amusement into hysteria. But if there'd been a humorous moment it was gone. She stood there awkwardly while Loopy wailed and, stonefaced, Pop demanded a detectivial assembly!

A noise disrupted everything then — a whooshing, a squawk, faces swung skyward and fingers pointed. Through the space where the statue should have been flapped what appeared at first another pigeon, but swooping back up over the trees it caught the light, blazing white against the blue sky. Through his viewfinder the photographer watched it loft higher and higher, zoomed in, at last snapped a picture.

Was that? said Debbie.

Yeah, said the photographer, lowering his camera. One of Raven's doves.

V

THROUGH HANDS cupped to the window Calum looked into the Room: lights off, benches up on tables, Debbie's deskchair wheeled back from her workstation, tilted at an angle that suggested a swift and drastic escape. And despite the CLOSED FOR LONG WEEKEND sign it seemed inconceivable that Debbie wasn't puttering around in the shadows. She was always here. He pounded on the door, shuffled back to the window, blocked the light, and looked again: nothing, just grey stillness.

Overhead a Yellowline train went clattering south. Calum looked up at the underside of the tracks, at the flashing shape of it moving along, and thought of the Hand — suspended in space, the train ziplining her along.

The cuts on his forehead, where the Hand's shirtless friend or brother had smashed the tube, were drying into a scabby acne, his left eye remained swollen shut. Moving away from the window Calum avoided his reflection for fear of what he'd see: a monster. But a very weak monster, weak as a slave, who'd stumbled bleeding and delirious out of the silos into Whitehall, and now found himself here, outside the Room, the slave who'd escaped, found the world too big, and dragging his chains returned to the only place he belonged.

But that was not the whole story. When his final throw had landed harmlessly in the girl's lap the silo had gone silent. Uh-oh, said the Hand, and a great crest of laughter rose up and came crashing down, Calum felt useless and stupid, dumbly confronted with what he hadn't done. The shirtless guy in the welding mask grabbed the Hand by the hips and pulled her onto his lap and said, Gotta break that thing on your head, those are the rules.

The rules. In shame Calum collected the tube from the girl's lap. She was chuckling. Her twin brother (were they twins?) was coming to on the floor, making soft groaning noises. She said, Nice shooting, and everyone found this very hilarious indeed.

Yeah, nice shooting, the guy said, lifted the Hand's shirt, his fingers scurried spiderlike up inside.

Calum's fingers closed around the tube. He stared into the girl's dark sunglasses, at the suggestion of eyes in there — he sensed scorn. Let's go, called the guy from the couch. Crack that thing on your face, he crooned, my sister here's dying to see it. Another surge of laughter — and Calum wound up and smashed the tube across the girl's face.

She wilted from the stool and lay there twitching on the floor. Half the tube remained in Calum's hand, the other half shattered into craggy bits. He tossed it, a faint tinkle of glass followed by a thick, brooding silence. And then there was a rush, like a flock of crows unleashed from a rooftop, and Calum turned, and, led by the guy in the mask, a faceless mob was descending upon him.

Now, moving down the laneway beside the Room, his vision kept clouding over, he had to shake his head to clear it. He reached the water, made fists, bashed his knuckles together in a hollow knock of bone on bone. Out on the lake someone's sailboat, a little white A, tacked across Kidd's Harbour. Calum watched until it moved out of view, then he headed back out to F Street. After a few steps the world reeled and swam, he staggered, had to regain his balance on a parked car. Halfheartedly tried the door: locked. Farther along was a payphone, which he checked for quarters. One sat in the slot.

Calum tossed the coin in the air, guessed heads — tails — flipped it twice more before he got heads, then fed the phone. But who to call? Not Debbie, he only had the number of the Room, not Edie, not one of their friends, not his mother. Not the Hand.

The money clunked down and was lost. He jiggled the cradle, no luck, took a measured step back, stomped the phone as hard as he could, his sneaker fell off on the backswing. Sullenly he fetched it. His stomach gurgled. He felt dizzy and sick. He leaned against the wall.

Where was Debbie? Calum thought about how giving she tried to seem, how generous and caring, yet she maintained a safe distance: he didn't even know where she lived. Who was she, really, this person who wanted everything from him, that he talk and share and trust her, for him to be better — and she believed this was generous, just to listen.

Calum headed south down F Street, his head humming a muffled, cloudy sort of tune, with nowhere to go and no one to see, and nothing to do with them when he got there.

AN ARTIST SPEAKS only with her hands, said Loopy, and displayed them: palms, then backs.

The Museum of Prosperity archivists stared.

Likeways, to exfabulate upon *my* hands, Pop said, laying them on the picnic table: My hands are my words. And my words are my hands. Therein lives the paradox.

The Mayor used her own hands to hide her face.

But back to this travestation, said Pop, and whom we can be sure is gullible.

The archivists met his knowing, shrewd look with equal bewilderment.

Do I have to spell it for you? The illustrationaire!

And to think these hands once sculpted his likeness, moaned Loopy.

Moreover! To think he has now, poof, into thinned air, envanished the only remaining relish of Lakeview Homes!

One of the archivists blinked. The other said, Relish?

Prehaps you need an illustration of my own! Pop thumped the table, held up his fist, rotated it slowly, almost forlornly. How are we to take back the night if the moon — the fist's rotations paused — has been conciliated by the irradiating sunshine — here he covered the fist in his other hand — of a forever-long day?

Pop concluded by exploding both hands outward, fingers fluttering, and then hid them under the picnic table. In his eyes was triumph.

Banished to the periphery among Friendly Farm's animaltronics were Debbie, Loopy's assistant, and Diamond-Wood. The latter's walkie-talkie buzzed, he listened, whispered, hung up, and tapped his crutches against a pig, its metal hide clanging, and shot the Mayor an urgent look.

What, she said.

Diamond-Wood ungagged himself. My people think it'd be a mistake not to rule out certain parties known for vandalism around the city. We —

Pop snorted. *Parties?* Perhaps your own party wishes the city's attentuations misguided? For was it not your party, sir, whom initiated the illustrationaire's pretence?

Excellent point, said the Mayor. Touch green.

Diamond-Wood staggered forward, bumping the pigs — which activated their animations: one mounted the other and began to thrust. Though their lovemaking began gently, almost sensual.

Ignoring the carnal whinnies and jigglings, Diamond-Wood hobbled up to the picnic table. Please, he said, Mr. Street —

Don't you please me! Aggregately, your organization has also empropriated my home! My home, Mrs. Mayor! You are savvy to this?

The Mayor said, Nope.

The mechanical coitus intensified, the pigs' prerecorded ecstasy escalating into howls, metal clanged against metal. Debbie and Loopy's assistant cowered behind a dromedary.

I can't speak to that, said Diamond-Wood, though the proper procedures —

My *home*, Pop roared. First my home, a quartered century hencefrom, and now . . . *Once again*, my home! Recurrently!

But —

As though time itself has too gone loopy!

Loopy leaned into the conversation, grinning benevolently.

But everyone's attention had been diverted by the pigs. Their squeals reached a pitch both tortured and rapturous, one slammed into the other with force adequate to either resuscitate it from near-death or kill it for good. And just as the frenzied creatures seemed ready to rip free from the cement, with a final heave they lurched to a stop. Everything was still. The creatures' eyes were stupid and oblivious.

Well, said Debbie, that was something, and everyone agreed.

HI ADINE. This is Sam.

Hi, said Adine. You're about two and a half minutes early, buddy. Give me one sec?

Through the phone Sam could hear his sister's TV, a voice was talking. He flipped around until his set's sound matched hers: channel 73. It was a boring show, just a woman at a table telling the camera about her sadness. Through the phone Sam could hear his sister breathing in the steady, in-and-out way of someone sleeping. Then the woman said goodbye and thanks for listening and there was a rustle on the end of the line and Adine said, in a small voice, Hey, buddy, sorry about that.

Hey buddy, said Sam. Are we watching *Salami Talk*?

Oh man. I guess. That's on 12, right?

That's on 12 right.

In the Know was wrapping up in a fanfare of kettledrums and trumpets. The closing credits rolled over images of kids splashing in the waves at Budai Beach amid frothy green runoff from Lowell Canal, and they ended with the We-TV logo, the screen went black, and here was Lucal Wagstaffe's mouth in extreme closeup, welcoming you to *Salami Talk* — and the mouth took a big bite of juicy sausage.

Today's intro montage featured images of magic through the ages. Witches are being burned Adine, said Sam. They're tied to tree trunks okay. But there's a guy now hanging upside down over the water. His hands are tied okay. He's escaping. There's some —

Let me listen.

Sam closed his eyes, just to see: Wagstaffe's was a voice you trusted. It wasn't lying. It talked about the history of magic. It talked about religion. Sam opened his eyes: the pictures on TV were of cloaked bearded men and miracles in the desert, then some grainy footage of soothsayers performing out of covered wagons, then fidgety films of a stage magician whisking a tablecloth out from a dinner setting, while women in bikinis smiled. And then there was a sound of wings and the screen went black and the black took the shape of a bird, flapping away from the camera toward a big white moon in the night, and on the face of the moon appeared: *Raven — Behind the Illustrations.*

Now Wagstaffe was standing in a dim brown library lit by brass lamps with jade-coloured shades, the books stacked floor to ceiling, speaking in a voice of liquid gold. Sam tried to explain the scene but Adine hushed him: It's Wagstaffe, I hate him, let's see what dooshy things he has to say.

This morning, Wagstaffe was saying, join us at *Salami Talk* for our exclusive, one-hour interview with Raven, live, from We-TV Studios.

The screen is black, said Sam. Oh. The videos are of Raven now. What's going on?

He's doing things with birds. Birds are appearing, disappearing. Everyone's clapping. It's in a place with rivers, boats, he's on a bridge. They're saying —

Shhh.

Sam waited, the scene shifted. They were back in the library and Wagstaffe was sitting in a big purple chair and in another was Raven. A fire crackled in a fireplace behind them.

Why is the TV telling me to live Adine? said Sam.

Sammy, no. It probably says *live*, said Adine, as in *alive*. Not *liv*, like . . . liver.

The host introduced Raven. Raven is smiling, said Sam. His smile is odd Adine.

Odd, what do you mean? Odd how?

Just odd okay Adine.

The interview began. Wagstaffe asked, How are you finding the city?

Fine, fine.

And your accommodations?

Adequate. What I require.

For those not lucky enough to attend last night's banquet, my colleague Isa Lanyess will be providing full coverage later today — you won't recognize your Mayor *by half*.

Only the beginning, said Raven.

And that bit with the trunk? Reappearing at the hotel? Pretty remarkable.

Trunking. It's a little ... theatricality, something I incorporate into every performance.

Could you trunk yourself anywhere?

With the proper image, yes, and the proper mental preparation.

So if you'd had a picture of a different hotel, you would have shown up there.

Exactly. The image I take with me into the trunk dictates where I will reappear.

Sammy, said Adine, you there?

I'm here Adine.

What about, said Wagstaffe, a picture of the moon?

Well then perhaps you'd find me on the moon.

Or my house, what if I put a picture of my house in there.

Then, Mr. Wagstaffe, you might very well come home to find me sitting at your kitchen table. With your wife.

That rattled him, said Adine, right, Sammy?

Sam was quiet.

And, because I'm sure our viewers are dying to know, continued Wagstaffe, can you tell us what you've got planned for tonight?

Ah. If I may be so bold: perhaps my greatest illustration yet.

Lucal Wagstaffe is staring at him, said Sam. But Raven's looking into the camera. His head is very shiny. His eyes are. I don't know what they are.

Odd?

Not just. More than that. Or maybe less Adine, maybe less.

Raven said, If I may? Let me explain not just this evening's illustration, but the grand oeuvre of my work. What I do is not magic. Magic is based in illusion, and illusion is based in lies. Visual fictions and other illusions, Mr. Wagstaffe, worry people who seek certainty from sight. But what I create are not fictions. They are not lies. They are, instead, revelations. I illustrate simply what already exists, by removing —

Yes, we know, said Wagstaffe. *The fog that obscures the truth.*

Precisely. The way we perceive reality is imaginative. People forget this. One's own imagination transforms what one sees into images, and then understands these images as things. We think of spectatorship as inherently passive, but it is in fact a highly engaged and active process. Your brain, for example, Mr. Wagstaffe, registers the pattern of light produced by this object you sit upon and translates it into some signifier, but this is not the lone process for your brain to understand it: chair. I do not wish to confuse that process, but merely to focus the brain, each of your brains —

He's pointing at me, said Sam. At you Adine. At us.

— to a new way of seeing. I wish not to create illusions, but to *illustrate*. Illusions are about faith, which does not interest me. Faith is only that faculty of man to believe things he knows to be untrue. I am not interested in duping or cajoling my audience. Seeing *is* believing, and seeing depends on an imaginative use of ambiguities.

Sausage? offered Wagstaffe.

No, said Raven. Further, you see half of something, or the vague shape of something, the brain can still understand it as a whole. And so what if the world the eye sees, or which the brain tells the eye it sees — or which the eye *tells the brain* it sees — what if it is only a partial version? My illustrations are an attempt to excite those ambiguities and *complete* the partial version of the world which exists in viewers' minds. Tonight, I wish to display a whole version of this city to everyone who lives here — the truth about this place, gentle viewers, where you live.

What is that nutcase talking about? said Adine. What *whole version of this city*? What *truth*? This is nonsense. It's psychobabble. Meaningless. How does anyone buy this?

Lucal Wagstaffe chewed thoughtfully on some jerky.

What's going on, Sammy?

Silence.

Sammy?

Yes.

You there?

Yes Adine.

You're quiet.

I'm letting them talk Adine.

Everything okay?

Yes Adine.

You seem . . . faraway.

I'm here Adine. The big clock is stopped but I'm still doing good communication Adine. I'm doing the work, he said, and he stared into Raven's hollow dark eyes and scratched the crust on his jaw until something jammy came dribbling out.

THROUGH THE PARK Debbie walked Pop back to Street's Milk & Things. Near the base of the Slipway, something white lay off the path amid the bushes. A shopping bag, or a sheaf of paper.

Lark, all these bins and still people strew refuse, lamented Pop.

Debbie moved closer: whatever it was flapped slightly, maybe caught in the breeze. She crouched. The white was feathers, the flap was the feeble lift and collapse of a broken wing. And here was the glossy black pebble of an eye, a beak. It's a bird, she said. It's hurt.

Don't touch it, said Pop. It's probably aswim with germinations.

Debbie knelt, placed her fingertips on the bird's side, felt a heartbeat as urgent as a drumroll. The whole creature seemed to be one trembling, feathery heart.

It's one of his, the magician's, said Pop, let it die.

It's a living thing! Can we take it to your store?

I've no time for resuscitations, I have telephonic appellations to dilate. My house, recall, has been abscondered. Though what make of revolutionaire are you, whom is more concerned with enfeebled birds than motorizing the wheels of restribution? Cause for disbarment from the Movement, prehaps?

We have to save it, said Debbie.

But Pop was lumbering away up the path.

In a nearby trashbin she found Havoc's placard — FUG THIS SHET PARK — discarded the day before, imagined him lisping his way through this slogan, suppressed a chuckle. She folded the cardboard into a little crib, lined it with crumpled IFC wrappers, and tucked the dove inside.

Pop was gone. Debbie imagined him in his store, ranting into the telephone. The thought exhausted her. So instead of joining him she climbed the slipway to Parkside West Station, boarded a Whitehall-bound Yellowline train, which she rode, with the bird in her lap, all the way home.

HOW ABOUT A little tour of the city? asked Starx, starting the engine.

As you wish, said the illustrationist, resuming his seductive pose in the backseat. Perhaps you could cool the air, though. I find it hot.

Starx cranked the dials, swung the Citywagon onto Entertainment Drive. Where to do you think, Bailie?

But Olpert was listening to the A/C. From it came a strange fupping sound. What is that noise, he said.

It's the car, Bailie, said Starx. And to Raven: This guy, eh — bit of a nervous bird.

Yes, said Raven.

How about a quick tour to the eastend? Maybe a jaunt through Greenwood Gardens and Bebrog, a stop for lunch in Li'l Browntown. Or we could head out to the Institute, go for a walk around the campus?

I'd prefer, said Raven, to first pay another visit to the bridge.

Guardian Bridge? Again?

Yes.

Whatever you say, said Starx. He turned onto Trappe Street and headed north toward Lowell Overpass. He glanced at his partner. Bailie, you all right?

The sound inside the dashboard was like paper rustling. From the vent what appeared to be a snowflake blasted out on a waft of A/C, performed a little loop-de-loop on the updraft, and settled on Olpert's thigh: a feather.

He closed his hand over it, shut the vents. The sound died — but Starx turned the fans back on. You deaf, Bailie? Our guest finds it hot.

Indeed, said the illustrationist.

The sound returned: the purr of playing cards threaded through a bike's spokes.

Don't you think it sounds weird? said Olpert. Maybe we should turn it off.

In the backseat Raven attended to his manicure with a nailfile. I'd rather not, he said.

See? said Starx. And what do you know about cars anyway, Bailie?

The sound grew louder, more urgent. A second feather came sailing out of the vent. And then another, and another — and with a mighty cough the vents spewed a sudden blizzard: hundreds of feathers swirled into the car in a white squall.

Starx yelled, What the fug!

Olpert was overwhelmed by the scratch and tickle of feathers, a swarm of clawfooted moths. One flew in his mouth, he gagged, batted at the air, and brushed madly at his face.

Starx pulled onto the shoulder and killed the engine. The fans died. The feathers settled. The car's interior suggested the aftermath of a to-the-death pillowfight.

Wow, said Starx. Weird.

Olpert swept a layer of down onto the floormats.

Most intriguing, said the illustrationist from the backseat.

These wagons, said Starx, they're communal, never know what other drivers have got up to in them. Maybe the last person tried to roast squab on the carburetor.

Ah, said Raven.

They sat for a moment before Starx restarted the engine, tentatively. Olpert kicked the feathers into a little pile on the floormat and placed his loafers overtop.

Hey, said Starx, mind if we crack the windows now instead?

Fine, said Raven thinly. Though such an episode does raise certain questions, wouldn't you say, Mr. Bailie?

Olpert made the mistake of checking the rearview: Raven's eyes were splashes of black paint eddying down a drain.

It's interesting, continued the illustrationist, holding Olpert's gaze, to consider how these situations might have come about, to speculate and wonder. Though I would argue it will be more interesting to see how they influence what comes next.

How's that then? said Starx, merging onto the Overpass.

Oh, just that any anomalous event — he twirled his hand absently — might have much larger ramifications than one might expect.

Like what? yelped Olpert.

Oh, Mr. Bailie, who can say? Raven looked out the window: Guardian Bridge rose into view. Who can say, ever, what might happen, to whom, and when.

VI

T STREET'S Milk & Things
the doorchimes dinged as usual, but instead of Pop lunging at Sam
for a handshake, a thin, hesitant voice wondered, Who's there?

Two men Sam had never seen before stood with Pop at the
counter. One was short, his eyes went two different ways, the other
tall and thin and from whose neck sprouted a silky yellow beard.
Spread upon the counter was an ICTS System Map. Something
was wrong.

Just entreating some friends, said Pop. Please, whatever you
need, it's on my house.

If you had a fuggin houθe, growled the thin man, and the little
one sneered.

In the back of the store the MR. ADEMUS'S THINGS shelf was
empty, surrounded by sawdust and building supplies and various
junk. Sam dug through the pile, found a hinge, pried it back and
forth, listened to it squeal.

At last Pop came over. Barely done?

Do you have locks? And those loops for locks. To hold locks okay.

Is this a constructional project?

Sam leaned in, whispered, I'm going to trunk him. But I need
locks.

Pop pulled out a combination padlock, which hung open. I don't know the code, he said, so unless you've an intuitional mind, once this locks, it's locked.

Sam was careful not to close it. The suspicious men watched. Sam pointed at them. Don't spy on me okay, he said. I'm just doing the work.

He's just doing the work! screamed Pop. One of my loyal customers, no one to dubiate, gentlemen, carry on. Once he's outfat he'll be on his way. And you — Pop lowered his voice — Mr. Ademus, recall: once that locks it *will* stay locked.

It will stay locked, said Sam. Forever?

Prehaps. Now, for further requirements, you should retail to the dumpster, you're welcome!

Pop walked Sam to the door, ushered him into the parking lot, and waved, grinning — but once the door closed his smile disappeared and his fat fingers trembled as they flipped the OPEN sign to NOT. And with heaviness and resignation Pop faced the cagey, tense men inside his dirty store.

BY MID-AFTERNOON People Park was bustling. Helpers draped the gazebo in black curtains, erected scaffolding rigged with floodlights and huge videoscreens, constructed a catwalk that jutted out to the barricades. Since Raven required more power than could be supplied by generator, the NFLM ran cables up the Slipway and through downtown to Municipal Works, where they tapped right into the grid. Meanwhile the common filled steadily with people, joy sparkled in the air, and the sun shone down upon it all.

A Helper strode to the end of the catwalk with a video camera. Its recording light came alive, and onto the screens, hazy in the daylight, appeared an image of the growing crowds. One family stationed front row, dead centre, jumped up together and began waving, pointing at their projected selves upon the bigscreen.

While other families jostled for attention this one was especially boisterous: the son, in a red cap, leapt up and down, his father hooted, coaxed the mother into a funny jig, while the small girl in the shot's periphery stood numbly with her face pointed into her purse.

The Helper zoomed in on the happy threesome. Even the wife seemed into it now, flashing little gunshot flourishes, blowing imaginary smoke from her fingertips, while the dad glared in triumph at the other, ignored families. Over his head the boy hoisted a book — Raven's *Grammar* — and even without sound anyone could guess whose name he was chanting.

Sam observed this wobbling down the path behind Street's Milk & Things, lumber stacked in his arms, a bag of supplies in each hand. Quickly gravity took over: his strides lengthened and gained a momentum of their own, the wood clattered, the bags swung, and as he reached the common Sam broke unwillingly into a full-on run.

Past the boathouse at Crocker Pond he sprinted, another ten yards and his feet could no longer keep up. He pitched forward: everything slid from his arms, one of the bags burst and its contents — tools and brackets and little packs of screws — splashed forth, and the other bag fell from his hand and spilled everywhere too.

Lying in the mud, surrounded by stuff, Sam raised his chin and saw before him a pair of pink leotarded legs. A little girl in a dress, holding a handbag, regarded him blankly — and then a screaming woman was upon them.

Elsie-Anne, are you okay? she cried, and shot Sam a scolding look, which shifted into confusion. Her eyes darted back to the girl, where they sharpened again. You could have been killed, said the woman — the one who'd been hotdogging on the big TV. My daughter can be a little out of it, sorry, she said, and took the girl by the hand and led her away.

Sam's supplies were everywhere. One of the bags was split and useless, he'd have fill his pockets. But when he stooped for a handful of screws, pain spiked his lower back and his neck felt stiff and wooden.

Now appeared a fatfaced child in a red cap — the son of that woman, the one who'd been chanting, still clutching his book. My dad told me to help you, he said. So here.

The boy held out a single lugnut, which Sam accepted and dropped in his pocket.

Are you building something, said the boy. What are you building?

It's for the work okay.

What's that on your face? He picked the combination lock out of a puddle. It had closed. Sam's stomach went hollow. The boy said, Oh, let me show you a trick, and held the lock to his ear, twisted the dial listening intently. Then, with a grin, the boy yanked the shackle — it didn't open.

That's okay, said Sam, and began stacking two-by-fours.

Let me try again, said the boy. It's hard to hear with all this noise here in the park, why do people need to make so much noise, gosh. He narrowed his eyes, the pink tip of his tongue appeared between his lips, and he set to twisting the dial again. He pulled and it didn't open. He pulled again. Nothing.

Sam put out his hand.

Hey wait, said the boy, opening the *Grammar*. I did something wrong, you're supposed to listen for clicks, I thought. He leafed to the back of the book, then from back to front.

Does Raven's book tell you how to break locks?

Ha, not break. *Solve*. You don't want to break them, silly. Haven't you seen Raven escape that time he went in space in zero gravity with almost no oxygen and *eight* or maybe *twelve* locks? But he got free. He always gets free. What's on your face? Is it a scar or leprosy or something? It looks like mushrooms. I had an abscess once, in my mouth.

He always gets free, said Sam.

We're on vacation here from faraway. We missed Raven's arrival but we got frontrow centre seats today so there's *no way* we'll miss tonight's show. Mummy's from here though. Originally. She was tied up but now she's back. She's sick though. Allergies. Sam nodded.

Now hush, I can't hear the clicks with all this talking!

A man came up, smiling and rubbing his hands. Gibbles, hiya. Everything okay?

I was helping. I was —

The man turned his smile upon Sam. Sorry if my wife was short with you. She tied one on last night is all.

My bag broke okay, said Sam. He poked his hand through the jagged hole, waved at himself. That's good communication, he said.

The man's smile faltered — and returned, blazing. He looked around the park, at the families and the trees and past everything, to the sky. Heck of a nice day, he said, isn't it?

Yes, said Sam. It's a nice day isn't it.

Gip leapt to his feet. I did it!

The lock hung open.

Wait, said Sam. How? What did you do?

The boy closed his eyes and in a low, sonorous voice said, I have removed the fog of obscurity to reveal the truth. I have only illustrated what you have always known to be true.

VII

T HE PHONE RANG and rang. Sometimes this happened, Adine knew, the connections on the Islet were dicey, when lines went down hours would often pass before workers and the proper equipment could be shipped out, plus whatever time it took for repairs. But there'd been no storm, it was late afternoon now, and Adine had been trying Sam since lunch.

The door opened.

Adine hung up.

Debbie came over, kissed Adine's forehead. You left all the bedding out?

Can't see, said Adine, tapping her goggles.

Right. Can't put the bedding away, can't clean the mouse-traps —

Adine sniffed. It smells in here. Your friend left his scent.

Debbie moved into the kitchen. Cupboards were opened, pots and pans clanged and rattled. Adine turned on the TV.

Where's that big casserole dish? called Debbie.

You're making a casserole? Is that my dinner?

More banging around.

What are you doing in there?

Adine felt her way to the kitchen. It smells even weirder in here. Are you cooking?

Nope.

Then?

It's probably the bird.

The . . . bird?

Yeah.

What, you bought a bird? To what — roast?

No, I found one. It's hurt.

Oh man. First that snoring monster, now this. It better not sing all night, because I can't take something tweeting and twittering —

No. I told you, it's hurt. I'm making it a bed.

And then?

And then we'll nurse it better.

Nurse it. At your bosom? Should I be jealous?

No reply. Adine felt they were on a raft with a slow leak. She stepped forward, groped, found Debbie's elbow.

I was just trying to be funny.

Were you?

Wasn't I?

The air shifted: she sensed Debbie facing her now, imagined those wide eyes all wounded and withering. She rubbed Debbie's arm, up and down, mechanically.

The arm slid out from under Adine's fingers.

I'm putting the bird here by the window. So watch out for it.

Adine said, Okay, and went back into the den. On the NFLM station was pingpong: the knock of the ball struck back and forth, a third man commentating — she pictured him clutching the table, watching almost greedily. Check out these dooshes, said Adine. Hey, Deb — help me out here. Does the third guy look like, greedy?

Debbie sat down beside her, the cushions split, Adine slipped into the gap, had to dig herself out.

So the protest? said Debbie. A bit of a bust.

I saw on *In the Know* about the statue. I'll flip to it, only the Up button works, hold on.

Yeah. That was sort of awesome actually.

Was it you guys?

No. This was important to Pop. He wouldn't have sabotaged it.

As the channels climbed higher the programming became more inane: a humming couple convinced they'd discovered an overtone that linked the universe, a man hosting a telethon to support his telethon, the Bookland channel where the shop's mousy proprietor whispered reviews of novels no one would ever, ever read.

So this thing I went to, said Debbie, last night. This thing they're doing in Whitehall.

What? You went to *Whitehall*?

Sure. It's fine, I don't know what the big deal is. People think —

At night?

Not alone! With Calum, from the Room. I thought maybe I could write about it, but.

About what? What would you write about?

Well this is the thing. They're doing something out there, those people — I don't know how to describe it. Like a noise . . . show. Sort of.

At channel 0 the set burst into static.

Hey, said Debbie. Don't change the channel, it's just like this —

But Adine kept flipping, the screen came alive with music and words, brief lucid flashes until she paused on channel 12, and Isa Lanyess.

Anyway, said Debbie, you need to see it. Or hear it. Or just come. I can't stop thinking about it. I hated it sort of but I want to go back — maybe tonight.

And you want me to come. Tonight.

Not want. Well sure, want. But more I think it's right up your alley. And also there's that potluck earlier in Bebrog? We could go there first, then —

Can't.

Why?

Tonight's Raven's big *illustration*. I mean, fug if I care, but it's important to Sam. He's out there all alone on the I. He hasn't got anybody else.

A rigid silence fell between them.

It's important to him, said Adine. He's my brother.

She let the words hang, knew they boxed Debbie into a corner.

I have to go, Debbie said, standing.

Well thanks for stopping in.

In the kitchen the fridge hummed, from down on the street came a mother's shout and a shrill reply from her child, and in the subsequent quiet Adine heard a sharp intake of a breath, either the inhalation of unspoken words or a stifled sob.

Fug, Deb! Are you crying now? What are you crying about?

I'm not crying! She paused. Adine? Please take off those glasses.

Adine laughed, turned up the TV. Isa Lanyess was interviewing Loopy about her missing statue: You must be destroyed, said Lanyess, which Loopy confirmed: Destroyed.

Adine? Please, come on. Take them off. It's enough.

Enough what? Enough me doing my job? I don't ask you to quit ... helping.

I miss you.

Right. You pop by to drop off a dead animal, then head right back out, now I won't see you till tomorrow morning. Seems like your heart's just bleeding to spend time together. Adine felt the current of her words hurtling her forward, she'd no idea what she might say next. Here it was, coldly: Are you sure you need me at all?

A jangle of keys, the deadbolt clopped open. As always, Debbie had locked them in.

That's it? You're leaving?

I have to *go*, Adine. People are waiting for me. I didn't even have time to make anything, I'm showing up to this potluck without any food —

Stick your new pet in the oven for fifteen minutes, howbout? The door opened. Into the apartment seeped the faintly fecal odour of some other tenant's cookery. Adine, sensing Debbie hovering in the doorway, told her, You know what you do? You look for holes in people and you just burrow your way in to fill them up, you're this little helpful worm. You need to start finding home in yourself, you need — Adine was interrupted by a great commotion coming from the tv. Loopy was livid: Of course I'll always have the *idea*, but you can't *show* people your ideas! It's the *thing* that matters! And no one ever got to see the thing!

You hearing this? Adine said. Unbelievable. Eh? Deb?

The apartment felt emptied — or, more, the apartment emptied itself into Adine.

Fine! she called. Leave me. I don't care!

Somewhere down the hallway, in another unit, someone sneezed. Adine was left with Isa Lanyess and Loopy, beseeching viewers to share with them, for one full minute, a ceremonious moment of hope and silence.

IS HE WALKING all the way across?

What? said Starx.

I can't see him anymore. Can you? He went out on the bridge and now he's just — gone.

Bailie, I don't know, maybe he's expressing himself over the side.

Peeing? You think?

No. No I don't *think*.

Then? What's he doing out there?

You're so curious, go see.

They'd parked again by the onramp to Guardian Bridge. Above the Citywagon the bridge opened up: the crosshatch of beams and girders, all that black-painted steel, the setting sun carved through it in coppery spears. The bridge looked unfinished, a skeleton yet to be draped with skin.

No, I'm okay, said Olpert. I'll wait here.

Me too, said Starx.

It was that time of day when the light seemed to slow and loosen before it collapsed into evening. Olpert always found this hour melancholy, maybe even nostalgic: before dusk, before nightfall, for a few careful moments the day took stock of what it had been.

He turned to Starx: What's your favourite season?

Why, thanks for asking, Bailie! Starx faced him from the driver's seat, the great bulk of him heaped there, head scraping the ceiling, arms wrapped around the steering column for lack of anywhere else to fit them. He seemed to be considering, his breath came in whistles and gasps. Finally he spoke: I think probably winter.

Winter. Why?

Oh, I don't know. Probably because I'm packing such a massive heater — Starx nodded toward his lap — and the cold makes it easier to heave this monster around.

I like fall.

I'm kidding, right? Bailie? That was a joke?

I like fall because it feels like the end of the day, all the time.

You like the end of the day? Why?

Why? Olpert searched his thoughts: he was sure, as the sun painted everything golden, that he felt in these cautious, delicate moments most at home in the world. He tried to explain this to Starx, but when the words came out they sounded inadequate, even false, and when Olpert looked out again over the Narrows the light seemed cold and harsh.

I'm a nighttime fella myself, said Starx. And the reason why is that's when I'm at my awesomest. But you? I can see it — the fall, twilight. They're like in-between. You're an in-between kinda guy.

Olpert pointed up the bridge: He's coming.

Back down toward the Citywagon Raven was moving swiftly, twirling his whip at his side, a self-satisfied smirk plastered across his face.

What I'm saying, Bailie — Starx started the car — is that you've gotta start *living*. This in-between shet? It's just waiting to die, man.

But you like the winter, Olpert said quietly. Doesn't that mean you're already dead?

Starx shifted into reverse. Shut your yap, Raven's here, he said.

Gentlemen! cried the illustrationist, sliding into the backseat. One final question, Mr. Bailie, a most simple question. May I ask what it is you want?

I . . . want?

Yes! What you most desire, Mr. Bailie — what is it?

Um. What do you mean?

In life, in love!

In love?

Mr. Bailie, would it be presumptuous to suggest that you are a man without desires? And, Mr. Starx, what about you? What about anyone here, in your nice-looking city?

Starx drummed the steering wheel. What do I want? Quite a question. I mean —

Nevermind! Raven was gleeful, bouncing around in the backseat. You and your fellow citizens are in for a visionary performance! Such a people of longing! Now, let's go.

Sure, said Starx, backing the car onto Topside Drive.

Mr. Bailie, please, activate your radio device. There are certain preparatory measures that I require. And then, my friends, all will be revealed.

What's that then? You wanna give us a little sneak preview?

Ah, Mr. Starx, you impatient rogue! I'll tell you only this: the people of this city strike me as wanting to wall up infinity. And you're afraid to look on the other side of that wall.

Gotcha, said Starx.

Olpert checked the rearview: Raven was swivelled in the backseat, watching Guardian Bridge recede from view. So you're going to show us, said Olpert, what?

Raven turned, caught Olpert's eyes in the mirror, and held them. Why, he said, what you have always known to be true, Mr. Bailie. Only the truth. And nothing more.

WITH THE TV chattering Adine tried her brother again — no response. She flicked channels, ended up back at *In the Know*. In her telejournalist's cadence, that exaggerated lilt only spoken on TV, Lanyess was amping the night's festivities. With We-TV eyes on *every* corner of the island, she cooed, Cinecity is going to be *the* place to be. And don't forget Saturday night's premiere of *All in Together Now* — the movie made by *you*, for *us*.

These vocal undulations faded into sinewaves, a boring music that had little to do with words. Adine's thoughts drifted to Debbie: she imagined her now arriving at some dim brown apartment that smelled perennially of stew. Around the dining table would be a bunch of sloppy moccasin'd *creatives* who subjected each new arrival to hugs, one of them would stroke Debbie's hair. The food: waterlogged salads and congealed sludgy putties flavoured with great ladles of cumin. And for flouting the rigour of cookbooks these ungodly repasts entitled Debbie's friends to an unearned, manic pride.

Oh, and the eye contact — incessant and creepy, and palpable behind every unblinking stare was a brain instructing: *eye contact, eye contact*. Like having dinner with a roomful of those portraits that seemed always to be watching you. Everyone was doing *great*, each self-celebratory anecdote was met with weirdly vicarious joy. Or, in the rare case of a grievance, a spectacular show of empathy — chests were clutched as though stabbed, then came the hand-pats and aphorisms: Well you're safe now — You're good though you know that right? — You are special, you are loved.

These people confused bohemianism for authenticity, homeliness for inner beauty, prolonged, distraught embraces for a communion of souls. And this blind faith in one another stitched their collective mediocrity into a tapestry of the somehow unique, the debatably valuable, the dubiously good. It all spoke to a shared hunger to believe they were loved, they were good, they were surrounded by good. And so when Debbie came home from these dinners Adine had to read the sated look in her eyes as a false light.

Though it was this hunger that Adine had first found attractive, and then fallen in love with. Debbie kissed with a passion approaching fury. In the middle of the night if Adine, overcome with some licentious urge, nudged her out of sleep, she was ready, right away, as though she'd been awake the whole time waiting for it. Her life seemed spent anticipating intimacy — at any chance to be loved, her whole soul sparked and blazed.

Sometimes this was nice. Sometimes it was what Adine wanted too, what she needed even. But quickly Adine learned that Debbie was like this with *everyone*, and their intimacy started to feel cheap. Just once, she wanted Debbie to say, Not now. Or: Ew your breath is gross. It never mattered if Adine's breath was gross or she had a little shred of food in her teeth or if Debbie was in the middle of something — a shower, making dinner, work. She returned Adine's kisses without hesitation, stopped only when Adine pulled away, and even then in her face burned a pleading look, craving more.

She never seemed to feel the frustration or invasion that Adine felt, sometimes, when Debbie snatched her hand or worked a knee between her thighs and Adine's mind was doing its own thing — contentedly, necessarily alone. Depending on her mood Adine would either ease away or bark, Not now. Rejected, Debbie would wilt a bit and Adine's frustration would dwindle into guilt, and back to anger for being made to feel guilty, so she'd kiss Debbie with quiet resentment sizzling through her body, and the kiss would feel empty — yet Debbie would still be going for it, all ardour and tongue.

There was something sad about Debbie's hunger, something desperate and grasping and tragically lonely, lonelier even than being alone. What if she *were* alone? Without Adine, what would she do? Throw herself into the arms of anyone? Those slipshod hysterical people at her potluck — they'd be there for her, *always* — and come away smelling of unessential oils? Fine, thought Adine. If that was what she'd rather, a great unwashed orgy of moaning ravenous kisses, a stewy kind of love, then she could have it.

Here was Jeremiah, the judder of him hopping up onto the couch. Adine reached across the cushions to pet her cat, though she couldn't find him, sensed maybe he was avoiding her hand. On TV some Institute kids were arguing about which bars poured the best cider — though of course their city comprised only the southeast corner of the island, plus maybe the Dredge, one daring young man suggested a spot in Bebrog and was mocked. Adine sprawled onto her stomach, called, Jer? grasped, snapped, clicked her tongue. From somewhere came a faint mewling. But her fingers swept empty air.

THE ARMOIRE WAS six feet tall, baroque and quadrupedal, its legs curled into calligraphic hooves, fronted with a pair of doors whose mirrors had long fallen off. Sam set to cleaning it out — a pair of dusty shoes, the bar from which four coathangers hung, a stray sock, he put everything in a shoebox. On the armoire's floor he laid an inch of yellow newsprint and a blanket, with a pillow at one end this made a decent bed. Next he drilled a hole in the top and dangled a bare bulb inside, ran it through an eyehook in the ceiling to an outlet by his bed. The light would just stay on, he figured, until bedtime. This is what they did in prison, yet this wasn't a prison. More a guestroom.

Next he sawed a rectangular hole at chest height in the door, laid runners so a drawer could be inserted to pass his guest essentials and messages. When this was accomplished Sam felt quite pleased with himself, how easily the drawer slid in and out, with a compartment for food and drinks. Above it he drilled a peephole, and looking in he felt proud, it really was like a little bedroom.

Collecting his tools he secured the outside, hammering two-by-fours over the doors, wrapping the whole thing in heavy chains, then produced the combination lock the boy had magically reopened, slid it in place, pinched it shut, and twisted the dial. Sam tried the doors. Solid. No escape. Yet the boy's words echoed: *He always gets free . . .*

The last stage was making the image. Sam got out the unused drawing pad and pencils that Adine had given him many, many birthdays ago — *You were such a good artist as a kid,* she'd said, you should do stuff. Finally he had something worthwhile to draw, though this picture needed to look as close as possible to the real thing, so Sam was careful and precise — the shadows, the woodgrain, the doorhandles' coppery gleam . . .

And then it was done. Sam folded the image into the breast-pocket of the khaki shirt which he'd found in the shower, and which lay, ready and waiting, upon his neatly made bed.

CALUM STOOD APART from the crowd, first in line in the yellow bevelled waiting area, hood up, his monstrous face concealed. From below came the knock of horsehooves on the cobblestones of Knock Street, Calum pictured a happy couple cuddled up in the carriage and hawked, watched his spit go arcing up and disappear between the tracks — maybe it hit them, maybe not.

From his pole position Calum was first to witness the white dot of the train approaching from UOT, the golden glowing strip above it that indicated the line (Yellow) — a cyclops with a caution-tape eyebrow swimming out of the dusk.

The gate opened, the moving sidewalk swept into motion, Calum stepped onto it as the train's hull formed around its head-light. A hiss of brakes, a blast of air, the train slowed to match the movator's speed as it eased into the station. The doors slid open with a singsong chime and people began to climb aboard from the moving sidewalk, everything synchronized and obedient.

No one debarked, everyone was heading to People Park. Calum found a spot inside the doors and the crowd oozed in behind him, bodies melted into one another, the air zinged with shared exuberance and joviality, there was nowhere to hide from it. Though the car was packed still more people piled into it, wedged into non-existent spaces. Calum, sandwiched between a man and a woman, cringed at the heat and tingle of strangers' bodies. Nearby two old ladies in matching Islandwear jackets had taken the Special Needs seats. Oh it's so nice to see all these people supporting their city, said one, and the other cawed, It sure is, it sure is.

The train hadn't yet exited the station, the doors hung open, though the platform was empty and the movator had stopped running. It would be a long, slow, hot trip to Bay Junction. And though they weren't yet moving, a man, pink-faced and grinning stupidly, reached over Calum's shoulder to clutch the handrail, squeezing them face to face. Calum shrank inside his hood.

Beside Calum was the ICTS map: all that city between Black-acres and People Park, a long way to ride with this guy in his grill. Squirming, trying to eke out a little space for himself, Calum thought he heard a woman saying something about him, about his hood being up: Not supposed to have hoodies on here, he thought he heard, but wasn't certain, everyone was talking, the air was a muddle of words. And then that gay little chime sounded and the robotic warning said to please stand back, the doors were closing, and the pink man announced, We're off! and everyone in the car but Calum cheered.

As the train picked up speed the pink man pressed even closer, his nose almost touched Calum's. A rubbery pink neck disappeared into a white shirt, collar yellowing, stained a deeper yellow in splotches at his armpits, a few stout black hairs investigated the outer world from his nostrils, the maroon crescent of a razor's nick scabbed his chin, his odour was sickly and moist as rotten fruit.

Then he spoke: You excited?

Calum's stomach lurched.

But it was the woman behind Calum who replied, You bet, speaking to the pink man not just over but through Calum, as if he weren't even there.

My wife and kids have been in the park all day, said the pink man, saving a seat for me, and the woman said, My boyfriend too, and someone else said, Lucky you guys, and people laughed and the laughter all around him made Calum feel hateful and small.

The train rocked along the elevated lines above Lakeside, to the south the smoke-coloured lake caught the setting sun in purple and pink streaks. Next stop, Budai Beach, announced the train. Budai Beach Station, next stop. And there was another cheer — from which a Ra-*ven* chant evolved, first a few voices and then the whole car in chorus, feet stomped and hands clapped. Calum's head throbbed, he looked down, the pink man's galoshes were toe to toe with his floppy sneakers, his breath drifted outward in a sweet-sour wash.

Amid all that joy Calum imagined the pink man saying something like, Young man, you're not joining us? You aren't excited for the big show tonight? And when Calum said nothing the pink man would say, Here's a young man who's not excited for the big show tonight, and at this the whole car would boo — and Calum would sweep off the hood, show them his ruined face, his monster's face, and smash the pink man's head through the window.

A fantasy. Instead the chanting eased as the train slowed into Budai Beach Station, and Calum hid inside his hood.

There was no more room, the stranded commuters swept past on the movator, faces dumbfounded, while the train slunk through the station. Next train, see you at the park, cried the pink man, and everyone laughed. At this a scream rose up in Calum — he swatted the pink man's hand from the handrail. An air leak of a voice said, Hey, and another said, Come on, kid, you can't just hit people. Meanwhile the pink man was puffing himself up, trembling. Animals, he muttered, animals. . . .

Animals? Calum laughed a little gunfire laugh.

But no one joined in. He felt an entire traincar's worth of eyes turning on him, everyone on the pink man's side, who was saying, They're just animals — and did this elicit a murmur of agreement?

Many faces glared at him. Calum laughed again, a lonesome yelp into the crowd. White stuff foamed at the corners of the pink man's lips. You animal, he growled, emboldened, you're just a animal, you're all animals, and Calum laughed again, but the laugh sounded forced and desperate, and his face was burning, and voices were saying, Get this kid off the train.

Hands fell upon him, he was guided to the exit doors, where a final shove sent him staggering onto the platform. He backed away staring at the people on the train, who stared back: all those eyes loathing his sad two own. The doors chimed, thumped closed, and the train sped out of the station. Across the tracks upon the westbound platform a few dozen commuters observed Calum with mild curiosity. He felt on a stage, humiliated.

And so he ran. Down the steps, into Mount Mustela, east along Paths that curled between houses and duplexes, along Crescents onto Trails and Ways, finally released into the open, lamplit swath of Mustela Boulevard. Here he headed north, passing the fur shops and Bookland, his sneakers slapped and echoed, his lungs burned, he couldn't stop. Through the Necropolis, he skirted the edge of the dump, climbed the pedestrian walkway over Lowell Overpass, took the stairs back down alongside the canal, which he followed in the growing dark, and at last emerged onto Topside Drive. Up ahead, in a golden ribbon, twinkled the lights of Guardian Bridge.

VIII

ROM THE SPOT he'd procured, front row, dead centre, Kellogg gloated as more and more people arrived to increasingly poor views of the stage. Spectators swelled up the hills to the north, east, and south, and beyond, onto the streets that circled People Park. Despite a handmade NO SPECTATION sign the parking lot of Street's Milk & Things hosted a tailgate party: in the houseboat's former site men dug ciders from a cooler and young mums suckled babies at their breasts. Latecomers packed the western hillock out back of the gazebo — though they'd see nothing, not even the videoscreens, at least they could claim having been there.

Look at these poor saps, proclaimed Kellogg, gesturing around the common. Not like us earlybirds, we got the worm! And by worm I mean *the best seats in the house*. He gave a thumbs-up to Pearl who sat with Elsie-Anne on their little blanketed claim, and landed a triumphant smirk on some lesser father a few rows back.

Gip took his father's hand. I know, Dad. Thanks.

The wild, panicked fervour that had the boy careening around the park all day had tightened into tenser, almost pensive antici-pation. He seemed subdued, or at least focused, leaning there on the guardrail, eyes on the trunk from which Raven would appear at nine.

The sun went down, the crowd pressed in, Pearl and Elsie-Anne joined Kellogg and Gip at the barricades. Gazeboside Helpers flitted around, walkie-talkies crackling: Keep your positions and maintain order — B-Squad ready? — Silentium, Logica, Securitatem, Prudentia — Absolutely retain *order* . . . The messages sputtered, all those bodies on the common disrupted the frequencies.

So, Gip, said Kellogg, any guesses what Raven's going to do? — a question he'd asked since noon to no avail. Might there be clues in your book? Want Mummy to get it out of your bag?

It wouldn't be in the *Grammar*, Dad, said Gip. As if!

No insights? Being his biggest fan and all?

Can't you just wait? You're so impatient. Gosh!

There's something to be said for surprises, said Pearl, handing Gip the day's final round of meds and a box of apple juice. No grape? he said, and Pearl said, They don't have grape here, only this. He washed down the pills, Pearl stashed the container in Gip's knapsack and dropped it at her feet. This is fun, she said. What a view! Thanks, Kellogg.

But Kellogg was distracted. At the back of the gazebo lurked one of the men in khaki, apart from the rest. Someone's camera-light, scanning the stage, shone upon him momentarily: a skittish character with a facial abrasion — the man from earlier, the one who'd nearly crushed Elsie-Annie with an armful of lumber. Kellogg waved, the Helper saw him and shrunk into the shadows. Who's that? said Pearl. He's . . . Kellogg began, but wasn't sure what to say.

WHILE A YELLOWLINE train swept from City Centre into Parkside West Station, at the head of the southbound platform a lone traveller sat motionless with a duffelbag between his feet. Dressed in black from head to toe, face concealed in a balaclava, this person watched impassively as the train slowed and unleashed a pack of Jubilee merrymakers and then slid off, evacuated and empty, toward Bridge Station.

Once the crowd had cleared, two figures — one tall and thin, the other stocky and manic, both in leather — approached the seated man. After an exchange of shifty nods, some furtive looks up and down the platform, and a few minutes of contrived estrangement, amid a clatter and screech and a funnelcloud of trash swirling up from the tracks, the PA announced a Whitehall train, the movator started up, and the men assembled to board.

In the first car the trio took seats adjacent to but not exactly beside one another. Hissing, the train eased alongside the empty platform. Through its open doors came the noise from People Park, an oceanic murmur, lunar and tidal and ancient. Then the doors played their song and closed and the PA said, Next stop, City Centre. City Centre Station, next stop, and they were heading off south into the evening.

In a low voice Pop said, Thank you for adjoining me.

Tragedy shook his fist. Fuggin justice, man.

Will be θerved, added Havoc, spat, and smeared the jiggling wad into a wetspot with a generic black sneaker.

BEHIND THE GAZEBO, at the edge of Crocker Pond, B-Squad stood guard outside the boathouse. A light glowed inside this ersatz greenroom: prior to each show the illustrationist required an hour, alone, to prepare himself with visualizations.

So, said Starx, I've been meaning to tell you — that dream you said you have?

Olpert was confused.

That dream you told *him* . . . Starx nodded at the boathouse.

Oh.

I have it too. Exactly the same. It was like you were telling him stuff from my own brain, Bailie. Superweird.

Well, said Olpert, that wasn't really my dream. I think he . . . put it there.

Whatever, right? I hate this shet about how dreams are supposed to reveal secrets. If you lie to yourself when you're awake, who's to say you don't lie to yourself in your dreams? So your dream, my dream, who cares. It's all made-up anyway, probably. Me, the only thing I like about dreams is they put me to sleep.

What do you mean?

I mean, if I lie there thinking about the day, or something that's already happened, I can't get to sleep. But as soon as I let my brain go off and make stuff up — fantasies or whatever — it shifts into dreams. Like I sort of dream myself to sleep. You?

I don't know. Olpert looked away, looked back, opened his mouth, closed it, and looked away again.

Something on your mind, Bailie? You've been weird all day. Still hungover?

No, it's just. I was. I don't know.

Talk.

Okay, said Olpert. Okay, I was just thinking about something. Or I've been remembering something. Because of what happened last night, at the bar. With . . . Debbie.

Yeah?

It's a long story sort of.

What else are we going to do, twiddle each other's dicks?

Olpert recoiled. Ew, no.

Then?

Okay, Olpert said, and sighed deeply, as if to refuel himself for what he was about to say. Then he spoke: When I was in fifth grade, a scientist came to our classroom. In, you know, one of those white coats? A real scientist. Anyway what he did was, and he probably did some other stuff first, some other experiments or told us some facts or something, but then he pulled a container out of his bag, a black medical bag, and he was very careful with it. It was that really cold stuff?

Dry ice.

No. A chemical, not nitrous oxide but . . .

Starx waved his hand: whatever.

So he opens the container and the stuff inside is steaming, there's fog coming out of it. Like a beaker in a mad scientist's lab on TV, like a TV version of science. Or witchcraft.

Right.

Then he, the scientist, asks if anyone's got a piece of fruit in their lunch. I put up my hand, and I don't know why because everyone, right away, all the kids, started going, *Olpert's got fruit, Olpert's got fruit.*

Starx snorted: *Fruit.*

And the thing, this is the main thing, so pay attention, okay? The main thing is I've got a huge crush on the girl I sit behind, who's in sixth grade, Katie Sharpe. I stare at her back all day long. Not even a crush, Starx. I love her. But back then that one year makes so much difference. Like she's on the other side of a river and there's no way across? But she has no idea I'm on the other side of the river, or there even *is* a river? I love Katie Sharpe and she has no idea I exist. The ground could fall away at my feet and I could get sucked into that river and drown and she'd — she'd have no idea.

Where is she now?

I don't know, married probably. Probably happy. But anyway, now you know about Katie Sharpe. So she's sitting in front of me and the scientist pulls out a pair of tongs and starts clacking them and goes, Okay, son, bring that fruit on up here, which was an apple.

Better than a banana.

So I took my apple up to him. And he takes the apple in his tongs and he does it all dramatic, he holds it up, he takes the apple and lifts it for the class to see, which is *agonizing*, Starx, especially because of Katie, and then he slowly dips the apple into the container where the fog is coming out of. And he holds it in there for a bit. And I'm just standing there the whole time, waiting for my apple back. Then he pulls the apple out.

How'd it look?

Maybe a bit white but otherwise the same. Then the scientist pulls a hammer, a little reflex hammer, out of his bag and hands it to me, and holds the apple in the tongs and he tells me to tap the apple with the hammer. So I do.

Hard?

No, regular. And it shatters! Like it's made of glass the thing breaks into little pieces all over the place — my apple! And I don't even hit it hard, just a little tap, and it just . . . It explodes. Everyone cheered. I remember that, how everyone clapped and I rushed to sit down, even Katie was clapping. I was so humiliated. All I could think was, that was my apple, that was my apple. I felt stupid and, I don't know . . . small.

Small. Yeah.

And a second or two went by, and I can feel it coming, but instead of going to the bathroom I open my desk and put my head inside, and then, can you guess?

No.

I puked, said Olpert. Splash, splash, splash, all inside my desk. And the room went really quiet and I know everyone's looking at me, and then Katie says, Are you okay, Olpert — and that's just too much. I run. I run, Starx, trailing puke through the room and down the hallway, I run out the school doors and keep running until I get to Bay Junction, and I ride the ferry across the Cove, and then run across the Islet, all the way home. My grandpa's out front raking leaves and he sees me, but he doesn't say anything. So I lie down on the lawn and tell him to bury me in leaves. And he does. He just piles them on top of me. It's cool in the leaves, peaceful. I don't remember much else after that.

AS THE POTLUCK wound down, to avoid the towers of stew-crusted dishes Debbie's friends put together an outfit to camouflage her in Whitehall. A game of dress-up: obediently she tried on an assortment of coats and blazers. Masks. A handkerchief tied around her face in the manner of bandits. And at last in the very back of the hall closet someone found a coal-black anorak, and they put it on and pulled up the hood and Debbie's face disappeared and everyone agreed: perfect.

Her last-ditch attempts to get them to come along were shrugged off — No, this is your thing, Tell us how it went, Just be safe — and Debbie hugged each one of them long and hard, her people, her community, she loved them, and they wished her well and she stepped out onto the street and the door closed behind her and she stood breathing the chilly night air of Bebrog for a quiet, still moment.

She was tired, the whole night had been tiring. When she'd arrived the potluck's hosts had made her tour their house, she hadn't been for a while, they'd amassed a small collection of Mr. Ademus originals. Aren't they great, she was told, and she had to agree, despite visions of Adine shaking her head in dismay and disgust. The whole night, really, she'd been thinking of Adine.

Throughout dinner the way they'd parted nagged her, she felt the tug of it from across town. What if now she just went home? No, she'd go home after: Adine would be there, she'd always be there, goggled and hermitically waiting, they'd make jokes and/or love, it'd be as if the fight never happened.

Debbie walked to Greenwood Station, transferred at City Centre, and Yellowlined past her stop at Knock Street and up into the Zone. In Blackacres she emerged again into the cold still night, looked north up F Street, back south — a fifteen-minute walk home. But she needed to see. So she flipped the hood of the anorak and crossed into Whitehall, down the murky serviceways to the silos and, finally, underground.

She'd forgotten a flashlight, had to fumble into the tunnel toward that ghastly screaming at its end, a factory of screaming down there in the dark. Along she went, bracing herself — and then with a sudden roar the cavern opened up, a formless howling washed over her, and she stared into the blackness and had to resist the urge to flee.

Noise was everywhere, shrieking, blistering, industrial, the grind and wail of some ruined machine. It stabbed into her ears and buzzed through her face, tingled down her limbs and collected throbbing in her hands and feet. Her skin seemed to surge with it, to expand and contract as though it were an organism apart from her, breathing. But this wasn't just noise, it was some sort of human music — she had to think of it as music.

As she might enter some black and churning ocean, Debbie stepped between two towers of electronics into the cipher. And here were people. Someone pushed against her, something electric zipped up her arm. Her instinct was to pull away but the person pressed closer. She waited tensely while their bodies touched, her skin humming. And then this person, whoever it was, released and drifted off into the crowd.

It had all been so intimate: contact, lingering, separation. The music suggested violence but among the people there was none. Everyone moved languidly, almost sleepily. She thought, They're all figures lost in the same dream. And wanting to join the dream Debbie unclenched her fists, tried to relax. The song, or whatever it was, had changed — now vaporous and airy, like, she thought ... like what? No words came.

Debbie moved deeper into the group, she was prodded and fondled, the sound transformed. Her emotions tumbled from fear to comfort to pleasure, someone stroked the back of her neck, and now she felt shy, though this person slid away and she was overcome with loneliness. Another step, everything changed again: a rotary saw tearing through metal, a shower of sparks. Hands were tugging her down. She crouched alongside someone who nuzzled into her, and she caressed this person, this faceless stranger. Whoever it was, their body was warm.

ON THE STREET outside City Centre Station people stood around with the awkward spacing of strangers at a bad party, watches were checked and checked again, toes tapped, exasperation and impatience abounded. Yet when a train arrived each face brightened: finally, the laggard might be here! And should this person come hustling down from the platform, all apologies and performed bluster, the other would sigh and tell them: It's fine, the park's full though, we're just going to have to watch in Cinecity.

Yet in Cinecity, with live coverage projected on the bigscreen, you were guaranteed a view not just of the stage, but of *everything*. All those cameras afforded perspectives unimaginable for a single human being, from aerial panoramas atop Podesta Tower to intimate handheld shots wobbling through the crowds. And in the theatre each set of newcomers delighted to discover revelry and anticipation equal to what they imagined down on the common, among those witnessing — or about to witness — the real thing.

The night's events were hosted gamely by Lucal Wagstaffe and Isa Lanyess, lofted over People Park in the basket of a crane-type apparatus. Trained on their faces was a camera at which Lanyess beamed and Wagstaffe tilted his head ponderously. The crane's arm swung at an elbowjoint and held We-TV's preeminent Faces in its fist, and in their own fists they held microphones, the bulbous foam tips pressed to their lips.

The atmosphere here at People Park is electric, said Wagstaffe, and Lanyess grinned a set of horsey teeth and whinnied, Just the sheer size of the crowd! It's — I don't have the words for how it feels out here! and Wagstaffe said, I've never seen anything like this in our city before. And we still don't know, added Isa Lanyess with a coy note of mystery, the answer to the question everyone's asking: what will Raven do?

Blow himself up, let's hope, said Adine to her TV. She picked up her cordless and hit TALK: only the dialtone. Where was Sam? Adine tapped the antenna on her teeth, felt her way over to the refrigerator, neither hungry nor thirsty, just to point her face at the cool air inside. A funny smell — though not from the fridge. Debbie's sick bird, she remembered, dying upon the window sill.

Just look at the number of people, cried Lanyess. What a turnout!

Simply amazing, said Wagstaffe. Everyone's here.

On the little TV in their kitchen Cora and Rupe were treated to a grandiose dollying shot over the common.

Rupe said, How come we can't go there too, Ma?

Hush now. We can see everything fine at home.

But this wasn't true: the picture was too small, identifying faces was akin to picking out raindrops from a monsoon.

Do you think Calum's there?

Hush.

If he still hasn't come home, Ma, don't you —

Cora swatted at him. I said hush!

Ma? Is that him? There! Is it —

There's just so many people, said Cora softly. There's too many people to tell.

THE NEXT DAY, said Olpert, the walk to school was the saddest walk of my life.

Yeah?

The whole way from Bay Junction I thought about that apple, the way it just exploded, and I thought — and don't laugh at me here, I was a kid — that my heart felt the same way. Like it had just . . . shattered. But with such a soft little tap.

Fug.

And, Starx? Is love like that? I figure it's that stuff, that steaming stuff, and you soak your heart in it, and then someone pulls out a hammer and smashes everything to pieces. And then you feel so so so so so so small.

Starx stared at him. He didn't say a word.

The light inside the boathouse clicked off. Raven didn't emerge. Instead, moaning: a mantra or a dirge.

Olpert turned back to his partner. Am I crazy?

Love's crazy, Bailie. Though Starx seemed to be talking to himself — No, thought Olpert, more a memory of himself. Love's a fuggin punt to the grapes for sure, he said.

BY QUARTER TO NINE People Park and its adjacent neighbourhoods were filled to capacity, there was nowhere else for anyone to go. And while Gip focused unwaveringly on the illustrationist's trunk, spotlit at the front of the stage, Kellogg was more interested in the shifty guy with the thing on his face, who emerged from the shadows every so often to examine the crowd. And each time he did Kellogg drew his family a little closer.

Everywhere people trained video cameras on one another. Eyebrows lifted, fingers pointed, lenses reflected lenses to infinity. There you are, people said, waving, Good to see you — Say something to the camera — I don't know you but hi! What boundless cheer, thought Kellogg, how good and decent a city could be. He wrapped his arm around Pearl, who hoisted Elsie-Anne on her hip, and she hugged him back while Gip chanted Ra-*ven* under his breath — what a champ! Had the Pooles ever had such a perfect, happy time? Not as a family, together, never. And the show hadn't even started yet.

NFLM Helpers moved through the crowd handing out sparklers. Go on, Annie, said Pearl, and warily Elsie-Anne shouldered her purse and took a sparkler and held it at arm's length, hypnotized by the flaring tip. That's not how you do it, Dorkus, said Gip. He snatched the sparkler and whirled it through the air: RAVEN, RAVEN, RAVEN. Easy now, said Kellogg. I just wanted to show her, said Gip, though he'd already lost interest. The sparkler was discarded, it fizzled on the ground into a dead tin stick.

IN MATCHING BLACK outfits Havoc, Tragedy, and Pop descended from Knock Street Station into Lower Olde Towne. At the station's entrance Pop removed his balaclava and glared into the security camera. I am whom I am, he howled. Envision me!

Tragedy elbowed into the shot, wonky eye shooting off lakeward, to shake a masturbatory gesture at the lens. Restribution, he said. Right?

Restri-fuggin-bution indeed, agreed Pop. Now let's get our moves on.

Lower Olde Towne was devoid of life, the tourist shops and artisanal craft stores closed, the B&B's along Knock Street seemed to be sleeping. From the station the trio pushed north, over cobblestones mottled with mats of hay masking paddies of horsedung. But the horses were stabled in Kidd's Harbour, their drivers downtown for the big show — along with, it seemed, everyone else.

The trio assembled under the awning of an Islandwear boutique. Pop opened his duffel, removed a can of spraypaint, puffed a bright green burst onto the wall.

Fuggin yeah, said Havoc, that'θ a θtart.

I've crafted a text, said Pop, removing a sheaf of papers from his pocket. He handed a section each to Havoc and Tragedy. I've divisioned it into chapters, one to each of us.

Tragedy leafed through the pages. Wow. We got enough paint?

Pop spread the bag open: it was full of cans. Absolutesimally, he said.

YOUNG PEOPLE occupied the common's eastern hillside. Most were drunk. Voices hooted, ciders made the rounds, empties were pitched into the orchard, bottlecaps flicked and forgotten. A small group started a lethargic and half-ironic Ra-*ven* chant, abandoned to apathy. The booze had them grasping at heedlessness and rebellion, despite curfews and homework in the backs of their minds.

Edie shared a flask of schnapps with a boy from school. He got hold of a sparkler, wrote, FUG, and a mum racing by with her daughters shielded their eyes.

Laughing, Edie handed him the flask.

Where's Calum, he said.

No idea, said Edie, I haven't heard from him since yesterday. Though if he wants to ruin his life, whatever, it's his problem, she said, watching the boy drink. He doesn't care about his future? Fine. I tried to help him, but you can only do so much, right?

What? the boy said.

Nothing, said Edie, and reclaimed the flask, and took another drink.

LESS THAN A MINUTE, said Wagstaffe, and Isa Lanyess neighed, The countdown's begun!

Adine checked the phone again — no Sam, no one. From the TV, kettledrums rumbled and a brass section belched its way through a melody that suggested some imminent triumph. She imagined spotlights dancing, the crowd tensing, the conjoined anticipation of cuddled-up couples. With this came thoughts of Debbie — so Adine reached for the remote and turned up the sound.

Isa Lanyess said, What a magnificent celebration of twenty-five years of this beautiful space, and Wagstaffe clarified, The park, yes, let's not forget — only thirty seconds to go!

Adine stared into the blackness of her goggles, images of Debbie flitting in her mind's eye: surrounded by friends, someone else holding her, an insipid snuggly orgy —

On TV the drums were intensifying. Isa Lanyess screamed, Ten seconds, and We-TV's co-hosts roared in chorus, Nine, eight, seven, six, five ...

Four, shouted everyone in Cinecity.

Three, said Rupe and Cora.

Two, thought Adine, grudgingly.

One, whispered Gip.

The drums stopped.

The lights went out.

Every clock and watch froze at once: it was nine.

From somewhere a lone trumpet wailed a single, sad note. The Podesta Tower searchlights swung over the crowd, illuminating thousands of expressions of rapture and wonder. The video-screens came to life in a grey mess of static, which organized into a shuffle of photographs meant to mimic movement. A ten-second, grainy loop played on repeat: the silhouette of a raven flapping across a colourless sky.

The trumpet paused. Into the silence pattered a drumroll, not just suspenseful but militaristic — a reveille. As it crescendo'd the birds on the videoscreens flew faster, faster.

Here we go, whispered Wagstaffe, and Kellogg, and hundreds of other dads.

The Podesta Tower searchlights, twirling like streamers in a gale, whipped together into a single spot upon the helicopter on the Grand Saloon's roof. The fat white band dragged through the orchard's drunk youngsters, down into the common, all the way up, slow as a sunrise, to the gazebo: the trunk opened and in this pillar of light stood Raven.

A roar rose up that Adine heard not just on TV, but through her windows, the whole island felt rocked by a seismic explosion. And the subsequent applause was the gallop of hot magma, thundering down.

Beaming at his public, arms wide to accept their adulation, Raven stepped from the trunk onto the catwalk. The stagelights came up. His tracksuit glowed, his baldhead was incandescent, he waved and blew kisses and grinned.

Yes, he cried into a headset microphone. Welcome!

Here he is, said Wagstaffe. Here's the moment we've all been waiting for.

Holy shet speak for yourself, said Adine, though no one heard her but Jeremiah.

WAY OUT IN Whitehall all Debbie could hear was a droning roar, changing as she moved through it, as she bumped against and slid away from strangers who fondled her and now she was fondling them back, and when a pair of lips came out of the dark and pressed to hers what could she do but return the kiss? For a moment she felt guilty, what about Adine —

But these thoughts were too distinct, too literal: they skidded away from her, lost in all that sound. She reached into the darkness for someone to touch. Hands found and passed her, one set to the next. And somehow the screaming began to disappear, to fold inside itself, becoming at once somehow bigger and smaller than silence.

The other people began to disappear inside it too: Debbie became pure sensation, she tingled and shivered, she was hot and cold and awake and asleep, all at once, and she knew that everything anyone had ever known could be found trapped inside this moment, this sound that was no longer audible, but something else.

Everything was *here*, everything was *now*. How could there ever be anything but this?

She felt her voice welling up. She too could make this sound, she understood at last how to make this essential sound, this non-sound, it gathered and swelled inside her and she opened her mouth to give it life —

And that was when the power went out.

ALL THE LIGHTS in People Park surged at once: the place glowed as if daytime had descended from the night sky. Kellogg reeled. Whoa, he said, that's bright! But Gip stared into it, wide-eyed and trusting.

Look at you, laughed Raven, indicating the screens on either side of the stage.

Upon them appeared the crowd, alive in that blaze of light. And from the crowd hundreds of cameras pointed at the screens, and cameras shot the people shooting themselves shooting the screen and on the screens everyone saw themselves and roared in one voice: Ra-*ven*, Ra-*ven*, Ra-*ven*.

Look at you, said Raven, you're beautiful, thank you!

ADINE TRIED EVERYTHING: when the remote failed she felt her way to the TV and twisted the volume, changed the channel, turned the set off and on — nothing. She picked up the cordless phone, hammered the buttons, listened . . . It was dead too.

THE LIGHTS DIMMED. Raven compelled silence. And so there was silence.

People! he said, speaking the word as an imperative. Tonight we have come to bear witness to something truly spectacular. I must admit I have never attempted anything this ambitious before, and I am honoured to try it, here, in your city — not great, indeed, but well built.

This elicited a dubious and scant ovation.

But, people! What is most important is that I have discovered a truth manifest in this land. By means of your solitary situation I fear you are to yourselves unknown, apt enough to think there might be something supernatural about this place. Am I wrong?

He quashed a Ra-*ven* reprise with an impatient wave.

No, no indeed. What I need from you, from everyone in your fair city, is to know you are the *right* sort of people — are you? Are you the right sort of people?

They were sure about this: Yes! hollered the crowd.

Raven's eyes widened. Are you *really*? Do you *believe*?

Yes! (Really! misspoke Kellogg.)

Because this will not work without the right sort of people — people who *believe*, people who are willing to open their eyes and *look*. None of us knows what the fair semblance of a city might conceal. Is it no better than a brushed exterior? A white sepulchre? Or perhaps rather illustrative than magical?

Cheers.

What you will see tonight will not be deception, nor an illusion, nor some spurious trick of the light.

More cheers.

It will be the truth! That is why I am here, that is what I plan to illustrate to you — humbly, of course. For many such journeys are possible. This is only one.

Again, in a single voice, the crowd performed on cue.

I've spent now two full days in your city. When I arrived I wasn't quite sure what I wanted to do. But, fortunately, I had some excellent guides who showed me around, and taught me some important lessons as well . . .

Backstage, Olpert felt a twang of anxiety that the illustrationist might mention him by name. He actually felt faint, swooned a little. But Starx caught him — Whoa there, Bailie! — and guided him pondside into a deckchair branded *Municipal Works*. You okay, pal? Starx asked, kneeling. If you're going to barf again, at least do it in the water.

Raven continued: But here we are! And what a perfect opportunity to reveal something deeply fundamental to what — I think, at least — this city is all about.

The crowd was buzzing now.

Wagstaffe said, Raven's making hints about what's to come, though at home in Laing Towers Rupe and his mother didn't hear this, Cora was smacking the TV to coax a picture back. But the set was out. The whole Zone was out.

What sounded like a bomb went off on the common. Olpert nearly fell into the pond.

Easy, buddy, said Starx. No war on yet.

Right, said Olpert. Just the show.

You want to go watch?

Do you?

Hey, said Starx, you make the call. We're B-Squad, right? Can't split up B-Squad!

B-Squad, agreed Olpert. Then: Do you mind if we just stay here, Starx?

I do not.

They gazed out over Crocker Pond, a sheet of glossed ebony.

I should pitch a fifth pillar, said Starx. Fidelititum, or something. Because isn't that what's most important, Bailie?

Fidelititum?

Exactly.

From the common, another roar. The illustrationist's voice echoed: Yes, yes!

So here's my story, said Starx, pulling up a deckchair. I told you I used to be married?

You did.

Well. So. My wife, my ex-wife, she ran this bookshop in Mount Mustela — Bookland.

She ran that?

Still does. Inherited it from her parents. Anyway she's working late one night. Just doing inventory or whatever. And man, I told her I don't know how many times it was a bad idea to be there all alone so late. Even though it's east of the canal.

I work alone late.

I know you do, pal. Listen for a sec though? So this one night she's there, this is two years ago, it's probably midnight or something, and she looks up and those people are doing that thing where they paint the windows black —

In *Mount Mustela*?

My lady, god love her, she's a tough bird, she goes right out front and is like, what are you doing to my store, I'm right here! There are maybe a dozen of those fuggin animals. And, sure, they stop painting. But then they just close in on her.

Oh no.

Starx stood, started pacing. I would have killed them, he said, wheeling at Olpert and brandishing one of his little fists. If I'd been there, I mean. You hear me?

What happened?

What the fug do you think happened?

I don't —

What happened was that she came home and told me, she's crying, and I'm — Bailie. I don't know what to do. I can't even describe this feeling. Not even *angry*. It's something way beyond that, like having some crazy evil part of yourself open up. Your brain starts shooting off in all these directions. I'm picturing finding these people, these animals, and tearing them apart with my bare hands. Just ripping them apart. You know?

From the common the Ra-*ven* chant started up again.

Starx continued: This lady of mine, Bailie, she was a fuggin spitfire. Lakeview-raised, the whole bit. But after this, after they *interfered* with her, she's half that person. I don't know what to do, so I call Griggs. He tells me to bring her right away, but she wants to take a shower. She goes into the bathroom and locks the door and I'm out there screaming we have to go, she can't do this — so what do I do? I break the door down.

Olpert thought, *Interfered.* What did that mean?

My logic is that we have to preserve all the evidence, so the HG's can do what they need to, so I can't let her shower. Right? And, Bailie, this is not a woman who anyone *lets* do anything. Nobody *didn't let* her do anything, ever. She just did or didn't. But now she's barely there, she's limp, there's nothing in her eyes. So I pick her up and carry her outside and — Bailie, it was horrible, horrible. I'll never forgive myself for that.

Starx stopped pacing. He stood at the pond's edge watching the water, his back to Olpert. Telling Starx about Katie Sharpe and the frozen apple seemed a terrible mistake now, so indulgent and pointless. The big man's whole world seemed coiled around that singled word — *interfered* — and when he'd spoken it everything had come unspooling: he appeared now smaller, drained, and spent.

From the common came another roar. Raven cried, Who will help me, who will help me, who among you will join me onstage and help me, here, tonight?

POP HANDED HAVOC and Tragedy a can of spraypaint each. He zipped the duffel, slung it over his shoulder, and flapped his manifesto. Restribution, he said, saluted, and crossed Knock Street at a low scuttle. While Pop stole around the side of the Temple, Tragedy pulled a radio from his jacket, held it to his face, and spoke: Griggs, it's Pea and Dack, the squab's in the oven. A reply came crackling back: Good lookin out. Bring him in.

KNEELING ON THE RUG by the dead TV Adine became aware of a stillness that extended beyond her apartment. A blackout, she said, aloud. She moved to the window, opened it, listened. Her neighbours were pouring onto the streets, Adine was struck by how many they seemed. Their voices were loud and curious, almost bold, and amplified as though seeking echoes. You without power too? asked someone and someone else replied, Yeah, right in the middle of the show, and Adine thought, Me too, but didn't call down to them, just listened as the two of them decided to head together to Cinecity. Adine closed the window, sat in the nook, pulled a pillow onto her lap and stared into the goggles. As always, everything was dark. But in a blackedout world, she wondered, what if anything did being blind mean?

SWELLED TO GARGANTUAN proportions on the videoscreens was the face of the boy, pudgy and astonished, the eyes of someone woken from a dream to live that same dream.

Yes, you, my friend, said Raven, you in the red cap.

With needless help from Kellogg (a hand on his son's rear), two Helpers lifted the boy onto the catwalk.

From the right sort of people, said Raven, the right sort of boy!

The crowd went berserk with envy and vicarious joy.

Please, now, silence, said Raven. Come, son. Yes. On the duck-tape X. Your name?

Gip Poole.

Hello, Gip Poole! Now, Gip Poole, are you the right sort of boy? Do you believe?

Gip looked at his parents. Kellogg shouted, Say yes!

Yes, said Gip.

Raven snapped three times. From the white trunk flew doves, he extended his arms, three landed on the left, two on the right. His expression clouded. He motioned with his fingertips, glared at the trunk. No sixth bird appeared. Snapped three more times. Nothing. The crowd shifted uneasily, the lack of symmetry was unsettling.

With a shrug, Raven lifted his hands over his head, the doves exploded into a shower of sparks. Kellogg screamed and lunged, a Helper straightarmed him behind the barricade. But Gip seemed less frightened than delighted: all around him fire came sizzling down, and he spun happily as though basking in the year's first snowstorm.

THE AIR IN THE cavern felt diluted, sapped. Debbie was bumped from behind. This time the touch didn't feel sensual, but urgent. People seemed to be congregating with new purpose, someone pushed her — and the whole group heaved and she was swept up, into the tunnel, bodies pressed around her on all sides.

And now they were running.

Down they went, zagging left, a hard right — starlings wheeling in a massive flock. No one said anything. The tunnel descended, swerved, Debbie tripped but she was caught and bolstered, there was no room to fall: a mad, wordless stampede down through the dim warrens of the city.

On they went, and then the tunnel seemed to angle upward again. Debbie's feet met stairs. She climbed, she was lifted. Ahead a shaft of light shone from some window or opening, and they reached it and burst into the night. The air felt sharp and cool. She looked around: they'd surfaced inside the gates of the Mount Mustela Necropolis.

Pushed up from underground — disinterred — here they were, a faceless horde, their numbers inestimably fading into the shadows. Everyone had gone still. The only movement came from a shirtless guy in a strange helmet, hoisting a lithe figure atop the roof of a little crypt. This person rose to her feet and swept back her hood: the girl with the handprint haircut.

Everyone pressed in close, leaving Debbie behind. The Hand moved to the edge of the crypt's roof, a pastor facing her parish. No one said anything. The silence reminded Debbie of that dreadful empty moment between a screech of tires and the explosion of steel and glass.

The Hand spoke: Look!

She pointed east, where a brilliant gloriole floated above People Park — the stagelights fanning up from the common in a silky wash. Then she pointed west: the entire Zone was cast in darkness, lights out all the way from Whitehall to Lowell Canal. And, finally, south: in LOT the Dredge Niteclub glowed in purple strips around its rooftop, the Mews sparkled and gleamed, Mount Mustela glittered like a circuitboard.

Here it's just darkness and damp cold, preached the Hand. There it's all sunshine.

Voices swelled in dissent — shouts, jeers, someone barked, someone squawked.

The Hand hushed them, beckoned them closer.

Debbie, abandoned on the periphery, realized the Hand was whispering. She caught a few chilling words — All their good deeds and dreams won't save them — and backed away, ducked behind a gravestone, crawled into a scraggle of shrubs, and lay there in the cool wet earth, her pulse throbbing through her entire body, while the Hand murmured instructions Debbie couldn't hear to the mob among the graves.

PLEASE, SAID RAVEN, Gip, reach into this trunk and pull out everything you find.

Gip produced a straitjacket, a half-dozen locks, various harnesses and clasps, leather straps, a length of chain that unravelled, yard after yard, into a pile. While this collected at Gip's feet, a Helper shuffled onstage — the sketchy character with the facial growth.

Raven covered his microphone, hissed, *Get out of here.*

The guy went scuttling past the trunk and off into the shadows.

Did that man drop something inside that box? said Kellogg. Pearly? A piece of paper? Pearl?

Pearl squeezed Kellogg. Pure delight lit her eyes. How about our boy up there, she whispered. Look at him! He's so happy. Have you ever seen him so happy?

The chain's end wriggled clanking onto the stage.

Kellogg, for the benefit of anyone within earshot, hollered, That's our boy!

Raven knelt. Gip, please install me in these restraints. Go on. Begin with the straitjacket. Yes, one arm here, the other here. Now these buckles, there you go.

Gip did as he was told. Closeups appeared on the videoscreens. Everyone watched.

Now test the clasps, said Raven. Make sure they're tight. How old are you, Gip?

Ten and one quarter, said Gip, yanking at an errant cord. Nearly two.

Ten and two quarters! Is that more or less than ten and a half? Obediently, the crowd laughed.

Gip straightened. They're all done.

Good, Gip! Good. Yes, they're very goodly tight indeed.

Isa Lanyess wondered, An escape trick? and Wagstaffe scoffed, You can bet he's got something a lot more exciting in store than that, and those watching had to agree. Those not watching included Cora and Rupe, flushed into the lightless courtyard of Laing Towers with a dozen co-residents: no one had any power, what was there to do?

Now, Gip, if you could just step back about five feet — yes, that's it, a bit farther...

Onto the stage came two Helpers (not the weirdo, noted Kellogg, he'd disappeared) to lower the bound illustrationist into the trunk. A camera swooped overhead and Raven appeared on the videoscreens, a mummy in its sarcophagus.

While my illustration transpires, said Raven, I will be in seclusion. Let good Gip be your guide. And remember: that which we see with our own eyes is the only *true* miracle.

From somewhere: drumrolls, a splash of cymbals.

The truth is nearly upon you! screamed Raven. I will reveal it from here, like this. Gip, good man, shut me into this box, lock it surely.

Gip closed the lid. The two Helpers swept up the chains, wound them around the trunk, helped him slide the locks in place. The crowd cheered.

Kellogg nudged Pearl. That's our boy!

Over the loudspeakers came Raven's muffled voice: Thank you, Gip! Everyone, a round of applause for Gip. Now, if I can direct your attention to the videoscreens . . .

FROM ITS ONRAMP Guardian Bridge reminded Calum of a woman, knees up and spread, and he smiled a little at the thought of a retreat down the birth canal — what a perfect way to start a new life. Lights ran along the suspension cables in lilting rows reflected shivering below in the water. Above: a starless sky, a faint moon like a pearl lodged in mucky riverbed. Across the Narrows was the mainland, so close.

From the loudspeakers in People Park Raven implored, Believe, believe . . .

With a great boom, the bridge disappeared. Where its outline had been traced in lights now hung only the night. For a moment Calum felt he might be falling — but the road remained steady under his feet. He was not floating in space. The bridge wasn't gone at all. The lights had merely been turned off. He stepped forward: solid ground.

Calum took another step, another, each one met pavement, and now he was walking out along the pedestrian concourse, gaining confidence. In fact this darkness abetted his escape. He even laughed, though nervously, it was eerie to be moving through such pitch.

A dozen paces out, twenty, fifty. He reached the bridge's midpoint — halfway there.

And back on the island the drums started up again.

Calum stopped. He turned. People Park glowed.

My friends, said Raven, his voice echoing, with the guidance of good Gip Poole, and bolstered by your nature, are you ready to believe?

The crowd roared.

Do you believe?

From the thousands in People Park came a frenzied bawling, beastly and primal, hungry and desperate. It chilled Calum. He couldn't move.

Then, please, believe, commanded Raven. Believe!

The drums became thunder — then silence.

Raven howled, *Believe!*

And Calum was swimming in light.

ON THE VIDEOSCREENS the searchlights swung over the water, the Narrows flowed obliviously along. No structure connected the island to the mainland. No craggy fragments jutted out of Topside Drive, the rest dynamited or concealed. Waves slapped the base of the cliffs on either side. Guardian Bridge had vanished, disappeared — it was *gone*.

At first the applause came almost tentatively. Gip, alone onstage, waved. People, emboldened by this, cheered. He climbed atop the white trunk and did a little dance, they looked from him to the screens — *there was no Guardian Bridge!* — and at once the whole park erupted with joy. People whistled and squealed and roared, the crowd thronged, Kellogg and Pearl fell grinning into each other's arms — their boy was a star! With little inward flicks of his fingertips Gip enticed the crowd's worship. Yes, he cried. Now you see the truth! Now you truly believe!

And here were the fireworks: the skies came alive with streaks of colour that ruptured in monstrous luminescent spiders of blue, green, red, purple, gold. More went up, great sparkling pinwheels, rockets, and rainbows, the reds volcanic, the whites like bursting stars, aquatic blues unleashed from the sea floor into the heavens. When the sparks fell tinkling down, everyone's attention returned to the videoscreens.

Raven's done it, said Wagstaffe. Oh my, said Lanyess. Oh my!

As he came into his unit Sam checked his third watch. The hands were stuck at right angles. Before he could turn on the TV, the phone rang. He picked up. Adine?

But Adine was fumbling her way down the stairwell and onto E Street, where the night air hit her face and the world seemed at once to tumble away and close in. She sensed her neighbours out there engaged in a sort of befuddled dance, moving one person to the next to confirm that, yes, the power was out, what had the illustrationist done, no one knew, they should all go to together to the park and see.

Gip continued to grandstand atop the trunk, ignoring NFLM commands to get down and move offstage. Though few people were watching him now — another burst of pyrotechnics was received with oohs and ahhs. Even his parents failed to notice two Helpers approaching the boy from the wings at a low, menacing crouch.

Hello? said Sam to the empty line. Time's machine is broken Adine. Hello?

A hand fell upon Adine's arm and she surprised herself by asking, Debbie?

But no, it was a man, an old man, the hand a gnarled and bony claw. We're going downtown, he said, the Yellowline's out, every-one's walking. Do you need help?

Adine shook her head. No, she said.

But, said the man, can you see?

Yes, she said. I can see.

He released her. Adine sensed him waiting. Out there was darkness, she knew. Though what was the difference between that and this *private* darkness? Her work seemed so vain now, so misguided and confused. Fug it, she said. And she took off the goggles. No light came searing in. The street was a sludge of dim, shuddery shapes — a crowd, she realized, squinting. People.

What a fantastic lightshow the NFLM are treating us to here tonight, said Wagstaffe. Truly a special night for the city, said Isa Lanyess, and a wonderful way to celebrate. And what an honour for us to share it with all of you, watching at home or in Cinecity.

Hello? said Sam again. No reply. Not even breathing. But the silence was that of a coma, secreting a dreamlife in another world.

The Helpers scooped up Gip and deposited him, squirming and reluctant, into his father's arms. Wow, champ, said Kellogg, you were amazing. But the joy in the boy's eyes had dimmed, replaced with a deadened gloss.

From the vacuum in Sam's phone emerged a voice, echoey and faraway. Hello? it said. Sam's breath caught in his throat. And the line went dead. Sam sat on his couch with the receiver in his lap. Slowly, he turned to look at the armoire, its doors barred and locked, and listened for any sound within. Nothing. Not yet.

Meanwhile as Adine joined the convoy trooping east from the Zone, and on the roof of the Temple Griggs and Noodles and Magurk cheersed schnappses to a job well done, and Cora dragged Rupe up the inoperative escalator into Blackacres Station, and in his cell in the Temple's basement Pop hung his head as Havoc — Dack — told him, Enjoy your θtay! and Tragedy/Pea added, You dumb fug, and Olpert and Starx sat numbly watching the fireworks' reflections shatter in Crocker Pond, and at last the hoodied mob disappeared — back underground? — and Debbie crawled out from the bushes, freed her face from the anorak's hood, looked across the city and saw the sky was on fire —

ABOVE IT ALL SPUN the Mayor in her tower, around and around and around.

IX

WHAT IS WAKING, waking is being born. The sky is pale, not the sky of day or night or dusk or dawn, not clouds, but more a lack of sky. A sky that isn't there. Or maybe this is what exists behind the sky, now Calum sees what has been there all along. Staggering to his feet he looks up and down the bridge, the road narrows to twin vanishing points in each direction, these distances feel infinite, the horizons look unattainable, as though they'd keep peeling back and away and on forever.

Calum goes to the railing, looks down. Below shrouded in mist might lie a river, if it is a river it disappears into thicker fog beneath the bridge. If it is a river then the river mirrors the sky, which is to say, colourless. If it is a river its surface is still. There is no current. Were Calum to fling his body off the bridge it would fall in silence and hitting the water not make a splash, if there is water, if not it would fall forever, tumbling end over end, a satellite dislodged from orbit in space.

So Calum steps back into the middle of the bridge.

And sits cross-legged on the yellow dividing line, and breathes short hollow breaths. And lays his hands on the knees of his jeans and looks at the palms of his hands, ridged with lines that mean, somehow, fate and love and health and life. He runs the fingers of one hand along the lines of the other. Squeezes the top knuckle of his right thumb. The flesh engorged with what should be blood does not swell purple, and when released no blood retreats, a rosy hue does not return.

Hello, Calum calls. The word disappears: no echo, no trace, it is as if another mouth has pressed to his mouth and eaten the word, swallowed the word.

Was there never a word?

Calum looks at the sky that isn't quite sky, along the bridge that stretches forever, down at his hands, into the fog that hides what might not be a river.

Hello? says Calum or does he. Does he say then, Hello?

Does he say hello does he not say hello has he not then ever said: hello.

SATURDAY

SATURDAY

What's a city without its ghosts?
Unknown.
Unknown.
Unknown.

— Guy Maddin, My Winnipeg

I

Here was the morning barely. Sometime in the waning hours of Friday night, those uncertain moments before dawn, the cloudcover sealed fontanelle-like over the island and snow began to fall. The temperature dropped and when the sun rose it did so with effort, struggling through fog thick as a pelt. Clouds drooped over the island, the sky nuzzled the ground, everything the same dirty white: the air, the thin crust of snow. Where did earth meet atmosphere, there was no telling.

It was this faint, hazy morning that greeted Kellogg. Waking felt akin to surfacing from the murky depths of a cave into an even murkier swamp. Outside hung that miasmic mist, and for a moment Kellogg had no idea where he was — and who were these people? and who was *he*? It took a moment before he recognized the children in the backseat as his own. The woman asleep in the passenger seat was Pearl, his wife, and he was her husband, Kellogg. They were a family, the Pooles, together, on vacation.

From the huge and vexing and open, Kellogg nestled into the sanctuary of the familiar. He looked from one dreaming Poole to the next, peaceful and perfect. But something nagged at him, watching them sleep. Elsie-Anne, Gip, Pearl, their faces were masks. Who might he be in their dreams, what sort of figure, a hero or villain, triumphant or shamed?

Though Pearl claimed she didn't dream, never had. But everyone dreams, Kellogg told her once, they'd had friends over for dinner, he looked wildly around the table for support. Not me, she'd said, and poured herself more wine. She could be lying: maybe her dreams were too weird to share. Or maybe she was oblivious to her own dreams, which was sad. Sadder: what sort of person had no dreams?

Watching Pearl sleep Kellogg wished for a device with which he could witness his wife's dreams — and then he could tell her about them. But such a device did not exist. Kellogg looked past her, out the window, where snowflakes like little flames tumbled through the campsite's lamplight, and replayed the final hours of the previous evening.

When the khaki-shirted men had escorted Gip back to his parents there'd been something almost apologetic in the way they handed him over — Sir, Ma'am. From that point things petered out: the last firework popped and splattered, the videoscreens shut down, an NFLM rep came onstage and offered a tepid, unmic'd, Thanks for coming, have a great night, and ducked behind the curtains. The crowd lingered with collective, discomfited confusion — there was a sense of unfinished business. Kellogg, though, remained ecstatic. With deep booming pride he hugged his son. You were amazing, champ, he gushed. Wasn't he, Pearly? Everyone was watching you. Everyone saw! But the boy seemed distant. He felt oddly limp in Kellogg's arms. He's tired, said Pearl, prying Gip away, petting his face. We've had a long day, let's get everyone to bed.

The crowd scattered, the air grew cold. Kellogg shivered as he hustled the family up the path out of the common. Along the way Gip kept silent as he was recognized and accosted: You were the boy onstage, how'd he do it? Pearl got snippy with one family who suggested Gip had been in on the trick and was now responsible for explanations. Leave my son alone, Pearl snapped, sweeping him under her arm while Kellogg shrugged and chuckled in a diplomatic way, he hoped.

At their campsite Pearl said, It's too cold for camping, my kids are not freezing to death in a tent tonight, and herded them onto Harry's backseats. Car sleepover, yelled Kellogg, fun! and grinned into the minivan. Gip gazed back blankly, his face emptied of life. What an amazing night! Kellogg roared, and Pearl said, Hush now, get the sleeping bags, you're letting the cold in.

He headed to the tent feeling unsettled. The night had been amazing — hadn't it? To think Gip had been centrestage alongside his idol for the whole miraculous thing, a dream fulfilled, before thousands of witnesses. Though why did the boy now seem so numb? The night struck Kellogg as a jewel — sparkling, perfect, yet flawed when tilted to the light. Worse: with some ghastly embryo fossilized inside.

Outside the tent Kellogg shivered, bedding heaped in his arms. Across the site, inside Harry, was his family, they couldn't see anything beyond the lit-up interior of the minivan. He watched Pearl blow her nose, excavate her nostrils, inspect what she found, and ball the tissue in her fist. The campground was quiet, everyone was going to sleep. The air felt wintry and thin.

And now, the next morning, winter had arrived. Kellogg turned the keys in the ignition, the engine growled and the fans came on with a blast of cold air. And yet still no one woke: cocooned within sleeping bags Elsie-Anne and Gip slept soundly, Pearl leaned against the frosted window, a little ellipsis of clear glass where her breath melted the ice.

Kellogg had to pee. He slid out of the minivan quietly, eased the door shut. A half-inch of snow covered the ground. In the fog floated dark forms that might have been trees, he aimed in their general direction, shivering, and as he zipped back up from the neighbouring site an engine came coughing to life. The red squares of taillights appeared. Holy, said a voice, can't see anything out here.

Another voice responded — quieter, murmuring, followed by the pneumatic wheeze of an opening car trunk. Kellogg moved toward the lights and voices, the squeak and crunch of snow and gravel under his feet. The trunk closed with a whump.

At the neighbouring campsite forms materialized from the mist: a young man, a green hatchback, a camping stove, blue flames wobbled around a tin pot. The car idled and chugged exhaust, the door hung open, and in the passenger seat a young woman flipped through a mess of static on the radio.

Morning, said Kellogg. Some fog.

The man — more of a boy, a fist-shaped medallion dangled from his neck — nodded down at the burner. I'm trying to make coffee.

Not going so hot? Heh.

Kellogg's joke went unheralded. The girl joined them. The radio's like, dead, she said.

The boy pulled the lid of the pot, revealing water as flat as glass.

My family's sleeping a few spots over, said Kellogg. We were camping, but —

Weird, said the girl. Look at the snow! Yesterday was so nice, then, bang, winter, just like that. You ever seen snow *and* fog at the same time? And this shet with the bridge —

What's the um, shet with the bridge? said Kellogg.

They're still blocking off the PPT and Topside, said the boy. I went for a walk up there this morning and a Helper-guy told me — the bridge is just *gone.*

What, still?

Yeah. I mean, it can't be *gone*, said the girl. How are we supposed to get out? We had camping plans this weekend, we aren't even supposed to be here.

Our stupid dorm's being fumigated, so.

And now there's no way off the island.

Could be worse places to be though? said Kellogg.

You're not from here?

My wife is. Originally. We're here on vacation. That was my son onstage last night!

We didn't watch the show, said the boy with pride.

And the magician? Maybe when he turns back up he'll fix —

The girl said, Do you know how much money they spent to bring that guy here?

No, said Kellogg. How much?

She looked blankly at her boyfriend, who offered nothing. Lots, she said. Money they could have used for more important things.

Such as?

Housing programs.

For?

People.

Gotcha, said Kellogg.

This water, said the boy, it's just not boiling.

What I'm saying is, said Kellogg, maybe the trick's not over.

I mean, they've got to do something, said the girl. She looked forcefully and with disappointment at Kellogg, implicating him in this *they*.

They will, he said.

From the fog a voice called, Kell?

He excused himself, discovered Pearl on her knees in Harry's backseat rooting through a mess of wrappers and juiceboxes and snot-wadded facial tissues. The kids were awake, blanketed to their chins and shivering.

Pearl stepped out, took Kellogg by the elbow. I can't find them, she whispered.

Can't find what?

His meds, she said. I can't find Gip's meds.

THE FOG FIT snug as a lid over the island, dying at its edges in raggedy wisps. As the view from Podesta Tower rotated east the Mayor, torso still estranged from the lower half of her body, was faced with People Park: the common was a bowl of milk overflowing into the city. Fog scudded along the streets and up the sides of buildings, thick all the way to the water in every direction.

The deck rotated: Fort Stone, Li'l Browntown, Bebrog, Greenwood Gardens, the Institute's campus knuckled into the island's southeastern corner — all of it hidden under a melancholy lather. To the south, Perint's Cove was also lost in fog, the Islet didn't exist.

To the west the fog spilled through downtown, connected in ropy sinews to the low-slung clouds concealing the office towers' tops, lapped up Mount Mustela right to the Necropolis, in LOT ignored and bounded over and through the gates of the Mews, engulfed Knock Street, threaded into UOT and Blackacres, the tenements swathed, the power still out, in the northwest corner of the island Whitehall was invisible too. And on the westside, as with the east, the fog stopped at the water. As if, thought the Mayor, a wall had gone up around the island.

Now she looked north: where Guardian Bridge had been was only absence. Across the Narrows, the mainland, was fogless and clear, not a wisp reached its shores. NFLM patrols clustered at either end of Topside Drive and at the opening of the People Park Throughline, into which snaked a trail of cars. That morning a queue had begun forming of commuters waiting for the bridge to reopen — or reappear.

Though this she couldn't see, and only knew from the memo Griggs had faxed over at dawn. The gist: At four a.m. some hysteric had broken through the barricade screaming, Smoke and mirrors, smoke and mirrors! and tried to sprint out over the Narrows.

There'd been no cartoonish moment of the guy suspended in space, he'd just plummeted straight into the river. The current had been particularly swift and *Luckily,* reported the NFLM, *there were no witnesses,* and the story had been swept away with him.

Phone, said the Mayor, and Diamond-Wood passed her the handset, retreated, the cord connected them umbilically. The Mayor coiled it around her finger, let it spring back and dangle slackly, listened to the steady bleat of the dialtone. She liked when expecting a call to ambush the person phoning, to pick up before it rang and disorient them, to always have the upperhand.

People who weren't quick and sharp infuriated her, inefficiency was the bane of any city. This was the reason she'd whittled her council in half her first term, why she'd cut the city districts to four, and now met only quarterly with representatives from each quadrant. The Mayor was methodical, which wasn't the same as slow: methodical meant developing a methodology and then operating, swiftly. If life were a minefield, the Mayor reasoned, you informed yourself and blazed into it, never tiptoeing along in meek, weak terror. If your leg got blown off you hopped. And now with a shudder the Mayor thought of her own legs: if you lost both, apparently, you found someone else to push.

Connect me to the Temple, she said.

Diamond-Wood dialled, the handset purred, the Mayor imagined the NFLM line jangling unheeded on some desk, the men asleep in bunkbeds — kids playing firemen but with hairier feet.

The view swung around to People Park. On its north side, the Thunder Wheel looked like a rusty sawblade lodged halfway into a robustly frosted cake. Beneath it, damp with fog, the rides would be shrouded in tarpaulin. Island Amusements was scheduled to open that evening, yet how could it possibly in this?

She let the line ring a couple more times, hung up, ordered, Hit PAUSE.

The deck stopped turning. Everything was still.

Look, she said, pointing to the Thunder Wheel. What a beautiful thing. Do you love this city? I love this city. I was born at Old Mustela Hospital fifty-seven years ago and I've lived here all my life. You know how many times I've left in those fifty-seven years? None. Why would I leave? I've never been on an airplane. On a boat exactly once — the fireworks barge during the centenary celebrations. You don't *need* to leave this place. So why get bent out of shape about being *trapped* here — where else would you rather be?

Silence from Diamond-Wood. The Mayor checked the phone again — nothing — handed the receiver to him, he deposited it into its console. Take off that tape, will you? she said. It's like talking to a coma patient.

He did.

Better?

Yes, he said. Thanks.

Anyway where was I? Oh yes — *trapped*, bah. The idea of being trapped here, it's like a child being trapped in a...in a...wherever children like to be. A store for children's things. Games or what have you!

The Mayor could hear the anxiety rising in her voice. Like a child in an adultless land, she decided, and continued with rekindled vigour: And while these aren't ideal circumstances, doesn't it offer the potential to bring the city together? Maybe it's *exactly* what we need to make us realize how lucky we are! So the bridge is gone, so what! Right?

Well, said Diamond-Wood, the power's still out in the Zone —

Those people are used to struggling! If *anyone* can deal with a little hardship it's them. Few people are aware of this, but I come from poverty.

Oh?

The Mayor peered over her shoulder at her aide: hunched upon his crutches, patchy stubble darkened his cheeks and chin, his uniform had the appearance of a rumpled paper bag. She looked away, continued: Touch green! Grew up in a trailerpark in what was then called South Bay. This was before the Lakeview projects. I was born in a house on wheels. Not literally, I was born at Old Mustela, but a trailer was where I spent the first few months of my life. So I think I know a little something about *struggle*. I *understand* people — rich, poor, young, old, fat, stupid — and that's what makes for an effective leader in times of crisis: empathy.

The phone burbled to life.

Give it to me! she screamed, nearly falling off the dessert cart.

The High Gregories sat around the speakerphone in their underground conference chamber — Griggs, Wagstaffe, Magurk, Noodles. Bean stood at the portal that led up into the Temple, hands behind his back in the pose of niteclub bouncers. In an adjacent chamber, Favours was having his morning treatments administered by two Recruits in latex gloves and surgical masks. From another came whimpering — tears?

Bad news first? said Griggs, his voice as inert as the basement air.

Fine, said the Mayor.

No sign of him, said Wagstaffe.

None? said the Mayor. What is wrong with you people? What did you —

It's nothing we can't sort out, said Griggs.

And Island Amusements? said the Mayor. It's expected to open —

Don't get your gitch in a gotch, said Magurk. That's the fuggin good news.

Everything's all set, said Wagstaffe.

Everything? said the Mayor. I wouldn't say —

Let's meet here for a face-to-face, said Griggs. There's a car waiting for you outside.

Now?

Now.

See you soon! said Wagstaffe cheerily, and the line went dead.

Griggs looked around the table. Anyone hungry?

Noodles nodded.

Bean, said Griggs, fetch us some flats. And wake B-Squad up. I'm sure the Mayor will want some answers from the dynamic duo meant to be keeping tabs on Raven.

SAM SLID BACK the cover from the peephole. The armoire was empty.

If you're there say something okay, he said, and moved his ear to the door.

Silence. Sam touched his face. The scab was dry.

I know you're in there okay, said Sam. I know you can make it look like you're not. But you can't go anywhere Raven. Sam tried the handles: the boards and chains and locks held fast. There's no way out.

Sam placed an apple on the tray he'd affixed through a slot halfway up the door. You can have an apple for breakfast. If you want more I can get more.

He pushed it through, heard the dull thud of the apple falling, put his eye to the peephole. From the bare overhead bulb fanned a cone of yellow light that dwindled in the dark corners. Upon the armoire's newspapered floor sat the apple, gleaming. There was no hint of movement from the shadows, darkness there and nothing more.

If the apple's bruised I can bring you another one okay, said Sam. Or if you don't like apples tell me what you like. I have juice. Or water. Or I could nuke you a meal.

Sam waited, eye at the peephole. Nothing.

The phone rang, the sudden burst of it a small explosion in the still room. Sam stood over the console. It alternated ringing and not — a tinny jangle, then silence, and the silence felt expectant, and Sam synchronized his breathing to it: inhale as the phone rang, and exhale between rings, not picking up because it would be the same voice, a deadened echo as though the call were coming from the bottom of the lake. Like speaking to his own drowned ghost.

The phone stopped ringing. The room waited. Then, from the armoire: scraping. Sam held his breath. A thump. And then something scrabbly and wet-sounding — the watery snap and crunch of a mouth biting hard with its teeth into an apple.

AT THE SOUND of fluttering Calum raises his head. Swooping down from above is a grey bird. A pigeon it seems at first but as it stills itself in the air with a slow backward beating of wings it might be a dove, though dirty or dusted with newsprint or ash, he thinks.

The bird, whatever it is, lights upon the railing of the pedestrian walkway, its claws curl around the metal bar, and tilting its head regards Calum with something evaluative or curious. He stares back. He feels cold. He laces his arms around his shins and pulls them close and wedges his chin between his knees. In the bird's pinkish eyes glitters something suspicious, he thinks. It doesn't trust him. It can't be trusted.

Calum says, Go away. And the words again are eaten.

The bird lifts one foot, then the other, puffs, shudders, but doesn't go anywhere.

So Calum lunges at it — though halfheartedly, if he caught it what would he do. The bird maybe knows this, it makes no effort to fly away. It only regards Calum steadily with those eyes like two droplets of something's pale and mucosal blood. Calum feints again to smack it but the bird holds its ground undaunted, so he lowers his hand and for a moment the bird looks familiar, he thinks, though his memory feels emptied and what he can't think is from where or when, or where where might even be or when, when.

He takes another swipe. Deftly the bird swerves out of reach, resettles on the railing, nods, caws, squawks, chirps, what does a bird think or mean to say, is it taunting him or only making noise for itself. Watching the bird gloat Calum feels repelled and repulsed.

Go on, he says, get out of here.

But his voice sounds like a tape played in reverse, each syllable sucks back into itself.

He looks up and down the bridge which narrows identically in both directions to little pinprick endpoints, tunnelling into a sky that has forgotten how to be a sky. Which way to go, does it matter. All that matters maybe is movement, away from this bird.

Calum picks a direction, he doesn't know which one, and begins to walk.

II

DEBBIE AWOKE ALONE. The covers on Adine's side of the bed were undisturbed.

Adine? she called, sitting up. Adine?

No reply. She got up.

In the den Pop's bedding remained heaped in the middle of the floor. The bathroom door was open, no one was inside, nor was anyone in the kitchen. Other than Jeremiah, blinking at her from the couch, the apartment was empty — Debbie did not count herself.

Normally the fridge hummed, the mixing bowls atop it jingled. But with no power everything was silent, the air brittle. From the couch Jeremiah, tail alert and coiled at its tip into a fiddlehead, watched her. Debbie shivered, scooped the blanket off the floor and took it to the window nook, swaddled herself, and curled up looking out over the street: but there was nothing to see, UOT was smothered in fog.

Across the room the blank screen of the TV glowed a greenish eggshell hue, it had a light of its own even when it wasn't on. Where was Adine? Out there stumbling through the city in her sweatsuit and goggles — Adine out in the city, how absurd.

Though there'd been a time when she'd loved the city and in a way the city had brought them together. When they'd met, Debbie had been still new enough to it, having spent her undergrad years mostly on the Institute's campus and in the adjacent student neighbourhood spoken of myopically as *the ghetto*. Everything west of the park seemed impossibly vast and intimidating and arcane.

Adine had spent her whole life on the island, she navigated it effortlessly, she knew things and places and secrets. Debbie's exuberance and naivety invigorated her and so the city came alive for them both. Though it wasn't just living in the city, it was talking about it: so much happened every day, hilarious and thrilling and sad. So they opened themselves to its people, its streets, its clichés and mysteries, and everywhere they found stories to recount to each other.

Once, during an early-morning Blueline commute, an elderly woman's newspaper-wrapped fish came alive between her feet, and the woman — *so old she was made of dust*, Debbie would later poeticize her — calmly took the flopping creature by the tail, beat it to death against the train's dirty floor, and reclined with a nonchalance meant to suggest the blood and scales at her feet had always been there. Witnessing all this from across the aisle Debbie was already skipping forward to that evening, when she'd tell it to Adine, and they'd cackle together in horror and delight.

Back then despite living on the opposite side of the city she spent most nights at Adine's, and every minute apart provided stories for their next meeting. But they never had enough time: there was always too much to tell, their voices bubbled overtop of each other's, everything frantic and urgent — *and then! and then! and then!* At night they had to start setting two alarms: one to wake them in the morning, the other to indicate a time they absolutely had to shut up and sleep, and after which they weren't allowed another word.

After a year of this Debbie moved in. Technically she and Adine began to share everything, though quickly there seemed less to share. Something happened: the city lost its drama, fewer were the moments of the sublime, the absurd, the ridiculous. In stitching their lives together Debbie began to fear they'd sealed the space, that chasm of mystery and possibility between them, where what was most alive about their relationship had crackled and zipped.

But if the real city no longer held any magic for them, Debbie had wondered, perhaps Adine's tiny replica version might. The first time Debbie suggested visiting her Sand City — *just to see!* — Adine had scowled and scoffed. But after some persuading, up there alone in the Museum's upper gallery they'd gone quiet before it, almost reverential. Adine ran her hand over the glass. There it is, she'd said simply, and Debbie had scooted up behind her and laid her head on Adine's shoulder so she could see what Adine saw and told her, It's beautiful. And then: I'm sorry.

Jeremiah hopped up onto the window ledge, mewling, back arched, tail rippling at its tip. Good dog, said Debbie, running her hand over the cat's spine. There was something in his fur, some dander or fluffy lint, Debbie plucked it free — a feather. For a moment she assumed he'd clawed open a pillow, something he used to do as a kitten, and then she remembered the bird. Oh no, bad dog, she scolded him, and went into the kitchen.

On the sill sat the newspaper-lined casserole dish into which she'd laid the dove. The window was open, mist hung thick and colourless over the street. In the dish were some feathers, a yolky smear of poop — but no bird. Oh, Jeremiah, sighed Debbie, taking his face in her hands. Did you eat that poor bird? The cat offered a slow, bemused blink, and flicked his tongue over his nose. Then he squirmed away.

Debbie looked under the table, behind the stove, anywhere the feeble creature might have been either dumped or gotten lost. From the kitchen window she struggled to make out the street below, let alone a carcass upon the sidewalk. The fog was solid as cement.

She removed the newsprint from the dish and unfolded it on the countertop as if it might reveal some clue. Maybe the dove had flown? The idea swelled from fantasy to probability. It had been simply stunned, Debbie told herself, and over the course of the night revived and, at some early morning hour, found the strength to push off out the window, caught an updraft that lifted it over the city, up through the clouds into the sky, where it wheeled and danced, maybe, once again free.

AT SOME POINT midmorning, time meant nothing in Cinecity, the images onscreen went live again: first-person footage of the downtown streets, fog whisking this way and that, a faint snowfall sprinkling down. The shot plodded along between office towers, everything silent save the rustle and squeak of popcorn breakfasts taken in the theatre.

These were the first live images Adine and the rest of the full house had seen since midnight, when she and her westend cavalcade had arrived just in time to watch a dishevelled Lucal Wagstaffe and a possibly drunk Isa Lanyess announce they were ending their broadcast. After the analgesic tone of an EBS test the colour bars were replaced with a title card in black and white: *The Silver Jubilee, A Second Look.*

This comprised hastily spliced-together We-TV footage of the previous night's festivities, and began with monologues performed in garages and bedrooms around the island, from the Mews to Fort Stone, the popular acumen of the masses, all those predictions and insights edited into one rambling overture that echoed and contradicted and befuddled itself before things cut to a happy Li'l Browntown family painting wings on one another's faces and chanting Ra-*ven* on their driveway.

Cut to a disembodied voice narrating tremulous handheld footage of the crowds descending into the park, hundreds of napes of necks and backs of knees with the view sometimes flashing skyward where sunspots seared the lens. A new voice took over, someone else shooting the opposite end of the park. All of this was set to a jaunty carnivalesque score, the time flashing at oddly progressing intervals: 13:40, 14:10, etc.

The daylight began to deepen. An extended segment featured a surprisingly well-researched and thorough tour of the Museum of Prosperity, right up to the top floor, and here was Adine's Sand City, and seeing it she felt a slight pang of — what? Something proprietary, violation, shame, yet beneath it an ember of pride. With the camera zooming in on her model it seemed unreal, or too real, the miniature buildings expanded to the size of actual buildings. Feeling overwhelmed, Adine's thoughts retreated into memories — of Debbie. Debbie who had once cranked a song on the radio, claiming it was *theirs*, and Adine had run to the bathroom and pretended to barf. But if anything was theirs it was the Sand City. Visiting the Museum's top floor had become the thing to do when there was nothing to do, they'd Yellowline over and Redline up and wave at the girls working ticketsales and climb the tower and there it was, under glass.

They'd tell each other stories then. When they ran out of stories they'd make some up: What if Isa Lanyess was actually sent here from some other planet to jellify our minds so she could plant her eggs into them and then all our heads would hatch millions of little space-alien babies? Adine suggested once. What if Lucal Wagstaffe's a secret vegetarian? countered Debbie. Adine had a key that locked the door, if she needed to. And sometimes Debbie would fix her with a sidelong lingering look, and she did.

Though these thoughts sparked irritation. The model wasn't Debbie's, it wasn't *theirs* — it was hers, Adine's, only Adine's.

Debbie was an interloper. She had so much else, all her friends and causes, her stupid cumin-drenched dinners and *community*. She shouldn't get to possess or even share the thing Adine had created before they'd met.

Debbie was the one responsible for its display now on the bigscreen — this violation, this corruption. Of course the public could visit the Sand City whenever they wanted, and that was bad enough, but simultaneously seen by so many people like this, with its creator reduced to another set of ogling eyes, felt cheap and humiliating.

But then the image dissolved: from the roof of the boathouse someone made wide sweeping pans of the mobbed park, which became a montage, one image flashed to the next, until the moment the Zone's power had cut out. All the westenders who'd missed the illustration edged forward in their seats. The tubby little superfan, Gip Poole, was brought onstage. The crowd went wild, the trunk opened, Raven got inside, the boy locked him in. Cut to one of those massive screens that flanked the gazebo, footage of the footage of Guardian Bridge, and the lights went out and came back on and the bridge was gone, and everyone in Cinecity gasped, even those not seeing it for the first time.

Cue fireworks.

Fade to black.

Credits.

The End.

And now this preamble to the main event, *All in Together Now*, the movie for the people by the people: a camera trolling the streets of downtown. South on Paper Street, out of downtown to Lakeside Drive, down to the shoreline, nosing out of the mist with the curiosity of a stage manager scoping the crowd between parted curtains. If this made the water an auditorium, there was no audience. The view was clear: no fog, no people, just the crimped steel of the lake all the way to the horizon.

Little flashes pocked the water where waves flared into white-caps. Otherwise it and sky were the same brooding grey, clouds too sullen to storm. No one was out boating or swimming. There was something soothing about the quiet chaos of the lake, undisturbed by human beings, wave after wave slicing up and frothing and dying. Adine watched. Everything was quiet. A pall had fallen over the theatre, silent and serene.

IN THE TEMPLE's basement, upon their respective wheeled devices at either end of a conference table piled with breakfast flats, trembled Favours, drool snaking down his chin, and the Mayor, whom a re-ducktaped Diamond-Wood had pushed right up to the table to conceal her lower half. To Favours' left were the High Gregories (Griggs, Wagstaffe, Magurk, Noodles), and to his right, the L2's (Bean, Walters, Reed). In the corner, with the guilty, squirming silence of two soot-smeared arsonists awaiting trial, on stools perched Starx and, like a child in his father's clothes, Olpert Bailie.

The air was thick with that stale cornchip odour that men exude in basements. Into the musty silence came a thumping sound from the other side of the wall, followed by faint chirps — someone crying?

Big fella, said Magurk, beckoning to Starx. Come with me for a sec.

Starx stood, bowed, and followed the Special Professor out of the room.

The Mayor spoke: Where is the magician.

Illustrationist, corrected Wagstaffe.

We have no idea, said Griggs.

No idea? said the Mayor. Not the answer I was looking for. He's just gone, poof, like the — like the fuggin bridge?

To be fair, Mrs. Mayor, said Griggs, Raven never told us how things were going to work, just his basic schedule. Our job was largely site logistics.

The Mayor opened her mouth to speak, but was interrupted by growling from the other side of the wall — then a dull whumping sound and Magurk's pennywhistle voice shrieking, You like that, fatty? There was a pause, an exchange of words — Olpert thought he heard Starx say, He's all right — a slap, another whump, and Magurk was back with Starx trailing after him, looking dismayed.

Magurk reassumed his place among the HG's: Sorry about that, me and the big fella here got things under control. Isn't that right, big fella?

Starx sucked his teeth.

So, continued the Mayor, despite shutting down the north shore to traffic, you didn't know the bridge was going to disappear. Nor did you have any idea that *he'd* disappear. And now — you're as lost as me.

Yes, said Griggs.

You pretty much nailed it right there, said Wagstaffe, beaming.

But your men were watching him! They didn't notice anything? Did they help him escape? Did the stage have trapdoors?

He doesn't use trapdoors, muttered Starx.

Helpers don't speak until told, said Magurk. Do we have to get the ducktape?

The Mayor eyed Magurk as if he were a slug she'd found in her salad, then spoke to Griggs: Who were the men in charge of Raven?

Him, Starx, said Griggs, pointing. And the redhead — Bailie.

Hi, said Olpert.

Raven works alone, said Starx, and we weren't ever privy —

Both of you! screamed Magurk. Silentium!

I don't care who talks, said the Mayor. I just want to know what's going on.

Everyone looked around the room at everyone else, but no one said anything.

Wagstaffe chuckled. Maybe it really was magic?

You hear that? the Mayor asked Griggs. Was it magic, Babbage?

Whoa, Mrs. Mayor, said Wagstaffe, that's the Head Scientist you're talking to. Patronyms, please!

Well, said Magurk, *something* made the bridge disappear. And your legs —

Griggs held up a hand to silence them both.

The Mayor scrubbed her eyesockets with the heels of her hands. Then, blinking, she looked from one High Gregory to the next: Wagstaffe (grinning), Griggs (ineffable), Magurk (nostrils whistling), Favours (sleeping), and Noodles, who had yet to speak, lips pursed within a bristly white goatee shorn into a perfect square. He stared woodenly at the Mayor, perhaps waiting to glimpse whatever hid behind her.

What about you, sir? Mr. — the Mayor checked her notes — Sobolin?

Noodles nodded once, slowly.

This one doesn't say anything? the Mayor said.

Noodles is judicious, said Reed, bowed his head, apologized for speaking.

The Mayor turned to Starx. Stars, is it? Billy? What. *Happened.*

Starx eyed Magurk.

Speak, said Griggs.

Mrs. Mayor, said Starx, we weren't assigned to do much more than make sure Raven was comfortable and that he got around to his events. In this city there's not much you have to worry about security-wise, which is such a testament to the NFLM's fine work —

The Mayor made an on-with-it gesture.

Starx continued: Maybe we haven't considered that this might all be part of the trick. Him disappearing, I mean. As in, there might be more to come.

Smoke and mirrors, said Wagstaffe, laughing. No one else laughed.

Tell me, Mr. Starx, said the Mayor, if we don't find this magician, am I going to have to see a doctor about my legs?

Starx caught Olpert sneaking a peek beneath the table and elbowed him in the ribs. His partner buckled, breath escaping in a woof.

Fug if it's fair we're being blamed for this, said Magurk, smacking the table with a hairy paw. Best event the city's ever seen. You ask people — he gestured vaguely at the surface — and they'll tell you they had the time of their lives last night.

Favours brayed. Olpert looked at him, expecting more: but the old man's head slumped to his chest, back into catatonia.

Griggs took a flat from the tray, nibbled a corner. I think, Mrs. Mayor, what we're trying to tell you is that last night was about giving something back to the people, and we did that. *We*, Mrs. Mayor, did that. *We* made it happen — *we* funded the whole thing, *we* organized it, *we* staffed it, and *we* made sure it went off without a hitch.

Without a *what*? The Mayor's voice was shrill. How about the teeny-weeny hitch that I can't walk? And, oh right, the other small hitch that the person responsible is missing? And the other as-of-yet-unrelated-but-it-doesn't-take-a-genius-to-do-the-math hitch that our artist laureate's memorial statue is *also* missing. And, oh! I almost forgot! That other barely-worth-mentioning hitch — anyone? *Anyone*? Allow me: Guardian Bridge is *gone*. It — the Mayor tapped the tabletop with each word — Is. Not. *There*.

She was on a roll: And I'm sorry, *event*? You make it sound like this was just a way to fill a weekend. Have you appleheads completely forgotten that the whole thing was supposed to be commemorative? Or was that *never* on your radar? It's not called a Silver Jubilee for the pretty name. There's, oh, a certain little park we're meant to be celebrating. A little park that transformed the city? Twenty-five years ago? A little park that is going to be here long after your stupid magician goes flying away in his helicopter.

The helicopter, said Noodles.

A miracle! said the Mayor. He speaks! He was listening!

Oh, the Imperial Master always listens, said Griggs.

I listen to all kinds of things, Noodles purred.

His sudden animation made Olpert uneasy. The room was already cryptlike enough, and now a corpse had leapt up off the slab to speak.

What are you thinking, Noodles? said Wagstaffe.

I think, said Noodles, that if Raven's helicopter is still here, then he's on the island.

Touch green, said the Mayor.

Quiet there, said Magurk. Noodles is speaking.

What else, Noodles?

The boy.

Which boy, Noodles?

The boy that was onstage. We must find that boy. He saw something.

And the Imperial Master bowed his head.

Mr. Noodles has spoken, said the Mayor. Amen and hallelujah.

The boy though, yes, said Griggs. Gip, was it? Goode?

Sorry, Griggs, just one second here, said Magurk. Can we backtrack for a moment? I resent the insinuation, Mrs. Mayor, that our organization doesn't value civic pride.

Don't talk to me about civic pride! I was *born* here. This is *my* city.

And I wasn't? yelled Magurk. And, I'm sorry, *whose* city is it?

Special Professor, please, cautioned Griggs.

But the Mayor was riled. You care about this city? she screamed, almost levitating off her dessert cart, neck strained into sinuous cords. Then where is he? *Where is he!*

And then she fell.

The room went still. The Mayor, or her upper half, lay by Olpert's feet, eyes closed. He gazed down at the greying half-woman discarded on the floor, struck by how drastically she resembled a seamstress's dummy.

I got this, said Starx, swept her into his arms and replaced her atop the dessert cart. From the table he took a roll of ducktape and adhered her torso and legs to their respective tiers. Everyone pretended not to watch, the air stiffened with feigned nonchalance, it was like a breastfeeding. Starx bowed, retreated, the Mayor coughed, smoothed the lapels of her jacket.

Into the silence from the next room came whimpering.

That fat sack of *shet*, roared Magurk, and stormed out.

Mrs. Mayor, tell me what you need, said Griggs. We're here. We can help.

This is my city. *My* city. I will not see it spiral into chaos. There was a plan for this weekend, an agenda. You've got your *Spectacular*, sure, but what about families —

Island Amusements is scheduled to open as planned, said Griggs. Why wouldn't it?

And the movie, said Wagstaffe. Don't forget! Our movie *for* the people —

By the people, chorused Bean and Walters and Reed. This time they were not scolded, instead Wagstaffe continued, beaming: *All in Together Now!* It's going to be great.

Griggs smiled thinly. Mrs. Mayor, while our men look for Raven — and we *will* find him — we'll send these two men, Starx and Bailie, to find the boy. A chance to redeem yourselves, said Griggs, and Noodles nodded, nodded, nodded some more.

Okay, said Starx, standing, hauling Olpert to his feet.

Magurk appeared in the doorway — shirtless, his chest so shaggily haired it appeared a rodent clung to his nipples.

Good luck, he said, sneering at Starx, finding anything in that fuggin fog.

III

THIS IS GOOD, finding my knapsack, Gip said, towed along by his mother as the Pooles marched in a tight grim formation through the foggy campground, the gently falling snow. So I can get the *Grammar*? And then I'll be able to figure out where Raven's gone? And maybe even how he vanished the bridge? And how he had me onstage? It was like he picked me because he *knew*. Like he knew, Mummy, are you even listening? Like he knew that I was his biggest fan so maybe do you think he wants me to put everything right? Like it was a sign? Like it's up to me now?

That's a lot of responsibility, honey, for a boy your age, said Pearl, blew her nose, tucked the tissue into her sleeve. Stay close, we can barely see anything.

We'll get your knapsack, Gibbles, don't worry, said Kellogg, with Elsie-Anne wobbling atop his shoulders.

Gip kept talking, his voice trembling and delicate. Every sentence swung up into a wavering interrogative, questions that weren't questions, questions that only demanded being heard. The boy had come to life a bit since breakfast, Kellogg thought, eyeing him warily, but still seemed less than himself.

The Pooles came out of Lakeview Campground at the Ferryport, no boats were running. A sinew of fog linked Perint's Cove to the

Islet, where it collected in a cataractal haze. Otherwise the view south was promise-clear to the horizon.

Beyond the roundabout where Lakeside Drive met Park Throughline lights stabbed through the mist in crimson spears.

Did someone crash? Kellogg said, and slid Elsie-Anne down to a piggyback.

The fog parted: one car sheared in half in the ditch, another upturned onto its roof. Around the accident gathered emergency vehicles, sirens flashed, pink flares sparkled, yet the scene was silent.

Good thing we walked, said Kellogg.

Except now my knee's bugging me, said Pearl, reaching down to massage it.

Is it, Kellogg said vacantly, watching two paramedics haul a stretcher out of the ditch and slide the body-shaped figure upon it into a waiting ambulance.

Limping slightly, Pearl led the family up the Throughline. Traffic was stalled bumper to bumper in the northbound lanes. To every car and van and truck corresponded a family, some huddled for warmth inside, others had unloaded lawnchairs and gathered around little bonfires on the shoulder. Farther along there looked to have been an accident, a white coupe angled into the ditch. Engines idled, but no one was going anywhere. There was no way off the island.

What's everyone waiting for, said Gip.

To go home, said Kellogg.

To escape, said Pearl.

But there's no bridge, said Gip, and don't you think I could save all these people, Mummy? We have to get my book, what if someone found it and they don't know that I'm the one who's supposed to finish the illustration?

Gip, said Pearl. We'll get your book. But this has to stop.

Kellogg set Elsie-Anne down. Dad's a bit tired, you mind walking?

It's okay, she said, hugging her purse. Familiar can help.

At the edge of the poplars the Throughline ducked underground and ran beneath the common all the way to Topside Drive, where it surfaced again at the gates of Island Amusements. The Pooles skirted the line of cars disappearing into the tunnel, climbed up top, and looked down into the park. Nothing below, just a milky wash of fog, the closest poplars appeared as shipmasts in a misty harbour.

Wow, said Kellogg. Think we can find anything in that?

I'll do it, said Pearl.

How's that, Pearly?

I'll go get his bag. If it's not there I'll find someone. Event staff or whoever. You take the kids to the Museum. We can meet back up later. Go to Island Amusements maybe.

Not a bad idea, said Kellogg, and pulled the CityGuide out of his backpocket. How about it, guys, want to see some exhibits? They've got a model of the city there, Gibbles — and hey look at this! Kellogg tore out a coupon. Two-for-one entry for kids! One of you guys gets in free!

Why does Mummy keep leaving us? said Elsie-Anne.

Leaving us? Ha, Annie, she's not *leaving* us. Just knows the city, she'll be back.

Will she? said Elsie-Anne. Familiar's not sure.

Kellogg frowned. I'm beginning to have it up to *here* with Familiar.

Yeah, Dorkus, said Gip, Mummy's our only hope of finding the *Grammar*.

That's the spirit, said Kellogg, wrapping his kids under his arms. This is Mummy's town! If anyone's going to find your knapsack, it's Mummy. Right, Mummy?

Let's hope, said Pearl.

A REAL WRITER, Isa Lanyess repeatedly told her staff, was meant to have a voice. Yet Debbie's writer's voice always felt distant, a vague echo toward which she'd only ever leant, squinting, like a deaf person with an ear trumpet. The voice was faint, or a hallucination, or there was too much clutter, too many other voices from outside and within, a cacophony of selves all clamouring for attention. All she could ever make out was its timbre: meek, timid and doubtful and meek.

The night before, down in the belly of the city, she'd gotten the closest she'd ever been to this voice, or something like it, before the power had gone out. Now Debbie sat in the window nook in a square of limpid daylight, the streets clogged with fog, trying to summon it back. But worry muddied her thoughts: where was Adine, had Debbie driven her away, would she come back? Over and over she replayed their fight, felt stupid for fleeing it, she should have stayed, said something . . .

Maybe things could still be fixed with words, thought Debbie, and she decided to write Adine a letter. She fetched her notebook and settled back into the window nook. But where to begin? What she wrote had to be genuine, from that essential part of herself she'd almost found in Whitehall, not as the cartoonish maudlin goof she'd come to play against Adine's cold cynic. But with the pen hovering over the page as always she was a little lost. What to say? How to say it?

All she could come up with were memories of happier times. Look, she wanted to tell Adine, see when we were happy, see how happy we can be? Though what was wrong with happiness, she thought. Maybe what they needed was exactly that — a celebration and reminder. She settled on a story: their first kiss.

They'd gone to Budai Beach so Adine could show Debbie how erosion would have swallowed her Sand City. The night was moonless. They slipped out of their shoes and sat where the waves swished up onto the shore and withdrew fizzing into the lake.

Adine's leg brushed Debbie's, retreated, then she reached over with her toes and playfully pinched Debbie's calf, and Debbie yelped and Adine leaned down to press her lips to Debbie's leg. When she came up her face was close. Neither of them said anything. Everything felt a little lost in the dark. Trembling, Debbie leaned in and — miracle! — Adine was doing the same. They kissed and Debbie thought, This is the most perfect kiss in the history of kisses. And after an instant or forever Adine pulled away and said, Fuggin *finally*, holy shet.

Debbie recalled a funny interpretation that had always batted mothlike around the fringes of this memory: *When we first kissed,* wrote Debbie, *it was like two halves of the same strawberry pressed back together.* Reading this over, her cheeks flushed. She could hear Adine's laugh, a skewer that pricked and went sliding into her heart, pictured her puckering her lips and teasing, Don't be shy, put my strawberry together. Don't make fun of me! Debbie'd wail. You're mean!

She dropped her pen. Here she was once again, performing herself in caricature. Always Debbie gushed and swooned, safely mawkish and too much, and Adine played the cruel realist, cutting her down with jokes. Though it felt good to make her laugh, and eventually Debbie would be laughing too. This dynamic preserved the illusion that they were still having fun — and it was, actually, fun. But also exhausting: fearing them corny Debbie buried her most heartfelt thoughts somewhere inaccessible even to herself. And Adine? She wondered if their theatrics had numbed Adine to her own heart entirely.

From the front door came a creaking sound.

Debbie sprung from the ledge. Adine?

It was only the apartment, its rickety walls spoke their own dialect of ticking and groans. *Adine?* echoed through the empty rooms. Debbie did this often, called her name, sometimes for no reason — it just came out, midsentence while reading or doing the dishes: Adine? And when Adine came harrumphing into the room, hands on hips, and Debbie would have to invent some excuse as to why she needed her. What was this instinct, akin to some nightmare-stricken child pawing for a parent in the dark: Adine, Adine, Adine?

But now she didn't come. The letter lay unfinished and abandoned somewhere between thoughts. Fog choked E Street. Adine was out there somewhere in it, thinking spitefully of Debbie. But where? To whom might she flee? At Sam's maybe — but the phone was dead, there was no way to call. The island suddenly seemed too huge, its streets sprawling in vast and terrifying catacombs within the mist.

Debbie tore out a page from her notebook, wrote a quick purposeful note: *Not sure where you are. Worried. Heading out to find you. Sorry about last night. See you back here if you come home first. Love, Deb.* This she taped to the TV, collected her jacket and keys, and with a glance over the apartment, taking everything in, realized that Adine might not be able to read it. But she'd left. She'd gone somewhere. She couldn't have done it blind. So the note was a gesture of faith, thought Debbie, as she headed out into the city, making sure to leave the door unlocked.

CALUM HAS NO idea how long he's been walking. The scene keeps repeating: the bridge is identical with the same beams and girders and lampposts and the smooth roadway split with the yellow dividing line, the horizon never gets any closer, there is no way to gauge how much distance he's travelled and no change in light to suggest the progression of hours. Also each step feels part of a steady fluid motion that his body performs outside of itself, churning along the bridge so along the bridge his body walks, toward — toward what, toward nothing.

He remembers hearing a voice, the voice hasn't returned. From which direction did it come and should he be seeking or escaping it, Calum doesn't know, he doesn't know which he is doing anyway. The silence out here is cottony, a river would make some watery whispering noise but whatever's below doesn't, it just hovers blackly beneath the mist and everything's dampened and the only noise sometimes is the bird: and here is the bird, the fup-fup of its wings as it flies by and disappears, where does it go, Calum wonders. All he sees is the sky, and the bridge, so he walks.

The air smells of water. Nothing is getting closer: there is no nearing shore, just the endless bridge which slopes gently to an apex beyond which it seems to slope down, though Calum is perennially on the upslope, the apex always just beyond reach, he feels himself chasing a wave as it rolls steadily away.

It feels, Calum thinks, like being on some enormous tread-mill. The girders and beams and lampposts he passes indicate momentum, yet they are the same, the same, the same. He seems to be a character, he thinks, in a piece of cheap amateur cinema with the scenery cranked around and around on an endlessly repeating scroll.

And if this is a film then Calum's body is just an illusion, he thinks, a mirage fidgeting in and out of existence, and if the projector breaks or stops Calum will shudder for a moment and then fade and cease to even be. Like something dreamed and destroyed upon waking. And so to exist he must keep moving, toward the bridge's peak, toward nothing, just on along the bridge and forever and ever on.

THE TRAY PUNCHED through the slot, a jeering tongue. Sam approached cautiously. Upon it was an applecore nibbled into an hourglass and already browning. He peered through the peephole. The armoire was empty.

You ate the apple Raven, said Sam, so I know you're in there Raven.

He shifted his ear to the peephole, listened.

Outside a sprinkler spat arcs of water over the roominghouse lawn.

I can't even let you out if I wanted to okay. I don't even have the combination of this lock. There's a way I guess of getting it open, a boy showed me how from your book. But I don't know how. I don't remember. I never knew.

Sam removed the applecore, pushed the tray in square with the door. From underground there was no sign of time's machine starting up again. The floor didn't judder or vibrate, the silence down there felt booming and hollow. And his third watch was still stopped. Now the end would be like a train barrelling headlong to a precipice, the tracks running out, and the whole thing hurtling over the edge.

You have to help us, said Sam. You have to okay. I've done all the work and —

From inside the armoire came the sound of a book opened in a windstorm, pages flapping madly. Sam peeked in. Something ragged and panicked fretted through the dim light: a bird. It bumped against the ceiling, flung itself against the door, settled. A few feathers puffed through the crack, drifted to the carpet.

I can't let you out okay, said Sam, even if I wanted to.

The armoire shuddered with another collision, the bird squawked, hit the door again, beak and claws ticking.

Please stop.

It seemed to listen. Stillness prevailed. From beyond the basement the sprinkler sputtered and hissed.

Sam stepped hesitantly toward the armoire.

The tray slid out of the door. Upon it was the bird — a dove — lying on its side, motionless and serene, eyes glazed, freshly dead, and served up as a dish.

ON CINECITY's bigscreen appeared another title card. It explained that before that afternoon's premiere of *All in Together Now* the theatre would screen a Best of We-TV countdown. This began with *Lakeside Drives*, an utterly unwatched show that consisted of a single tracking shot of the eponymous thoroughfare's centreline, inch by inch of yellow paint striping black bitumen, from one end of the island to the other, and back — meant, Adine guessed, to be experimental, but without explanation only boring and bad. Everyone booed.

Next: the island's community theatre troupe. Strange and solemn music played while shadowy figures in black undulated around a royal banquet, and just as the King opened his mouth to speak he was replaced with grainy film of a *Y's Classic*, all that maroon and white thronging in the stands as time wound down toward a championship, and that became two matronly looking women poaching themselves in a hot tub and reciting highlights from their daughters' diaries, and that in turn transformed into something else, and then something else, and so on.

It was weird to be *watching* TV again, thought Adine. And while this was exactly how she'd always navigated channels at home — relentless flipping — experiencing it at Cinecity, on this scale, in a roomful of strangers, was much more disorienting. With the images so enormous and the sound stereophonic and everywhere, her senses were overcome. She felt trapped on some endless babbling stream, forced to leap from stone to stone before each one flooded: establishing a foothold then plunging ahead to the next, just hopping along without a purpose or destination.

But more than that, the swift flicking through all those lives seemed deeply sinister. Each fleeting glimpse of existence suggested not only mortality but the expendability of people too. This was made even more tragic when shouts of recognition rang out in the theatre (Hey it's me! — Hey it's you! — I know that person, hey!). People delighted in seeing themselves or someone they knew up there, gigantic and famous, each a bit more popular than the last. But celebrations were brief before each station was supplanted with something better.

Listening to voices exclaim and rejoice and awkwardly fade, Adine forced her mind to cloud over, to abstract the people and places onscreen into shapes, shadows, patterns of colour. Wasn't that more honest? Those weren't people up there but pictures, illusions of life. So she let them be that — just light — and let the sound also blur into formless noise. Every so often this reset, nonsense hiccupped into more nonsense, the rhythm soporific, lulling Adine into a dreamy stupor.

She sank into her chair. The theatre faded. She felt removed from everything. If time in Cinecity had become an abstraction now so was space. She had only a peripheral awareness of having a body. Her mind was a whitewalled room. And then into the emptiness stabbed a voice. And though it was hushed the words were clear: *I don't think I can take much more of this.*

Adine blinked. Up there onscreen was Faye Rowan-Morganson.

It's just too much, she said, twisting a lock of black hair around a finger. *I know no one's watching,* she said, and paused.

Adine sat up, moved to the edge of her seat.

No one at all.

Faye Rowan-Morganson was younger than she'd had imagined, the cheekbones a little more drastic, and darker, and she wore makeup. But that was not the biggest surprise — most startlingly, she was naked. Or at least appeared to be, visible only from the shoulders up, the camera in tight, the background blurred. Even so, Adine felt she was meeting a long-lost childhood friend, now an adult — not an exact equivalent of the version in her mind, but the essence matched: mournful, fatigued, unmistakably her.

No one in the theatre spoke up, no one seemed to know Cinecity's latest star. Or if they did, like Adine they didn't say.

Well, Faye Rowan-Morganson told the camera, *tomorrow's Thursday.* Her tone was one of resignation. *As I've been saying, that'll be it for me, and by the time you see this —*

The channel flipped: a woman in a yellow bandana and a heavily bearded man, cross-legged, bongos in their laps, were providing heartfelt tips on how best to transmit the Essential Soul through percussion. Their eyes were intense. You have to be one with the drum, advised the woman. I snuggle mine, said her husband. Yes, she said, nodding sagely, it's a very good idea to snuggle your drum.

IV

13

BY MIDDAY ALL that was left of the flats was a puddle of grease, and Magurk — still shirtless, distended belly resembling a lightly furred, bulbous gourd — had popped the top button of his khakis. Since her fall the Mayor had retreated into an almost barometric silence that loomed at the edge of the conversation in a grey solemn wall. She sat pushed away from the table with her arms crossed while Griggs outlined the NFLM's plans and Noodles presided behind tented fingers — nodding, always nodding.

We'll open Island Amusements at six, Griggs explained, and channel all the traffic up the Throughline into the parking lot. He dispatched Bean to oversee the operation of rides and concessions. Silentium, Logica, Securitatem, Prudentia, advised Griggs.

Good lookin out, said Bean, puffed his inhaler, and hurtled eagerly up the ramp.

The next order of business was the ICTS. Power was out only in UOT, Blackacres, and Whitehall, but because no trains could turn around in the Barns the whole Yellowline was frozen. Walters and Reed and their moustaches were sent to figure this out.

You see? said Griggs, sealing the portal from his control panel. We're on it. This is how we do, Mrs. Mayor — we run the city so you don't have to.

Primly she brushed flat crumbs from her jacket.

The final issue: communications. While the NFLM's internal radios were working fine, both the phonelines and We-TV's closed circuit were out. Which actually isn't such a bad thing, explained Wagstaffe, since it likely means we'll get better crowds at Cinecity. To, you know, distract people a bit. From what's going on, I mean. And with that Wagstaffe excused himself to oversee the film's final cut.

Around the table only halfnaked Magurk, enigmatic Noodles, incontinent (probably) Favours, Griggs, the Mayor, and her mute and crippled aide, Diamond-Wood, remained. The adjoining room had gone silent since Magurk's last visit.

And the final order of business, said Griggs: Raven.

The Mayor sighed. And?

A trapped animal, murmured Magurk, is a dangerous animal.

What? said the Mayor. What does that even mean?

Special Professor, *please*.

So? said the Mayor. What's the plan?

Noodles held up both index fingers.

The Imperial Master has some thoughts, said Griggs.

Oh, good old Noodles, said the Mayor. Cuddle me up to a whole forest of green.

And yet Noodles' thoughts are his own, explained Griggs.

Oh, said the Mayor. Of course.

Noodles nodded, twice. And sat back, having said nothing. The room felt like the inside of a steadily deflating balloon.

Anything else? said Griggs.

The Mayor shifted into a stern, authoritarian pose, leaning forward — but before she could speak an alarm went squawking throughout the Temple.

Code 42! said Magurk, jumping to his feet.

Favours whipped to attention, eyes full of fire. Code 42! he cried in a phlegmy warble.

Code 42? said the Mayor.

A breach, muttered Griggs. From the main floor came thumps and shouts, a crash. Footsteps pounded back and forth. The alarm howled, the stomping thickened into rumbling, a mob of dozens, crashes and whoops.

In the corner of the room, Favours had never seemed so alert, eyes darting around the room, a smirk playing at the corners of his lips. They've come, he chortled. Code 42, Code 42! They've come!

The Mayor looked from Favours to Diamond-Wood to Griggs to Magurk to Noodles, who returned her bewilderment with a curt, officious nod.

Magurk rose, knuckling up. Those fuggin animals, he sneered.

They've come, sung Favours. Oh my yes Code 42 they've come!

Who's come, old man? demanded the Mayor.

Kicking his feet in their stirrups and cackling, Favours threw back his head to reveal a rubbery yellow neck laced with purple veins.

For fug's sake, growled the Mayor, what kind of loony clubhouse is this?

Application forms are upstairs, said Griggs coolly. He pressed a button on the console. The alarm died, the lights in the basement extinguished. After a moment of total darkness, a generator stirred to life somewhere within the Chambers, and the lights returned, though duller, tinting everyone beige.

The noises above weakened into a faint scuffling.

Griggs lifted the phone to his ear. His face sagged. He tapped the console, once, twice — then hung up, sat back, and rapped his fingers on the table.

Did they cut the line? screamed Magurk, and then he stamped off to the adjoining room yelling, Is someone here for you, you fat sack of squatter trash? Who the fug is it?

If there was a reply to this, it was drowned out by a gentle explosion from the Great Hall. The conference chamber shuddered. From upstairs came another rush of footsteps.

There must be a hundred of them, said Griggs.

Favours howled.

Who's *them*? hollered the Mayor. Who are *they*?

A smoky odour began seeping into the basement, acrid and sharp.

Magurk reappeared drawing a sword, long and parabolic, with a slippery shink of metal. Slicing through the air, he shrieked a feral battle cry.

Oh come now, please, said Griggs. With the portal closed there's no way anyone can get down here. Sheathe your weapon, you're embarrassing everyone.

Griggs, said the Mayor, tell me right now: who's attacking you?

Oh, it could be anyone, said Griggs, almost sadly. There are just so many people, he sighed, so many people it could be.

WHAT DO THEY EXPECT? said Starx. That we'll get out and check every site?

Maybe we should have told them we don't even know what — Olpert checked their notes from Residents' Control — *Gip Bode* looks like.

And what? Also tell the HG's we didn't even watch the show? Terrific idea, Bailie. Crazy Magurk'd cut our fuggin eyelids off.

Ha, said Olpert — though this time Starx didn't seem to be joking.

They drove at a crawl through fog-soaked Lakeview Campground. Around every bend the Citywagon's highbeams appeared as twin dabs of yellow paint on a blank canvas, illuminating nothing, while the wipers scrubbed lethargically back and forth, smearing the scant snowfall into wet streaks across the windscreen.

Starx steered them into a Scenic Vista at the edge of the poplars. Though the vista was of fog. Above the treetops this bled into a grey cloudcover in parts tinged bluish. Around the Citywagon the fog churned, coiling and uncoiling, a thicket of pale snakes or the fingers, thought Olpert, of many many searching hands.

Know what I think?

Okay? said Olpert.

I think this guy, Raven — know what he's doing? He's hanging out somewhere right now, maybe in his hotel room, having a laugh at all of us.

You think?

Starx tapped the walkie-talkie: just a dull drone, not even static. Weird, he said.

So do we go to the Grand Saloon?

No, it's not our job to look for him. They'll have dozens of guys doing that. We're supposed to find the kid, right, but how can we? I'm not a fuggin detective. Are you?

Starx put a hand over Olpert's mouth. That was rhetorical, you scrotal pleat.

He let go. A taste of soup lingered.

Tell you what. Let's get a cider.

Starx! We haven't had lunch yet!

Fine, you get lunch, I'll get a cider. Though if you don't drink then you have to drive.

Oh, said Olpert uneasily.

The Golden Barrel it is, said Starx, firing up the ignition. On the dash dials spun into place, the Citywagon's headlights splashed onto the fog. Starx pointed at the dashboard clock. See? It's nine o'clock, Bailie. Perfect time for a drink.

Starx, wait, said Olpert, pointing through the windshield. Look.

Something was happening in the headlights, mist swirled into phantasmal forms.

Pictures? said Starx.

They're moving, said Olpert.

What is it? said Starx. Can you tell?

A series of indistinguishable images played holographically out of the highbeams, skipping one to the next — a slideshow of strange shadows marbled with light, just figurative enough to suggest people maybe, or animals. The pace quickened, then the figures began to sputter into motion, invoking those halted jerky images from the advent of cinema. But quickly they sharpened, the animation smoothed, and a scene took shape . . .

Is that? said Starx.

I think so, whispered Olpert.

And —

It can't be!

But —

Oh god, said Starx. Oh no, oh god.

Olpert's face had gone the colour of the fog.

No, said Starx. Bailie, no.

The two men watched, rapt. The film's refracted light danced over the Citywagon's hood. Neither spoke, neither blinked, neither budged a muscle. The film blazed into a final searing swath of white, and in an instant everything was gone. The highbeams left a yellow stain on the wall of fog.

What was that? said Olpert. What did we just watch? Starx?

Starx shook his head as if to dislodge something from it, slung an arm around the passengerside headrest, put the gearshift into reverse, and floored the gas. Olpert lurched forward, the seatbelt sliced into his neck, gravel shrapnelled up the sides of the Citywagon, and they went screeching out onto Lakeside Drive.

At the roundabout a Helper lowered his traffic batons and leaned in the window.

Nothing on my radio, he said. Your guys's dead too?

Starx nodded so slightly that Olpert felt the need to pipe up: Yes, ours too.

Where you headed?

Special mission, said Olpert.

Special mission, repeated Starx, and fixed the Helper with a blazing, wild look. Going to let us through, brother? B-Squad's got places to be!

The Helper removed himself from the car, called, Good lookin out, and waved them through the barricade, around the traffic jam up the Throughline, and out of People Park.

IN THIS MOVIE or is it a dream the bridge has been empty, that sort of huge and booming emptiness that could never have been anything but empty, who else could be out here and where would they come from. But there it is bobbing at the horizon, a fleck, what might be just a spot in Calum's vision or a reflection or a trick of light. From this distance it could be anything small, a mote or mite or flea, maybe not a person at all, this little blip of matter exactly at the point where the bridge narrows and vanishes. Amid all that emptiness here is this *thing*, whatever it might be, a blot or a mistake, a puncture or a speck, now visible and now not, flickering. It seems less present than projected or imagined. It is a dot, a period, the end.

Calum keeps walking and holds up his hand to gauge perspective: the shape has curled into a comma half the length of his thumbnail. Some indefinite amount of time later it has fractured into a top and bottom, a semicolon, twice as big. Calum seems to be closing the distance at a rate incommensurate with the speed he's walking. He squints but doesn't pause. The shape bobs on the horizon. It is moving. It is growing. It is, he realizes, approaching.

He squints again. This thing seems to be human, or at least human-shaped, and coming at him very, very quickly, now the length of a knuckle. And though the shape of this thing is human there is something inhuman about it, about the way it moves and its spectral presence and the shimmer of air between it and

Calum, a dream's air that thickens into tendrils that slip and tighten around his neck.

Also as this person approaches, the bridge behind it, in fact everything behind it, even the sky, seems to be disappearing. It isn't going dark. What was there a second before vanishes. And for a sky that was already an absence to cease to be even that — it becomes nothing, there's just nothing there. As this person moves the horizon recedes, closing in, a hand curling around a camera's lens, shrinking the image, choking what can be seen until, eventually, it will be just Calum and this person, alone, and everything else a void.

Calum backs away from the yellow line. His first step is deliberate, but then he staggers, legs twisting, and everything goes slow and soupy, this can't be a movie, it has to be a dream. The encroaching figure nears, the emptiness swells behind it — and Calum stops walking. He steps off the yellow line. He backs up against the bridge's railing. There is nowhere to go. He looks down into the mist and what is maybe a river's shadow beneath and above at what remains of the colourless sky, swiftly vanishing.

And the figure comes closer still, swallowing everything in its wake.

AT BLACKACRES STATION train 2306 sat on the southbound tracks, doors open. The platform was empty, the movators motionless. Debbie boarded the lead car. Two passengers sat down at the far end: a kid, maybe eight years old, and his fatigued-looking mother with a handbag in her lap.

Standing over her, the kid kicked his mom's feet, she told him to sit down. He crawled up on the seat opposite and from his knees looked out the window and said, We aren't going anywhere, we've been here forever, what are we doing. Sit down, Rupe, his mother said again, and he said, I am sitting down, and pulled himself up as tall as he could on his knees and stared at her stonefaced. She had nothing to say about that.

Normally the neighbourhood's tinny din would drift up from the streets into the station. Instead the car filled with a silence that came thudding into the ears, at once thick and hollow, everywhere and empty. Outside the mist swirled past the windows of the train and over the roofs of Blackacres, between watertanks resembling the hulls of fogged-in ships, grabbing and releasing the phonelines and electric cables that lolled between rooftops. They were dead: the power was out, of course the train wasn't moving.

Yet Debbie didn't leave. Stray bits of mist nudged through the open doors. At the far end of the car the kid got down and went back to kicking his mother's feet. I said stop it, she said, and he kicked her once more, and she said, I'm warning you, and he kicked her again, giggling — and at this she sprung forward and smacked his face. The kid held his cheek. He looked stunned. She shrunk away, seemed to reconsider, grabbed him roughly by the arm, and shook him. Are we supposed to walk to find your brother? she screamed. All the way all across the city, are we supposed to walk? The boy started crying. Rupe, no, said the woman and hauled him into her arms. I'm sorry, she whispered, kissing his face, his mouth.

Stiffly, Debbie watched. Sometimes at the Room she was privy to corporal parenting, almost always interrupted by a realization of witnesses. Then came excuses and embarrassment, the family slunk out the door in shame. But to this mother, now coddling her boy, Debbie seemed invisible, their world didn't include her or her judgments. What was wrong with these people, didn't they know they were in public? Had they no shame?

But what bothered Debbie most was feeling excluded and ignored. With nothing to say and no way to help, she slipped back onto the platform and down to the street. A Citywagon idled in the depot opposite. Debbie approached, waved. The driver, bundled in furs, face taut as a canvas and primed with powder and rouge, rolled down her window. Yes?

Hi, said Debbie. Sorry, could you help me?

Help you what? I can't drive you anywhere. I have to get home.

In a rush Debbie explained her predicament, that her phone was out, that someone was missing and —

And so?

And she's blind, said Debbie — which, really, might not have been untrue.

Oh, said the woman. Blind?

Yeah. All I need's a ride to Canal Station, maybe the Redline's running . . . Listen, I can pay you, she said, producing her wallet as proof — the woman snickered — and shamefully pocketed it again.

Can't you get your own car? said the woman.

I don't have a Citycard. I don't know anyone in the um, men's league.

Yeah, see, my husband . . . The woman trailed off.

The engine idled, chugging exhaust.

Debbie felt cornered. She sighed, could hear the self-disgust in her voice as she said, Listen, I write for Isa Lanyess —

Oh? said the woman. Sudden interest glinted in her eyes.

Debbie felt filthy, but blundered on: Yeah, and if you give me your information I bet this is just the kind of feel-good story she'd love. You know, power out in the Zone, kind benevolent citizen makes generous act . . .

Benevolent, murmured the woman. I like it!

She was already out of the car, handing Debbie a business card, eyes glazed with fantasy, projecting herself onto her friends' TV screens, basking in their awe and envy. She spoke in a rush, every moment here delayed her taste of fame: Keep the engine running, you won't need to log in. There's a lot by Canal Station, park it there. Or I'm going to have to pay for it, understand?

Of course, said Debbie, sliding behind the wheel. I appreciate this so much.

And I'll hear from you soon? About the show?

Debbie nodded. You bet.

Gosh, little old me on *In the Know*, cooed the woman, who would have guessed?

V

PEARL STOOD at the top of a staircase that vanished into People Park as a swimming ladder into a frozen pond. The fog collecting on the common didn't shift or swirl or embody any of the vaporous properties it did elsewhere in the city, but seemed instead a solid stagnant mass. Down there somewhere was the gazebo — and, with luck, Gip's knapsack and his meds. The air was icy, the light a sort of non-light. It had stopped snowing, what had fallen layered the ground, pebbly and granular, half an inch thick.

Pearl imagined herself heading down into the misty park, swallowed up, never coming out. But that was ridiculous. She dangled a toe until a snowy stair responded with a squeak and crunch. And down she went, tentatively, by feel and sound, imagining Gip and Kellogg and Elsie-Anne browsing the Museum's exhibits, her husband flapping his guidebook and raving about the place as if it hosted miracles.

A dozen careful steps later the stairs flattened into a Scenic Vista, the fog so thick she crossed the platform at a crouch, feeling ahead with her hands. In the snow her fingers quickly went cold and stiff, she brought them to her mouth to blow on them, reached out again — but what if she encountered something cold and wet and fleshy lying on the deck . . . Pearl recoiled. A chill passed through her, deeper than the cold, it iced her heart.

Kneeling, she checked her watch: dead, the hands stuck at nine and twelve. She thought of Gip. Her bad knee twitched. In inclement weather and with stress, acting as a vane or gauge, the restitched ligaments often tightened. Though this felt different, not stiffness or pain, but a strange, electrical tingling.

She stood, shook her leg out. Her knee was swollen to twice its normal size. Water retention usually came on over hours, if not days, and only after a workout. She hadn't done much lately but sleep and sit and stand. Fluid seemed to be collecting at an abnormally drastic rate, and the joint pulsed, and despite the frigid air wasn't cold at all, but oddly warm and soft, almost spongy — and it was inflating.

Her jeans stretched, split, the denim tore with a zippery sound and out the knee crowned. Pearl stumbled, the entire leg was numb, she had to hop. Finding the deck's railing she leaned against it: the knee had gone hydrotic, big as a toddler's head. Weakly Pearl called for help, her words slipped into the fog and were lost.

She waited. There was no pain. Instead the numbing fizzled into lightness. And the knee, a globelike bloom, began lifting, and behind it went her leg, unencumbered by will or gravity. The rest of her body followed: her right foot peeled from the deck, there was a weightlessness and ease to the whole thing. Pearl went limp, her worry drained into the fog. This must be a dream, she thought. She never dreamed, now she felt herself a tourist in her own subconscious. What to do but give herself over to its magic? And so she floated, her kneecap the puffed-up bladder of a hot air balloon, the rest of her body dangling beneath, out into the pillowy air over the common.

THE FIGURE IS CLOSE enough that on its face Calum can make out shadowy splotches of eyes, a nose, a mouth. Its clothes are white. And as it advances it draws a curtain upon the world — no, a curtain would be something. This is just oblivion: everything behind it is swept from existence. The bird, the pigeon or dove, swoops down from somewhere, the airy splash of its wings, looping up and circling above. Calum tries not to think of vultures. And still the figure approaches, sweeping with it that great wave of nothingness. It is a man, a brownskinned baldheaded man in white moving with brisk strides, and as he closes in Calum sees upon this man's face, grim and dark as a ditch: a grin.

ONCE THE NOISES upstairs had calmed, Magurk raised his sword. Who's got my back? He pointed the tip of the blade at Diamond-Wood. Recruit, you ready to earn your schnapps?

The aide glanced at the Mayor, who waved him away. My sword's got a jones, screamed Magurk, blade in disembowelling position. Griggs, sighing, opened the portal from his console: no one waited there ready to pounce.

Magurk crept up the slope at a crouch, Diamond-Wood followed awkwardly on his crutches. A tense sort of hush poured down from above. The Mayor waited, listening. They've trashed the place, cried Magurk. My people, are you with me?

Griggs and Noodles exchanged a look.

We should probably get the radios back up, said Griggs, and Noodles nodded, and together they headed upstairs to join their brethren.

The Mayor eyed Favours in his wheelchair. Should we have a race or something?

Code 42, chuckled Favours, they're here, at last!

From upstairs came moans of dismay, disgust, barks of rage from Magurk, the sound of the men moving room to room, surveying the damage.

So what next for your little boys' club? said the Mayor.

His eyes widened — in *anticipation*, it seemed.

And the portal banged closed.

Favours squealed.

From the hallway that led to the other chambers came a whooshing, fluttering sound. Out of the darkness flew a bird. It circled the room — the Mayor ducked — and returned down the hall. From the shadows came a patter of footsteps and in the next chamber the man hollered, Lark! My liberationeers have arrived!

In a rush of black six hooded figures spilled into the conference room. Before the Mayor could cry for help, hands were upon her, a strip of ducktape was slapped across her mouth. Favours was spun around in his wheelchair, the old man clapped and hooted in delight, and then he was shuttled off into the Chambers.

The Mayor found herself wheeled past barred cells and bunk-rooms, down a ramp into an unlit corridor. Favours' whoops faded as he was swerved along another passageway. The abductors piloted her in silence, eerily purposeful, careering around a cor-ner — a flash of light from some hatch above, they were entering a stormdrain. Things went dark again. The air warmed, infused with a mustardy, sulphurous smell . . .

The floor degenerated from concrete to gravel, juddering through the cart and rattling the Mayor's teeth, she held on for dear life. My legs, she screamed, make sure you don't lose my legs — but beneath the gag her words sounded submerged. On they went, hairpinning into a passageway that angled up toward streetlevel.

Some light splashed weakly from the end of this tunnel: in it the Mayor tried to get a sense of who her kidnappers were. But their faces were mysteries inside their hoods. They drove her headlong up toward the watery brightness — a glimpse of the surface in some distant corner, who knew where, of her city.

THE FIGURE STRETCHES from the tips of his fingers to the heel of his palm and suddenly Calum is outside it all. He has a bird's-eye view. From high above Calum sees himself upon the bridge and sends frantic thoughts to this person who is some version of himself to run, but the body is frozen, leaning against the railing, staring at this person, whoever it might be, barrelling over the bridge and inhaling the visible world with him.

That purple-lipped grin shadows the lower half of its brown face, the grin of some sinister and weird anticipation. Here are the eyes, dark and glittering. The baldhead sings with a dull sheen. The legs move in great strides but the upper body is motionless, almost rigid, the man less runs toward the Calum on the bridge than glides.

And this Calum is up against the railing, on this bridge from nowhere to nowhere, with even that nowhere becoming some farther and deeper sort of nowhere, and the man closing in of course must be a dream, the whole thing must be a dream. The skybound Calum watches himself look over the railing: hundreds of feet below, a swath of gauze.

The figure is big and close, hovering, and overhead Calum as a bird traces looping circles against the shrinking sky, and where will he go when there is no sky left. A vast negative halo surrounds this approaching figure. It brings nothingness into Calum's dream — but then Calum thinks no, this is not his dream, it couldn't be his dream. Calum has invaded someone else's dream and now that person is coming to banish him from it.

From above Calum watches himself watching — the figure is almost upon him, moving swift and slick, no sounds of footsteps, no sounds at all, just those blazing black eyes and monstrous joyous grin, legs stabbing in front and sweeping away behind him, and this man is big, he is so big, and he is reaching for Calum with long thin brown fingers, and the fingers seem to be growing, stretching into tentacles twisted through with veins.

Things start to swirl and twist and eddy and Calum, soaring, can imagine this man's hot breath on his own face, those fingers lace snakelike around his wrists, almost gently, and he feels his knees go weak — but then with a last desperate surge of strength Calum watches himself tear free, climb up onto the railing, and launch himself off the bridge.

But then Calum is climbing up, closing his eyes, and jumping off the bridge.

Closing his eyes, Calum climbs onto the railing and jumps.

Before the man is fully upon him, the man's fingers are curling around his wrists and he feels the feathery touch of something else wrapping his ankles, the mouth opening from a grin to something far more sinister, he is trying to devour Calum, Calum shakes his arms free and leaps up onto the railing and propels himself off the bridge.

In silence Calum jumps off the bridge.

Eyes closed, Calum jumps, and for a moment finds himself floating.

And he is back inside his body and falling. The wind whistles into his ears and his head fills with a sort of screaming, all he can hear is screaming, his guts tumble, and down he plummets, not quite a swan-dive but flattened out, all swimming limbs, the tug of gravity, Calum's body, the water and meat of it, falling, and it feels endless, this fall, down and down he tumbles toward the possible river below. He braces himself for the smack and icy rush, time will slow as the water catches him, then he will sink, and his crushed and ruined corpse will be buoyed back to the surface and swept away. And if this is a dream Calum will instead of dying hit the water and wake.

THAT'S HIM, said Starx. That's the kid.

What kid — oh. Him?

That kid on the corner there. The one who spat on you.

Across the intersection of F and 10 the fog opened to reveal the Golden Barrel Taverne. From the Citywagon idling at the corner Olpert watched: onto the sidewalk stumbled a someone in a black sweatshirt, hood up. His movements were a sleepwalker's — that sludgy, heavyfooted trudge through one's own inner world.

Same shirt, said Starx, same slouch. Though, fug. All these people look the same to me.

Olpert squinted. The fog swirled, the figure disappeared. Are you sure that's him? What's he doing?

Take the wheel, said Starx, unbuckling his seatbelt. I'm going.

A lump bobbed in Olpert's throat.

These animals, they need to pay.

Starx flew into the street like a great khaki bat, the fog closed around him. A scrabble of footsteps, muffled shouts, Olpert thought he heard his name, opened his door, reconsidered, and slid into the driver's seat. As he edged the Citywagon forward, the passengerside door flapped and creaked. A misty whorl shivered up over the hood. Olpert eased on the accelerator, couldn't see anything.

And then a person came reeling out of the fog, right in the path of the car. Olpert yelped, stomped the gas. The figure, black as a shadow, thumped into the grille, flipped over the hood, and amid a screech of brakes rolled up and wedged between the open door and the windshield.

The car idled. A jagged hypotenuse cracked the glass. Beyond it the fog tumbled and seethed. Half lolling into the car, half dangling outside, hung a boy.

Starx appeared, stared at the body, at Olpert, and back.

Olpert felt he'd swallowed a handful of tacks and his stomach was a clothesdryer, tumbling them around.

Starx spoke — Holy fug, Bailie — and some part of Olpert released and drifted off into the mist. He felt light, watching Starx peel the kid from the doorframe and lay his body, limp as a sack of flour, on the hood of the car. Starx listened to the chest, felt for a pulse inside the hood. He's dead, said Starx, eyes wide and astonished. We killed him.

We? said Olpert.

We.

Up and down F Street, nothing but fog.

Open the trunk, said Starx. His voice was solemn.

Olpert did.

Now help me.

Together they hoisted the body into the trunk. Gently Starx folded the kid's legs, crossed his arms on his chest. Around his left wrist, a fork. The hood came loose: one side of his face was a mess, the left eye swollen shut, the cheek stippled with dried blood.

At least it's him, said Starx, the kid who spat on you. See?

Olpert's vision swam. The tailpipe spewed exhaust against his legs, pleasant and warm, he didn't want to move. Starx closed the trunk and guided Olpert into the passenger seat. But the door wouldn't close properly, it kept popping open.

Just hang on to it, said Starx.

Olpert did.

Listen, Bailie, this is the reason we're in this organization. You have a problem, they take care of it. We'll take him to the HG's. They'll know what to do. Right?

Okay.

He handed Olpert the walkie-talkie. You talk though. Your gramps an OG and all.

Okay.

Bailie, it's going to be fine. It's an accident. I pushed him, sure, but I didn't realize you were — not that it was your fault ... Starx massaged his temples with his thumbs. Just an accident, he said. They'll take care of it.

Starx turned onto Tangent 10. Waiting for a response over the radio, Olpert stared at his reflection in the sideview mirror. A smudge marked his jawline from ear to chin: he wiped at it, but the mark remained. Vaguely aware of Griggs' voice — *What is it, B-Squad* — calling from his lap, Olpert peered at the mirror: the mark wasn't on his face at all. It was the glass, he realized, smeared with something red and sticky-looking and wet.

VI

EVENING WAS coming and the armoire was empty. Or it appeared empty, it was possible that if Sam looked one place then Raven went somewhere else, that he could somehow read Sam's thoughts and knew where his eyes would go and bounce from that spot to another. The door was secure, the lock held fast, there was no chance the illustrationist could have tunnelled his way out, what would he have used?

Sam had trunked him, the illustrationist had told him how: *The image I take with me into the trunk dictates where I will reappear.* The image had been of the armoire. Sam had drawn it. But what if his drawing hadn't been perfect enough? Maybe the perspective was off, or he'd gotten the shading wrong... Where might Raven have trunked to instead?

Sam rapped on the door. It's dinnertime okay.

No answer. Yet the basement felt different, emptier somehow. Sam pressed his ear to the door, heard only wood.

Outside the light was shifting, the sprinkler hissed and sputtered across the lawn. And time's machine was still silent.

Sam said, Okay I'm nuking dinner.

He carried the dead bird upstairs, struck by the weightlessness of it, a pocket of air wrapped in feathers, and put it in the kitchen trash. From the freezer he took two trays of nuclear dinners, punctured the cellophane lids with a knife, and while they were nuking he took the knife in his fist as a murderer might and stabbed twice at the air. He pressed the blade into his fingertip, felt the sharp prick, pushed until it punctured the skin and a droplet of blood swelled and ran down his finger in a twisting ribbon.

With the nuked dinners stacked in one hand and the knife in the bloody other he went back downstairs and stood before the armoire and said, I have your dinner but I cut myself okay.

No reply.

Sam closed his fingers around the handle of the knife and made a stabbing pose. He said, I cut myself, I need your help, come on out. Help me.

The sprinkler on the lawn stopped. The silence was absolute.

Raven I'm just trying to do the work okay. You stopped time's machine before the third hand came all the way around. Monday the work's over though right Raven? I'll let you out then. But I need your help okay. Please Raven. Please okay?

Nothing.

Sam went at the armoire with the steak knife: he stabbed, the handle snapped, Sam kept stabbing the door clutching just the blade. Blood ran down his arm and smeared his fingers and he kept stabbing and scraping, shearing wood from the door, saying, Help me, help me, help me.

He stopped. The pain in his hand was a sharp wet twang and he uncurled his fingers with difficulty. He'd buried the blade into his palm, he had to wiggle it out, the sound it made was gristly. The blood was sticky and hot and everywhere. Sam took off his three watches, lay them side by each on his bed, the third hand stuck at nine. Then he wrapped his wounded hand in ducktape, thinking as he did of Adine's face in the hospital, swathed in bandages, the eyes hidden somewhere deep inside, seeing nothing.

CAN I GET you a drink, said Wagstaffe. Or something to eat — sausages maybe?

Griggs eyed the NFLM's Silver Personality, whose face glowed an ungodly russet in We-TV Studios' halogen-lit hallways, chin jutting from it in a dimpled, tanned promontory. He had the eager look of a camper on parents' visiting day, standing there with his hands clasped, rocking on his heels. The unsolicited and disarmingly thorough tour was finally over, here at the control room.

Noodles checked his watch. Tapped it. Held it to his ear. Didn't nod.

We're fine, said Griggs. Let's proceed to the task at hand?

Of course! Head on in, I'll get you guys set up.

Wagstaffe wheeled two chairs up to the console, patted them for Griggs and Noodles to sit, flicked a switch, and a bank of monitors came to life.

Grab headsets, said Wagstaffe. They're tuned to the NFLM frequency. What else?

As long as we can monitor all the Squads, said Griggs, we should be fine.

Wagstaffe puffed his chest. Well with ten thousand cameras — Eyes on the City, as we say! — feeding live right here, you'll be able to see anything you want. Actually, he said, tweaking a knob on the console, for a little *intimate entertainment*, if we switch over to the live We-TV feeds, there's a lonely Fort Stone housewife who —

That won't be necessary, said Griggs, smacking his hand away. Now, shouldn't you get back to your movie?

Our movie, Griggs — *All in Together Now*, right? We're almost done the final cut! It's going to be —

Noodles nodded curtly toward the door.

Mr. Imperial Master, said Wagstaffe, retreating. Mr. Head Scientist — good lookin out!

Though the monitors displayed the whole city — the Institute's Quad, the parking lot of IFC Stadium, a rooftop camera surveying People Park from the Museum of Prosperity — every view was obscured by fog. Even the Knock Street Station security camera across from the Temple revealed only a faint glimpse of Pea and Dack standing sentry on the front porch.

Griggs pulled a list and a pen from his pocket. Let's see . . . Magurk's got the roundup underway — anyone not from here, anyone suspicious, they'll be taken in — check. D-Squad is looking for Favours, Diamond-Wood's going to find the Mayor, bridge access is still blocked, check, check, check. Radios are back up. Wagstaffe's — sorry, *our* — movie is almost ready to go, Island Amusements is set to open for families, check and check. Starx and Bailie — no word yet, but they're on the hunt for that kid. And then there's Raven . . . Anything else?

Noodles motioned for the list and Griggs' pen. He made an addendum, and with a long-nailed index finger tapped the freshly bulleted point:

· *Revenge.*

UP OVER THE common Pearl floated, pumpkin-sized knee dragging her beneath it. Along she scudded, sweeping the occasional languid backstroke or, with her good leg, whipkicks that stirred the fog into spirals.

Her mind was so blank she was unaware of its blankness. Everything was airy, empty, nothing mattered. She had a vague impression of the ground hundreds of feet below, and yet with this realization came no fear, only lightness, the heedless ease of a sleeping child.

She drifted out of the park's northern side, a sign emerged out of the mist: STREET'S MILK & THINGS. As she swept past, Pearl reached out and grabbed its corner, hung on for a moment, her knee tugged her away. There was no breeze to speak of: the knee seemed to enjoy a velocity and volition of its own.

Pearl was lofted out over Street's empty parking lot. East along Topside Drive the rollercoasters of Island Amusements appeared in silhouette, skeletal dinosaurs prowling the fog. Across the road she was carried, distantly aware of people below, the faraway sounds of idling engines and horns and voices.

From above came a fluttering sound. A bird swooped down, disappeared, circled back, and, as Pearl reached the far side of Topside Drive, made another pass. At the shoreline the fog parted: mist swirled around the bushes on the chalky hillside but ceded abruptly at the water. She floated out over the Narrows. The opposite bank was low and flat.

The bird returned, soaring up from below and gliding for a moment alongside, a flock partner or mate. It seemed to regard Pearl with curiosity, this bird — a pigeon. Then it did a little loop and landed on her inflated kneecap, adjusted its footing, ruffled its feathers, and settled. In tandem she and this new passenger traversed the slate-coloured channel over which Guardian Bridge had once risen. On the far shore an airplane was taking off from the airport. The skies above the mainland were blue and clear.

The pigeon seemed both wary and dismissive of the human being connected to its roost. It clucked. The Narrows rippled along. A slight breeze ruffled Pearl's hair. She waited, watching the bird, should she shoo it away or let it rest? But before she could decide, it straightened, fluffed its wings, extended its neck, and, with a swift, downward stroke, drove its beak into her knee. Chirruping gaily, the pigeon lifted and flapped madly back to the island.

Air whistled out of the hole, the balloon began deflating, Pearl sank toward the water — fifty feet up, now forty, she could smell it: clamshells and rust. The current rushed swift and purposeful to the east, a branch went whisking by, thirty feet below. The skin around her kneecap had gone baggy and loose.

She had to get to shore, either the mainland or the island, she was halfway to both. One was home, the other — something else. Wheeling, Pearl paddled the air, arms thrashing, lowered ever closer to the murmuring Narrows.

THE THUD AGAINST the side of the Citywagon at first struck Debbie as a hiccup in the exhaust. But then figures swarmed out of the fog, surrounded the car. How many people, a dozen, it was impossible to tell, one stood at the car's fender, holding a plank with spikes at both ends, there was nowhere to go, they were everywhere.

The driverside door was pounded, voices were hollering. Debbie fumbled with the locks — and something smashed into the window, crinkling it in a greenish web, and she screamed, and the pipe or crowbar was swung again, and the window caved inward, greenish glass sprinkled her lap.

A high, childish voice cried, Out of the car, out of the car!

Debbie went foetal, the door was opened, hands undid her seatbelt and dragged her out and shoved her ass-first onto the tarmac, and for a moment everything went still.

Over her stood a figure, hood pulled tight around its face, holding a mophandle with bike chains attached to one end.

The trunk was opened, slammed shut.

No one in here, called a second voice — flatter, kazoo-toned, but also very young.

The figure pulled her hood aside to reveal hair shaved into a handprint. But the Hand made no intimations of recognition, just flicked her weapon between Debbie's outstretched legs: the chains jingled, brushed her thighs.

Please —

Again the Hand whacked the chains against the pavement.

The first voice, shrill as a whistle, demanded, Where is he?

Debbie raised her hands in a pacifying gesture. Who? I don't know. Please.

Your car took Calum, said the second voice. Your car hit him and took him, it said, moving out from behind the Citywagon. We saw it happen.

We see everything, said the first voice.

The speakers appeared on either side of the Hand, tiny creatures each carrying makeshift weapons: two-by-fours with metal prongs ducktaped to both ends. Ten years old, Debbie guessed — and only three attackers, she'd assumed a mob of dozens.

Calum, said Debbie. I know Calum. Who took him, what are you talking about.

The Hand stared back, unspeaking.

The kid on her left said, What do you know? Can you help us?

Tell me what happened, maybe I can —

He was hit by a car like this one. This car.

No, this is a Citywagon, they all look the same — wait, he was *hit*? Is he okay?

They took him, said Right. They put him in the back part.

Oh god. Was he alive? Is he all right? Where did they go?

We don't know.

The Hand shifted. The bike chains clinked.

We'll find him, said Debbie. I can tell you care about him, and I care about him too —

Shut up, said Left. We need to find him.

We need to, said Right.

I know. I didn't know — but yes. We need to find him. There's a Citywagon depot —

We're taking your car, said Right. Drive us.

I can't, it's not my car —

The Hand lashed the ground again, Debbie sprung away. The girl's eyes were hateful.

Okay, said Debbie, hands up, placating. Let's go, we'll find him.

INTO THE DUSK they sprung, up through the bowels of Whitehall and south on F Street beneath the Yellowline tracks, three phantoms in hoods pushing and the Mayor white-knuckling the dessert cart, rumbling over the uneven sidewalk, jarred by potholes and cracks in the road. The fog had lifted to form a cloudbank into which the day was fading, inky shadows spilled from the feet of the Blackacres lowrises, the twilight pixelated and staticky and through it the hooded triumvirate rolled the Mayor, past darkened derelict housing all sad old ghostfaces on the eastside of F.

At Tangent 18 a sour, chemical smell swelled up — Lowell Canal. The Mayor's eyes watered and nostrils burned, her tear-streaked cheeks whipped dry by the wind. On she was driven, down F past a blur of descending east-west Tangents — 17, 16, 15 — and three-storey walkups, some with plastic sheeting for windows, others freshly painted with windowboxes sprouting green shoots. A Citywagon whipped past at F and 12 and was gone.

Two blocks south, passing the Golden Barrel Taverne, the pace slowed. The Mayor checked the lower tier of the cart: her legs were still there, ducktaped down. And then the slap of feet on pavement silenced and she was released. She rattled along for another half block before the cart slowed and banked left and bumped up to the curb. She faced the depthless shadows of an alleyway.

A block north her hooded abductors collected in the middle of F Street, conferring in low voices — a fourth figure had joined them, big and shirtless and wearing a strange helmet. They seemed to have forgotten about her entirely. She listened, could make out nothing distinct, just low muttering. She got a fingernail under a corner of the gag, and was just beginning to peel it away when lights flooded F Street.

There was a roar and a screech of brakes, the blare of high-beams. Doors opened, two Helpers tumbled out shouting, Hey you — Θtop there — Get them! But her kidnappers had slipped off into the shadows, or become shadows. The Mayor struggled with her gag, thrashed atop the cart to draw attention, but the streetlights were out, she was lost and mute in the pitch. The partners piled back into their pickup truck, which went squealing up F Street.

But before the Mayor could feel too dejected, she was bumping up over the curb. She looked around: no one was there. The cart seemed to be moving on its own — rolling forward, very slowly, over the sidewalk and into the alley. The air felt thick. The shadows enfolded her, it was like entering a mine or a cave. No, a lair: something huge and horrible made its home here.

As she thought this a humid and foul-smelling breeze washed over her face. Then another in a rotten swell — breaths, she realized. The cart pushed deeper. She seemed to be teetering at the edge of a slope, the front wheels angled over. A pause. The Mayor gripped the sides of the cart. The moment stretched out, expanded. Another breath gusted up from below. And then the cart tipped over and she was plummeting headlong and reckless toward whatever lurked in the depths of that terrible dark.

VII

FTER SOME indetermin-
ate amount of time, the We-tv countdown in Cinecity reached
the Top 10. Each clip was met with cheers and groans, fans and
detractors trying to drown out the other. Top 10 status was the
province of the truly sensational. At #5, on the Devourers' channel
three men had set fire to a car and were eating it, piece by flaming
piece. People howled.

At #4: *Stupid Fat People Humiliated in Public Bathrooms by
Drunk Babies*.
At #3: *The Lady Y's Lingerie Pillowfight Extravaganza (Semi-
Finals)*.
At #2: *Isa Lanyess, In the Know*.
At #1, of course, was *Salami Talk*.

Lucal Wagstaffe grinned. I'm very happy to retain my *position*
at the *top* of your charts. Nice to know you all still *like to watch*. (A
slow lick of his upper teeth, the tip chomped off a pepperette.)
But this isn't about me. I'm only here to introduce one of many
highlights of the Silver Jubilee weekend, and also an amazing
example of our citizens coming together in harmony. What you're
about to see has come from you, dedicated viewers — a movie *for*
the people, *by* the people. The result reflects not just who we are,

but what we all want to be. So sit back, relax, break out a sausage, slide the sausage slowly into your mouth, bite down, slowly, allow the juices to burst over your tongue, and enjoy.

Cinecity buzzed as the film began.

THE NEW FRATERNAL LEAGUE OF MEN AND WE-TV PRESENT:
ALL IN TOGETHER NOW
A SILVER JUBILEE SPECTACULAR

Through a pair of binoculars Gregory Eternity gazes squintingly, like a moustachioed and gunslung nearsighted person, though he isn't (nearsighted), he can see really great, out over the roiling black waters, which are also white where the waves lick like black yet white-tipped tongues into whitecaps, of the Lake.

He lowers the binoculars as a look of consternation sweeps over his face at the same time as a cloud sweeps over the sun, metaphorically. What could be out there? his scrutinizing gaze seems to suggest. Something, suggests his gaze, as he squints and looks through the binoculars again. Maybe something evil . . .

Something's out there, he intones brassily, and his second-in-command, a buxom and curvaceously sensual yet with a look in her eye that says, *Just fuggin try me*, woman named Isabella who wears bulletbelts crisscrossed over her torso, combat boots, and cool reflective shades behind which it's impossible to tell what she's thinking, says sultrily, I think you're right.

He turns to Isabella and kisses her, hard, his moustaches smearing against her soft, creamy skin like a broom pressed against a wall and smeared around as though to scrub something gross off of it.

Take me, she says. So he does. Gregory Eternity takes her, right there, soft and then hard, poetically on his mother's grave in the middle of the Necropolis.

But while they are taking each other something moves on the horizon — something black, something not quite human, something with the reek of the inhuman about it like a stinky halo of otherworldly danger and evildoing. Something evil.

What are we doing? says Gregory Eternity, withdrawing briefly from Isabella, already well on her way to her sixth climax. She is a woman ripe in her prime.

Isabella climaxes anyway, then collapses on the bed of flowers they laid there earlier — the reason they've come to the Necropolis being to lay flowers for Gregory Eternity's dead mother, who passed quietly at her own home surrounded by friends and family, except Gregory Eternity, who was out drinking cider with his buddies, and now carries guilt like a bag of rotten squab because he could have saved her with one of his kidneys, but didn't, for reasons unexplained. Probably medical.

Danger-slash-evil is moving closer.

Who is it? says Gregory Eternity, who quit drinking through a supportive twelve-step program at the Museum of Prosperity (Sundays 2–4 p.m.). But it must be a rhetorical question, because then he answers himself sort of: It's not human.

Isabella shudders visibly. What do we do? she asks questioningly.

Gregory Eternity squints again, putting his pants back on. We defend this place, he growls. This is our home and no outsiders will ever come here and take it from us. This is where we live and so do our friends and families, except my mother, who is dead, RIP. It's the best city in the world. Do they think they can come here and take it from us?

I don't fuggin think so, says Isabella, producing a huge gun from somewhere, cocking it, and glaring with a come-and-get-it look at the encroaching boats (they're actually boats). She focuses her aim on the lead boat, which sails a flag featuring a foreign symbol that is inhuman and alien (not necessarily of the outer-space variety) but most of all, undoubtedly evil.

This. Ends. *Now!* ejaculates Gregory Eternity.

Isabella echoes, Now!

But the boats aren't in range yet, and first they'll have to call a town meeting to assemble an army to defend the island. But it will end soon. Very, extremely soon.

PEARL'S GAIT SEEMED even more laboured than usual. From the steps of the Museum of Prosperity Kellogg watched her approach from Topside Drive: dragging herself along, heaving one step to the next. Her jeans were torn at the knee, the hole gaped raggedly. But, most important, she didn't have Gip's knapsack.

Pearly? Hey, Pearly, we're up here. Kellogg stood and waved. Look, kids, it's Mummy!

We are wasting valuable *time*, said Gip. How many times do I have to tell you?

I know, champ. I know. But know what? When you're old like me you're going to look back on this and think, gee, it was so great to have that time with my family, so great to spend time with my parents now they're dead.

Dad? said Elsie-Anne.

Ha, no, I'm not dead yet, Annie, don't you worry.

Not . . . yet, she whispered.

Kellogg ran at Pearl, a plastic bag from the Museum's giftshop swinging in his hand, and hugged her clumsily. Pearly, he said, I got you a present! He produced a sweatshirt. Islandwear! You're a local, figured you should dress the part.

No backpack, she said. No meds.

Aren't you going to put it on?

Maybe later.

Okay. Kellogg took it from her, held it up to his wife's chest, his own. But hey, mind if I wear it? Getting a little chilly out here with the sun going down and all, is all.

Sure.

Kellogg disappeared inside the shirt, struggled to find the arms, popped his head out the top, and announced, Well hello again, Family Poole!

Gip came down the steps. Mummy, did you find my book?

I —

Well obviously not, since you don't have it. How am I supposed to take over for Raven if I don't even know what Situation this is? You *promised*, Mummy, that you were going to come back with my book, I went through that whole stupid Museum with *him* — he jabbed a thumb at his father — and the Sand City model isn't even *working*, it's just covered in fog like outside, and here you are without my book even though I thought you knew what you were doing, but look, you haven't even done your *job* and —

Pearl's open palm connected with a sharp smack. The air seemed to fall apart: it was as though a blade had sliced down and guillotined the space between her and the rest of her family. Pearl's hand shrank to her side, its imprint reddened on Gip's cheek, the Pooles tableau'd: mother and father and son, Elsie-Anne talked to her purse on the steps.

Gip didn't move, didn't make a sound.

Pearl buried her face in her hands, then gathered Gip in her arms. Kellogg checked up and down Parkside West: a family watched from the opposite side of the street. He stepped into their sightline, turned his back, widened his stance. This was private.

I'm sorry, Pearl said, stroking Gip's cheek. I'm feeling a little ... off. I shouldn't have —

Well no kidding, Pearly, said Kellogg. I mean, sheesh.

Gip whimpered. Pearl held him close.

From the steps: Did Mummy hit Stuppa?

Kellogg wheeled. Hey! No way, Annie. The Pooles don't hit our kids. Right?

But, Dad, I —

Nope! Gip had a bee on his cheek is all. Can't ever be too careful! Right, Pearly?

Kellogg smiled broadly, eyes blazing. And watching his wife and son, their arms around each other, he felt certain that it was not Gip who needed holding. If released, Pearl seemed ready to collapse. And so Kellogg joined the huddle, wrapped and squeezed them tight. Everything's going to be okay, he whispered. I just love you guys *so much.*

THE HAND TAPPED the passengerside window with a fingernail.

Right, said one of the kids from the backseat.

Debbie killed the lights and turned onto Knock Street, jostling over the cobblestones. The streetlights were on here, it was disorienting after piloting through the murk of UOT.

Stop here, said the other kid.

She parked at the entrance to Knock Street Station. Across the road, the Island Flat Company flagship restaurant, a two-storey complex that occupied half the block, glowed in twin golden stripes from each of its floors. High above the IFC logo flashed, one letter to the next, over a flatlike obelisk. *At the edge of forever* buzzed beneath in orange squiggles.

Beside it the NFLM Temple looked abandoned, the flickering bulbs on either side of the S I A I O N sign seemed the faint lifesigns of a comatose patient. Debbie laughed: the windows had been blackedup.

And another lot north was the Citywagon Depot, a grid of three dozen vehicles, identical and silver and sleek. Each car was plugged into consoles upon which greenly blinked the time: 9:00. Though it wasn't nine.

Okay, said Debbie, here we are. I don't know how you expect to get into the trunks —

One of the twins, halfway out of the car, said, Let us worry about that, and the other said, Leave the engine running, and they followed the Hand into the Depot, leaving their weapons in the backseat.

In the IFC's upper-floor window, two men in NFLM gear were sitting down with trays of flats. There was something familiar about them: one presided over his food with a simian sort of hunch, his partner, lanky and blond-bearded, demurely tucked a napkin into his collar. The stockier man angled his head, jaws unhinged, to stuff a flat halfway into his mouth, while the other deposited unwanted toppings into a napkin and inspected the offal as a virologist might some rare and curious disease. Then he spoke, and though his lips blubbed silently, each s whistled between his whiskers as: Θ.

Tragedy! Havoc! Snitches!

In shame and dismay Debbie laid her forehead on the steering wheel, playing the previous two weeks over in her mind: the two men's sudden materialization, no one had ever heard of them before, their all-round shiftiness, such a performance of rage and militancy — and so it was. But what of Pop, his *restribution planifications* of the night before alongside these two infiltrators? Debbie had abandoned him. She felt sick.

A Citywagon's window exploded in the Depot. An alarm wailed and blared, the car's trunk flapped open, the shadows shivered with movement.

Up in the second-floor window of the IFC, Havoc — or whoever he was — cocked an ear like a tracker. Another window smashed, another trunk opened, another alarm joined the first. The other man stood, wiping his mouth with his sleeve, moved to the window, cupped his hands to the glass — and Debbie slid down in her seat, out of view.

From the Depot: the puff and tinkle of another window knocked in, a trunk opening. The night air throbbed with honks and sirens. Debbie peeked out: the shadows seemed to fracture and shift. Meanwhile, the snitches had disappeared from the IFC's upper window. What purpose did they serve the NFLM — undercover operatives, provocateurs? They'd comprised a third of the *entire Movement*, nearly doubled its size! Spies? Even the idea seemed absurd.

At the restaurant's front doors the Helpers were accosted by the hostess and held up while the one who called himself Tragedy went digging through his windbreaker. Havoc moved to the window, gazed out, Debbie ducked.

A voice cried, Calum's not in this one either! In the sideview mirror Debbie watched the Helpers leave the restaurant and creep across the Temple's front yard, the shorter man, scuttling buglike alongside his gangly companion, produced a walkie-talkie: Pea and Dack here, he shouted. It's them!

At this the Hand rose out of the shadows, illuminated by a streetlight, with the vexed alert posture of a startled animal.

What happened next Debbie could only process in fragments: a surge of adrenaline — the engine roared — Havoc and Tragedy frozen in her headlights — the car swerved — two men diving out of its path — the Hand and the twins piling into the backseat — Havoc and Tragedy getting to their feet in the rearview — a screech of tires — kids' voices: Where are we going? Where are you taking us? — and maybe Debbie said something, maybe she didn't. Then she was swerving north onto F, over Lowell Canal, leaving behind the lighted streets of LOT, swallowed into the sheer slick darkness of the Zone.

VIII

BY THAT EVENING the fog had thinned to dewy gossamer. Through it cars and vans and trucks stalled all day down through the belly of People Park were directed along the PPT and east on Topside Drive into the IFC Stadium parking lot. Marching alongside the slow-moving traffic the NFLM provided encouragement: Family-friendly entertainment! — Free rides for all! — Better than sitting doing nothing! — Come on you appleheads, let's have some *fun.*

With Harry bunkered away at their campsite, the Pooles walked west along Topside Drive, and as they passed the Stadium Kellogg said, There it is, and Pearl said, Yup. Helpers directed them toward the entrance to Island Amusements, over which coloured bulbs twinkled in kinetic patterns, back and forth. High above brooded the Thunder Wheel, a huge blank clockface stripped of the time.

Why are we here? said Gip.

This is where all the kids are going, said Kellogg. Free rides! See, there's Mummy's puking one.

Why though, Dad? I can't help from here. Raven's gone and I'm the one —

I bet they have flats at the concessions too, guys! What do you say, Annie?

Familiar has to pee.

Familiar or you, Annie?

Same thing. He's living inside me now.

Kellogg knelt in front of his daughter. Enough of that, eh? It's getting a little weird.

While Cinecity hosted entertainment for the island's eighteen-and-overs, Island Amusements' free entry was attracting families by the hundreds: with the arrival of each Redline train more parents and their children poured down from Amusements Station, the lot reached capacity, to avoid double-parking along Topside Drive the NFLM allowed traffic onto the pasture reserved normally for vendors.

Helpers wielding plastic orange batons directed drivers into a grid. One Helper, face as luminescent as his sticks, screamed, Free today, kids, rides're free! and in a panicked semaphore ushered the Pooles through the turnstiles onto the midway. Here the night seemed to open up and come alive. Everything glowed and sang and burbled and flashed, the air redolent with caramel and deepfry, beneath which festered the porcine stink of the portable toilets upwind by the treeline.

In a tight, tense voice Kellogg said, Everyone stay close, and took Gip's hand and, prying it from her purse, Elsie-Anne's. Pearl drifted alongside, gazing around with astonishment. Everywhere was something: games of chance, the yelps of vendors and hawkers, the booming evil laughter of Broken Hill Haunted House, the Atomic Canyon and Holy Road and Kicking Horse (Love the Horse or leave the Horse, threatened a Helper) rollercoasters whipped and roared and looped to the delighted terrified screams of their riders, over Rocket Falls' *Get shot thru tubes!* sign had been posted an apology: SORRY, NOT TIL SUMMER – MGMT.

Daunting queues threaded from every ride, but the two most impressive led to the washrooms and concession stands. These dipped and twisted so circuitously that newcomers assumed positions beside those at the front. You waiting for food or the toilet, a woman asked Kellogg, and he grinned and told her, Neither yet! The woman frowned and was bumped by a man reeling past balancing a tray of ciders and greasy island flats.

Annie wants the bathroom, said Kellogg. Pearl?

She was staring at the Thunder Wheel, its apex lost in the low-hanging clouds.

Pearl? You want to take Annie, or —

No, she said, Gip and I will ride the wheel.

Gip cowered behind his father. The boy's face was still faintly crimson where she'd smacked him. Pearl reached for him, stroked his cheek with the back of her fingers.

Great idea, said Kellogg. A chance for you two to, you know ... Gip? Go on, take Mummy's hand.

The hand that hit me?

Shhh, now, said Kellogg, and nudged him at his mother.

He joined her grudgingly, watching as Kellogg and Elsie-Anne were folded into the crowds, their spot assumed by a teenage couple lugging unwieldy inflatables won at games of chance.

Come on, said Pearl, eyes on the Thunder Wheel, and dragged her son across the midway.

A bored Helper told them, Ride now, you'll get it solo.

Pearl looked up: every Thundercloud was empty.

No view, explained the operator, clouds're too low. Still fun to go up though ... I guess.

Pearl said, Remind me how long the ride is?

Six minutes, fifteen seconds.

Exactly?

Usually each Thundercloud gets less than thirty seconds at the top. But since you guys'll be alone, I'll give you five minutes. Quite a while to be up there, eh, kid?

Gip, what do you think, want to ride it with Mummy?

But —

It'll only take a few minutes. Maybe from way up there you'll be able to find Raven?

Gip gave her a skeptical look.

Okay, said Pearl, we'll go.

Congratulations, said the Helper, helped Pearl and Gip board a Thundercloud, buckled them in, and closed the gate behind them.

AT THE BOTTOM of the Slipway Starx and Olpert Bailie sat in the Citywagon facing Crocker Pond. Or the misty enclosure over it. Despite thinning at streetlevel down here in the park the fog had the opaque gloss of a gessoed canvas. This is good, whispered Starx, just how Griggs said. He led Olpert to the car's rear and opened the trunk: there was the boy, his hood pushed back, gaping at them with one glassy eye.

Hold on, Starx said and went off somewhere. Olpert didn't know where to look — not at the boy, that waxy cycloptic stare, not at the fog, who knew what horrors might appear within it. So he looked up through the hazy ceiling at the darkening sky, the moon nudging into view.

Starx returned pushing a wheelbarrow lined with a tarp and bags of salt. He set the wheelbarrow down, tore the bags open, dumped the salt into the barrow. Then he brought Olpert around to the trunk, reached in, and took a sneakered foot in each hand.

Get his top half, he instructed. We'll wrap him up, the salt will weigh the body down.

The boy was heavier than he looked, his head lolled against Olpert's chest, the jaw clacked open, Olpert staggered and dropped his end. The kid's skull knocked off the pavement with a dull, nutty sound.

What the fug, Bailie, hissed Starx, and all the way across town sitting on the motionless train at Blackacres Station, with Rupe sleeping in her lap, Cora looked up sharply. Something hitched in her throat. What was happening out there in the dusk?

Starx scooped up the body, folded him into the wheelbarrow, arms and legs sagging over the sides, and bound him in the tarp. As he was manoeuvred toward the pond one of the boy's shoes jostled loose, which Olpert fetched and, cradling like a magic lamp, brought to Starx at the end of the launch.

The boy's unshod foot dangled, a hole in his sock revealed a rosy coin of heel, and all the way across town the stabbing in Cora's throat went twisting down into her chest. She gazed out over the roofs of Blackacres to the wall of skyscrapers downtown. Into the twilight appeared the night's first few stars, and in the moon's pale light down in the empty pit of People Park Starx said, Help me here, and Olpert tucked the shoe under his arm and took Calum's feet, the spot of exposed skin clammy to the touch.

Got him? said Starx.

It's because he doesn't wear shoelaces, said Olpert.

What?

That's why his shoe fell off. Olpert nodded toward it, wedged in his armpit. See?

Out in the Zone the moon painted everything silver. Rupe moaned in his sleep, and in his face Cora saw his brother's face, and her heart felt ravaged by little scrabbling fishhooks. The downtown office towers struck her as dominoes, she imagined them toppling, one felling the next until they were rubble.

Starx said, On three. Olpert nodded. One, said Starx, and as two butchers with a side of meat they rocked the boy, salt sprinkling from the tarp. Cora shivered. Two, said Starx, the body swung pendulously out over Crocker Pond, and back. Rupe woke and said, Ma, are you crying? And Starx yelled, *Three*.

The body flew. The tarp unfurled. Salt scattered, arms and legs flailed, and everything disappeared into the mist.

There was no splash.

What the fug? said Starx. He toed the water: frozen solid.

Olpert still held the boy's shoe. He looked from it to Starx.

He's on top of the ice out there somewhere, said Starx, squinting.

The fog was without depth, a wall of white.

Starx took the shoe from Olpert, knelt, and slid it along the surface. For a second or two it swished over the ice — then vanished, went quiet.

Cora said, No, I'm okay. She petted Rupe's hair, eased his head down to her lap. Go back to sleep, we'll find your brother tomorrow.

The mist domed Crocker Pond. Everything was silent.

Fug it, Starx said. Ice has got to melt sometime. There's salt out there too, right.

Olpert peered into the fog. Shouldn't we go out there?

But Starx was on the horn with Griggs: Good lookin out, it's done. What now?

And now? said Griggs. And now, Starx, B-Squad must disappear.

WITH THE WAXY white stick Sam marked two bright flecks on the door of the microwave. (Its clock too was locked at 9:00.) He pressed his forehead against the plastic, lined up his eyes: a match. Next were the holes. With his ducktaped hand Sam guided the drillbit into the door — a grinding sound, a smell of burning plastic, crumbly twists twirled onto the floor. Sam blew out the dust: two eyes stared back.

Next, putty. Sam pinched a grey gob out of the container and sculpted a half-inch volcano shape over the left hole, leaving the top open, and then the right, smoothing the ridges. He put his face up to them, the putty nestled perfectly into his eyesockets, he stared into the oven's shadowy inside and moulded the two little mounds tighter, it was vital that no light or heat escape, or any air get in, and he smeared the putty onto his cheeks and up to his eyebrows, along the bridge of his nose on both sides.

He felt for the power dial. Found it. Paused. Okay, he said.

Sam breathed in with a great chest-filling gulp, and out, and thought of Adine's face after the explosion: that raw pulpy mess, that death mask, that mask of blood.

The work was about returning to nothing. And as Sam stood there ready to rewind everything, staring into darkness, he wondered when it was over what he would see. Even darkness was itself something — nothing would be like space, in space it was always night. But no, night was something. Nothing was what you couldn't see. Nothing was the space behind your head — if there was no space, if you had no head.

OLPERT FOLLOWED his partner into the boathouse, the wood splintered where the big man had shouldered the deadbolt through the doorframe. Starx groped in the dark for a lightswitch, flicked it on: the room was a jumble of nautical equipment, life preservers and flutterboards and oars and paddles and various small watercraft — rowboats, canoes, kayaks, pedalboats in stacks. It smelled of sawdust and mould.

Starx came at him with a pair of denim jumpsuits. Griggs said to get disguises, he said, handing one to Olpert. Starx's uniform fell to the floor in a heap of khaki. He had nothing on underneath. Olpert was transfixed: so much man stood before him, everything so broad and fleshy and thick. Wrestling that massive body into the jumpsuit seemed equivalent to squeezing a ham inside a sandwich bag. In the end the pants clingwrapped his calves and the top flopped at his waist.

You too, candynuts, Starx grunted, we can't be in uniform for when they ship us out tomorrow. Don't look so forlorn, pal! Just a little break, a little holiday, till this all blows over. I need a different shirt though, maybe there's a lost and found here or something . . .

Starx wandered off and reappeared in a maroon Lady Y's Back-2-Back Champs T-shirt, which fit him as a tubetop. Not ideal, he said, but better than —

Olpert was gone.

Bailie?

Starx stuck his head out the door, looked left, right, up the hill: mist, mist, more mist.

Bailie? Starx's voice rang out over the common.

And then, to the north, he saw movement — a figure flitting down the path from Street's Milk & Things. Starx nearly called out, but it wasn't Olpert.

This person was small, a child, a tubby little guy in a red cap who descended with purpose at a light gallop. He reached the bottom of the hill, paused, transfixed by the cloudy bubble over Crocker Pond — waiting, maybe, for a sign.

GRIGGS.

Walters? said Griggs, chair-wheeling beside Noodles before the Orchard Parkway monitor.

And Reed, he's down in the truck. Cathedral Circus is cleared. Only business with anyone in it was Loopy's — she was in there, crying, but we sent her to the pub. Reed gave her a fivespot, told her to get a cider on us. Everything's ready.

We see that. We've got cameras on the street and — he flicked channels — garden.

I'm up on the roof. Of the Grand Saloon. With the chopper. It's clearing down on the street but still foggy as shet up here.

And you're sure he hasn't returned to his suite?

Raven? No, no way. We've had men in there all day. I mean, he didn't have any luggage or anything like that but —

Fine. Is everything set?

Yeah, pretty much. The chopper's rigged and ready to go. Hitch looks good, should be a breeze.

Good lookin out.

So do we go ahead? With the um, demobilization?

It's going to land in that little parkette, correct? To the north of the Hotel?

If Reed guns it, it should, yes. Provided the chains hold.

They'd better hold!

They'll hold, they'll hold.

Griggs lowered the walkie-talkie. Noodles had wheeled away from the monitors to a corner of the control room. Feet up, he massaged his temples, a soothsayer conjuring a vision, eyes closed. Griggs hit TALK: You're sure no one's going to come through there?

No chance.

Okay, I guess we're good to go then.

We're good to go?

We're watching, Walters, keep in mind.

So should we go ahead?

For fug's sake, said Griggs, yes, go ahead.

Good lookin out, said Walters. Talk in a bit.

From the pickup's trailerhitch a towline lifted and disappeared two storeys up the Grand Saloon Hotel into what was either sinking clouds or rising fog. A thumbs-up flashed out of the driverside window, the engine rattled to life, and for a moment nothing happened. Then Griggs' walkie-talkie crackled. Okay, all set, said Walters, here we go.

The pickup's engine roared, the tailpipe belched exhaust in a sooty plume, the towline snapped taut, twanging.

It's moving, yelled Walters, the chopper's moving, it's dragging it to the edge!

The pickup inched forward, the chain trembled.

It's about to go over, said Walters. Griggs, are you there?

I'm here, said Griggs. Noodles and I are watching.

The pickup strained, the towline flexed, Walters screamed, It's going over!

The chain went slack. The pickup, released, went tearing up the road. Griggs waited for the crash as the illustrationist's helicopter fell groaning over the side, plummeted six storeys, humbled to earth as an elephant to its knees.

Instead the towline came whipping out of the fog and thrashed in the Grand Saloon's parkette. No chopper followed. Noodles opened his eyes. Blinked. Did not nod.

Walters?

Griggs, it's done!

No. Nothing came over.

What?

The towline came loose. Ask Reed, when he returns from his joyride.

Wait — Griggs? No way, I saw it go over. What?

IX

WHAT DO you mean he's gone?

He's — Pearl began, but she felt emptied, incapable of words.

In his free hand Kellogg held a tray of flats, the cardboard sagged and dripped grease. He handed this to Elsie-Anne. Around them the midway blared and jingled. What happened, Pearly? Where's Gip?

I got on the Thunder Wheel and he was beside me and —

And?

I look away for a moment, and then I look back, and we were moving, and Gip...I started yelling for them to stop the ride but it just kept going up and up.

You checked lost and found?

No. We should.

And the bathrooms. Or some other ride? Or — whoops, Annie!

The flats slid from the cardboard tray and landed in a soggy heap on the sawdusted path. I bought dinner, said Kellogg, pointing. I thought maybe Gip could use something to eat.

A fly landed on the flats. Then another. And another.

No problem, Annie, said Kellogg. We can get more. But first —

Where's Gip? said Elsie-Anne. Mustard streaked her dress.

Kellogg wiped his hands on his pants, left greasy streaks, lifted his daughter into his arms. Mummy just lost track of him, Annie.

We'll go make an announcement. He can't have left! Where would he go?

Pearl followed her husband, the midway clattered and brayed. They passed beneath the Kicking Horse's loop-de-loop, a train-ful of riders hurtled around it screaming and yanked away, a hawker brandishing two ungodly stuffed bears, eyes thyroidal and bulging, two kids about Gip's age lapping candyapples with sugared frenzy.

Kellogg stopped a youngish couple walking arm in arm, opened his wallet, dug out Gip's school photo, wagged it at them, they shook their heads. He moved to an elderly gentleman hobbling along with a fistful of balloons. About yay tall, Kellogg explained, red hat, healthy, um, girth? Raven's co-star last night? The balloon man apologized, wished the Pooles luck.

Pearl watched this hazily. As the Wheel had first begun to turn she'd gazed out over the island with melancholy. She tried to locate the view of the carnival below as the echo of some memory, but couldn't. There was the story of her poor date throwing up, but though she remembered the details enough to tell it, the actual memory didn't exist. She couldn't recall the boy's face, let alone his name, what the weather had been, how she'd felt before or after. All that remained was the disgusting, dramatic climax. She'd been happy to entertain her family with this, but now she wanted everything else: who was the boy, what had that night meant to her as a teen?

It was then that Pearl realized the seat beside her was empty. The wheel kept climbing. Her stomach flipped. With panic rising into her throat, choking her, she scanned the fairgrounds. Maybe she'd find Gip flashing a cheeky grin and waving as the ride lifted her skyward: what an illustration, vanishing like that. But the crowd shuffled along, no one looked up, no one was anyone she knew — besides the ride's ambivalent operator, face cupped in hands lighting a cigarette.

Her cries of, Stop the ride, stop the ride, were lost amid the roar of the midway and the honks and shrieks of looped calliope. A metal bar pinned Pearl into the Thundercloud, though even if she could escape it was too high to jump, especially on her bad knee — she imagined it popping off like a bottlecap.

The world shrunk away beneath her. At seventy feet it became impossible to pick out faces from the crowd. Another twenty feet up what filled the midway ceased to be people, more a hive teeming with bees. Past one hundred feet their movements resembled a sheet rumpling in a slight breeze. And another fifty feet higher Pearl passed into the clouds, and through the other side, and everything below disappeared.

The wheel stopped with a shudder. She was alone up here — again. (Though that flying episode must have been a dream, surely . . .) This was real: the Thundercloud swayed and creaked. The night was speckled with stars. The moon was colourless and ghostly. She breathed the crisp, clean air. Dread drained from her body. Her shoulders loosened. Her whole body loosened, a tight icy coil within her loosened. Despite the sounds of the fair filtering muffled through the fog, Pearl felt beyond everything, giddy and light, yet serene. She wished, or longed, or pined, to never come down.

What would she return to? A scenario began to play out in her thoughts: if Gip had run away or been kidnapped — hoping of course he would turn up, eventually, safe and sound — she imagined a scene, some months later, returning home from work to Kellogg and the kids standing grimly at the end of the driveway with boxes and luggage. She would be deemed negligent and unfit. A judge would award him custody of the children. She pictured herself in the living room, emptied of everything but her reading chair, sitting there in the dark, deserted and mercifully alone. Just like this.

At this came relief — followed immediately by shame, but the initial response was undeniable. It was a terrible thing to wish for, to abandon your family, or have them abandon you. But she was tired, always tired, and tired of being tired. Conversely there was freedom: no medications, no slogging alongside Kellogg's manically blazing happiness while inside her glinted something black and mean. Pearl imagined her family as a brick and her life a balloon, the brick squashing and squishing and contorting the balloon, the balloon curling up in little rubbery swells around the sides of the brick, always on the verge of popping.

Pearly! cried Kellogg. Come on!

He was lunging past the balloon man, Elsie-Anne in tow. Pearl caught up at Lost Property. The calliope died, the PA crackled to life, and the guy working the booth struck up a little handheld radio. While Kellogg whispered dictation, out rattled a monotone announcement: *Gip Poole, your father is looking for you ... Please come to Lost Property ... Not that you're property ... Gibbles, Dad's here ... He loves you ... Champ ... Everything is going to be okay.*

OLPERT STOOD across the roundabout from Bay Junction, hiding in the shadows from the couple waiting at the Ferryport. They were that headscarfed woman and her husband, a burly creature of beard and fleece, who lived on the Islet's southernmost point in a home built from trash scavenged from the beach. They existed without electricity or running water, grew all their food in a solar-powered greenhouse, hosted gatherings at which visitors orbited a bonfire tapping homemade drums. One night Olpert had watched in secret from among the reeds, found the rhythm soporific, fallen asleep, woken up cold and hungry, the bongos still tocking.

This couple, toiling at land's end with their compost bins and trellised veggies, were worrying: they seemed apocalyptic and crazed, harbingers of some social collapse to which no one else was yet privy. Even so Olpert usually braved a sidemouthed Hi when he bumped into them. But now he hung back, skulking within the shadows while the ferry came chugging into dock and the apron lowered. Only upon the foghorn warning, low and mournful and ghostly, did he race aboard, all the way to the bow.

The engines roared and off they slid toward the Islet. At night the crossing seemed slower and lonelier than it did during the day, a sluggish grumble through the dark. Though tonight Olpert hardly noticed time passing or the lakebreeze batting his face. Starx's huge domed head kept rearing into his thoughts. And with him came the boy, or not the boy, just that single glazed and horrible eye: *You did this to me, Olpert Bailie, you.*

He felt gutted. All he wanted was sleep. Even the prospect of being pulled from bed, handcuffed, and escorted back to shore seemed worth it to collapse into his sheets, slip away, and, if only for a few hours, be nothing but not awake. But handcuffed by whom? His uniform precluded him from justice. Or the forces of justice had deemed him just — they'd even abetted his escape.

The water slurped the sides of the boat. Olpert pictured himself in a limp, tired way tipping over the railing — the icy throttle of the water, sucked under, the peace of sinking to the Cove's dank, cold bottom. He'd never been much of a swimmer, it wouldn't take much to drown. The engines chugged, the water churned. And just as Olpert was gathering himself to mount the railing the Islet's lights shone down, the woodsy couple sidled up, and the ferry bumped into port.

OTHER THAN THE milky hump concentrated over Crocker Pond, the fog on the common had almost completely dissipated. The thinning clouds exposed a dull and flat and sparsely starred sky, not the big wet-seeming messy sort of night Gip was used to back home, which suggested other worlds and dreams. This was muddy, the low moon a halved apple afloat in a bucket of muck. It was in the light of this moon that Gip found his knapsack stashed sidestage.

He opened it, riffled through all the junk his dad had packed — and, with a grin, pulled out the *Grammar*. Yes, he cried. Yes!

Then he climbed into the gazebo. The illustrationist's trunk sat front and centre where he'd left it, or it'd left him, the lid gaped, locks busted into useless tin crabclaws. Standing upon the ducktape X, Gip examined the trunk: its velvet lining was scuffed and threadbare in parts, but there was no sign of any trapdoor or hatch through which Raven might have slipped away. Such trickery wasn't how illustrations worked anyway, Gip knew.

Gip tilted the *Grammar* toward the moonlight and flipped through to the 10th Situation: Abduction. A succession of line drawings presented a figure beside the trunk, brandishing an image, and the second —

The light extinguished. Someone had turned off the moon! No: a hulking figure had appeared stageleft, his torpedo-shaped head concealed a section of sky.

Gip Goode? said a big, round voice. We've been looking for you.

Gip Poole, said Gip.

Whatever, said the man. He was dressed strangely — coveralls that sagged at his waist, a tiny shirt that struggled to contain his massive torso — and approached cautiously, saying something about people who had questions for Gip. The moon peeked over the top of the man's head, illuminating a scrap of paper tucked into a corner of the trunk.

My people just want to know what you know, said the man, plodding across the stage.

Gip hopped into the trunk, took the paper in his hands. Faintly he could make out an image: a drawing of ... furniture?

No, hey, pal — the man's voice was rushed and panicked — what are you doing?

Gip grabbed the leather thong hanging from the lid and pulled it down. Darkness enclosed him. He could hear the big man charge across the stage, fists banged on the trunk, a voice hollered, Open up, you little knobdiddler! And then it all faded: the trunk's bottom dropped out, the sides fall away, the lid lifted, and Gip hovered in space, and then through it he was falling.

WITH HIS FACE pressed to the microwave, eyes inside each of the structures he'd puttied around the holes, ducktaped hand on the POWER dial, Sam waited. The kitchen was still. There were no machines, there was nothing. If Sam had ever trunked him, Raven was gone. Only nothing remained. All that was left was to join this nothing. Sam wasn't frightened: this is just what it was. This was the work. The house was quiet. Upstairs the others were in their beds. But now there was a noise outside — footsteps. Someone was coming up the walk. He'd have to hurry. Okay Adine, said Sam, and sucking in his breath widened his eyes until they ached and cranked the dial as far as it would go and the microwave hummed, and all Sam could see was light.

SUNDAY

SUNDAY

Thus is a life brought to ruin —
Street by dreaming street.

— Kevin Connolly, *Drift*

I

ON THE KITCHEN tiles lay the man in Olpert's stolen khakis who'd said his name was Sam, though that was all he'd said. When Olpert had arrived home he'd discovered this Sam staring into the microwave, his face pressed to it, the oven hummed, a smell of burning plastic and something wet and hot filled the air. Olpert said, Hi? and Sam wheeled to face him. His eyes were strange. They seemed to be bubbling. With horror Olpert realized he'd been cooking them: they hissed and sizzled while the microwave whirred and light streamed from twin holes bored in its door.

What are you doing, said Olpert, who are you, what are you doing?

I'm Sam, said this man in a hoarse, sick-sounding whisper, and fell to the floor.

Olpert unplugged the microwave, it died, and he knelt over Sam. His pupils were pinpricks, the irises glossed with a milky mucous, the whites raw. Olpert dampened a teatowel and pressed it to Sam's eyes. Again he asked Sam what he'd been doing, and why. But Sam didn't make a sound, even of pain.

There's no ferry till morning, said Olpert. I'll take you to hospital then. Okay?

He pulled the towel away. Sam's eyes had the look of scorched jelly. You need to keep this on them, said Olpert, and he wrapped the towel around Sam's head as a blindfold for a party game of bluff. He swept up the twists of plastic that littered the floor, sat in a chair at the kitchen table, and, with Sam sprawled at his feet, waited for the sun to come up.

Hours passed, the tang of burnt flesh and molten plastic faded, Olpert nodded off, awoke to the rattle and scrape of Sam's breathing, noticed one of Sam's hands was wrapped in ducktape — had it always been? — and dozed again. Morning arrived: through the blinds light striped the kitchen gold and grey. Sam sat up, turned his face toward the window, said, I can see it, it's daytime, I can see the light! Though the hitch in his voice suggested dismay.

There's a seven-o'clock ferry, said Olpert. We can walk out there now and wait for it.

Sam scratched at a scab on his jaw with his ducktaped mitt.

We have to get you to the hospital. Your eyes —

Shhh, said Sam, an ear cocked at the floor. He might be down there okay.

You need to go to hospital. It's not my business but if you want me to take you I will. If not I'd like to go to sleep. Okay? I'm very tired. Are you all right?

The fridge came on with a hum.

Sam said, Help me, and extended his arms.

Help you, help you what.

Go to my room. Downstairs.

You're in the basement? That's your unit?

Olpert pulled Sam to his feet, his face came close, it smelled of broiled meat. Olpert said, You can't see anything, can you?

I can see it's light okay, Sam said.

You need to go to the hospital.

But Sam shook his head. No, my room, he said. The work's not done. Help me.

OLPERT STEPPED OUT the front door with Sam on his arm. The sky was opening up into a clear and pretty morning, yet the lawn was sodden. Olpert's first thought was that the septic tank had ruptured again. But this was surface water: at the southern edge of the property little waves rippled up from the lake.

The Islet had flooded once before, when Olpert was nine. He and his grandfather and the other residents had been rescued by ferry. The flood itself hadn't been frightening. Coming ashore the real terror had begun: a fleet of ambulances screaming out of the city, a storm of flashbulbs and jabbing microphones, a gawking crowd from Lakeview Homes as the Islet's evacuees were lined up like hostages and tallied.

Why are we standing here, said Sam. What's happening?

Nothing, said Olpert, and looped his arm around Sam's neck and helped him around back where steps descended to the basement unit.

Opening the door released a damp and earthy aroma, inside this soured into a yoghurty bouquet of mildew and infrequently washed man. Olpert set Sam down on the couch, a plastic approximation of leather, flaking and lumpy, greasy and stained.

You okay?

Sam said nothing. The compress seeped through in twin damp ovals.

Olpert had never been in one of the other residents' units. He took a moment to appraise it: bags of garbage positioned into hedgerows, a bed neatly, almost institutionally made, junk strewn everywhere — broken toys, kitchen appliances missing key parts (a bladeless blender, a toaster oven without a door), stripped car stereos, a heap of sawdust, lumber, a toolkit, a saw — and a huge armoire against the far wall, the doors boarded up and chained in what resembled braces against invasion.

From inside this armoire, someone knocked.

Hello? called a faint voice — a child's. Hello?

Sam tensed.

Let me out, whined the voice.

Who's in there, said Olpert. You've got a kid in there.

Sam said nothing, jaw clenched, teeth gritted.

The child knocked again and called for help, its voice as detached as waking-world sounds to the sleeper slipping into dreams.

I don't know who you've got in there, but I'm going to let them out, said Olpert. Okay?

Sam seemed to be listening to something else. Olpert heard it too: a glubbing sound. Water bumped against the basement's groundlevel windows. From the bottom of the windowframe a lightning-shaped chute jagged down the wallpaper.

First, the kid in the cupboard.

Do you have the combination to this lock?

There's a way but I don't know it okay. The work was not letting him out.

Well we're letting him out now.

Sam pawed the crust on his jaw.

Olpert stepped to the armoire, spoke to it: Don't worry, I'm here to help.

Who are you? replied the child's voice.

He didn't know what to say to this. In the toolkit he found a hammer and pried the boards off, knocked the bolts from the hinges, the door folded open. A fattish boy drifted out from the shadows. He wore a red cap and matching knapsack and he moved with the sludgy gait of a sleepwalker.

The boy sat on the couch. Where is this? he asked Sam. Did I trunk here?

Did you change into a boy, said Sam, or did you take Raven's place?

Yes, I'm taking Raven's place! My name is Gip Poole, said the boy. Don't forget it!

Gip...Poole? said Olpert. You were onstage? Not Bode?

Poole, said Gip firmly. Gosh, why does everyone — he looked hard at Sam. Hey, I know you. You're the one with the lock. Why do you have that thing on your eyes? Are you sick?

People are looking for you, said Olpert.

I trunked! said Gip happily. Didn't I?

Sam shrugged. If you say so okay.

Olpert peeked into the armoire: yellowing newsprint, a splotchy pillow. What make of kidnapping was this? The boy hadn't rushed to freedom, Sam seemed only perplexed. There was nothing nefarious or sinister between abductor and abductee, side by side on the couch. They looked like strangers waiting for the same latenight train, bewildered that anyone else might be taking it too.

From upstairs came footsteps — the other residents collecting in the kitchen. The floorboards creaked, voices muttered, water trickled in through the window.

Sam, said Olpert, do you know the other people who live here? What time is it, he said.

Time? I don't know what time it is. Morning! Time to leave! Your eyes — and you, Gip, what about your parents?

My parents are Kellogg and Pearl. And I have a sister Elsie-Anne but I call her Dorkus and she calls me Stuppa because she couldn't say Stupid when she was little and it stuck.

From between the couch cushions Sam dug the TV remote. The set burst into static.

I think it's broken, said Gip.

Overhead the footsteps moved across the floor to the front door, and through the basement window Olpert watched two men and a woman go highstepping across the flooded lawn. The leak was thickening — tributaries into a forked river, all the way to the carpet — while Sam flicked through fizzing, broken channels.

We need to get out of here, Olpert said.

We *do*, said Gip. We have to go because *I'm* the one that's supposed to finish the illustration. Because he chose me. I'm the chosen one. Raven —

Raven? said Sam. He turned off the set. In the TV's empty face, bowed and grotesque, hovered his and Gip's reflections. What do you know about Raven?

What do I *know*? Only everything! *Nobody's* a bigger fan than me, mister, got it? Maybe you didn't see me trunk here? Now can we *go*, please? I've got work to do!

Work? said Sam.

Quiet, both of you, said Olpert.

The water had submerged the basement window. And now Sam's front door was leaking too. On the other side Olpert imagined a little tiered waterfall cascading down the steps, pooling at the bottom, seeping greedily under the door.

The water's coming in, it's flooding, said Olpert. I'll take you both. We have to go.

AFTER AN ENDLESS tumble through the darkness, the cart stopped with a judder. The Mayor pitched forward, clutched the sides, somehow didn't fall. The air was black, it seemed both sprawling and to compress around her. Tilted on an incline, she realized someone or something was holding the cart: a foot against the wheels, a hand upon the edge, inches from her own hands. And even before he spoke, she knew who it was.

Greetings, my queen, said the voice — that creamy, sleepy voice.

The Mayor sighed.

Can you see me?

It's too dark.

Look at me. Try.

I don't go in for this sort of craziness. I can't be party to it.

Nor I, Mrs. Mayor, nor I. But please. Focus your eyes. Allow them to acclimate.

She closed her eyes, opened them: and saw less than when they had been closed.

And now? said Raven.

Is this where you've been hiding? A hole in the ground?

Is that where we are? A hole? It seems to me more complicated than that. But what do I know, this is your town —

City. This is a city. My city.

Pardon me, of course. *Your city, your* splendid metropolis, *your* great megalopolis. I trust you're aware what comes next.

Feeling herself easing downward again she grabbed the sides of the cart. The movement halted. Raven rocked her softly, back and forth, like a babe in its cradle.

What are you doing, she said. What have you done.

Done?

Done!

Ah. To tell you the truth, I thought this would be amusing. I didn't know that it would be — that it would be, well . . .

Well what. A disaster?

You think it's that? May I ask, Mrs. Mayor, what you think existed here before us?

Where does it go, this tunnel.

Oh, don't worry. For certain, we are totally alone.

Yes, but where *are* we. Where is *here.*

Such a question. Have you considered that perhaps *this* place does not exist even now. Perhaps it never has? Perhaps *we* never have.

I exist! Aren't you talking to me?

Yes! Such sagacity, such simple truth. You exist in your words, and I in mine.

The rocking stopped. The stillness and darkness were absolute.

Everything pitched outward into oblivion. When Raven spoke next it was in a whisper: We do indeed exist, all alone down here, wherever we are. We're unique in that, Mrs. Mayor — so dreadfully unique, you and I.

DEBBIE WOKE to cricked pain through her body, a stiff neck, her left leg numb from foot to buttock. All night she'd bounced from dreams into waking panic. She unfolded herself from the beanbag chair and on creaking limbs hobbled to the Room's rear window and parted the curtains.

Dawn was breaking over the lake. But something was wrong. It took a moment: the breakwater was submerged, waves swept all the way to shore. The water, level with the piers' edges, was starting to trickle over. From below came a pocking, suctiony sound — surf slopped up against the building's underside.

She found the Hand sleeping on the floor of her office.

Hey, said Debbie from the doorway, we've got to get out of here. There's flooding.

The girl stretched, yawned, blinked, so innocent and girlish that Debbie looked away with a flash of guilt — it was too cute, nothing she was meant to see, this gentle kittenlike awakening before that hard mask came growling down.

The door slammed: Debbie was left staring at a poster about how to build community. She moved to the main room, where the twins slept head to toe on the couch. Their eyes fluttered open and regarded Debbie, hovering over them, with suspicion.

We have to go, she said. The lake's flooding.

The office door opened, the Hand padded to the bathroom. A swishing sound — puddles splashed into the Room. She followed behind, kicking water in front of her.

See? It's flooding, Debbie repeated. We should leave. I want to help you.

With a snort the Hand turned to her friends. You hear that? She's going to help us. How? Teach us to glue macaroni to a paper plate?

Debbie glanced at the gallery wall, at all that macaroni glued to all those plates.

No, said the Hand. We don't need help. Let's go.

She led the twins to the door. But she couldn't figure out how to unlock it, so Debbie stepped in, the Hand stood by stiffly as she flipped the catch. None of the three youngsters acknowledged Debbie on their way out — but on the sidewalk they stopped short: a Citywagon idled in front of Crupper's store. A Helper got out, leaned on the roof of the car, called, These kids with you?

Me? said Debbie.

Yeah, they yours? We were getting ready to grab them.

What do you mean, grab them?

We're doing sweeps. There've been . . . incidents. So we're scooping anyone suspicious — nonresidents, whoever, just taking people to the Galleria to ask them some questions.

What sort of incidents? Debbie stepped boldly in front of the Hand and the twins, hands on hips. You don't have anything better to do?

The guy's tone remained lethargic: If they're with you, don't worry about it. Just doing what we're told. Then his expression changed. What about you, you local?

Me? said Debbie. She shrank a little, then gestured to the Room: I work here.

Sure. But are you *from* here.

Of course I'm fuggin *from* here, said Debbie.

Oh. Well make sure you have your papers ready, we'll be doing sweeps all day. And we're still working on the power out, but the trains'll be up again soon. Good lookin out! He saluted, got in the car, and drove off.

Debbie turned to the Hand. Well, she said, maybe we can help each other after all?

The Hand stared back. Her eyes were savage. From the back of her throat came a gravelly sound, rising up — and she spat. A fat wet glob smacked Debbie in the chest and clung there like a mollusc. Debbie's arms floated down to her sides, a faint whimper sounded between her lips. One of the twins laughed. The Hand shook her head, gestured to her two friends, and they moved off up F Street at a jog, down an alley, and Debbie was left listening to the swish and plop of waves slapping underneath the Room.

II

FTER PASSING through the phalanx of Helpers that ringed the Galleria, Kellogg, Pearl, and Elsie-Anne found the end of the surnames N–S queue at the south entrance. Noticing the other legal guardians — some alone, some in anxious-looking pairs — eyeing Elsie-Anne covetously, perhaps even in a predatory, kidnappy sort of way, Kellogg sandwiched their daughter tightly between him and Pearl. Watch out now, he whispered.

From their eyes drooped purple sacks, the skins of spoilt plums. As had many of these parents, the Pooles had spent all night dealing with Residents' Control before being directed downtown just before dawn. For reasons unexplained, a number of young people and nonresidents had been rounded up and detained in the Galleria's upper floors. There was a chance, the Pooles were told, they'd find their son among them.

I have to pee, said Elsie-Anne.

Soon as we've found your brother, Annie, said Kellogg. He's got to be here.

Real bad, Dad.

This is no one's fault, okay? Sometimes stuff just happens.

Pearl blew her nose, tucked the tissue into her sleeve. The line edged forward, the Pooles took a half step into the mall.

Day was breaking over the city. Honey-coloured blades of light sliced between the skyscrapers, the streets flushed pink, the pigeons were up and clucking. More people joined the line. The Pooles moved into the Galleria, the doors closed, and everything outside was gone.

Here we go, said Kellogg. Closer and closer. Gip's going to be so happy to see us!

The mall smelled of nothing. The air was stagnant, the lighting jaundiced. The N–S queue snaked in a slow trudge by Citysports and Bargain Zoom and Horizon Systems and other shops of various merchandise and services, Kellogg whistling tunelessly and Pearl groggy and distant while Elsie-Anne cupped her crotch.

From each quadrant of the mall four such queues (A–G on the north side, H–M to the east, T–Z west) converged in the Galleria's foodcourt, where a glass ceiling admitted a crosshatched quadrilateral of daylight. Here at four desks sat Helpers, each with a Residents' Control registry open before him. By the time the Pooles were a dozen spots from the N–S desk, the morning sun gleamed merrily down into the mall and Elsie-Anne had buckled into a pelvic-focused hunch, knees locked, purse dangling off one shoulder, head bobbing to some inaudible, mictural rhythm.

From the middle of the foodcourt, escalators cycled in opposing ellipses, hypnotic to watch. Pearl watched. The foodcourt was a grid of empty tables and chairs. The unattended restaurants wore slatted masks. Security cameras shot the scene from domed bulbs in the ceiling. No one was eating. No one was shopping. The Galleria, normally packed on Super Saver Sundays, had been repurposed into what some agitated parents had started calling the Kiddie Fuggin Jail.

With each set of legal guardians or worried spouses moving to the front of the line to ask after their child or partner the Pooles inched closer. After rummaging through his ledger the N–S clerk might say, Yes, we've got him/her, at which point two Helpers took off up the escalator and returned minutes later with an exhausted-looking detainee (sometimes two, even three), who were reunited with their family and ushered from the mall — where? Somewhere, with purpose.

Occasionally the reply was: No, sorry, maybe try again later. At this the searchers would either slink away defeated, or stand unmoving with a look of incredulity, or fly into a rage that prompted NFLM interventions: the upset party was escorted down the hall to a special office from which they'd emerge ten minutes later looking not unlike reprimanded children themselves.

Dad, said Elsie-Anne, tugging on Kellogg's sleeve, I really have to *pee.*

Upstairs, said Kellogg, that's where Gip'll be. See, Pearly?

From the second-floor mezzanine a pair of Helpers observed the proceedings below.

Check it out, guys, we're moving again. Only one family before us!

A fax machine propped beside the desk came to life, a sheet of paper curled out, lifted, and flapped down upon a pile of ignored memos. A flustered pair of men stormed past, one muttered, Well where the fug else do you think she'd be then? and the clerk called, Next, and the Pooles were up.

Hiya, said Kellogg, and in his friendliest voice explained who they were looking for.

The Helper leafing through the registry paused, inspected Kellogg, scrubbed at his moustache with a knuckle. Come again? You mean the kid who was onstage?

That's our boy! As you can probably imagine we can't wait to see him. Quite a star, must have been flummoxed by all the attention . . .

The clerk — *Reed,* said his nametag — eyed Kellogg, forehead scrunched into a show of deliberation. Hang on, he said, and chair-rolled over to a man in an identical moustache kicking unread faxes into a pile. He whispered in this person's ear, pointed at Kellogg, and the second man waved the Pooles around the desk.

See, Pearly, said Kellogg. These people are reasonable.

Where are your permits? said the second helper — *Walters.*

See, that's the problem, he's got them, said Kellogg. My son, I mean. They're in his knapsack. Which he might still have! But if he's *here* —

Dad? whined Elsie-Anne, and Kellogg told her, Shush.

This your daughter?

Gip Poole's our *son,* Kellogg said. He's the one we're looking for. But you might have him as Bode. Or Boole, was it, Pearly?

Goode, said Pearl, I think.

What are you talking about, said Walters, crossing his arms.

Reed crossed his arms too.

You guys messed up the permits, said Pearl, and Kellogg leapt in: An easy mistake!

Walters closed the registry. We don't have him. If we did, we'd know.

We're also looking for him, said Reed. Your son.

Kellogg cocked his head. Oh?

I have to pee, said Elsie-Anne. Really bad.

You always have to pee, said Kellogg. She always has to pee, he told the Helpers.

Where do you live? said Walters.

They're not residents, confirmed Reed.

My wife is! Kellogg nudged Pearl. Tell them.

I was born here, she said.

Walters nodded. And your husband? And your child?

We live out of town now.

We're making arrangements, said Walters, for nonresidents to leave.

But our *son*, said Kellogg, is still *here*. We can't leave!

Well your *wife* can stay, said Reed. But you and your daughter, without permits —

Do I *have* to stay? said Pearl.

Of course, said Walters, grinning nicotine-stained teeth. You're a resident.

Or were, said Reed. And I'd hardly say *have* to!

Kellogg swatted his daughter's hand away. Annie, quit tugging my sleeve, okay? We'll take you to the bathroom in a minute. Can't you talk to Familiar? How's he doing?

He's gone, said Elsie-Anne, for now. Dad, I have to *pee*.

Oh, said Kellogg. Did Familiar go back to Viperville?

Elsie-Anne's face contorted, panicked and pained.

Sir, said Reed, we can't help you.

Our son needs his meds, said Kellogg weakly.

What kind of meds?

The type that without them he'll definitely have an Episode!

From Elsie-Anne: a feeble whinny. Then she froze. Wetness bloomed upon the front of her dress. Her expression was conflicted: horror, shame, relief. The stain spread, pee streamed down her legs and puddled around her shoes. No one moved — not her parents, not the Helpers — and the sound was gentle, like distant windchimes, the odour sharp and sour amid the non-smell of the airconditioned mall.

GREGORY ETERNITY and Isabella are busy assembling an army — a lot of work! — from the roof of the Galleria. The streets below are full of people cheering and putting their weapons in the air like they don't care about anything, except fighting for everything they believe in probably.

Something's coming, bawls Gregory Eternity in a voice that echoes the fire burning inside the spirit of every man, woman, child, and cat in the whole city.

Something alien, supplements Isabella additionally. Something that thinks it's going to take our city!

Boo, boos the crowd.

Are you with me? To stop it? inquisitively howls Gregory Eternity.

Also me, adds Isabella moreover, thrusting her gun outward in a display of it.

Yeah! enthusiastically shrieks the crowd, drunk with the taste of the attackers' blood in their collective, gaping, and toothy mouth. And though they can only imagine how this blood might taste, the taste is quite visceral, as though they've once before torn open some invader's throat to feast on the clots of putrid gore that froth forth like the carbonated eruptions from a thousand shaken-up bottles of cider.

It's really obvious that the people are willing to do anything they can to stop the evil force from taking away everything they believe in. Even risk their lives. Even kill. That is just how much the city means to them.

That is. How much. It means.

Are we all in together now? questioningly bellow Gregory Eternity and Isabella in stereophonic dual tonality.

Yeah, deafeningly responds the crowd in kind.

Then to the shores, thunders Gregory Eternity, for that is where we shall meet them!

OLPERT COULD NOT recall the last time he'd held hands with anyone, let alone a grown man, let alone a strange boy. A classmate's maybe, buddied up on a fieldtrip as a kid. Had his grandfather ever held his hand? No, it seemed impossible — in fact up sprung a memory of trying to take the old man's hand in the crowd flooding out of a Maroons game. He'd recoiled and growled, What are we, going steady?

Thirty-some years later, here Olpert was hand in hand with Gip and Sam wading across the Islet. The water had quickly reached halfway up the ground floor of every permanent residence and summerhome and cottage and cabin and beach house. In the deepest spots Olpert wrapped an arm around Gip's waist and heaved him out of the water, placidly the boy allowed himself to be moved. From the ticket booth to the ferrydock arched a little bridge, now each end disappeared into lakewater, the docks were submerged. Olpert led Sam and Gip up to the walkway's midpoint, let go of their hands, and said, We're okay, it's dry here, we'll just wait for the ferry across.

We'll wait here, said Sam. The towel frothed over his eyes, and from the breastpocket of his stolen NFLM shirt protruded the TV remote.

Olpert looked across the Cove: islandside the Ferryport was empty, no one lined up, there was no ferry in sight. Bay Junction seemed closed. Beneath the walkway flowed a river, household items floated past: a wicker trashcan, an empty pack of Redapples, some sort of manuscript, all those pages ant-trailed with type, plastic bags by the dozens — most from Bargain Zoom.

Hey, look, said Gip, pointing. People.

Around the Islet's eastern promontory appeared a strange convoy of watercraft. Roped to a central rowboat heaped with boxes and furniture were four canoes, two paddlers in each, a passenger hunkered amidships. Bongos harmonized each paddlestroke as the flotilla progressed into Perint's Cove.

Hello, hello! Olpert shouted. Help, help!

Gip echoed him: Hello, help!

The southerly wind caught and swept their voices back over the Islet. None of the canoeists broke rhythm, the drums kept time.

Shrill clear instructions came across the water: Stay together, everyone stay together!

The woman in the yellow bandana sterned the lead boat. In the bow, digging into the water as though trying to tunnel out the other side, was her grizzly partner. Between them someone's child knocked bongos. In another boat were the two men and the woman who'd fled the roominghouse that morning. Twelve people in all: the entire Islet community, save Olpert and Sam.

Face pointed toward the Cove, Sam was shouting, his words garbled.

Save us please, called Gip, his voice reedy as a blade of grass and just as effortlessly rebuffed by the wind.

They can't hear you, said Olpert.

A pillow floated past.

Across Perint's Cove the silver miracle of the city gleamed against a cerulean backdrop of sky. The drums were fading. A seagull screeched by overhead, two sharp cries of despair or mockery, and swooped out over the lake.

What do we do? said Gip. I've got to get back, I told you. I'm the one!

Sam said, I don't know how to swim okay.

Olpert stared at all that water. I don't know if I know how to swim.

Sam said, We need a boat.

Do you have a boat? Where can we find a boat?

I could build a boat.

What? You could?

If there was time.

Olpert looked back over the Islet. All that remained were treetops and the second storeys of the taller houses. He imagined the roominghouse on the far shore, waves nudging the upstairs windows, begging to be let in. Maybe even pouring in.

Oh no, he said. Jessica.

Jessica? said Gip.

She's trapped. We've abandoned her. I —

Olpert pictured her terrarium churned to mud, a little mole-nose valiantly sniffing for air — and water smothering it. He reached for the bridge's railing for support. And, steadied, discovered something bright and brave shining through his despair. It took him a moment to identify: courage.

I have to rescue her, said Olpert.

You can't leave me! wailed Gip. I have to get over there and finish Raven's illustration because I'm *the one*, he told me so.

But Olpert was already wading back into the water. I'll be two minutes, he said, just wait here. And, in a voice he hoped was not ridiculous, but the brassy baritone of a hero, he added, And then I'll take us across!

LET ME GO, said the Mayor.

You're certain? If that's what you wish, Mrs. Mayor, of course, I'm happy to set you loose. You're aware what's below, I assume?

Wait.

Yes?

Where does it end.

This? Oh, you know. I'm not sure it exactly *ends*. Though I can't say for sure.

What does that mean. Can you say something that's an actual *thing*, please. Everything's just words with you.

Words are things. Words aren't things?

Answer my question: if you let me go what will happen.

Oh, I don't know. Who can say? Doesn't what happens just *happen*?

The Mayor was silent. Raven rocked her gently, almost lovingly — with a hand? a foot? Or might this just be some telekinetic capacity he had? With a tremor of horror, she wondered if, beyond a voice, he was even there at all.

Ventriloquist, spectre — whatever he might be, he was speaking again: It's hard enough to just *be* somebody, let alone try to make everyone else a little bit more of themselves. What do people want? How can one know when *they* don't even know?

What are you talking about. I want my body back. I want to get out of here. I didn't want any of this. I just wanted everyone to have a nice weekend. I even thought it might be fun. Make it normal. You need to fix what you've done. That's what I want!

What's normal? Isn't normal what I've been trying to show you? And by normal I mean the *truth* — the normal, quiet truth beneath the clatter of your busy city lives. Though did I achieve such truth this time? I have my doubts. I can't judge it myself, as I'm within it, you see? Who knows, I say what I do aren't illusions, but maybe they are. Maybe they're just lies. Don't truths which no longer entertain become lies?

You've put an entire city in chaos. That's what I think. *That's* the truth.

Surely it is the acts of people that destroy them? At most I merely provide the means.

This is pointless.

I wonder, the people — are they at least afraid? Are they truly afraid?

You need to put right what you've done.

No. Mrs. Mayor, I shan't. Not yet. It's so delightful down here, away from it all, and it's good to chat with you. I'm in no hurry to go anywhere. Are you? To what?

The Mayor sighed.

Ah, life, Raven said.

What will happen if you let me go.

I told you, he said, I never know. I just don't know.

III

1

N BLACKACRES STATION sat train 2306. The platform was empty, the movator immobile, the escalator — stairs. The station held the air with the sterile expectation of an empty operating room. Debbie ducked inside the first car, where, in the gloom at the far end, were that same mother and son, food wrappers and empty drink containers heaped at their feet.

She was just in time: the lights came on, the train began to hum, the woman reclined and drew the boy's head into her lap. You see, Rupe? she said softly. Here we go.

As the train wobbled out of Blackacres Station Debbie moved wide-legged, as though wading, down the car. Yet when she reached the mother and son she had nothing for them, nothing to say. Instead it was the PA that spoke: Next stop, Upper Olde Towne. Upper Olde Towne Station, next stop.

Debbie sat. The train moved at a deliberate, measured speed. Sixty feet below, the blight of Blackacres yielded to the gentrifications of Upper Olde Towne. UOT Station slipped by: the tarped platform, wires in capillary bundles bursting from holes in stripped cement walls, a sense of desertion, and then they were through and the PA claimed Knock Street Station would be next.

A toxic odour rose up as they lumbered over Lowell Canal, Debbie gagged. The woman across the aisle seemed unperturbed, just stroked her son's face, the same hand that had smacked the same cheek only the day before, now so loving and gentle. Each caress made Debbie feel lonely and extraneous. She looked away.

On the streets below appeared the Citywagon Depot, the Temple, and IFC. The previous night's events felt so profoundly in the past — such revelations! Debbie thought of the snitches Havoc and Tragedy and laughed bitterly to herself. Though what might they have done with Pop? Possible NFLM vendettas wheeled in her mind, and with them came guilt — she had to do something. But the train moved through Knock Street Station and out the other side.

We're not stopping, said Debbie. I need to get off.

Next stop, Budai Beach, said the PA — it sounded chiding now, somehow. Budai Beach Station, next stop.

How absurd, thought Debbie, to imagine the prerecorded announcements were mocking her. Yet, really, was it? Though the ICTS claimed full automation, things had to be *somehow* run by people: someone had once spoken these words, as someone now decreed a straight shot through — to where? She pictured a phantom behind a vast, flashing circuitboard, taunting them with each station stop, steadily hauling them in.

Out in Kidd's Harbour flashed squares of silver: the roofs of Citywagons in the Budai Depot. The flooding spilled over Lakeside Drive to the base of the bluffs. Debbie turned to share this with her co-passengers, but they seemed to exist in a separate reality, the woman stroked her son's face, eyes vacant and forlorn.

The train entered Budai Beach Station, a bubble of concrete and glass, hawk decals deterred the kamikaze of muddled gulls off the lake. Again the train slid through. 72 Steps Station, they were told, would allegedly be next.

The woman was asking her something.

Sorry? Debbie said.

I asked where you're going.

Oh.

Downtown to look for someone too?

I'm — yes.

Who?

Someone, she said, but her throat was tight and the word came out strained.

Us too, said the woman, and went back to petting her son.

The tracks skirted the bluffs into Mount Mustela, where hundreds of people crowded the boulevard. As the PA announced 72 Steps Station a banner unfurled from Bookland's roof: FINISH THE TRICK! Placards were lofted — WHERE'S RAVEN? and GIVE US BACK OUR BRIDGE. And a chant began, less reverent now than incantatory: Ra-*ven*, Ra-*ven*, Ra-*ven*.

A protest. Debbie smiled ruefully and thought, So here's what it takes.

We're stopping, said the woman.

The train heaved as it braked, the lights went out, the engines died. And sat unmoving in the station, while down on the street khaki uniforms infiltrated the crowd — Helpers handing out sparklers and streamers to help soften people's ire into cheer.

They're trying to make it a parade, said Debbie.

That's nice, said the woman. Hear that, Rupe? That'll be nice for everyone, she said.

AROUND ANOTHER corner of the Galleria's back corridors Pearl crept, into the service elevator, she pressed the TWO button, winced as the doors banged closed.

The elevator seemed to conspire against subterfuge, grating and groaning as it cranked its way up. Yet no Helpers were waiting for her on the second floor. The hallway was identical to the one downstairs: a storeroom of cardboard, staff washrooms, the same lifeless quiet all the way to double doors with windows laced with wire. Lit with blue emergency halogens, the mall's upper level had the ambience of a bunker or submarine. The shops were shuttered and dark.

She chanced cracking the door. Clothing racks and shelving blockaded the mouth of the northern quadrant, guarded by a single Helper, arms crossed and staring into the middle distance with a look of dutiful vacancy. Two men rose out of the foodcourt on the escalator. Good lookin outs were traded, the watchman ushered his comrades past, resumed his post.

A scream pierced the air — followed by chuckling, then silence.

Was it Gip? No, the voice had sounded older, thicker. Pearl held her breath, listened. The escalator droned and ticked. Her throat felt dry, her nose ran, her eyes itched — Kellogg had packed the antihistamines in Gip's knapsack, wherever it might be . . .

The lookout adjusted himself, resumed his stoic watch. Pearl considered various strategies of how to make her approach: with authority — *They told me to come up here myself and find my son* — or cutely, with fluttering eyelashes, or a sad trudge that suggested distress, she'd beg, *Help me, please, my son.* Or she could just dash at him shrieking, knock him down, and hurdle the barricade . . .

Something settled on her shoulder: a hand.

It belonged to the Residents' Control guy, Reed, from downstairs, offering his best expression of rebuke, halfway between a hammy scowl and pained constipation. Behind him Kellogg stood looking sheepish with Elsie-Anne. The pee-soaked dress discarded, Pearl had bundled her daughter in Kellogg's Islandwear sweatshirt, toga-style.

Hi, Pearly, said Kellogg. He found us hiding in the garbage room.

You can't be up here, said Reed.

Pearl sighed. So now what?

Well, said Kellogg. He says Annie and I have to go home.

All nonresidents are being — Reed struggled for the right word — *extradited*.

But not me, said Pearl.

No, you're from here. Reed brightened. Which means you can go watch the movie!

ORGIES AREN'T PLANNED. Everyone knows they just happen, as with the endless turn of the seasons or getting pooped on by a bird. So when the orgy on the city streets begins it's a surprise to Gregory Eternity, if he's honest with himself he kind of suspected something like this might happen, especially with bloodlust as thick in the air as homicidal pollen. But it isn't just bloodlust. It's sexlust too, apparently.

While people on the street begin to seductively disrobe, Isabella turns to Gregory Eternity, standing beside her on the roof of the Galleria, and demandingly queries, Do we have time for this?

A light shines in Gregory Eternity's eyes not unlike the sort of light that might shine on a porch if you are inside waiting for someone to come home to have sex with them. Why don't you tell me, he slurs suggestively, and then comes at Isabella with his tongue protruding beneath his moustaches.

She takes him, right there on the roof. First she's on top, then underneath, then they're doing it in a sideways fashion with their limbs sticking out like the blades of a multipurpose knife splayed for cleaning in the dishwasher. Below the streets roil with body fluids and desire. People incorporate all the positions they know, and when those run out they make up new ones: Up-from-Under, Dirty Squab, the Bonnet & the Bee.

Where are the children?

Anyway, more urgently the attackers are steadily and stealthily approaching in their craft from the lake, so at some point Gregory Eternity dismounts and screams, Okay, everybody finish up, and he starts counting and at, One hundred! everyone climaxes at the same time. It's indubitably the most beautiful moment many people in attendance have ever seen or heard or smelled or in which they've partaken, even former members of the glory-days-era Lady Y's, Back-2-Back Champs.

Okay, say Gregory Eternity and Isabella, together and all at once. Now let's go show these invaders what tough meat we're made of.

WITH JESSICA RESCUED and tucked inside a Y's cap pulled down to his ears, in the roominghouse's flooded yard Olpert discovered the armoire's doors bumping against a tree. He pulled the boards off, split them in two halves, and, repressing pained memories of forced swimming lessons, lay upon the less damaged side and tried a few flutterkicks: the door held.

Upon this dubious watercraft he paddled back toward the ferryport. Jessica's initial panicked scrabble had subsided, all he could feel was the rapid stammer of a heartbeat against his forehead. It's okay, Jess, he whispered as he swam, pushing off on ground gone mucky and soft.

This was not what a hero looked like: a skinny man in too-big clothes and a rodent tiara drifting atop cheap timber. And what hero would abandon a corpse, the one-eyed teen, had Crocker Pond melted, had he gone down? The sunlight soaked the water's dark surface in an oily sheen. He imagined it sucking him under, he could taste the tar.

He'd left Gip with the strange man, Olpert's housemate, was he a kidnapper? A terrible, dangerous mistake: it reminded him of a riddle from his childhood, how to cross a river with a boat that fit two and not three among a falcon, chickadee, and sack of seed, the goal was to have nothing eaten, he'd been first in his class to solve it, Katie Sharpe had been impressed — where now were those smarts? He'd spent too much time browsing magazines and living indoors and going pale, everything about him had paled.

But here he was at the Ferryport, and Sam and Gip were waiting. The water made suckling noises against the walkway's underside. The boy waved.

He keeps saying he has to finish his work, Gip said, but *I'm* the one. Raven chose *me.*

Great, said Olpert. Listen, Sam, I've got the door from your wardrobe, we'll use it as a raft to get across the Cove. We'll just hold on and kick. And, Gip, you'll ride it, okay?

But I'm the one, right? said Gip. Can you tell him?

Sure, said Olpert. Sam, he's the one.

I just want to finish the work okay, said Sam, and patted the TV remote in his pocket.

Okay, said Olpert, and slid into the water.

Perint's Cove was the colour of steel. Across it the Islet flotilla reached Lakeview Campground, the lake so high they boated right into the trees.

I can't really swim, said Gip.

You don't need to swim, you're going on this raft.

That's not a raft. It's a door.

It used to be a door. Now it's a raft.

Olpert stood nipple-deep in the flood. He realized his Citypass lanyard had come off at some point and disappeared into all that water. Past him flowed debris, each cluster telling a little story. Here was a ruined party: balloons, streamers, a slice of cake topping a paper plate — and plastic bags by the dozens.

Gip, said Olpert, climb down, get on the door.

The boy swung over the railing and dangled a hesitant foot. Just step down, Olpert said, steadying the door, I'm right here. Gip said, Sure? and Olpert said, Sure, and the boy dropped, landed on his knees on the door, which wobbled but didn't tip, then flattened onto his stomach, knapsack riding his back. I'm on it, he said.

Sam, come down, said Olpert. This is the only way across. If you stay you'll drown.

I can't swim, he said.

It's not swimming, you just have to kick.

Sam picked at his facial wound, sniffed what smeared his ducktaped fingers. A pause. And with a shrug folded over the railing and flopped into the water below. The door nearly capsized, Gip clung to its edges, and when Sam surfaced his blindfold had gone askew.

Olpert pulled the wet rag over those dead pink eyes and placed Sam's hand on the door's handle. Next he whisked a Bargain Zoom bag through the air, tied it swiftly: an inflated bladder. Hold this with your other hand, he said, passing it to Sam, then made a similar float for himself and moved to the door's opposite side.

We're going to cross now, said Olpert. Sam, kick. Gip, lie there and hold on. Okay?

The current carried them briskly into the Cove. Gip sprawled facedown, white-knuckling the door's edges, while Sam and Olpert paddled. The temperature of the water plummeted. Sam, yelled Olpert, keep kicking! We'll stay warm if we keep moving. And though with every swell and dip the raft pitched and icy water washed over the sides, the waves felt to Olpert like hands, passing them shoreward all the way to the city.

IV

THE FATHER-DAUGHTER Poole duo was escorted first to Lakeside Campground to gather their luggage (the minivan could be collected, they were told, upon the bridge's . . . rematerialization), then down into People Park. The previous day's snowfall had melted into a brown gravy, Kellogg and Elsie-Anne found a dry knoll behind the gazebo where they sat upon their bags. But as more evacuees arrived they were forced to stand, penned in by Helpers stalking the periphery like bored shepherds.

A man with a camera asked to take Kellogg and Elsie-Anne's picture, they complied, he furnished a business card: *Ruben Martinez, Photographer.* He'd come here solo, he told them — Kellogg pulled his daughter a little closer — and had been staying at the Grand Saloon until getting tossed that morning. Two of those guys in khaki came to my room and were all, You're going home, and I was all, But I've paid for tonight, and they were all, All nonresidents are going home, get your stuff together, and that was it, and here I am, said Martinez brightly, as though being interviewed for TV.

My son went missing, my wife's looking for him, Kellogg said, and held up his wedding band as some sort of proof.

Martinez nodded. I mean, as far as a refund goes I don't really care. I can afford it. But this is supposed to be my vacation, know what I mean? Those permits were a hassle!

This was supposed to be our vacation too, said Kellogg. And then my kid goes missing! I mean, he's got to be somewhere, right? My wife's from here, she'll find him. I'm not worried about it. Though we did have to abandon our car too . . .

Thing is I can't even say for sure if they credited my account. I mean, not that I care. Money's just paper. But it's annoying, know what I mean?

Yeah, said Kellogg, fanning himself. Getting hot out here, huh?

I got some great snaps on Friday night. Pretty spectacular, that stuff with the bridge.

That was my son up there.

Where?

Onstage. With Raven? Gip Poole, our little guy! He's the one missing though.

So was he in on it?

No, no.

But you said he disappeared too.

What?

Like the magician, like the bridge.

Wait. A bead of sweat scurried down Kellogg's spine. No, wait.

From the gazebo came a siren: a Helper stood atop Raven's trunk with a megaphone. You're all going home soon, he shouted, the amplification tinny and weird. We've got water for everyone, we — his words were lost in a honk of feedback.

Six people clapped wanly.

The morning's placid obedience was souring, the air prickled and itched.

Martinez knelt to shoot a pair of Helpers, was bumped from behind mid-photo, and, teeth bared, wheeled at his aggressor — a young mum wearing a baby in a sling. To Kellogg he said, Soon as people get a little stressed they start acting like animals. Though what's the order here? There's no line! When it's time to leave, who goes first?

Kellogg didn't know.

Helpers moved through the crowd handing out bottled water. Kellogg took two and said, Hiya, any idea what's going on? You'll be going home soon, recited the Helper, and turned away. Kellogg gave Elsie-Anne one bottle, the other he splashed onto his face, the water was lukewarm and brackish, bloodlike. Martinez sipped his gloomily. No point holding a spot if there's no line, he said, hoisting his camera, gonna go get some snaps.

He disappeared into the crowd.

The air had thickened into a clammy goo, in it limbs jellied and even breathing took effort. Kellogg looked around: every face shared the same droopy look. Across the pond he recognized the young couple from the campground. Annie, look, there's shade with those folks by the boathouse, I know them, Kellogg said. He took his daughter's hand, shouldered her bag, and wheeled his suitcase at the closest thing he had to friends.

Hi, we met yesterday? At the campground? We were the next site over.

We're not even supposed to be here, said the boy.

It's because we were camping with tourists, no offence. And we're not residents, is what they're saying, even though we fuggin live here.

But all we have is Institute ID. And since we're not from here originally —

They consider us nonresidents, the fuggin appleheads.

They'll make us leave and once things're back to normal we'll just come back.

It's so senseless.

Fuggin senseless is what it is.

Kellogg nodded.

You heard about the flooding?

We were just at the Campground, said Kellogg, to get our bags, the beach is underwater but —

Not just there, said the girl. At the Institute too. The lake's coming up.

Also they're saying there are riots in the Zone, said the boy. His eyes glinted with — what? arousal? People are attacking people and looting. So we hear.

The megaphone wailed: Hi, okay, listen up, we're about set to begin this ... evacuation, or I mean extradition — the Helper lowered the megaphone. The crowd waited. Finally he spoke: Your free trip home.

Since the Slipway would be the evacuees' route out of the park, those assembled at its base were deemed the front of the line. Complaints — But I've been here since dawn, etc. — petered into subdued grumbling, it was too muggy to put up much of a fight. From the Slipway the crowd wrapped around the gazebo, across the common to the far side of Crocker Pond, where Kellogg and Elsie-Anne found themselves at the end of the line.

Kellogg folded a sweat-sodden braid behind his daughter's ear. His own clothes had gone heavy and damp. The air felt tenser, somehow jagged, now that the dull throb of waiting had sharpened into anticipation.

Soon, Annie, said Kellogg, taking her hand. Mummy'll find Gip and we'll all be home.

Elsie-Anne blinked. In Viperville only the baby eels survived. All the grown-ups died.

Is that what Familiar says? Is he back?

Not yet, she said. But he's coming.

From behind them rose a sudden commotion.

The photographer, Ruben Martinez, had been pulled aside by two Helpers, one muttonchopped and grim, the other smiling amiably. While his sideburned partner exhaled hot oxen snorts and smeared a fist into his palm, the friendly one told Martinez, No photos allowed, sorry, we're going to have to take that!

As if disqualifying a recent medallist, the Helper de-garlanded him of his camera. Then he was escorted up the Slipway, to street-level, out of sight. A family of four assumed the free spot in line.

Where are they taking that man? Kellogg asked the students.

Fuggin appleheads, said the girl. Shame!

Shame, agreed the boy.

Kellogg gazed out over the crowd marshalled into rows. The sun pounded the common. He felt dizzy and delirious, and at first thought he was hallucinating when, high above everything on the northeastern corner of the park, the Thunder Wheel began to turn. He couldn't see from that distance, of course, but packed snug into a Thundercloud was the foursome of Griggs, Noodles, Magurk, and Wagstaffe.

The former three men sat buttoned into pockets of silence, while Wagstaffe videoed the scene and in his narrator's brogue announced what he saw: Flooding on all sides of the city! Water really coming up! Nonresident evacuation's underway —

Wagstaffe, said Magurk, shut the fug up, will you?

No need to get all dooshy, said Wagstaffe, just because you're scared of heights.

Reaching the Wheel's apex the Thundercloud wobbled to a stop.

Griggs' walkie-talkie fizzed: It's Bean. First trains arriving into Parkside West.

Good lookin out, said Griggs. He surveyed the island's northern shore: the Narrows swelled halfway up the cliffs. Westward along Topside Drive, where the land dipped to meet the water, waves spilled into the opening of Lowell Canal. The torpid olive-coloured strip cut south alongside the Zone and jagged west between Upper and Lower Olde Towne to dump its sludgy effluent into Kidd's

Harbour. And with the Narrows flooding one end and the lake the other, the Canal was rising.

If it overflows it will go downhill, said Griggs. Mount Mustela and the Mews will be fine. The Zone though — not so much.

Is that our problem? said Magurk, glanced down, and retreated, yellowing.

Well, said Griggs, do we have any idea what's in that water?

Actually, said Wagstaffe, lowering his camera, we do. Isa did a special on it.

And?

Oh, awful things. Lots of awful things.

I'm going to barf, said Magurk.

Well for Gregory's sake do it over the side, said Griggs.

Noodles seemed oblivious to all this. With a blank expression, he watched the sky.

Wagstaffe shot the park, the crowd a patchwork quilt fringed with khaki. And so the crowd readies, he said, and the evacuation begins!

Don't call it that, said Griggs, and struck up his walkie-talkie: Bean, start moving the nonresidents to Parkside West. Then he switched channels: Is the ferry in Whitehall?

Ferry's on its way, came a reply.

Everything's proceeding according to plan, narrated Wagstaffe.

Except finding fuggin Raven, said Magurk, his head between his knees.

Noodles gestured at the horizon, above which floated a handful of black specks.

Your people? said Griggs.

From across the water, said Noodles softly.

Choppers, bellowed Wagstaffe, zooming in. Exciting!

Here to help? said Griggs.

Noodles didn't nod.

Then?

To watch, said Noodles, with a twitch of his lips just short of a smile.

SOPPING AND SHIVERING, Olpert and Sam bumped the door up against the bottom of the 72 Steps. Waist-deep in the encroaching lake, Olpert lifted Gip onto the bottom stair, guided Sam alongside, and there the three of them huddled, the lakebreeze a swarm of prickling insects, waves slopping at their feet.

The lake had swallowed Budai Beach, Lakeside Drive was three feet underwater: out in Perint's Cove the Islet, reduced to peaked roofs and scraggly treetops, resembled some strange forested tanker run aground on its way to port.

Despite the sun Gip's teeth chattered, Olpert tucked him under an arm. With a purple, trembling finger he pointed to the top of the bluffs. Let's go, he said.

Up they went, slowly. Halfway Sam stopped, palms pressed to his eyes.

Hey, said Olpert, come on, we're taking you to hospital. Get up. You can't stay here.

Sam knelt, tucked his head into his chest. This is as far as I can go okay, he said.

Down below waves slung the armoire's door against the bluffs. The water was rising.

Go, said Sam. I'll be okay.

You'll be okay?

I'll be okay. But this isn't the work. The work's different.

Right, said Olpert, and tucking Gip against him they left Sam behind. Each step stung, his bare feet were swollen and the colour of veins.

I'm so cold, said Gip.

We'll get out of these clothes, said Olpert, and get furs, they'll keep us warm —

Fur: his stomach dropped. He felt for his hat — miracle, it was there. Within its folds he found Jessica, an icy nugget, little jaws frozen in a cry of anguish. She'd chewed holes in the wool, evacuated her bowels in a greenish dribble.

Gip said, What's that.

Jessica.

Is she dead?

Olpert pocketed the hat. Twenty steps down, Sam had gone foetal.

Hey, Olpert yelled, the lake's coming up, you can't just lie there. Sam?

Sam didn't move.

Gip tugged his sleeve. Should we help him?

No, said Olpert, turning. We have to go.

At the top step, Olpert looked back a final time: no sign of anyone. The water sliced the stairs in half, steadily rising.

TRAIN 2306 had the look of something discarded or forgotten, sitting there inertly in 72 Steps Station. Below in Mount Mustela things were bustling, the NFLM ensured order and joy, while other Helpers performed random citizenship checks and marched those without papers off to the park. Along with placards (RAVEN, RETURN! and WE NEED CLOSURE and THIS ISN'T MY TRUTH, I WORK AT THE AIRPORT, etc.) people lofted glowsticks and sparklers, a jaunty music played.

Debbie searched the crowd for familiar faces — Pop maybe, safe and sound and back to his old tricks. Instead, climbing atop a Citywagon appeared Loopy, instantly recognizable in her beret

and caftan. With rhythm, perhaps trying to provoke a correspond-
ing chant, she pumped a sign demanding, WHERE'S MY ART? But
she was ignored, the parade headed up Mustela Boulevard, steered
by Helpers across Paper Street toward People Park.

There they go, Debbie said, and sat down again across from
the mother and son.

The woman nodded — not quite an affirmation, her chin
dipped robotically. There was nothing agreeable in her eyes, nor
even camaraderie, just resignation. She seemed accustomed to
being abandoned: at the mercy of forces beyond her, as always
she waited patiently for the world to have its way.

Debbie wanted to say something to either breach or access
this, such faith seemed both admirable and sad. She said, Maybe
we're being held here for a reason?

Maybe.

Sorry, said Debbie, leaning in, I don't even know your name.

The woman blinked.

I'm Debbie. This is Rupe, so I've heard. Hi there, Rupe. And
you're?

Me? Cora.

Cora. Hi. I'm Debbie.

Yes.

Hi. And you're looking for —

Look, said Rupe, someone's coming up the bluffs.

Debbie joined him at the window. Directly beneath the station
two people, a man and a boy, both barefoot, were summiting the
72 Steps. The man took the boy's hand and led him up Mustela,
behind the last few stragglers trailing the parade.

Where'd they come from, said Debbie. A boat?

No boats, said Rupe. But look.

Perint's Cove extended emptily to the horizon. It took Debbie
a moment to realize what was missing.

The Islet, said Debbie, did it flood? It just seems ... gone.

Maybe it sank, said Rupe.

I have a friend who lives there, said Debbie.

Maybe they sank too, said Rupe, and grinned.

But those people, said Debbie, they would have been taken to safety, right?

You'd hope, Cora said.

A chirp, the vents whooshed, the lights came on. The train hummed and shuddered and began to move.

There, said Cora, patting Rupe's knee, see? We're off.

The PA announced: Next stop, Bay Junction. Bay Junction Station, next stop.

And Debbie, rocked gently down into a seat, watched the swollen lake slide by, with no place to go but wherever the train was taking her.

THE PEOPLE EMERGING from the poplars were a shabby, shaggy crew that didn't seem cityfolkish to Kellogg, nor the sort of countryfolk he was used to back home. They seemed wild, the children had a feral affect, the sight of them felt anthropological somehow, ten of them standing atop the park's southern hillock with the look of captured prisoners of war. Last to appear were a bearded man and a headscarfed woman dragging a rowboat jacked up on axles that bumbled over the roots and rocks. At the slope's edge they halted, but the boat kept coming, the mooring lines tautened and dragged them a few steps before they let go and the boat crested the hill — down it came, ropes flailing like tentacles.

Safely on the far side of the pond, Kellogg and Elsie-Anne watched: the crowd on the common's southside scattered, the wheels hit an exposed gnarl of treeroots, the boat lurched free, out spilled cardboard boxes, a TV, which smashed, a suitcase that split and gushed clothes, a pair of chairs, a tricycle, machines, boots, sheaves of paper, food in tins and boxes and jars. The axles bounced off in opposite directions, the boat kept coming, sliding down the hill on its keel and across the mud-slicked common, hit the concrete banks of Crocker Pond with a ripping sound, pitched on end, cartwheeled twice, and came crashing into the water, where, remarkably, it righted itself and glided out over the surface with almost defiant serenity.

A miracle — or something like it. Everyone save the hilltoppers broke into applause. Wowee, yipped Kellogg, Annie, did you see that? A handful of Helpers dispatched to the poplars ordered the boat people into a tidy line to be counted or ID'd — but the man who'd been hauling the boat refused to line up. He shook his head, indicated all their ruined things strewn down the slope. His partner took off her yellow bandana and wagged it in the Helper's face.

Let's not worry about that, Annie, said Kellogg, and he lowered his daughter and pointed at the boat, sailing calmly into the middle of the pond. Hey, he said, wasn't that amazing? And turning to confirm this with the student couple Kellogg discovered that he and his daughter had lost their spot in line.

In front of them was a huge man in a too-tight T-shirt (Back-2-Back Champs, it bragged) and coveralls meant for labour but, flopping from his waist, possibly misworn for style. Where'd he come from? And how could the NFLM ignore such recklessness? This sort of behaviour might ignite chaos, this was all it took: one instance of defiance and another person saw it and thought it was okay, and then another, and that was how order became anarchy, how a peaceful gathering degenerated into a frenzied mob.

Kellogg stared at the back of this interloper's neckless head: the man feigned an ornithologically nonchalant gaze toward the treeline, where sparrows twittered and chirped. Did this bullish renegade assume he could do as he pleased unpunished? Was he brainless or bold? His presence was like a massive flaming boil bloomed suddenly upon clear smooth skin. He was immense and strange, smelled of mildew and sawdust. He had, Kellogg noticed, for his size, alarmingly tiny hands — and this was emboldening.

Clearing his throat, Kellogg tapped the man's mountainous shoulder and said, in a voice of authority, Hey. The guy didn't even turn. And the young couple offered no solidarity: their position hadn't been compromised, they watched Helpers wrestle the bearded man and bandana'd woman to the ground and kneel upon their backs.

And so Kellogg was alone — but no, he had Elsie-Anne! He set her down in an illustrative way, as per the humanity-eliciting properties of small girls, or as though she were a bomb. Hey there, excuse me, Kellogg said, my daughter and I —

The big guy muttered something about it being no fuggin cataclysm, though he addressed Kellogg over his shoulder, as one might a drunk begging for change. How wrong! What about the protocol of women and children first, and if not *women* then certainly children, and alongside them their guardians? Such as Elsie-Anne and Kellogg, for example. But wait, was the big guy singing now? He was, gently, under his breath: *Drag you down, drag you down, drag you something-something down* . . .

Rage simmered through Kellogg's body. And yet it was a trapped rage, a rage without outlet, an impotent rage that festered and fed upon itself, and now Kellogg was shaking. The line advanced. Kellogg rolled their luggage forward and enthused, Here we go, Annie! Though it came out choked. He stared at the point where the interloper's weirdly bullet-shaped cranium sloped down into his shirt, imagined striking the top vertebrae, the spine snapping, the man crumpling, dead . . . But he couldn't. This was how life went: in exchange for his dignity Kellogg was so often handed something putrid and fecal, he grinned and offered thanks while the mess of it oozed over his fist. I'm a good dad and husband,

I'm taking my daughter home, he wanted to scream — to whom? Who would listen or care? No one was even looking.

And then with a nod to a nearby Helper — acknowledged, Mr. Summoner, good lookin out — the big man insinuated himself between an elderly couple stooped over matching walkers. Who, aside from a brief flutter of disconcertion, said nothing, did nothing. What could they do?

A gust of wind scuffled the Jubilee banners hanging from a nearby lamppost. The birds sang, the sun shone down, the weather was a mildewed blanket draped over People Park. Overhead, a helicopter made a pass, the air thrummed. Kellogg looked up: with his feet dangling from the cabin, a cameraman filmed the scene.

OUTFITTED IN A knee-length fur coat and shearling chaps and mohair slippers, wet clothes discarded in the alley out back of the Mount Mustela Fur Concern, Olpert Bailie told Gip, Wait here, and edged back out to survey the street. He slid behind the rack from which he'd stolen the furs, and flinched at a sudden burst of gunfire — no, only an ineffectual dappling of fireworks shot into the daylight. The tailend of the parade at last moved off along Tangent 10, vacuuming sound with it.

Two Helpers lingered in the Citywagon Depot, packing up pyrotechnics. Otherwise Mustela Boulevard, from its bottom end, where the lake was beginning to spill over the bluffs, all the way up to the iron gates of the Necropolis, was desolate. A light wind stirred the parade's detritus of cardboard platters and softdrink cups, paper streamers, Redapple butts, dead sparklers and confetti, then settled, and everything was still.

Olpert ducked back into the alley. Gip wore his knapsack overtop a stole and fleece bodysuit. For headwear he'd insisted on a pillbox hat, cocked jauntily.

Warmer? said Olpert.

What about that other man?

He's off on his own now. He'll be okay. We've got to get you to your parents.

But —

No buts. There are bad people looking for you, and two of them are out there. I can drive us, but I need to get a pass first and it's a bit of a walk from here. Can you make it?

And then? You'll take me to the bridge so I can finish the illustration?

I'll take you to your parents, said Olpert, and they'll take you home.

Oh, said Gip. I'm hot.

Keep the furs on until you warm up.

But I'm already hot!

From the sidewalk came footsteps. Olpert whisked Gip down the alley, out into the Courts and Paths and Crescents and Ways of Mount Mustela, west toward the Temple, abandoned save the Hand and the twins, loading tools into a great canvas sack, and, locked in his basement cell, Pop Street, who moaned, I can hear you, please help me, I'm subterrained below. Please help me. Please.

V

RS. MAYOR, perhaps I too
have failed at the task of living.

You . . . *too*? Are you suggesting I've failed? I haven't failed. You
cut me in half, that's not failure — other than failing to stop you.
No, I've not failed. What are you talking about.

If I put you back together it's just so *predictable*.

But it's the right thing to do!

The right thing. Who decides what is right and wrong? It's
just tradition, that's all.

Tradition — what are you talking about. It's my body.

It's my body too.

No. No it is absolutely not.

No?

You can't come here and perform these tricks —

Tricks? I beg your pardon? What a rude suggestion. My illustrations are the honey of adventure with which I sweeten life's
bitterness! Whomever they do not please doesn't deserve the
status of human being. People —

People? You don't care about people. All you want is to be looked
at, to be watched, to hear them chant your name.

But Mrs. Mayor, up there onstage, I was actually watching
them.

Why?

To observe, to . . . see. To witness their wonder. For my goal, as ever, was not merely exhibiting wonder, as some hawker or showman, but the revelation of a truth that, when one turns away, provokes more profound wonder. Did I do that, Mrs. Mayor?

I don't know. I didn't watch.

She who believes the world's secrets should remain hidden, Mrs. Mayor, lives in mystery and fear.

But you said this was *about* fear. You said you wanted people to feel afraid!

Well perhaps I was misguided.

I would say so.

I almost feel bad about it now.

You should.

I said almost.

WHAT WAS THIS place, thought Pearl, moving west through downtown, and where might her son be in it? After so many years away, the city's connective tissue — every corner that meant nothing to her, every neighbourhood in which she'd never known anyone — dissolved to nothing. In her mind the island had shrunk into a few neighbourhoods enjambed one to the next, condensed and imaginary, a shrunk-down dreamscape inhabited by a distant past version of herself. And Pearl ruled every inch of it.

That was not the case as she pushed along Trappe against the crowds flooding toward the park. A parade, she realized, but solemn, almost funereal. There were no floats. Just bodies trudging through the tropical heat. As they passed she searched for someone she knew, someone to help her find her son. But the faces were faceless. The crowd treated Pearl as a stream treats a stone, oblivious and flowing resolutely on its way.

There'd been a time when Pearl's picture regularly graced the front page of *The Island Word*, she was interviewed or discussed on IBCTV, kids felt bigger having met her — adults, a little small. Now she was no one, ignored and irrelevant, foreign and strange...

The skyscrapers less scraped than hung from the sky. The city made her long for home, her real home, what kind of way to live was this, everything cement/steel/glass. The spindly trees wavering out of the sidewalk were cruel jokes on nature, leafless and bare, summer's sad ghosts. And all these people! How could humanity exist in a place where a person was just another piece of the scenery?

Where was Gip, where had he gone, had he been taken. He could be behind her now, swept along on that tide of bodies, Pearl couldn't look everywhere at once, only drift and hope that chance would carry her son into her arms. But the city was too huge. Faith in a place like this was stupid and vain. She needed a strategy, something firm and real. If he thought Raven had chosen him for something, what would he do? Where would he go?

Into Mount Mustela the crowd thinned. From a sidestreet a couple about Pearl's age appeared rolling a wagon loaded with bags and boxes — and kids. She watched them, pressed together in a tight little bundle — father, mother, offspring — as they crossed the street and hustled past. Pearl headed north up the Boulevard, past Inkerman's, a tailor, a rug merchant, a travel agent. And then, just before the fur concerns began, here was Bookland: a squat hovel, ramshackle and ancient.

In the front window, atop a velvety black cloth and eponymously topping a pyramid of copies was Raven's *Illustrations: A Grammar*. Pearl tried the door — locked. The lights were off, the shelves cast in a dusty grey pallor. Yet deep within the store was movement. A woman poked her head out between the stacks, and disappeared.

Please, said Pearl, knocking again. Please, I know you're in there, I'll just be a minute. The woman moved in a cautious hunch out of the shadows, fiftyish, in a cardigan, skirt, and slippers. She stood behind the window display assessing Pearl, a hand at her neck, possibly taking her own pulse.

I'll be quick, said Pearl. This was met with a stony look. She took a different tack: My son's missing, she said, loud enough to be heard through the glass, yet with softened eyes, hands clasped in an imploring gesture.

The door cracked. I'm only open by appointment, she said through the gap.

I just need that book, Pearl said gently, gesturing at the window. Oh?

Please, Pearl said, producing her wallet, peeling off bills. I'll buy it. I can pay. See?

And the door opened a little more.

WITH THEIR GLORIOUS hearts blazing in their eyes Gregory Eternity and Isabella lead the bloodthirstily heroic and still somewhat aroused mob through the streets of the city toward Budai Beach. Under all those thousands of stampeding feet the earth shakes like a weeping child who stops crying for a moment when offered candy but then has the candy whisked away and eaten, right in front of his/her face, and so erupts into a fit of such violent, wracking sobs that his/her body shudders like an earthquake. Or else is just shaken for being obnoxious.

Halt, cries Isabella, and takes up the binoculars she has procured from Gregory Eternity and through which now she peers.

They're closer, she imparts. The invaders, she clarifies.

Gregory Eternity nods sagely, armed with the knife of this knowledge. Send in the airstrike! he screams with the authority of a man without a drop of fear in his 100 percent brave and fearless blood. Then he pulls out his actual knife, which he knows how to hold properly so as to punch and cut, and does so, examplarily. (This fugger's ready for *anything*.)

Overhead some helicopters lope chopping along and hover above the gathered mob like hovercrafts except in the sky. The lead pilot leans out the window and jabs a thumb-is-up gesture to the crowd, which (crowd) cheers with the mania of a hundred thousand people who are really, really excited about something: vengeance.

Go get 'em, screams Gregory Eternity, stroking his moustaches pensively.

The helicopters sweep out over the Lake like a flock of bees through a hole in a window screen that someone has punched there in blind rage, probably because her daughter is journalling about her, and here now the bees come, hungry for the succulently spoiling contents of the fruitbowl. Only this time the fruit is going to be blown to smithereens.

Let's keep going, screams Isabella.

While the helicopters go out over the Lake to bomb the invaders, the mob moves down Parkside West toward the shores of the very same Lake. Their weapons are poised. Their readiness to fight for everything they believe in has not abated, nor been replaced with mutinous laziness, which in this particular case would amount to sedition.

Out over Perint's Cove the helicopters' machine guns start blazing a rat-a-tatting chorus. One of the invading boats explodes in a ball of orange, hot flames, then sinks. The crowd explodes in exultant eruptions that spray everywhere in a scorching lava of joy. But when that lava cools it becomes the hard and uncompromising bedrock of stick-to-itiveness. Eyes narrow. Fists clench. Resolve is up-plucked.

They're at the beach now. As the helicopters dodge retaliatory fire from the evildoers, Isabella licks the barrel of her gun, as is so often her wont.

Gregory Eternity flexes his considerable pectoral muscles, one then the other, as though they're in conversation. In fact he's having an imaginary conversation in his brain between them: Let's do this, says the left one. Okay, replies the right, let's. And so forth. Then he twirls the ends of his moustaches into points sharp enough to impale cubed squab, kebab-style (squababs, his favourite food). Then he dons shades that match Isabella's, and staring at her reflection in his lenses, she says, Do we have time? He knows exactly what she means. Do we have time not to? he replies, coolly unzipping.

While Isabella and Gregory Eternity are taking each other the rest of the crowd strip and follow their masters as guides. Yet no one can quite achieve the same range of positions or heights of ecstasy. If ecstasy is a ladder Isabella and Gregory Eternity are balanced way, way up on the top rung and whoever's holding the bottom better not let go, because the lovers will come hurtling down and crack their skulls open and splatter their brains like cerebral cortical stew all over the pavement.

THE OVERALLED line-jumper had wheeled to the front of the line at the base of the Slipway, a few hundred spots ahead of Kellogg and Elsie-Anne on the far side of Crocker Pond. Kellogg's wishes upon this man for a lonely death were interrupted with a honk from the NFLM megaphone. All right, people, shouted its operator, we're ready for the first wave!

Helpers ushered a hundred-strong contingent up to Parkside West Station, the big guy leading the way, clapping his tiny hands, whistling and jolly as could be.

The queue shuffled forward. Four helicopters now circled the park, each bearing the insignias, Kellogg noted, of mainland TV networks. A train slid into the station, loaded, headed off south, another group was led up the slope. The sun beat down. Kellogg sweated through his shirt in abstract patterns, Elsie-Anne drooped at his side.

The boyfriend half of the student couple returned from some reconnaissance mission. The riots in the Zone are coming this way, he said. Gangs trashing the city as they go.

It's those people who live in Whitehall, said the girl.

It's finally happening, said the boy.

It is, she said.

It: the pronoun lodged in Kellogg's brain. Whatever was happening was becoming an *it*, an *it* that history would later name more specifically. For now it was *it*, and the careful order of the people, their submission to the uniformed authorities, suggested that everyone recognized they were living an *it*, helpless and servile to *it*, whatever *it* might be.

Exciting, said Kellogg, and the students' expressions wilted into disgust.

Another train arrived, collected passengers, the line moved forward.

We're next, Annie, said Kellogg, and Elsie-Anne said, Yes, it'll all be over soon.

They were relieved of their luggage — You'll get it on the ferry, explained a Helper — and directed up the hill. The air felt tight, the heat stifling, their ordered march regimental.

At streetlevel the group collided with an incoming mob. The rioters, Kellogg assumed, and braced for confrontation. But no, this was a parade, subdued and behaved and NFLM-sanctioned. Still, there were suddenly people everywhere, and amid the confusion, as Helpers struggled to segregate the evacuees, the student couple slipped into the procession north to the Narrows without a word to Kellogg, who watched them go feeling abandoned, though he'd never gotten their names.

A Helper hollered, Nonresidents, keep going, take the escalators, and Kellogg and Elsie-Anne went where they were directed, rode the escalator in silence, waited at the turnstiles for further instructions.

As the movator began conveying people out to the platform, Kellogg thought enviously of the students. If this was an *it*, he reasoned, shouldn't he be more of a participant in the drama? Like those young folks, stealing off to a new adventure. But what about Ruben Martinez, the photographer, whose defiance had only gotten him punished . . .

Maybe action was too dangerous. Instead Kellogg entertained fantasies:

Sir, he imagined a Helper saying, we're not letting you leave.

But, Kellogg would scream, my wife's from here!

Only people who have gone through the proper channels, sir, are getting priority clearance now. And if your wife, as you say, is a resident —

Former resident. She *used* to live here, and doesn't now, because we live elsewhere, and her name like mine is *Poole* but you've got it as *Pode*!

Sir, if your papers aren't in order there's nothing I can do.

Our child disappears and no one will help us, and *look* at my little girl — Kellogg would gesture at Elsie-Anne, an ammonial scent sifting from beneath the Islandwear sweatshirt.

But the Helper would be heartless: You're not boarding this train.

Pushed to the brink, Kellogg would grab the guy by the throat, Helpers would collapse upon him, he would shatter windpipes and sternums and storm off into the city with his daughter in his arms to find his missing son . . . What drama! That was more like it.

He felt a hand on his back. Ɵir, said a lean, whiskery Helper, let'ɵ go, move ahead.

Way down the tracks, a train was rounding the bend from Bay Junction. Kellogg apologized, took his daughter's hand, did as he was told.

When Familiar comes back we'll go to Viperville, she told him.

We will?

Not you. Just me and Familiar. Then we'll be together forever, she said.

Kellogg stroked her cheek. Shush now, the train's coming.

Forever, Dad. Forever and ever and ever.

VI

T HE TEMPLE DOOR was open, Olpert stepped inside, called hello, sensed the word drift through the Chambers like a loopily thrown paperplane, skidding uncaught onto the dais of the Great Hall.

A flick of the lightswitch achieved nothing. Slowly the foyer came into view. Shards of the smashed Hair Jar gleamed within its furry contents, Olpert's own orange leg hair would be somewhere among them. Solid black rectangles had been painted over the foyer's twin windows — from inside. Cast in shadows, the place had that amplified stillness that prevails after destruction, phantasmal, absence so palpable it becomes present. Olpert ushered Gip in from the chortling floodwaters and closed the door.

The library was trashed. One of the recliners had been sliced open, foam frothed from the wound. The shelves had been emptied, strewn everywhere were dozens of defaced (pages torn out, covers ripped to strips) editions of *How We Do*. Olpert picked one up, flipped through. The pages were blank. He tried another. Empty. He'd seen men writing and reading feverishly in here, had they been faking? But then he shivered: the words might somehow, amid everything, have been erased.

Gip called, Someone made a mess in here.

Olpert discovered the boy in the kitchen. The cupboards had been dumped out, a split tin of corn-in-a-can dribbled mucous all over the counter. Various other foodstuffs littered the room: a confetti of cereal and rice, various energy-drink powders in neon trails and sprinklings, anthills of coffee grounds, what Olpert hoped was chocolate pudding piled beside the upended trashbin.

In their furs Olpert and Gip moved into the Great Hall. The pews were upturned, the Original Gregories' portraits hauled from the walls or spraypainted black, or both, and the faintly marine odour of urine hung stale and salty in the air. By the Citycard cache Olpert discovered his grandfather's picture torn in two, the old man's halved visage seemed to glare at him even now with disappointment: *Where were you to save me, boy?*

But of course he'd never been able to save him.

During its innocuous initial stages, his grandfather's illness had been a relief. Instead of attending that week's NFLM meeting, they'd watched a Y's game on TV. The old man shivered under blankets and turned his head occasionally to hawk clots of black guck into a shopping bag. Something viral in the chest, a break from routine and nothing more. Two weeks later, Olpert was visiting Gregory in hospital, and then two months after that interring him in the Mustela Necropolis, the headstone emblazoned with the NFLM crest and the title GRANDMASTER AND CO-FOUNDER in a reverential-looking font. After the funeral, Favours had laid a claw of a hand on Olpert's shoulder and wheezed, You've got a lot to live up to, carrothead.

From the recesses of the Temple came a weak voice: Is someone there? Please, aidance, please, I'm subtrained, please.

The portal was open, the ramp sloped down into shadows.

Olpert took a Citycard from one of the hooks. Listened.

Gip appeared. There's someone downstairs, he said.

I know, said Olpert.

Well we can't just leave him, how we did the other man, the one with the thing on his eyes.

No, said Olpert. You're right. We can't.

They descended into blackness. As the ramp levelled off the basement trembled with brownish light. The conference table was underwater, chairs afloat. Deeper in the Chambers the generator hummed faintly.

Hello? cried the voice. Is someone there?

Wait here, Olpert told Gip, rolled up his fur pants, and waded in. Around the corner, cell lit with a guttering yellow lamp, there he was. Pop surveyed Olpert with ambivalence.

So you've retailed for me, said Pop. Was it guilt? I envisaged as such.

I didn't, said Olpert. I'm not really one of them.

A likewise story. And what now, evil one?

Now I'm going to let you out.

With the Citycard Olpert swiped the security box. The door slid open.

At last, justification, said Pop. Yet how estranged it feels to be rescued by an evil one! I'm aligned onto the side of the behooded revolutionaires. Still they left me. You all left me. And only now you enfeign restribution.

Olpert said nothing, led Pop to the ramp, collected Gip, and headed up into the Temple, past his grandfather's halved portrait, and outside. Water, seeping in blackly from the west, hid the cobblestones of Knock Street.

We can't drive in this, said Olpert.

Ah, but evil one, said Pop, if only you'd not abscondered my watercraft!

Your houseboat, said Olpert. They took it to the dump.

They? Pop eyed him. Are you, evil one, not one of them? Or not?

No. I'm not. It's complicated but I'm not. It's just me and the boy —

Not?

No.

How do you know?

That I'm not one of them?

Where I might find my boat.

Olpert gestured at Gip. I want to get this boy to his parents.

If we get to my boat, I can transpose him to safety.

You can.

I can, said Pop, puffing out his chest. With absolutesimal certainty, yes.

THE MORE I talk to you, Mrs. Mayor, the more convinced I am that you are very intelligent.

Oh, well gee. How kind.

I've made a decision, with your help: from this time on, I'll... I'll ... what? What will I do? I'll try to look at people differently. With more kindness. Maybe. But after all I still have my illustrations to do. So I'll do them, but with a little more kindness.

What about my people.

Do you mean *the* people, Mrs. Mayor?

Yes, of course, the people. The people of this city.

I'd say they're all going under save me and you.

What do you mean, going under.

What do I mean? What does one ever *mean*?

This is hell. I'm in hell.

Hell, Mrs. Mayor?

What was the point of all this? This — this *show*?

Oh, nothing, Mrs. Mayor, but to delight the mind. And to let everyone see what magic can perform. But you say you find yourself in hell? Where hell is, I'd suggest, is where you'll ever be. Aren't all places not heaven in some way hell? Doesn't knowing there is some other paradise make this a hellish reality? But don't little glimpses — *illustrations* — of that paradise give us hope?

What do you mean?

That question again! I mean perhaps, Mrs. Mayor, only when you cease to be will you find yourself anywhere else. And yet can you not find glimpses of heaven here on earth? What's happening up there on your city's streets, say. Is there any other truth than that?

The Mayor looked into the dark, squinted. Nothing. She spoke carefully: And what is this then? Where are we now?

Why, under the heavens! Under everything.

I thought it was everyone else who was going under?

Yes, he said, I do think that's the truth, Mrs. Mayor. Though there is some joy to be found in where we are. Perhaps *this* is the kindness I offer. Speaking with you here and now, at least does, I believe, feel a truer truth. So you ask me where we are, yet you've answered your own question. You know the truth yourself. Hell, stated Raven simply. Truthfully, we are in hell — with glimpses of the other side.

ONE OF THE helicopters explodes terrifically. It just pops in the air like a piece of popcorn with a very, very small stick of dynamite inside. Gregory Eternity rises to his feet, erectly. Isabella pulls her legs from behind her head, climbs down from the tree around which's low-lying branches she'd been coiled, and, smoothing her bulletbelts, assumes her rightful place beside him. Slowly everyone else withdraws or untucks, as flaming debris hurtles down to the Lake like bits of chopper-shaped meteor.

Another helicopter explodes, then another. Mayday, utters the lead pilot as his flying, propellered steed bursts into a ball of flames and he's flung down insolently to a watery grave, in the water. One by one all the helicopters explode, until there is none left, not even a single one. The pinballs of hope bouncing around everyone's stomachs vaporize and through the principles of evaporation become gasps of disaster that go wheezing up their cardboard-lined, dry throats, and out into the world between parted lips in brown, thin clouds of sadness.

With nothing stopping them now, the boats sweep fast toward the island. But how utterly weird, they aren't coming to Budai Beach at all! They're turning left!

They're aiming to half-circumnavigate the island, as though it's a halved apple lying facedown on a plate in the fridge and some bees, right before they die of frostbite, are climbing over its peel. Except upside down. They're heading to the north shore!

They're going to try to destroy the bridge! screams Isabella.

Oh shet, responds Gregory Eternity, though his moustaches turn upward at each corner, revealing impeccably bleached teeth, into a smile. Truth is, he's impressed with Isabella's prescience, though beneath that smile, or entering his smile and tunnelling down inside Gregory Eternity's pulsing innards to someplace that we can only call his soul, we might find a dark, viscous blob of something called jealousy. We've got to get over there first to defend it, he manages to spew forth from his mouth.

Isabella steps in front of him. The crowd goes quiet. She holds her arms up in a V that could stand for Victory or Vengeance, take your pick. Are we all in together now? she bellows in the voice of a thousand war trumpets played by a cyclone massively. And the crowd bellows back just as loud times however many they are (thousands).

Now the citizen's army (because that's what they're calling it) has to run all the way back across the island. There's no time to dress! Will the naked army get there in time to meet the invaders' boats/bees half-circumnavigating the island's upside-down apple peel? Only time will tell. But how much time? (Same answer.) These are the questions asking themselves of each person as they run north with the hunched-over trot of old people with bowel obstructions, inside each of their own, private minds.

Let's save the city! screams Isabella. It's as clear as a freshly unclogged drain that, between the two of them, she's the one in charge now.

Running along beside her, Gregory Eternity's moustaches droop shamefully. But he's not ashamed. It's hard accepting his position in the reformed hierarchy of authority between him and Isabella, which now posits him beneath her, and her on top. But Gregory Eternity is a modern, accepting man. It will just take time.

The sound of the boats churning their way up the western shore of the island fills the air. Though it might sound improbable, this is how the crowd intuits that whoever is invading them represents an especially despicable breed of evil, one they've not encountered here before, even when rival fans come to town for Y's games and do appleheaded things like litter all over Cathedral Circus, the fuggin dooshes.

At the northern shore the mob arrives just as the boats are coming around the corner by the Whitehall Piers. Their engines rape the air.

Everyone in position, screams Isabella. (She's explained everyone's positions along the way through a system of pass-it-along. Simple.)

Maybe a third of the people march out to the clifftops and stand there in a nude line with their guns trained on the Narrows to the west and the approaching invasion, another third scamper up behind them as reinforcements, and a third contingent gambol onto the bridge like a train of ants wandering out onto an island flat that has been folded and laid over a small stream in the manner of a bridge.

Isabella and Gregory Eternity climb to the top of the Thunder Wheel. She starts screaming at everyone through a megaphone. He abides at her side, trying to look proud.

Out on the bridge the people are ready. Yet one weird woman is apart from everyone else. She climbs down under the bridge. She walks out on a trestle. She has no gun. She just stands there, facing west, pale and naked, and the wind tussles her hair like a drunk uncle's hand, though benign, into a mess of black scraggles.

The boats are fast approaching. The air fills with the clacking clamour of a bunch of guns cocked fast. But the woman apart from everyone doesn't move. She seems oblivious to everything: to the invaders, to Gregory Eternity trying to get a U-*nique!* chant going, clapping his hands like someone's too-keen, embarrassing dad, oblivious to her fellow citizens poised to kill, to the world and all that is in it.

GOOD LOOKIN OUT, Bean, said Griggs, and clicked his radio off.

From the top of the Thunder Wheel the view was astounding. The lake nibbled its way inland. The streets in the eastend's farthest reaches had become a grid of black water from which houses and trees struggled, and upon these impromptu canals residents of Fort Stone and Bebrog and Li'l Browntown and Greenwood Gardens boated and swam and waded inland toward People Park.

The westend too was a swamp. From Lowell Canal ribbons of green sludge threaded into LOT and UOT. Residents who hadn't joined the exodus surveyed this warily from upper-storey windows and roofs and the top of the Dredge Niteclub. Only the Mews, swelling bubblelike from the island's southeast corner, remained, for now, dry.

As from the east so from the west, people were escaping to People Park — great convoys of them on foot, grimly splashing through the water, in and upon various watercraft (rowboats, surfboards, planks) they fled the Zone. Meanwhile, the protest/parade had reached Topside Drive, discovered it flooded, and disbanded — some people had relocated to the common, others milled aimlessly around downtown.

Yikes, said Wagstaffe, lowering his camera.

Too late to sandbag it, said Griggs. Once people are downtown it should be fine but —

Wait, said Magurk, what do you mean *should*?

Look at the water, said Wagstaffe. It's still coming up. Look!

I'll take your word for it . . . Lucal.

Whoa, who are you calling *Lucal*? I'm sorry, things go a little wonky and suddenly we forget protocol? What is this, *How We DON'T Do*? What if — he swung the camera at Magurk — we were actually broadcasting?

But Magurk had gone quiet: all this commotion had got the Thundercloud rocking and creaking, he gripped his harness, face as pale as paper.

Griggs spoke into his radio: Walters and Reed, any word on Favours?

No sign of him.

Good lookin out, sighed Griggs. He eyed Magurk, then Wagstaffe. Guys, he sighed, please, remember the fourth pillar. Try to maintain decorum.

Wagstaffe trained the camera west, zoomed in on Laing Towers, where a few dozen residents congregated, safe for now, the water six floors below.

They're spelling something, he said. With the letters from the building sign.

What does it say? said Griggs.

WE . . . ARE — but just a letter R . . . wait . . . wait. Oh.

Oh, what? said Magurk. *WE R O?*

No, that's it. Just *WE R*. They don't have the letters to spell anything else.

Laing Towers, Laing Towers, said Magurk. They could write: *WE R LOST*.

They're not lost, sighed Griggs. They're on their own roof.

How about: *WE R LOST AGIN?* said Wagstaffe. Misspelled, but still.

But if all they're after is help, said Magurk, what the fug does it matter what their sign says? Don't they just need to be noticed? I mean, they could write *WE R* — he paused, his lips moved, the other men waited. The wind blew gently. At last he spoke: *GOAT SIN* if they thought it was going to get them rescued.

Goat sin, yucked Wagstaffe. Is that what you're up to at the Friendly Farm afterhours?

I swear, once we're off this ride —

Enough! bellowed Griggs. Please. Would everyone just *shut up*. I'm sure Noodles too would appreciate a little silence.

But Noodles' attention was turned skyward: a newscopter went puttering past, off to the westend, to video the helpless folks stranded atop their tenements.

AT LAST TRAIN 2306 entered Parkside West. After riding through so many vacated stations Debbie was stunned by the waiting crowds. Even at rush hour such a crush was rare. The doors opened, a Helper stepped into the far end of the car to instruct everyone how to board.

Debbie called, Can we get off first?

He looked at her in disbelief. How the fug did you get on here?

And then he was demanding to see her papers, so Debbie slid into the crowd and, with Rupe and Cora trailing her, carved a path across the platform, singsonging, Excuse me, excuse me, feeling like an enemy of the world. Quickly, she lost sight of her co-passengers amid the bodies closing in and pushing past and draining into the train. Who were these people, she wondered, where were they all going?

At streetlevel she waited for Cora and her son. No one came down. The parade had dwindled, stragglers drifted about, with nowhere better to go they descended the Slipway into the park. Up top, the train heaved out of the station. And still no sign of Rupe and Cora. Debbie climbed the escalator: the platform was empty. South along the tracks, the evacuation passed through City Centre Station, picked up speed around the bend toward Bay Junction and the drowned south shore, and disappeared. Debbie was deserted trackside. Across the street, the lights of Cinecity's marquee flashed and twirled.

FROM THE FLOOD beneath Upper Olde Towne Station the Hand and the twins scrambled up the scaffolding into the half-renovated platform, climbed over great coils of cable and stacked girders onto the tracks, swung underneath and hung there digging drills and electric screwdrivers from pilfered toolbelts. Motors whirred and the process began of grinding out screws and rivets, each one crusted with rust and hardened paint. They worked in purposeful silence and only when the first of the huge lugnuts wriggled loose and tumbled down to the flooded street, landing with a plop in the black water, was there a hoot of triumph, before they went back to work.

WITH RAVEN'S *Grammar* tucked under an arm Pearl waded down to the bottom of Mustela Boulevard, followed people hopping the turnstiles, climbed the dead escalator to the platform, and joined the waiting crowd at 72 Steps Station. The atmosphere was tense, the air clammy and thick. Everyone seemed to exist inside a column of solitude, even family members seemed somehow estranged from one another, the lakewater slapped at the station's struts below.

Eking out elbow room, Pearl opened the *Grammar* and examined its Table of Situations. The chapters were titled arcanely — Supplication, Daring Enterprise, The Enigma. Where to begin? Only Disaster seemed relevant, but all she wanted was to find Gip, not solve the whole city's problems. Even if she could.

Train, called a voice from the far end of the platform — echoed, Train! — and the mood lightened, hope bloomed. The platform rumbled, a galloping sound came from the east. Someone hollered, We're saved! and everyone cheered.

Turning to face her, an old man shot Pearl a gaptoothed grin. Been waiting here forever, he said. Didn't think we were ever going to get out. I've got the ground floor at E and 9, totally underwater when I left it. But as you can see — gently he knocked his cane against Pearl's leg — I'm not exactly fit to walk all the way across town.

The whole westend is flooded? said Pearl.

Flooded? Missy, I've *seen* flooding! This isn't flooding. Sinking's what we're doing. The man winked. Get out while you can!

Sinking? What's sinking? The island is sinking?

Look, he smiled, twirling his cane, here's the train!

A clatter as it neared. When the movator didn't come to life, people stepped into the bevelled warning area. But the lead car reached the end of the platform and failed to stop. One by one, each car flashed by, close enough to touch, packed with people, the faces of men and women and children inside mirrored Pearl's astonishment — *What are you doing there?* — until finally the train slipped off to Budai Beach.

Not again, said someone.

What now?

I've been here twenty minutes! Nothing's stopping either way!

It's not like the trains aren't running.

I mean, was that a train?

That was a train. So was the last one. And the one before that!

So what are we supposed to do? Wait here to drown?

No one's going to let us drown.

What the fug is going on?

Pearl hugged the *Grammar*. The old man leaned on his cane. And somewhere nearby two angry voices clashed like blades.

What about the riots? What if they come here?

There's no riots! Our houses are underwater!

There's riots, people are looting, there's —

There's no riots! Understand me?

The crowd surged, Pearl was pressed against the wall.

Get your hands off of me, said the first voice.

Hey now, break it up — a new voice, booming and paternal.

There's riots, there's riots! Everyone knows! Admit it!

You touch me again the only riot'll be my fist through the back of your fuggin head.

Silence. Expectation. A general, tingling excitement at possible violence.

Tell me this, said the second voice, why riot when the whole city is drowning?

Or sinking, the old man whispered to Pearl, winked, and twirled his cane.

THIS WAS NOT an illustration, said the Mayor, not a trick, not even a spell. It was a curse.

A curse?

You put a curse on this city.

Ah. Oh.

You must put it right.

Put it right. If only, Mrs. Mayor.

What. Why not.

Oh, you know. I have only certain powers and only those at certain times. So, this is to say, that even if I wanted to —

You don't want to.

I'm not saying that. What I'm trying to express is the fear — yes, *my* fear — that I've brought things to a point beyond my control. I can't fix anything now. They must just go, they must just happen. Whatever happens, happens.

For a reason.

For a reason? No! For what reason? What reason could there possibly be?

You don't believe in anything.

Not true. I believe that nothing is what it seems. It's always something else. Or at least we must understand it in terms of something else. The thing itself, Mrs. Mayor, is never quite enough. We must always examine it sideways. We must —

Please, just stop it.

Oh, Mrs. Mayor, are you the duck who cannot imagine herself a hunter?

What.

At any rate, I won't be around here for a while.

And I —

And you, Mrs. Mayor, you should join me. Let me be your gateway.

Gateway? To what?

To your own past, if you wish.

The Mayor's throat hitched. She bit her lip.

Well, said Raven, I do believe it's time for me to go. Will you join me?

Will I? Go with you? No. No, I can't.

Ah. No?

No.

As you wish, said Raven.

Whispering, rustling. A sucking sound of water sucked down the drain.

Then silence.

A breeze gusted over her.

And the Mayor was released.

The cart began rolling down the slope, that sudden urgent tug of gravity. She picked up speed, was soon hurtling down, the wind whipped her face and whistled in her ears. As she plummeted the blackness filled with shrieking. This grew: louder, hysterical, she felt it inside her bones, her teeth, her arteries and veins — and then it stopped, she was lifted, or dropped, the cart tumbled as if into a void. The Mayor felt disembodied, light. She was floating, drifting, like a rogue planet through a galaxy without stars.

And then a voice spoke and broke the spell: Goodbye, sweet queen. I'll see you in your dreams.

VII

ADINE STOOD UP. Ignoring the crowd's scolding — Sit down! — What the fug! — You'd make a better flat than a window! — she was hypnotized by the image onscreen: the naked woman at the edge of the trestle, black hair dancing around that gaunt, haunted face. A hand grabbed Adine's arm, tried to tug her back down into her seat, but those huge and tragic eyes onscreen were too much: they released something from Adine. She felt released.

But then with a great upward sweep of black hair the face was gone. For a moment empty space consumed the screen, then the film cut promptly to Gregory Eternity and Isabella and the remaining unkilled members of their entourage being driven back from Topside Drive into People Park, where the treetops are ablaze with flaming fires like tall, skinny, brown and bark-skinned people with their hair on fire, except not running around but just standing there stupidly, because they're trees, and amid a crackle of gunfire the invaders advance, dozens of shadowy figures like the somehow cloned shadows of something evil's melena-black shadow —

Enough. Adine squeezed out along the aisle between knees and chairbacks. Heads craned, voices hissed: Hey! — Get out of the way! — We're missing *our* fuggin movie here!

In the lobby sunshine came streaming in, garish and disorienting, the first daylight she'd seen in months. Through it Adine stumbled to the bathroom, splashed water on her face, her vision adjusted, shapes defined, the pain faded. She observed herself in the mirror, hair a limp greasy mophead, colour had deserted her face as light from a waning day.

The only sound in the bathroom was the dripping tap. Adine tightened it. The dripping continued. And the sink to her left started dripping, and so did the one to her right, and all the faucets were leaking thin streams, then torrents, cranked open by unseen hands.

She stepped back, her feet encountered more water: the toilets were overflowing, a slimy puddle crept from the stalls. Adine tracked sneaker-prints to the bathroom's exit and out into the foyer. From the men's room water was oozing too, the same dark water, the sickly whiff of sewage beneath it.

The box office was empty, no ushers were about, no one worked the candyapple counter. Adine stuck her head back into the theatre: It's flooding, she warned them, is there someone who works here, the bathrooms are flooding. A few scattered shhhs replied, no one turned from the drama onscreen: bombs explode like detonating broken hearts and Gregory Eternity rages alongside Isabella, the love of his life . . .

Back in the lobby Adine tried the payphone: dead. She left the receiver dangling and headed for the exit, the rug squelched underfoot in a buttery frogspawn, a bubble lifted, and as she pushed out into the crowds on Parkside West it burst and released a little waft of yellow gas as if hatching a ghost.

AS IT CAREENED around the bluffs the train's doors bulged, the NFLM had packed in too many passengers. Kellogg could feel that odd alien hum of a stranger's flesh upon his own, he offered the woman beside him a tired smile, she returned it reluctantly and looked away. The air was warm jelly, skin stuck and peeled off skin with a tacky, ripping sound.

Kellogg's shirt was drenched, Elsie-Anne's hair sopping, the sweatshirt slathered to her as wet leaves over a rock. The speaker system announced the next stop, Budai Beach Station, but the Helper assigned to this car, a rasping character behind Kellogg (nametag: *Bean*) corrected it: No stops, folks, just straight around the Yellowline to Whitehall, a ferry'll take all you mainlanders home.

This failed to raise morale. The human cargo rocked silently in a steady, sloshing rhythm as the train travelled alongside the lake. Kellogg hooked his daughter into a gentle headlock. This is it, he said. They're taking us home, Annie. Home.

OVERTOP OF WHAT had once been Lakeside Drive Sam paddled the door, naked. The pain in his face had dispersed into a dull throb through his body. He'd wedged the remote in the dry spot between his chest and raft. He saw only light, the microwave's blazing, the last thing he'd seen was all he'd ever see. Yet within this were shades: the view to his left darkened where the bluffs blocked the sun, to his right was the greyish wash of the lake.

The light to his left brightened, what he saw now looked bleached. Bay Junction, Sam figured, the bluffs flattening. Were he to cut north he'd be heading into downtown. He was close. Sam felt tired — tired of this work, which was over. He'd not known how it would end. But so this was it, time's machine sucking everything under.

Soon he'd be home. He could smell the earthy potatoey rot of the dug-up ground, the sour gasoline odour of the diggers and bulldozers, the dust of crushed and ruined buildings scratched his throat. Up he'd go, enter the A-Blocks and swim north along the Throughline, and at home in H-Block, Unit 53, he'd find Adine, watching TV, and together they'd wait for time to wheel all the way back to the beginning, to the end.

THE CROWDS COLLECTING on Parkside West had begun to tip into People Park. Debbie considered joining the convoy down the Slipway, but Helpers were among them, randomly checking papers. Instead she fled to the Galleria, where an anxious-seeming woman in a postalcarrier's uniform held the door open and asked, You looking for someone? Debbie nodded. Friend or family? She stared. Well whoever you're looking for, said the postwoman, they aren't here. No one you'd know is in here. And she joined the procession descending into the park.

The Galleria offered a reprieve from the crowds and heat, yet suggested the choked stillness of an aftermath. The storefronts had been smashed, goods rooted through and taken. Debbie hoped pillaging had at least remained practical — food, water, emergency supplies. Though as she was thinking this a young man trotted past shouldering a TV.

In Bargain Zoom a woman was dumping tins of corn-in-a-can into a shopping cart also shared by two children. Debbie called, Is it upstairs they're holding people? The woman spun, eyes narrowed, and screamed, You can't stop me, what's to stop me, her kids kneeling wide-eyed amid a clutter of tins. It's everyone for themself, she hollered, and wheeled down the aisle.

Each store bore evidence of looting, shelves upended, racks overturned, cash registers hung open like skulls with their tongues lolling out. For some reason a small fire smouldered on the reception desk of Horizon Systems, and the lottery booth had been relieved of all its tickets — to which lottery now? As Debbie reached the foodcourt a group of four middle-aged people went racing past, arms full of boxes of cider powder, followed by a friend wearing eight pairs of sunglasses and lugging a bulging knapsack.

Debbie walked the out-of-service escalator, climbed over spilled clothing racks up top. The first store was Baldini & Vogl's Music. She peered through the lock-down grate into the gloom. At first all she could make out were the coffinlike shapes of pianos. But something stirred: the murky lumps lining the aisles were people. They sat on the floor in rows, dozens of them, faces indistinguishable. No one spoke. The only sound was the whisper of a ventilation duct.

I'll get you out, she said. Don't worry, she said, I'll get you out.

No response. Not a word, not a flinch. Did they even see her? And then one of them stood and came lurching out of the dim. Shirtless, wearing a welding mask, he stood unspeaking on the other side of the grating . . . staring at her? In the visor Debbie saw only herself. A chill slithered through her body, as a ghost through a wall.

I'll get you out, she said weakly, backing away, and ran down the escalator and into the northern quadrant, where water was flowing in from Topside Drive, deepening as she went. From Citysports emerged the four-legged beetle of a portaged canoe. The canoe was lowered, flipped with a splash onto the shallow water, its liberators stood over it wielding paddles. And Debbie was relieved to see familiar faces: the most recent additions to the Restribution Movement, the student couple whose names she'd yet to learn.

Guys!

They looked at her blankly. And, with recognition, impatience.

There's people upstairs, Debbie said. We need to save them.

The only person to save is yourself, said the girl. No one else will.

Not the NFLM, not Raven, said the boy. They were trying to deport us!

This boat's only big enough for us though, said the girl. Sorry.

I mean, we're sorry, said the boy, steadying the canoe as his girlfriend climbed aboard.

It's okay, said Debbie.

Water gushed into the Galleria from the north. From their seats, bow and stern, the students looked up at her. Give us a push? said the boy. Please, said the girl.

Debbie swivelled them north. Straight across the Narrows, she said. Good luck.

We'll see you on the other side, said the girl.

For sure, said the boy.

They went paddling out the doors and out of sight. Water rippled up Debbie's shins. She thought for a moment to just lie down, let it wash over and take her wherever it might run. But there were people to help. She procured boltcutters and a flashlight from Citysports, went back upstairs — and discovered Baldini & Vogl's empty.

Empty, yet without any indication of forced entry or escape. The flashlight danced up and down the vacant aisles. The store's austere duskiness suggested a widow's parlour. Debbie squinted, maybe they'd made their getaway through an air vent. But the ducts were bolted closed from inside the store. Had she imagined the captives? Had the gloom played tricks on her eyes? But what of the shirtless guy who'd come to the grate? He'd been real. Debbie had seen her own reflection in his mask.

She sensed someone behind her, tensed, turned. Only the woman from Bargain Zoom, the one with the shopping cart, though she'd ditched it, and seemingly also her children. She pointed at the boltcutters. You using those?

They were eased from Debbie's hands. The woman grinned wildly into B&V's, at all that stock for the free-and-easy taking.

I'm not a musician, she explained, as she set to shearing the lock, but this shet's worth its weight in schnapps.

THE DECISION was sudden and collective: people started climbing down onto the tracks, hands were offered, children were passed below into strangers' arms and reunited swiftly with their parents, the exodus downtown began. A contingent chained up to block the electrified rail. Just keep going, someone advised, stay calm, stay together, we'll get there together.

The old man couldn't get down. Blocking Pearl's way, he wagged his cane into the empty space, crouched, extended a foot, retracted it again. Someone pushed past Pearl muttering, Enjoying the show? This person took the fellow under his armpits, two other people supported his legs, together they lowered him down.

The first person asked him, You okay to walk? and the old man laughed, twirled his cane, said, You go on, don't worry about me, I got here fine, I'll get out at my own speed. But they wouldn't, instead yoked his arms over their shoulders. Am I a wounded soldier? the man laughed, embarrassed, yet allowed himself to be carried.

Ignoring a woman asking for help with her stroller — why'd she bring a *stroller*? — Pearl hopped down, she had to find her son. As she walked she leafed through the *Grammar*, though this was dicey, she had to keep checking her footing from one tie to the next, and the text was a mash of arcane language — An Object of Whose Possession He Is Jealous, A Victim of the Mistake, A Cause or Author of the Mistake . . .

Gip's face hovered in her thoughts, a pleading look in his eyes, but she couldn't picture the rest of him — bodiless, an apparition. She returned to the Table of Situations, and there it was, the book's final chapter: Recovery of a Lost One. Pearl flipped to it greedily.

But the section was blank, all the way to the end, page after page wiped clean.

Pearl stumbled, nearly fell, someone seized her arm, told her, I gotcha — probably best to save the book for later, to which Pearl replied feebly, I'm trying to find my son. Someone passing heard this and laughed: She's trying to find her son! and someone else said, You're the only one, lady! And the person who'd helped her, a woman in a Y's cap, suggested, We're all trying to find someone, hey?

Shaded by the cap's brim the woman's eyes were kind: she'd spoken not from scorn, but solidarity, and her grip was gentle. People streamed past, giving them room. If you're all right, said the woman, we should get going. Looping arms she and Pearl, as teammates in a three-legged marathon, rejoined the march.

Y's fan? Pearl asked. The woman said, You bet. I used to play for them, Pearl said shyly, and her arm was squeezed and she was told, I know, I know who you are . . . Pearl, right? This was dizzying — her own name, spoken aloud, amid all this! Like being kissed. Yes, she said, with the grace of a prayer: Pearl. That's me, yes.

They spoke of their families — the woman was searching for her two girls, they'd stayed over at friends' places in Bebrog. While she'd dispatched herself to find them her husband, an NFLM Helper, was rescuing stranded westenders in a catamaran. People Park's where everyone's going, she said, that's where I'll find my daughters. What conviction, Pearl thought, tightened her grip on the *Grammar*, leaned close, and said, What about my son? Don't worry, the woman said, he'll be there too. Everyone will.

Pearl's spirits warmed: such faith! And all of these people, together, how could they be wrong? But after a few minutes of walking in silence the woman tensed. Up ahead, where the tracks curled inland, more walkers joined the procession at Bay Junction

Station. So many, whispered the woman. Her grip loosened, her pace slowed. And here they were, hundreds of refugees, from both sides of the platform, pouring onto the tracks.

Keep talking, Pearl wanted to say, tell me it's going to be all right. But the crowd had become oppressive, each person's mouth pressed to the back of some stranger's neck. No one could speak, the tracks were so full of people, all those people, still more people . . . With a sudden heave from behind, Pearl's arm was knocked free. She reached for her friend, but the crowd enfolded her, the Y's cap slipped away.

Stopping was impossible. People were wedged in so tightly Pearl couldn't even turn to look back. Already she struggled to recall the woman's face, her voice, the hope shining in it, the warmth of her body against Pearl's — gone, all of it gone. Except the cap, the logo, that last image of it sucked into the mob. And now she was trapped alone inside this mechanical push toward People Park, the site of the crime, and the only place her son might be.

AS A GUNSLINGER with a pair of pistols, Noodles pointed two fingers, thumbs extended, at the sky. One of the newscopters was swooping down toward the Thunder Wheel.

What's happening? said Wagstaffe, videoing. Are they going to take us out?

What do you mean, *take us out*, said Magurk, glancing around for a weapon.

Rescue us.

Oh. Are they?

Griggs said, Noodles?

Noodles nodded, nodded.

Wait, are you just nodding, or is that a yes?

He nodded some more. The newscopter hovered, gusts from its propellers flattened the men's khaki jackets. Griggs' crusty hairdo twitched as if electrified.

A rope ladder flipped out of the chopper's cabin, unfurled, and hung.

We can't get out, said Wagstaffe, because of these fuggin harnesses.

Noodles stopped nodding. He frowned.

Isn't this what Helpers are for? said Magurk, snatched Griggs' walkie-talkie, shouted into it, Hey, who's there, who's this?

It's Walters. And Reed. Is that the Special Professor? Good lookin out.

Right, right, good lookin out, said Magurk. Silentium too, and all that.

Sorry, we still haven't found Favours. We're hoping someone scooped him up —

No, no, this isn't about that. Though, hey, keep trying. Listen, we're stuck on top of the T-Wheel. We need someone to let us out.

We?

The HG's.

Oh. All of you?

The rope ladder dangled. Griggs strained for it, couldn't reach.

Walters, said Magurk. Do you have a boat?

Yeah. Reed's skiff. That's how we're looking for Favours —

Listen, forget Favours. Get over here. Bring a saw.

But what about —

This is an order, growled Magurk. Favours will be fine. You need to let us out.

Good lettin out, said Walters with a sad laugh.

Hurry up. People are starting to notice us.

THE TRAIN ROUNDED the island's southwest corner and dry land appeared: high on a hilltop a cluster of huge houses sat untouched by the floodwaters, beneath it the neighbourhood was lost under a leaden swamp laced with emerald veins. The smell was sour, it flooded Kellogg's nostrils and made his eyes weep.

I'm not actually crying, he assured Elsie-Anne.

The PA announced Knock Street Station.

Ignore the announcements, gasped Bean, between pulls on his inhaler. We're not stopping anywhere, it's just straight through to Whitehall, and the ferry —

And then we'll go home, cracked someone behind Kellogg, and grim laughter flitted batlike through the car.

Well of course, said Bean. That's the plan: then we'll ferry you home.

The train whisked through Knock Street Station. Below a trio observed this from the roof of a house. Their faces were invisible inside pulled-up hoods, they seemed relaxed despite the water rising all around. They seemed, Kellogg thought, to be waiting for the train, watching it expectantly — almost hungrily — as it headed into the Zone.

Next stop, Upper Olde Towne, said the PA. Upper Olde Towne Station, next stop.

Nope! screamed Bean.

On they went, clacking and swaying. We'll be there soon, Kellogg told Elsie-Anne.

Very soon, Dad, she said, and closed her eyes.

From the tracks came a thunderclap. The train lurched, skidded, all the riders were pitched forward and cried out in one voice. Kellogg turtled over Elsie-Anne to shelter her from the pile-on, bodies heaped upon his back, a foot connected with his face, his mouth filled with a tinny taste. And then they lurched to a violent, screeching stop.

Everything was still. Resting at a crooked slant, the train hissed.

A few yards ahead and above was the half-built dome of UOT Station. Gingerly, people disentangled themselves from one another.

Is everyone okay? screamed Bean, and fell into a fit of coughing.

There was a streak of blood on the floor beside Kellogg's head, was it his own, he couldn't tell. Annie, he said, you okay?

We're okay, Dad, she said. But —

A savage groan of metal, the struts buckled, the tracks fell away. As a child released into its bath, the train slid into the flooded street. Riders scrambled away from the bottom end as it went under, water swam up blackly around the windows, the car filled with screams.

Kellogg grabbed his daughter. Annie!

The train eased to rest: half-submerged, half in the open air.

The water's coming in! — Help! — Everyone stay calm!

A mad scramble. The sounds were primal, shrieks and yelps and groans, panicked babbling. And the water gurgling in.

With Elsie-Anne in his arms, Kellogg climbed to the top of the car, someone grabbed him and pulled him up, he was being helped! He huddled among strangers on his knees, someone climbed over him, someone else was sitting on his back. Beneath his body he shielded his daughter.

Please! — Holy fug someone open the doors! — Don't do that! You'll flood the car! — Not at this end, we're out of the water here! — Let me out before we sink!

Kellogg dabbed blood from his teeth. Annie, he whispered, it's okay, we're going to be okay. But his daughter didn't respond, she'd gone limp in his arms.

The doors were pried open. In came a stench of sewage and rot. Everyone out, someone cried. In pairs people jumped. With grim purpose Kellogg crawled toward escape, Elsie-Anne held close, two by two people went tumbling from the train, vanished — where? And then he was next.

A tepid breeze. Hundreds of people splashed around below, the train drooped from the tracks like a vine from a slack wire. A voice yelled, Go! Kellogg was pushed. The slap of the water was sharp and quick. It knocked Elsie-Anne from his hands. Kellogg sank, reaching blindly for his daughter, he screamed a torrent of bubbles, the sour dark water filled his mouth, somewhere in this abyss was a city, drowned and pulling him down.

VIII

A WALL: the cart struck it hard and the Mayor tumbled free, arms scrabbling to break her fall — and found herself landing soundly on two feet. She kicked her left leg, then the right, wiggled her toes, sidestepped, shuffled back, did a little jump. And then, restraining her happiness, she narrowed her eyes and declared, As well it should be, touch green.

An overhead light came on. She was in an elevator. The doors closed, the cables cranked into motion, and up it took her. There was no gauge of floors, but the little tin box accelerated, faster and faster, lifting her higher. The lights flicked off, then on again: the elevator, now glass, rose out of Municipal Works and climbed the Podesta Tower with views of the city all around, most of it submerged under black lacquer.

They're all going under save me and you.

To the west, yachts and various pleasurecraft had formed a leisurely armada, abandoning Kidd's Harbour on strips of white wake. Upon the roof of Old Mustela Hospital patients and staff waved vainly at the media helicopters making passes above, but they just swooped away, onlookers only, not here to intervene. Farther north, at Upper Olde Towne Station something had gone wrong, the Yellowline had collapsed, a train was upended into the swamped street.

There was movement out there too, a cluster of multicoloured dots, people spilling from the train. Some climbed up to tracklevel, others dropped into the flood. And as she reached the viewing deck, with a shudder the Mayor thought of the bottomless alleyway at F Street and Tangent 10: underwater now, while chaos raged on the surface.

She walked out onto the deck, still hesitant, stockings torn. Though she felt hungry. Or not hungry, but hollow. She touched her midsection. Nothing there. She patted, passed a hand through: just space — no torso at all. She was two arms, two legs, and a head, her jacket drooped emptily.

The deck turned. Gloomily the Mayor surveyed the eastend. The incoming water had almost reached Orchard Parkway, chasing residents inland. Cars, their roofs loaded with suitcases and boxes, had been abandoned amid thousands of pedestrians, some pushed shopping carts or pulled wagons loaded with parcels and bags and boxes, others floated rafts buoyed with dumped-out bleach bottles, all of them converged on People Park.

IFC Stadium's parking lot resembled a beach at high tide. The rides at Island Amusements seemed to struggle out of the water, gasping for air. The deck rotated west, toward the setting sun: the Necropolis evoked a kneecap jutting from a filling tub. Nothing looked like itself, everything looked like something else. Though maybe it was just easier to make sense of things that way.

Some of the Mews escapees doubled back to help with the UOT Station rescue. One lavish pleasurecraft stopped to collect folks stranded on the Dredge's roof. But instead of bringing them to People Park, it shuttled them off to the mainland. Rats, thought the Mayor, abandoning a sinking ship.

The elevator whirred to life, zipped down to the lobby, collected someone, brought them back up. The Mayor tensed. The doors opened. Standing there was Diamond-Wood, heaped over his crutches. He grinned sheepishly. Draped over his shoulders was her mayoral sash. You're okay, he said. Good.

IN SINGLE FILE Gip and Olpert followed Pop from Mustela Boulevard through the gates of the Necropolis, Olpert had shed his chaps, they'd gone sodden and heavy, he traipsed along shyly in his skivvies and the shaggy coat. Pop lectured as to why, historiographically speaking, the squabs were flying home to roast.

Speaking of aviants, you are savvy to the birds that used to impersonate these here tombs? An urbane legend, prehaps, though valid.

I don't, said Olpert.

Not *you*. It was the boy upon whom I requisitioned.

Gip blinked.

Young man, said Pop. Bend me your ear! And you too, evil one, whom might learn a thing or two things.

But Olpert's thoughts were elsewhere: his grandfather's grave was nearby — where? He looked around, felt disoriented, it'd been so long since he'd last visited . . .

Well these birds, said Pop, they had gotten lost on their way enmigrating somewhere else, or had been someone's pet, or came over on a ship, a stow-in. But on any rate, it was very colourful, a parrot of some sort, to actualize there were in fact two: a male and a female. Now the male only had one wing, on the right side, and the female only one wing, on the left, and where the missing wings should have been, you see, the male had a bit of bone in the shape of a key. And the female, do you see whence I'm getting toward, young man? The female of course had the enmatching *lock*.

Gip's eyes filled with light. Wow.

Shall I continue, said Pop.

Yes!

Well, said Pop, how do you think they flew?

They locked together, said Gip.

And then?

And then the one with the right wing —

The man.

He did the flying for them on the right side.

And the woman?

She did the flying on the left.

And thus way they flew. Betrothal'd.

Gip nodded.

Should we go? said Olpert, with a glance at the darkening sky. Night's coming, he said.

Pop glared at him. *I say when we sully firth* — he paused — and hence? It is now.

But wait, said Gip, what happened if one of the birds died?

Well, said Pop, that's exactly what transposed. One of them died, and so the other couldn't fly, and so he was, I believe the anecdote finalizes, forewhence the ban on such animals in our fair city, plucked from his nest and eaten by a dog.

ARMS AND LEGS thrashing, Kellogg scanned the water for Elsie-Anne. All around him people scaled fences and lampposts, others grasped at anything floating by — planks, water jugs, other people. Across the street, a woman atop a schoolbus stared with astonishment at the jagged bone poking through a hole in her forearm. Beside her five people in a huddle formation were either scheming or praying.

The names of missing loved ones rang out, Kellogg joined the chorus: Elsie-Anne! Annie! But there were too many people, he couldn't see anything, the water roiled, the world reeled, the reek of the flood so thick in his mouth it seemed a dead and festering thing had been laid on his tongue to rot.

Though maybe she'd never jumped. At tracklevel two cars remained railbound, from which the other four hung. Up top people gazed dazedly across the chasm that separated the severed section and where the tracks resumed on the far side of UOT Station, there was no way to Whitehall except by water. Helpers began pulling them away, steering an exodus back downtown. Might Elsie-Anne be among them somehow?

An aristocratic-looking couple breaststroked past as if out for a leisurely dip at the beach. In Kellogg's periphery someone floundered in the water, a gargly voice choked, Help me, help me, was sucked under, came up sputtering —

Kellogg swept his arms over his head and dove, saw nothing but murk, veered in another direction. The water had the odour and consistency of that foul brown juice that collects in the bottom of trashbins. It tingled on his skin, stung his eyes. It was too much. He surfaced, gasping, Annie, Annie!

An eerie hush closed around his voice. All around people slopped and splashed through the water, calls for help, yelps and shrieks and sobs, but nothing lingered, the air seemed incapable of sustaining sound.

Annie! he cried again, but the word was vacuumed up and lost. Then: Dad.

There she was, on the balcony of a Laing Towers apartment. Kellogg swam toward her, climbed up, took his daughter's face in his hands, and kissed her, long and hard.

Annie, I'm sorry, he blubbered, hugging her. I'm sorry, honey. I'm so sorry.

Familiar saved me, she said. He carried me on his back.

You're such a good swimmer. I forgot. I'm sorry I forgot, Annie.

Kellogg let her go — she was bone-dry. The sweatshirt was slightly askew, her left nipple winked at him, he adjusted it for modesty. But otherwise Elsie-Anne appeared unscathed, in fact she seemed to have never entered the water at all.

Her eyes were distant, those of a war orphan in some televised campaign. Who was this girl, this ghost of a child who drifted through the life her parents laid out for her? A stranger. She gazed through him, past him. Kellogg shivered.

People were climbing up from the flood to join them on the balcony and those of the adjacent apartments, a Helper — *Dack*, his beard wilty and dripping — among them. Dack knocked, then shouldered the apartment door open and ushered everyone inside.

Let'θ go, Dack lisped. Water'θ riθing. Get to the roof. We'll radio a pickup.

While people squeezed past, Elsie-Anne stared dreamily into the floodwaters.

Annie, said Kellogg, come on, it's flooding, we've got to go.

Not flooding, Dad, she said with a canny smile. It's sinking. The city's sinking.

Θome kid you got there, fella, Dack told Kellogg, and disappeared into the building.

SAM WAS AMONG the poplars, branches scrabbled the underside of his door-raft. The light was deepening. Soon it would be night, soon he'd enter the south side of Lakeview Homes, and as he paddled he thought of Adine, waiting for him in the living room, there'd be no one home but the two of them and whatever was on TV. Okay Adine, he said aloud, I'm coming, the work's almost over and we'll be together soon okay.

IGNORING THE WATER seeping now up to its edges, still more people headed down into the park. From the top of the Slipway Debbie surveyed the thousands gathered before the gazebo, assembling as they had for Raven's arrival and illustration. A tepid Ra-*ven* chant rose and died listlessly. Gone was the anticipation, a muted dread hung heavy in the air, when they called his name it was only in vain and despairing attempts to summon him.

Up the Slipway a couple was dragging a paddleboat purloined from the boathouse, two kids in tow. They reached Parkside West, pushed it into the water, the kids got inside, while the man and woman rolled their pants to their knees. They looked like people Debbie might know, friends of friends, maybe they'd met at a potluck or some such thing. Her mind riffled through a catalogue of names and faces: nothing, they were no one she knew. Right now, it seemed she'd never known anyone.

Look at them, said the woman to her husband. Don't they know he's not coming?

He's not coming! he hollered.

Another family turned and regarded this man bitterly, then kept heading down.

Fuggin appleheads, said the husband. As if this is magic, as if some clown in a sweatsuit can fix it with a wave of his whip. No one's going to save you! This is *real*.

Hey, we can make room, said his wife, if you want to come across with us.

Debbie realized she was being spoken to. I'm sorry, she said. Across?

To the mainland.

The strangers' faces were tired but kind.

You can't stay here, said the husband. You've got to get out while you can.

This — *while you can* — was chilling: it inferred a time when Debbie, or anyone else, wouldn't be able to . . .

Thanks, she said, but I need to find someone first.

Godspeed, said the wife, and her family joined the brigade crossing the Narrows.

Though dusk was descending the streetlamps remained blank-faced — no power, no power anywhere in the city. The NFLM no longer seemed to be checking ID, in fact no Helpers were visible down in the park at all. Meanwhile the flood had discovered fissures in the Slipway and descended in thin dark gunnels, fed Crocker Pond, Debbie watched it bloat and threaten its banks . . .

A hand settled on her shoulder, her heart skipped: such timing, it had to be Adine. But this woman looked haggard and shabby, grey wilted hair like the fronds of a dying plant. Debbie, said this person.

It was Pearl. Or some phantom of her, wild-eyed and waving a book. I have to get down there, I figured it out, it's called trunking. Situation Ten: Abduction, Deb. That's where Gip is. He trunked. That's why he's gone and —

Pearly? Sorry, I'm not following you. What's going on?

I need to get down there, she said, gesturing anxiously at the gazebo.

Hey, I don't know, it might make sense to try to leave —

No, not without Gip. I have to find him. She tapped the book's cover. It's all in here, Deb. It's called trunking, I know how to do it now, I can find him . . . Her voice faded. My daughter's gone, my husband's gone, said Pearl. Gip's all I've got left. I need to find him. What about you, Deb? Who are you looking for?

Debbie looked around wildly. All those nameless faces spilled grimly past. Wait, she said, focusing again on Pearl. What do you mean, *gone*?

Gone, gone, gone. She stepped into the water streaming heartily down the Slipway. Bye, Deb.

Dragging her bum leg along like a dead branch, Pearl disappeared into the swarm tumbling into the common from all sides, some with boxes and bags of belongings, most empty-handed, each face pasted with dazed grief that had yet to sink soulward. High above People Park circled a dozen newscopters shooting footage. Did their viewers wonder who all these people were? Debbie doubted it: this was likely only thrilling, a good show on TV.

IX

FROM MIDWAY up the rope ladder Wagstaffe pointed his camera down at Griggs, who lingered stubbornly in the Thundercloud, flouting his harness sheared in half, walkie-talkie in hand. High above, Noodles was pulled aboard, then Magurk.

Wagstaffe hollered something lost in the helicopter's roaring.

Griggs shook his head dolefully. Far below the Institute's swimteam, in matching bathing caps and trunks, converged upon Reed's skiff. Walters yanked the ripcord, the motor coughed but wouldn't start, Reed took up the chainsaw with which he'd freed the HG's and wielded it at the students closing in.

Wagstaffe gestured frantically: *Come on! Come on!*

Again Griggs shook his head.

The chopper dipped, the ladder swung, Wagstaffe scrambled, caught himself but dropped the camera. It tumbled past Griggs, three hundred feet down, knocked the chainsaw from Reed's hands, plopped into the water and sank. Reed cast an incredulous look at the sky, Griggs followed it: Wagstaffe and the ladder were pulled aboard, the hatch closed, and the helicopter lifted and wheeled away over the lake.

Back down below, the swimteam, emboldened, were once again on the offensive. Just as they seized upon the skiff its motor whined to life and the two men absconded into the Narrows. The swimmers treaded water in a sharky shoal. And their attention shifted to the top of the Wheel, at the lone figure sitting up there, safe and dry.

Griggs spoke into his radio: How are things going, Dack?

Lotθ of people up top of Laing Towerθ. Θomeone'θ coming? We heard the ferry θank —

Sit tight, Dack, have faith. Someone will come. Remember: Silentium. Logica. Securitatem. Prudentia. Griggs switched frequencies. Pea?

Pea here. Still waiting on the roof, water's coming up ... What's this about the ferry?

Griggs repeated his advice, changed channels, checked in with Bean — no signal. The common was an inky muck seething with people, from all sides the water chugged steadily in. He changed channels, repeating the four pillars to himself, while the angry swimmers collected at the Thunder Wheel's base.

Diamond-Wood answered: Yes?

And where are you?

With the Mayor.

And how's she?

Diamond-Wood tapped the Mayor's shoulder. How are you?

Fine, fine, she said, absently stroking her sash. Just watching everything go under.

It might be time to get out of there, said Griggs.

Yeah, said Diamond-Wood. What about you?

I'm the Head Scientist! I can't leave ... Griggs sighed. Besides, where would I go?

Diamond-Wood waited.

You're young, Recruit. Save yourself.

And the Mayor?

Does she want to be saved?

Diamond-Wood looked at the Mayor, the sagging shape of her silhouetted in the light of the viewing deck, the sash an empty bandolier, the sunset streaming through her midsection as a bulb through a lampshade. Maybe not, he said.

I can understand that, said Griggs.

Want me to ask her?

No. No, that's okay. And D-W? Tell her one thing, will you? Tell her we're sorry.

AS THE SUN SET the air cooled, Olpert was glad for his jacket, though his bare legs were goosefleshed. He and Gip followed Pop Street out the gates of the Necropolis and down into the boggy dump. The smell here was sour and yellow, the water oily, silky mats of gas floated atop its surface. Gulls watched and squawked mockingly as the threesome waded down a channel between mounds of trash.

Pop shrieked, Lark! and gestured grandly before him: his houseboat was lodged between the rusted-out shell of an old Municipal Works snowplow and the dump's back fence. Thar she goes, he declared, wading toward it. My home!

Overhead a helicopter peeled off toward People Park, where Olpert watched it join dozens of choppers tracing interweaving loops in the dusky sky.

Hey, mister, said Gip, it's okay, that chopper's not Raven's.

Raven?

The illustrationist! He's gone, I think.

Oh.

I thought maybe? Since I was the chosen one? I could do something? But —

Hurry! Pop called, heaving himself up the ladder. Restribution awaits!

Gip was pulled aboard and ushered inside the cabin. Olpert went to follow him — but Pop stepped to the gunwales with an oar and blocked his way.

Not you, evil one, he said. You're one of them. An esquivalient.

What?

Not with us, said Pop. Not here. *Not this time.*

Olpert stared.

Ah, and now at last he sips the cruel cider of justification! Pop seemed to address an imaginary audience that might not have included Olpert. No, we shan't save those whom propetuate the substantiation of a people's past. You don't care about history? Well now, Pop snarled, *you're* the one whom is history.

He beat the water with his oar. For a moment, delight twinkled in his eyes, then a stony facade slid overtop. Expunge yourself, he growled.

Please, said Olpert, come on, I'm not the enemy here, I'm not with those people —

Expunge!

But I helped you. I helped the boy, and I freed you. I'm not one of them.

Pop raised the oar above his head, menacing a deathblow. Bygone, be bygone!

Olpert sank back into the water. The highest dry land was a mountain of junked appliances — rust-scabbed fridges and stoves and washer-dryers missing doors and dials. He climbed atop a dishwasher, his own wake slurped at the pile, and sat there, quietly.

A fine place for you, evil one, said Pop, amid the city's refutations. Then he joined Gip inside the cabin, slamming the door behind him.

Olpert's heart skipped beats. Though, wait — something actually twitched and jumped around inside his jacket. Jessica! But in the pocket was not a mole, but a bird. He set it down, it toggled from one foot to the other, shuddered with a sort of mute sneeze, and took to the air: an m-shaped silhouette, then a speck, then vanished. Another newscopter passed above, from it a spotlight searched for — what? Bodies, survivors, stories.

Pop came out of the cabin, went to push off, and discovered that, despite the rising water, the houseboat was stuck fast on a reef of trash. He dug his oar into a pile of softened cardboard, tried to dislodge the boat. Grunts, groans, splashing . . . failure. He knelt, catching his breath. Olpert watched. And Pop met his eyes. Help me, he gasped.

Olpert didn't move.

Evil one! I am immobilized without another helmsman, it seems. Hence you may come onboard, yet don't envisage yourself anything but enemary. For you are only such.

Sure, said Olpert.

As Olpert climbed the ladder Gip's face appeared in the cabin's porthole: he observed the action on deck with the aloof interest of a gossipy neighbour.

All right, evil one, said Pop, handing him an oar. If you're with us be at least aidful.

From either side of the houseboat they heaved at the sludge, the boat creaked in protest, or encouragement. At last with a scraping sound they dislodged, coasted out into the floodwaters, and Pop swung them round toward Topside Drive.

Where to? said Olpert. Should we try to find the boy's parents first or —

Neigh! Initially — Pop adopted a preacher's cadence — one last trip home. For though the day enduskens, still the blazing sun of restribution beckons beaconlike my soul.

THE WATER POOLING in the Museum of Prosperity lent it the look of a marble-pillared bathhouse. Debbie sloshed through the rotunda, climbed the stairs out of the water to the second floor. Footsteps echoing with the promise of a secret knock, she passed through Loopy's retrospective — busts of the island's rich and famous, dozens of self-portraits, the Faces of Us: had been transplanted here too — to the room that housed the IAD's modest collection of Mr. Ademus's work: four rusty sculptures on plinths.

And here she discovered the island's artist laureate, slumped against a wall. Debbie stopped. Loopy regarded her idly, beret twisted in her hands.

Hi, said Debbie.

No, said Loopy, low. I'm feeling very low.

Oh yeah?

All my work, said Loopy, with a sweeping gesture toward the adjoining galleries, is going to be destroyed. And then what will I have? What's an artist robbed of her work?

I'm actually looking for someone, said Debbie, inching past.

Wait.

Debbie froze.

Listen to me, said Loopy. All of you, you thought I was serious. The whole time, you never knew. This, all of this — none of you ever saw what it was.

What was that? said Debbie.

You think I didn't know how absurd I seemed? I mean, *Loopy*? This ridiculous outfit? Paintings of people on TV? Not that it matters now. It's all amounted to nothing, anyway.

Yeah, said Debbie, edging up the spiral staircase, that sucks, good luck.

Nothing. *Nothing! NO-THING . . .*

Debbie climbed, Loopy's squawking faded as she curled up and up, the tap of her sneakers, the swish of the banister under her hand, spiralling all the way to the towertop gallery. She tried the handle: locked. Her legs weakened, her spirits felt punctured —

A voice called, Who is it?

And Debbie said, It's me.

Silence. A whispering of feet. A pause.

The catch clattered, the door opened, and standing there was Adine.

It's you, she said.

Hi, said Debbie.

They stared at each other for a moment.

You're not wearing the goggles, said Debbie.

No, said Adine. I took them off.

From somewhere in the Museum came a feeble, plaintive keening.

I guess you saw Loopy? said Adine.

Debbie grinned. Nothing, *nothing*.

No-thing! laughed Adine. And they kissed.

You found me, Adine said, pulling away. You came.

Of course, said Debbie. Of course I did. I'm sorry.

It's good to see you, Deb.

Yeah. It's good to see you too.

Check it out, said Adine, Sand City's finally getting its due.

The model had melted into sludge inside the glass cabinet. The city's topography endured in two lumps — the Mews and Mount Mustela — and a divot where People Park had been. Everything else was mud.

Magic, said Debbie.

Oh well, said Adine. I suppose it was always meant to be like this, wasn't it? Before you stopped me, I mean.

Yeah. Debbie watched her. I knew you'd be here.

Adine moved to the window. Not much sense making up stories now, with all that's happening. Was it him, all this ridiculousness, do you think? Or just nature?

Whose nature? said Debbie.

Adine laughed thinly.

Hey, we should probably go, said Debbie. The water's coming up.

Go? Go where?

Onto the roof?

And then?

And then, I don't know, wait to be rescued.

By?

By whoever! Why does it matter?

Where will this whoever take us? To wherever, right?

Adine's hair drooped, gone was its usual ecstatic frizz. The sunset highlighted the puckered flesh across her forehead and around her eyes, those scars from a lifetime ago, her half-buried life, preserved in wounds.

Debbie said, Are you worried about Sam?

A pause. A slow blink. A swift sharp dip of her chin.

You shouldn't, I'm sure he's fine. They got all the people off the Islet, I heard. And over on the mainland I'm sure they'll reunite people with one another —

Who's this *they*? The NFLM?

No, not just them. The rescue people. Other people. Everyone.

That's this mysterious whoever, right? *They* is just whoever, to take us wherever. Well *they* might as well take us nowhere. We might as well stay.

Hey, no, come on. Debbie moved beside her. But Adine pointed her face at the setting sun, which lowered blithely, almost obstinately, into the swollen lake.

Come on, said Debbie again. We'll find Sam on the other side.

Deb, can we just not, for a second? Can we just wait here? I'll go, I'll go. I'll go when we have to. But for now can we stay, just for a minute? And watch the sun go down?

Okay.

Will you stay with me?

Yes.

Say it.

I'll stay with you.

They stood together at the window and watched the last dim shreds of daylight wane. People Park was gone. Cinecity was gone.

A few buildingtops resisted the water, boats whizzed among them collecting survivors, and Podesta Tower rose defiantly above it all, a fist holding aloft a single finger — exultant maybe, or a last act of dissent before the end.

The dipping sun striated the sky: a pink ribbon upon the lake, up to deeper reds, then blues, before everything dissolved in blackness.

They waited.

The colours drained.

Everything darkened.

The sun was a wound replicated in the lake — then a slice, then a nick. At last its final sliver and reflected double swallowed each other. But before darkness fell completely, a vein of green light flashed across the horizon, sudden and blazing, then instantly gone. Did you see that, said Debbie, and Adine said, Yeah, a comet or something, and they pressed close and peered hard at the skyline. But the miracle was over: a brilliant, ethereal shiver, vanished, and all it left behind was night.

WAVES SWILLED into the tenement's upper floors, Kellogg and Elsie-Anne were pushed to a corner of the roof of Laing Tower South. He held his daughter, she let herself be held, though her eyes fixed upon the IFC billboard ten blocks north, the top of a mainsail lifting from the shipwreck of the Golden Barrel Taverne. Walkie-talkie held high, Dack strode all over the roof, flipping through static to find a signal, while the lake came up and up and the crowd waited, hushed and helpless.

WATER CASCADED into People Park in syrupy chutes. Crocker Pond topped its banks, gushed into the common, sending the empty rowboat, floating there since midday, out with it. Screams were silenced as it bowled three people under, they came up spluttering and bloodied, the park's basin filled rapidly, there was nowhere to go. Helpers in rubber dinghies and canoes and kayaks offered rescue at the hilltops. But how could anyone swim up waterfalls?

The only high ground was the gazebo, toward it the crowd moved through the churning current, Pearl among them. A girl struggled along beside her — and a sudden swell took her out at the knees in a flailing of limbs. The *Grammar* was swept away too, but Pearl kept going, reached the stage, climbed up.

A man was trying vainly to open, dislodge, or destroy Raven's trunk. He hammered his fists on the lid, kicked its sides, the metal dented but the thing didn't budge. Fug you, fug this, he screamed, a hopeless character with HOPE tattooed on his knuckles, then flung himself into the water and started swimming — where? Pearl took his place upon the ducktaped X. She tried the lid. No luck, shut tight.

Past everything, up the northern hillock, the Thunder Wheel arced out of the flood. From its highest seat Griggs watched the Institute swimteam coming for him, one Thundercloud to the next, teeth gritted. They'd formed a human ladder, leapfrogging their way up. And now others were chasing them: a middle-aged woman in workout attire reached the lowest student and savaged him with a chop to the kidneys, he dropped into the water. Resurfacing he clambered after the woman, grabbed her by the ankles, her face smacked a rung as she fell, and when her body hit the water it didn't come back up.

Meanwhile escapees fled to the mainland by the dozens. The haphazard armada included bodyboards and buoyed shopping carts and a group of fours in a racing shell (the coxswain's chants — *S-troke! S-troke!* — variously interpreted by his rowers), inflatable rafts with the Municipal Works logo on their helms, some brave swimmers plowed into the Narrows, frontcrawl devolved to breaststroke, then to doggypaddle.

Above it all the sky seemed indifferent, the night's first stars perversely sublime in the face of the chaos below. For a moment Griggs allowed himself to enjoy the evening: up there things were vast and beautiful, perfect and serene — and shattered by newscopters training spotlights on scenes of drama: a heroic windsurfer rescue of an infant from the branches of a poplar, a half-dozen families trapped in a rooftop garden, with their own clothes they'd spelled out HELP and waited shivering and half-naked to be saved.

And still People Park filled with water, pouring down from the surrounding streets in torrents. From the gazebo Pearl watched Helpers lower ropes, but even the heartiest citizens couldn't traverse the churning currents. Out on the common surfaced the girl who'd been knocked off her feet, slogging toward the gazebo. Pearl lay on her stomach, extended a hand, hauled her onto the stage. Before Pearl could ask if she was okay, the girl cried, You're alive! and rushed into the arms of another girl who was weeping.

The water came in, the water came up. When it began to wash onto the gazebo people shrank to the middle of the stage, from the shadows they cursed the airborne newscasters. They're just watching us drown, someone said, and someone else suggested, You think it's just them watching us? and a third person said, Wouldn't you?

Yet Pearl, sitting amid puddles by Raven's trunk, felt a sudden calm.

Water swam warmly up to her hips, stroked her kneecap through the hole in her jeans. Some people threw themselves past her, screaming, Save yourself! and frontcrawled to the bottoms of the hills, rebuffed by whirlpools like mismatched magnets. Helpers up top threw down lifevests — not donned but shared, two people to each one.

The gazebo had become a trap, people climbed onto the roof only to find themselves marooned, while Pearl rubbed her knee and waited, as Griggs, watching the dozen-strong crowd scale the Wheel, waited: she for magic, he with the defenceless surrender of a web-trapped fly, and here come the spiders, scrambling and famished.

FROM AHEAD, murmuring. The current tugged, the door slipped over the water, Sam didn't need to paddle, it carried him along. The noise amplified, a hundred voices begging one another for quiet. Sam's breath came easy. He was close, he knew it. With his ducktaped hand he held the remote ready. The door slid toward that rushing, shushing sound, a television on channel 0, the surf of static, a screen sparkling with a nonsense of nothing. This became rumbling, his ears filled with thunder. And Sam was lifted, he seemed to hover for a moment, everything stopped, a clear cool wind hit his face. And then the door angled down sharply and was falling. With his thumb he hit POWER, and held it, and the raft was gone and the water hurtled him down, and he was inside the roaring, and all he could see was white, and he fell and fell and at last Sam crashed grinning into —

THE YACHT POWERED through the Zone, *The Know* calligraphied on its hull, engines trailing yellow froth. Its single headlight illuminated the hundreds of people stranded atop Laing Towers, they responded with cheers of joy and relief.

Iθa Lanyeθθ, cried Dack, and a chant went up: Lan-*yess*, Lan-*yess*, Lan-*yess*!

Kellogg squeezed Elsie-Anne's shoulders. There, Annie, you see? Just in time. We'll be okay. They'll take us to Mummy and Gibbles, don't worry.

Edie Lanyess stood at the boat's prow, hands on her hips, looking every part her mother's daughter. She spoke in a matronly singsong: We've got room for everyone, don't worry, just stay calm. We're here! We're going to get you all out safely!

This inspired a reprise of the Lan-*yess* chant.

Kellogg went to join the movement shipward, but was held back.

Elsie-Anne pointed in the direction of the IFC billboard, a ridge in the water swallowed even as they watched. There, she said.

Annie, he said, no, the boat's here. They're here to rescue us. We're going to be okay.

But she wouldn't look.

The first few people were helped onto the yacht's deck. Boisterous cheers!

Annie, said Kellogg, look, everyone's leaving, we have to go.

Plenty of room, called the girl, joined now by her mother, beaming, whose beauty, despite the chaos, remained undisturbed. Listen to Edie, whinnied Isa Lanyess, no need to push! Helpers too, Mr. Dack, easy now, there's room for everyone.

Kellogg reached for Elsie-Anne, caught her arm. Come on, Annie, he said.

But the girl stood fixedly in place. She seemed apart from everything, facing north, almost hypnotized.

What's out there, Annie? said Kellogg. If you're looking for Mummy —

With a surprising burst of strength she squirmed from his grasp, stepped into the eavestroughs, and dove off the roof. A frothy channel furrowed the water as she zipped away into the flood.

Annie! Help! Someone, help!

Heads turned, Kellogg was regarded with mild confusion, but the line pressed forward as more folks were rescued. Kellogg peered into the dark. His daughter's trail was fading. What could he do? He jumped in after her, swallowed a great gulp of bitter water, came up gargling.

His daughter's purse appeared with a plop.

He splashed toward it. Behind him the yacht's engines chugged, the stranded became passengers, celebrations abounded. The purse bobbed just beyond reach, the flood's oily sheen pocked with reflected stars.

A ripple, a pause — and the purse was sucked under.

Annie?

Something brushed his feet. Down in the depths the purse whisked by. Sucking in a lungful of air he dove, swam, saw nothing, surfaced, wheezed, dove again. A shaft of light from the rising moon illuminated the IFC billboard: the screen in some subaquatic drive-in. Beyond it the water was bottomless.

Kellogg swam deeper down, lungs tightening. Far below something wriggled in the gloom, thick and serpentine, and released — what? A jellyfish maybe, which fluttered past. No: an Islandwear sweatshirt. Kellogg snatched it — empty — screamed his daughter's name, three syllables the water muddied to bubbles. His face and throat had gone taut, his lungs burned. He looked down and up and around and everywhere was the same vast void.

And now the snakish thing appeared again, uncoiling. Was it summoning him? Kellogg's head tingled, the blood fizzed through his veins, he felt limp and not quite there. Something ropy and thick tightened around his ankle and began almost tenderly towing him down, and the blackness opened up, it was ravenous, he had nothing left, he'd forgotten everything, why was he here, for whom, his vision blurred, and the last thing Kellogg saw, hauled down toward it, were parallel white bands aglow in the darkness. The lights of a bridge maybe. Or were they teeth.

ONE OF THE newscopters flew low over the Museum's roof, nosing down for a spotlit shot of the two women waving at whoever might be watching, so whoever was watching might wish them saved. The water slavered between the turrets in a black skim, wetting their feet. The camera rolled. One of the women flipped an obscene gesture and the chopper whirled away into the milky night.

Fuggers, said Adine. They're not going to help us. We have to get higher.

The Grand Saloon, Debbie said, pointing across the street. The clocktower.

Do we swim?

Can you make it?

Stay close to me, said Adine.

I will.

The building dropped into the water, reeflike. Somewhere down there was Orchard Parkway. But now it was a river. The flood had reached the terrace of the Grand Saloon Hotel's penthouse, emptied into the suite. Copper gables sloped into the old cathedral's spire, and the bare clockface resembled a tired moon lapsing into the sea.

Hurry, said Adine.

They jumped, twin splashes, neither's head went under.

Okay? said Debbie

Adine said, Okay.

The current swirled. The flood felt unsure of itself, directionless, waves buffeted them from all sides as they doggypaddled across. The only sounds other than the gurgle and plop of their strokes were the newscopters overhead — though these were fading, heading to the mainland to shoot the escapees as they washed up on the pebbly beach.

THE PIG APPEARED just as Pearl was beginning to slip under. Her knee had failed her, the flood had filled the common, she'd been forced into it with everyone else. All around her people struggled to stay afloat, calling to one another, Keep paddling — Head up — Stay with us now. As the water reached streetlevel some swam off, Pearl wasn't sure where or why, past small boats loading survivors, kids first, which then shuttled off with promises of a swift return.

But they didn't come back, and treading water among the abandoned hopefuls she felt her soaked clothes grow heavy. She kicked off her shoes, yet still some invisible weight dragged her down. She wouldn't last, she was weak.

And then bobbing along: the pig.

It was a hollow thing of pink plastic. Pearl caught it, slung an arm around its neck, clung there with closed eyes, opened them to discover animals all around: a matching pig, two sheep, donkeys, cattle, lions, a whole zoo's worth of creatures swimming up in pairs.

The Friendly Farm! someone cried, wrangling a goat.

They've come to save us!

There's room on my rhino, come on!

Nearby a family climbed aboard an elephant, a kid to each leg and the parents on either side of its trunk. Its mate was mounted and claimed as an explorer might some new planet, a woman knelt upon it, arms raised, howling at the moon. More people found floatables, a fleet of them bobbed in the water. Pearl held on, waves buffeted her from all sides. It's a miracle, someone cried. A miracle is what it is!

This was all drowned out with a fat band of light and a purr of engines. Out of the dark appeared a mirror-windowed and sleekly aerodynamic yacht. A teenage girl waved from its helm. We're here, she cried, the Lanyesses are here!

Pearl was pulled aboard, the pig went spinning off. Below decks, dozens of survivors wore matching stunned expressions and housecoats. Many sat with teacups dangling from their fingertips, others drifted in and out of private berths, from the lavatory emerged a bearded man in a white bathrobe monogrammed ISA.

A woman was close, eyes wide and empathic, hand out. Pearl took it to shake, realized it was clenched in a fist and holding a marker.

Hi, said the woman, I'm Isa Lanyess. Now, actually I was just going to number you so we don't go over capacity. Turn your hand over?

She wrote the number 16 on the inside of Pearl's wet wrist.

Still room for one-thirty more! We've already rescued our full capacity once, just getting everyone safe. Doing our part because we can. The woman turned to address all the newcomers, dazed and dripping. Good luck with the animaltronics, huh? Now, I'm out of robes but towels are coming out of the dryer soon. Anyone care for some hot cider?

Lanyess, said Pearl.

That's us! We've got the yacht so we figured we might as well help —

You used to be a ballplayer. For the Y's.

Maroons, pre-Y's. Funny you'd know me *that* way ... Anyway it's a small world!

A small world, said Pearl, and this small world responded by tilting vertiginously, swirling into a kaleidoscope of her family's faces: Kellogg's, Elsie-Anne's, Gip's. Lanyess caught Pearl by the elbows and said, Okay there, I got you, and a sob swelled and burst in Pearl's throat. There, said Isa Lanyess, yes, let it out, holding her while she wept.

As *The Know* prowled People Park, scooping survivors from the water, the Podesta Tower's rotations finally shuddered to a halt.

So that's it, said the Mayor.

With the solar power exhausted the elevator was out too, Diamond-Wood stabbed vainly at the CALL button, shot the Mayor a look of panic and dismay. She blinked, her eyelids so heavy it was a struggle to raise them again. She'd never felt so tired.

If you want to leave, she said, there's always the stairs.

The *outdoor* stairs?

Off the viewing deck was a door marked EMERGENCY EXIT with a diagram of a man fleeing flames. Diamond-Wood pushed it open: an alarm would have normally gone screaming through the building, instead the only sound was the muted putter of helicopters. Gripping the doorframe in a skydiver's pose, Diamond-Wood gazed down into the floodwaters.

Go, said the Mayor, go if you want to. But do you see how they've abandoned you?

A soft wind rumpled his hair.

Go!

He paused. But then where, he said. How will they know where to find me? I get to the bottom and then what? And then I'm stuck there, and then the water keeps coming up . . . look, everything's gone — look!

Into the room drifted chemical vapours churned up from Lowell Canal. A trio in a bathtub paddled past, a shower-curtain sail bulged and hustled them toward the mainland, where the newscopters stroked the beach with fingers of white light.

Mrs. Mayor, I'm scared, what should I do?

She shrugged, turned away, looked out over the city.

Her view was that of a ship captain up in the bridge. Other than Podesta Tower only a few structures broke the flood's surface: the tallest skyscrapers, the spire of the Grand Saloon, the top of the Thunder Wheel, where bodies swarmed and seethed.

How many hadn't made it? There was no telling. The Mayor thought of elderly couples entombed in Fort Stone attics as the water crept upstairs, covetous Bebroggers who, retrieving jewellery, had fallen through sodden, wilting floors, or, citywide, the irrevocably lonely who'd spent lifetimes waiting for a chance to end it all — and here it was, dribbling obligingly up to their front doors. The trapped and stubborn, the stupid, the unlucky, the vain … All those quiet secret deaths, happening unknowably in the night.

After this, she said, we will be even stronger as a city. This is just a test. It'll pass.

She looked to Diamond-Wood for corroboration, but his back was to her. The smell from outside was ammonia, human waste, spoiled meat.

There's a boat coming, said Diamond-Wood. I'm going. I'm sorry.

Okay, said the Mayor. Go, ye of little faith. She smiled. Yes, imagine us after this! Just like now, but better, touch green. Imagine it: a place like this one, but everyone's happier. Or at least they believe themselves to be. What else do people need?

But, turning, the Mayor discovered the boy already gone, helped onto the deck of *The Know* by Edie Lanyess. The yacht went churning north — leaving Diamond-Wood's crutches twirling in the water like the hands of a crazed malfunctioning clock.

WHAT ARE YOU doing, why have you sojourneyed from your stroking?

Olpert gestured with his oar: There's people there, on the spire.

What do you conspire, evil one?

No, the cathedral spire. The Grand Saloon's. They're on the top of it.

And?

And we should rescue them.

Pop stared.

What? We shouldn't? We should just leave them there?

Ah, and so now after a lifetime of esquivalience you wish to play the hero! You pretensualize restribution! Well fine, prehaps this will envisage the airs of your ways!

With an ironic curtsy Pop steered the boat south.

All around them watercraft loaded with people and belongings were crossing the Narrows. A little outboard-fitted junk putted by loaded low with people, sad and weary, eyes wide but unseeing.

Rats, said Pop. Desertioneers!

Olpert paddled. As they closed the distance he could hear the people — there were two — clinging to the spire calling, Help, help us, please.

The boat glided up alongside. Olpert looked at the two strangers, tried to show something firm and authoritative in his face that suggested all was okay. And then seeing who it was, his oar slipped from his hands into the water.

And now this, Pop howled. Some hero, he can't even get a grip!

Debbie clapped. Pop Street, she said, Pop, you came for us.

The small woman beside her said, Who would have guessed?

Yes, said Pop, whom?

Debbie, said Olpert. I know you. We met. At the Taverne? On Thursday . . .

Of course, evil one, we all are recognitive of every each other. This is some great phenomenology? Bah. It is life!

Olpert reached over the gunwales, steadied the houseboat against the spire, extended a trembling hand to Debbie.

Thanks, said Adine. Fiercely she levered herself past Olpert and aboard. Then she turned to help Debbie and Olpert stepped between them. It's okay, he said. Let me.

Debbie eyed him curiously. She took his hand.

Hi, he said. I'm Olpert.

Olpert knows you, Deb, said Adine. A fan maybe. You sportos get all the love.

As Debbie climbed aboard the boat yawed, she lost her balance, fell into him.

Olpert folded her into his arms. She squirmed, he held her tight. Destiny!

Their mouths were close. He pressed his to hers, the blows upon his back and shoulders had to be of passion, he kissed her harder, everything in the universe had converged in this final moment and here it was, one big yes —

Something sharp and hard stabbed his lower back. Olpert crumpled, released Debbie, he reached for her, clawed only air. What was happening?

Standing above him the small woman and Pop brandished oars like truncheons. He was aware of Debbie shrinking behind them, wiping her mouth with the back of a hand. Olpert rose on shaky legs, offered a pacifying gesture, his spine ached.

Pop and the woman advanced. Her eyes were fierce, his manic, he was whispering, And so we see your truthful colour, evil one. They backed him up against the railing. The small woman was saying something, her lips moved, yet the words were drowned by Olpert's booming heart.

Debbie went inside the cabin. She watched from a little round window. Olpert implored her with a desperate look. She pulled away.

Animal, the small woman said. You fuggin animal.

An oar came at him. Olpert dodged it, but he lost his balance and tumbled over the side, surfaced, grabbed for the first thing floating past: a grey shoe, the tongue lolled, it had no laces. Olpert looked at the shoe, dumbfounded, and then up at the houseboat, which was pulling away.

Gip, watching from the porthole, told Debbie, He fell overboard, that man fell overboard, and Debbie, sitting on the floor, released her face from her hands. What?

He's in the water, said Gip, we're leaving him —

Debbie rushed to the porthole. Adine and Pop rowed at opposite gunwales. She looked around the cabin, snatched up a lifepreserver from the wall, barrelled out onto the deck, and, though in the dark she couldn't see the man — Olpert — flung it into the water, and watched with desperate hope as it floated off, almost idly, in the houseboat's wake.

THE MAYOR DOZED shallowly, dreaming of the sky, being inside the sky, not flying but just existing there, with no earth below, all there was was sky. At the slop of water against the windows her eyes opened. At last the flood had reached her.

Gone was any impression of captaining a galleon to port, this was more akin to a periscoped glimpse of open water from a submarine. The lake stretched west, the moon carved a silver tunnel to the horizon, spectral and grand. Yet it was the stars that amazed the Mayor. The night was full of stars and stars.

She'd never seen a sky like this. Evenings thudded down upon the island in a dim curtain, waxy and purplish with the moon throbbing dully behind. But this night was a living thing, it seemed to pulse and breathe. The Mayor was in awe. Awe at the spectacle of it, at that immense luminescent fury, awe that such astronomy had always existed — she'd just never been able to see it.

This view, though, was shrinking. In a trembling line the lake bisected the viewing deck and crept higher up the glass. She was sure of it now: the island was sinking, the tower lowered (or *was being* lowered), the whole city swallowed into some subterranean layer amid the bottomfeeders and the lakefloor's churning guck.

The water swelled muddily up the glass, opaque and blotting out the cosmos inch by encroaching inch, there was nothing to look at inside it, not even fish. It seemed to eat the sky. The Mayor had stayed expecting to feel noble and proud, possibly even martyred. Instead, as she watched the water swell up over the stars, she was consumed with longing and melancholy. She was alone, hopelessly alone. And soon there would be nothing left, nothing but water. Still, before it was gone, she relished that last visible band along the top of the window, a final jangling dazzle of that silken miracle of sky.

X

CAMERALIGHTS LIT THE beach like intermittent signal fires. In each islanders gave enthusiastic accounts of their escapes for mainland TV. Survival conferred the status of hero, everyone was championed as brave, resilient. You're an inspiration to our viewers at home, one of the reporters told a humbled family, and passing by Adine couldn't help herself: Not like those sad fuggers who didn't make it, and Debbie shushed and manoeuvred her down toward the water.

Hand in hand Debbie and Adine weaved through the crowds, between the medical tents and media and boats along the shoreline, calling, Sam? Sam? But they'd searched the entire beach twice, on each pass enviously eyeing reunited families and friends. Fellow searchers passed them wide-eyed or squinting, in their faces were both camaraderie and estrangement.

As the crowds thinned a figure materialized out of the dark, stumbling up from the water's edge. They rushed to him: not Sam, this man was in NFLM khaki — and for a moment Debbie blanched that it might the strange man they'd flung from Pop's boat. But it wasn't him either, this guy was taller and sad-seeming, in his eyes was the same defeated look in Adine's.

Sorry to run at you, he said, I thought you might be my daughters. It's okay, said Debbie, we thought you were someone too.

We're looking for my brother, said Adine, guy about my size, short hair, probably wearing a suit? The Helper shook his head. Adine continued: We've been up and down the whole beach and haven't found him, so if he isn't here then where the fug is he? And once again Debbie had to steer her away and on along the beach.

For the third time they reached the edge of the inlet where the pebbles swelled into boulders and still they hadn't found him. Out here, the tinny smell of the lake drifted ashore with each crashing wave.

Let's go out on those rocks, said Debbie, we'll be able to see the whole beach. Yeah?

Pebbles and stones chiming beneath their feet, they moved out on a little promontory that sloped down from the cliffs into the Narrows — misnamed now that the lake sprawled unperturbed to the point it folded into the starry sky in a sort of crease.

From the outcropping Debbie surveyed the shore: the sporadic glow of cameras, TV vans in the parking lot of the airport motel, antennas blinking and jettisoning signals into the ether. It's dark, she said, there are thousands of people, he could be anywhere, let's wait for morning. I'm sure they'll have a station set up to reunite people —

But Adine wasn't listening. She watched the water. What's that? she said.

Something floated out there in the moonlight. Debbie's first instinct again was that it might be the man they'd turfed overboard, and at the sight of it she felt both relief and shame. Though it wasn't a person, too boxy and bright. A little boat, maybe a raft, carrying the flood's last survivors? But it wasn't really boat-shaped, and no one rode aboard — a coffin?

Whatever it was, riding a crest and ducking down, vanishing, then reappearing on the peak of the next wave, it was coming ashore.

What is that? said Debbie.

Adine shook her head, looped her arm through Debbie's.

The white box lifted on a swell, dipped into the trough, came up again. It was the size of a coffee table and advanced with the resolve of something driven or steered.

The night was cool, the surf hissed. The lakebreeze smelled of pennies. They waited, watching the odd little craft bob and dip. Thirty feet out it caught on a fallen tree, the branches held it fast — as a gift, thought Debbie, dangled tantalizingly before a child.

What do we do? said Adine.

We go see what it is, said Debbie.

She kicked off her shoes, hitched her pants, and waded out, the icy water stinging her shins, sand swirling with each step.

And then she was upon it: a trunk — somehow dry all over, though it swam, fashioned from some material that was not glass, metal, or ceramic, but perhaps an amalgam of all three, sheer to the touch, dented in spots, and which repelled water as if coated in wax.

Debbie took hold of one of the handles and pulled. The tree groaned, the branches scraped the trunk's sides, before it slowly, almost reluctantly, eased free. She pushed it toward shore, not heavy, though it did drag in the water in a somehow solemn way, and in the shallows the trunk lodged in the sand.

Adine waded out to help. It looks like a treasure chest, she said. Wait, I wonder —

From the trunk came a snapping sound. The latches flew open. Debbie recoiled, Adine crabwalked frantically back up onto the beach. The lid opened, fell, bounced on its hinges. A figure all in white unfolded from the box — and rose to full height, grinning, arms wide to command applause.

When there was none, Raven frowned. Debbie joined Adine on the shore, where they watched the illustrationist remove his whip from the bottom of the trunk and lash the water. The shallows parted into a narrow path to the beach, which he took, then whipped again, and the water collapsed into place with a plop.

There you have it, he said, sweeping his whip over the lake. What do you think?

Adine said, I fuggin don't —

She was interrupted by a humming, sputtering sound. A helicopter dipped out of the night blinking red lights. This provoked a clamour on the beach, the TV crews wheeled to shoot its sweep to the Scenic Vista eighty feet up the cliffs, where it settled and perched. I believe that's my lift, he said, pushed between Debbie and Adine, and headed up the slope.

Do we do something? said Debbie.

What?

All eyes and cameras were on the helicopter, it gleamed under all those lights, sitting there insouciantly at the bottom of the boardwalk. They seemed to be waiting for its pilot to appear. Meanwhile Raven skirted the crowd, scaling the cliffs in the shadows.

He's not in there! cried Debbie. He's here!

But the crowd was surging toward the helicopter, howling (No! was all Debbie heard — No! No! No!). Some people threw stones, these arced up haplessly and had to be dodged on their way back down. The illustrationist's helicopter seemed to smirk in defiance.

Look at him, said Adine.

There was nothing magical about his scramble up the cliffs: just the hunched and shaky ascent of someone not used to climbing for anything.

Still the cameras hadn't found him, their lights focused on the chopper. Some enterprising broadcasters up top were hanging over the cliff's edge and shooting it from above, others were lugging equipment down from the motel's lot. Some particularly enraged islanders began scaling the cliffside, though it was sheer, the rocks slick with moss, many missed handholds and fell to the pebbles below.

Listen, said Adine. She cocked an ear.

They're angry, said Debbie.

No, not them. Something else.

Debbie listened: a windy sound, whistling and whispering in her ears.

It's coming from up there, said Adine.

Raven had reached a walkway that traversed the cliffs — a path dug out to allow easy maintenance on the drainpipe twenty feet below the Vista. He strolled across, was at last discovered and spotlit, the crowd below howled, he waved and curtsied and flourished his whip, and kept going across, illuminated in cameo.

It's getting louder, said Adine.

Beneath the crowd's hysterics the whispering had thickened into the gentle roar of surf. It seemed, Debbie realized, to be coming from *inside* the cliffs. Adine confirmed it: Something's in that sewer, she said. Look, his helicopter's moving.

It was, juddering slightly on its skids. The whole cliffside was shaking.

Raven, a hundred paces away, stopped.

The crowd went quiet.

The drainpipe rumbled and shook, the helicopter jostled to the platform's edge, nudged against the railing — and the railing tore free and came tumbling down. The crowd at the base of the cliffs bolted. With nothing to secure it, one of the chopper's skids slipped off the side of the platform, began to tip, and as the rumble within the cliffs swelled into thunder, the helicopter was knocked from the Scenic Vista. It dropped, end over end, in almost exquisite slowmotion, and crumpled at the base of the cliffs.

People dove for cover, expecting an explosion. There was none, just a little plume of smoke. And the drainpipe kept rattling, the roar now deafening, cameras zoomed in, everyone — including

Raven — watched and waited, hushed.

The drainpipe hitched. From it poured something thick and dark.

Is that sewage? said Debbie.

No, said Adine. People.

It was: all in black, bursting by the dozen from the end of the pipe. And the sound wasn't just the thunder of their footfalls. They were screaming.

So many people, said Adine.

The noise intensified as the mob rode little avalanches of sand and rock, hundreds of them tumbled down the banks. Raven fled. Still more and more figures surged out in a great phantasmal mass, the air electric with their screaming. They were like the shadow cast by a sudden violent storm, or an eclipse, or a creature, huge and black and hungry, and they swept down the path after Raven, over Raven, inhaling him — a flash of white and he was gone.

And the mob kept coming, scorching the air with their voices, sweeping down the cliffs in a vast dark wave, out onto the beach, where we could only stand and watch as they fell upon us all.

O

Printed in the United States
by Baker & Taylor Publisher Services